Intimate Terms

INTIMATE TERMS

A NOVEL

Elaine Gordon

LYLE STUART INC.
SECAUCUS, NEW JERSEY

Published by Lyle Stuart, Inc.
120 Enterprise Ave., Secaucus, N.J. 07094
In Canada: Musson Book Company
a division of General Publishing Co. Limited
Don Mills, Ontario

Manufactured in the United States of America

Library of Congress Cataloging-in-Publication Data

Gordon, Elaine.
    Intimate terms.

    I. Title.
PS3557.0654715   1988   813'.54   88-2132
ISBN 0-8184-0458-2

For BURTON

who transforms dreams into realities
and is able to make the realities
even sweeter than the dreams

A note of special thanks to a few people:
To Jane Stanley for being such a loyal friend.
To Carole Stuart for her creativity and sensitive understanding.
And finally to Deborah Chiel who was the one editor in a million that every writer hopes to find. My gratitude extends far beyond the final page.

Everyone knows what he is
  fleeing from
But only a fortunate few
Know what they are fleeing to

Prologue

Marriage.

To a sixteen-year-old girl.

He would be absolutely mad even to consider it.

Although within the four walls of Salah Shawak's study, Salah had made the plan sound so logical.

Marriage.

The only one of life's experiences that held no allure for Dolph Robicheck. For Dolph, freedom was the ultimate pleasure.

He followed the curve of the Kowloon waterfront, absentmindedly kicking stones along the cobbled street. Though not a conventionally handsome man, Dolph Robicheck had a commanding presence. His slim, muscular frame made him seem taller than he was. With his gray-blue eyes and slightly wavy light-brown hair, he looked typically English. In fact, he had been born in London, but his parents had been Austrian Jews, and Dolph had been brought up to speak German almost as well as he spoke English.

As usual, he was dressed in a fashionable Savile Row suit, which he wore with great style. Even in this moment of extreme anxiety, Dolph's symmetrical features gave no clue

11

as to what was going through his mind. He had long ago learned from his mentor, Salah Shawak, to mask his emotions.

At forty-two, Dolph Robicheck presided over an ever-expanding financial conglomerate. The British-Orient Limited was his most consuming obsession. He had had no formal financial training, but Salah Shawak had been his university as well as his mentor. Had it not been for their remarkable friendship, Dolph might never have reached his current prominence.

Dolph took orders from no one. But Salah, accustomed to being obeyed, had always wielded a powerful influence over him. Dolph's destiny was entwined with his. The fate of Salah's fortune affected that of his own.

Salah had little patience with indecision. Dolph could give only one answer to his proposal.

Dolph walked inland, following the silvery trail of the full moon. The pungent odors of food, animals, and dust, the bustling sights and sounds of early evening Hong Kong all reminded him of the year he and Salah had first met.

BOOK I

Chapter One

1937.

The world was wobbling on the verge of a violent upheaval. The Jews of Europe scrambled madly for visas and travel permits. Desperately, they sought to escape the relentlessly tightening noose of Nazi domination.

Dolph Robicheck's world came apart that year. Seventeen years old and the only child of Isaac and Rose Robicheck, Dolph had learned to play the piano almost before he could walk. Music was the family's *raison d'être*. Isaac was a brilliant violin virtuoso, Rose an acclaimed pianist who accompanied her husband. The Robichecks' charm and spirit held their audiences captive, and their concerts received uniformly rave reviews.

On a glorious late August afternoon, they performed an all-Debussy program at an open air concert in Brighton. Never before, reviewers were to say later, had they played so brilliantly.

But it was to be their last performance. On their way back to London, a delivery truck collided head-on with their little red convertible, and Isaac and Rose were killed instantly.

Dolph moved in with his only living relative, Maurice Robicheck, a philosophy professor at Cambridge. Maurice was as devoted to his academic career as his brother had

been to his music. He had never married, but his comfortable little house was a magnet for the campus radicals who
hung on his every word.

A short, stocky man with thick, curly white hair and a
generous beard, Maurice Robicheck was the very picture of
the learned professor. But he had an impish side to his
nature. He was a ruthless flirt, much to the frequent distress
of his more dour colleagues.

Dolph had no heart for playing the piano or for continuing to develop his growing interest in musical composition.
But Maurice's small cottage buzzed with the discussions of
earnest students, and Dolph's education took an abrupt turn
that was to change his life. Despite his grief and an aching
sense of displacement, he gradually began to immerse himself in university life. He found himself drawn into the spirited conversations and endless debates about the approaching war in Europe.

Maurice was an ardent socialist and Zionist. The Jewish
people were in peril, he argued, and their only hope was a
Jewish homeland. For the first time, Dolph began to take an
interest in his own Jewishness and the political future of
Europe.

One of the most articulate of the regular visitors to the
household was Christopher Brooke, a young man about four
years Dolph's senior whom Dolph particularly admired.

Christopher was that rare combination—a mother's dream
and a daughter's fantasy. A product of England's finest
schools, he epitomized the shining example of young upper-
class British manhood.

Sir Aubrey Brooke, Christopher's father, was slightly
amused at his youngest son's taste for radical causes. But as
long as Christopher didn't disrupt the household with his
ideas, or bring his rather scruffy friends home for weekends,
there was no harm done. Although Sir Aubrey wouldn't
have admitted even to himself that Christopher was his
favorite, he knew it was just as well that his pompous eldest
son would inherit the family title.

Christopher had an almost uncontrollable penchant for
adventure. He never ran to where the action was—he
created it himself. He was the acknowledged ringleader of

his group at school. Fortunately, his excellent grades often saved him from punishment for his pranks. No matter what the mischief he devised for himself and his friends, not only did he avoid getting caught, he also somehow managed to twist a sticky situation to his advantage.

A natural athlete, he had a healthy, ruddy complexion and a muscular build from many hours spent outdoors. His tow blond head stuck out in a crowd, for he towered a good six inches above most of his peers, and his disarming smile came so readily that his intelligence was often under-estimated.

Stories about Chris's exploits regularly made the rounds of London society. Women were immediately drawn to him, taken in by the innocent stare of his huge blue eyes. All it took was one hour, and the mesmerized lady was positive that only she interested him. And for that one hour, she was right.

One rainy afternoon, around teatime, Chris came pound-ing at the Robicheck's front door, looking for Maurice. With a dramatic flourish, he flung his muffler on a nearby chair.

"Hallo, Dolph," he said. "Where's the Professor?"

"Out for a bit. He'll be back shortly, though. Want some tea while you wait?"

"Damn, I wish he was at home," Chris went on, ignoring the invitation. "I have an idea that I wanted to thrash out before I commit myself."

"Oh?" Dolph said, immediately curious about Chris's latest scheme.

"It's a chance to help save some lives," Chris said excit-edly. "The hitch is I'd have to leave Cambridge before the end of the term . . . though with war about to break out, I'd probably enlist before graduation anyway."

"Leave Cambridge? Are you out of your mind?" Only a fool, he thought, would give up his chance at a Cambridge degree.

"Dolph, we've all been hearing the horror stories about people being shipped off to internment camps for what the Nazis call 'reassignment.' I'm tired of sitting here in a com-fortable chair and philosophizing about what's going on over there. Somebody has to take a stand for human rights. I want to get involved, Dolph. Christ! I'm not even Jewish. What do you, a Jew, think about all of this?"

The question stunned Dolph. The emotional drain of his own problems had left little room for those of anyone else, but he had listened to endless discussions about the Jewish question. Certainly he cared deeply about what happened to the Jewish people—his people.

"I don't know what to think," Dolph said slowly. "Tell me more about your plans."

Chris sensed his glimmer of interest. He settled himself near the fire and began to talk enthusiastically.

"I've just heard of a group of chaps preparing to leave England in a week. A whole network has already been formed. They call themselves 'partisans,' and their purpose is to train men who can work underground to get the Jews out of Europe. I've pretty much decided to join them. Some of us will be sent into the occupied countries to provide counterfeit documents and smuggle these people as far as the borders. The overland routes are quickly being sealed off, so others will be responsible for leading the refugees to whichever ports are accessible. Italy, France, Spain, and Portugal are still open and safe. The lucky ones will be able to emigrate to England or America. The others . . ." He shrugged his wide shoulders. "Who knows?"

Dolph shook his head. "The whole thing sounds damned dangerous, Chris. You could be killed. Is your life that cheap?"

"I love my life very much, Dolph, but I'm willing to risk it for a cause I believe in. Otherwise, it's not really worth living, is it?"

Dolph leaned forward, his eyes bright with interest. "You've got a point, Chris," he said.

"Life is full of chances," Chris continued. "Some people know when to grab them. Some sit back and just let them drift by. As for me, I want to clutch life with both hands."

"What's all this about life?" a voice boomed behind them.

They'd been so deep in talk that they hadn't heard Uncle Maurice coming into the room. As Maurice fixed himself a sherry, Chris repeated the discussion he'd just been having with Dolph.

Dolph stared absentmindedly at the glowing coals in the fire grate. Up until his parents' death, his life had been predictable and secure. Even now, he was living an altogether pleasant, sheltered existence. He had never had to endure the injustices his fellow Jews were suffering at this very moment. And what Chris said was so true. He had never thought of it before—being involved in something one truly believed in made the quality of life more valuable.

The words tumbled out of his mouth before he realized it. "I'm going with Christopher," he announced.

Maurice and Chris looked at him sharply.

"What are you talking about, Dolph? You're far too young! I will not have it," said Uncle Maurice.

"What difference does my age make?" Dolph countered.

"It's more than a question of age. You're all that I have left. And I have a responsibility to your parents. I can't let you go."

"I want to do something for my people. I don't think my parents would have stood in the way. They believed in taking chances, and they were dedicated to what they believed in. As you are, Uncle."

Maurice twisted a lock of his thick, white hair around his forefinger, and said pensively, "I wonder if they could use someone of my estimable talents. Or do you suppose I'm too old?"

Dolph grinned, knowing he had won. "Uncle Maurice, you're not only too old, but quite frankly, your physical condition leaves much to be desired."

Maurice laughed. "The first premise of debate is never ask a question that you don't want to know the answer to," Maurice laughed.

"Well, Uncle, if that's the case, I'll forgo my next one and simply tell you. I'm going with Christopher."

Maurice swept a gnarled hand through his hair.

"God forgive me," he said in a low voice, "but what else can I say? I will pray for the both of you."

The following week, Dolph, Christopher, and fourteen other young men sailed from Dover for France.

The group was met in Le Havre by a gaunt, coarse-faced

man of about forty, Constantine Perez, who was to be their leader during the two-month training period. Their camp was located just north of Bayeux, on the windy, rock-strewn Normandy coast. Because it was late October and the cold, rainy weather had already moved in, the volunteers were bivouacked not in tents, but in an enormous, starkly furnished abandoned barn, a shocking contrast to Uncle Maurice's cozy cottage.

The new recruits had barely settled in before Constantine summoned them to the farmhouse that served as headquarters and briefing room. He paced heavily as he lectured them in a voice that was surprisingly quiet for a man of his size. Constantine ended his brief description of the training the recruits were about to undergo with a warning.

"We appreciate your efforts, but volunteering isn't enough. If you don't pay close and careful attention, and learn to follow orders without any questions asked, you'll be of no use to us as a member of this rescue organizations. And if I decide that you are useless, out you go.

"There's a war going on. Never forget that. And if you insist on acting like you're at a school outing, you'll sacrifice lives. Many lives. Including, most certainly, your own. If you manage to learn what we're trying to teach you, you could be of some use, maybe even save some innocent people."

Constantine paused. "Got it?" he asked, his eyes scanning the room, holding the gaze of each member of the group long enough to read an answer there.

"Just one thing more, gentlemen . . ." Again, the steady, searching gaze. "Good luck to you."

The group was divided into smaller units, depending on their language skills and previous experience with guns. The days began before dawn and lasted well into the evening. First-aid procedures, communications, infiltration methods, target practice, map-reading, handling explosives—so much to learn. And just one mistake could mean the difference between life and death.

All too soon, Dolph discovered he wasn't cut out for soldiering. But he couldn't help but admire Constantine, who was a tough bird. Exacting as he was, nothing fazed him.

He never seemed to sleep, and appeared to be an expert in every aspect of their training.

Dolph sensed that beneath the Turk's tough outer skin was the soul of an idealist. He wished he could penetrate Constantine's armor. Christopher already had, of course, but people were always drawn to Chris and revealed themselves to him unwittingly.

Dolph stared forlornly out the rain-spattered window. Every bone in his body ached. Who was sitting in front of his uncle's blazing fireplace at this moment? he wondered. The prospect of another starchy supper made his stomach feel queasy.

He looked down at his grimy, chapped hands. The rough soap they'd been supplied with made them raw and stiff. Would he ever recover his former dexterity? Hell, that was the least of it. He'd settle for getting back to England alive!

Damn Chris for making this sound so heroic. Once the excitement had faded, there was nothing left but the misery. Well, life was full of choices. And he had made his.

By the end of the first month the atmosphere in the camp had loosened up. As the men relaxed into the routine, their talk drifted to the subject of sex and the girls they'd had back home. Dolph sat silently, listening with poorly disguised curiosity. Ever sensitive to a companion's feelings, Christopher took pity on his young friend. Obviously Dolph was completely ignorant of the opposite sex. Chris decided to remedy the situation as soon as possible.

One night, after the snores and deep breathing of the sleeping men had blended with the sound of the wind moaning through the cracks of the drafty old building, Dolph and Christopher put their newly acquired skills to the test. They quietly slipped out of the barn and sneaked past the sentry on duty.

Dolph's heart was pounding. In the darkness he was having trouble keeping track of Christopher who seemed to know his way through the overgrown apple orchard. The scraggly branches scraped at Dolph's face as he struggled to keep up. He felt as though he were already on his way to meet the enemy in battle.

They came out onto a dusty lane, and continued on for another twenty minutes or so. Christopher took turn after turn without a moment's hesitation. Finally, he motioned toward what looked to be a solid hedgerow, and slipped through an inconspicuous opening. A narrow path led them to a cluster of cottages.

Chris waited for Dolph in the shadow of a small grove of tree-sized shrubs. He tapped him gently on the arm as he caught up.

"All right, Private Robicheck," he whispered, "we're within sight of our objective. When we get closer, give me some time to let loose with my heavy artillery and soften up the resistance. When I'm ready for reinforcements, I'll send up a signal flare. Better take some of this," he added, pulling a small flask from his breast pocket and unscrewing the cap. "Good for a soldier's courage going into battle."

Dolph was hit by the pungent odor of cheap brandy. He obediently raised the flask to his lips and took a healthy draught, managing to swallow the burning liquid without choking. His eyes watering, he handed the flask back to Chris.

"Well done, comrade," murmured Chris. "Let's go."

They covered the last hundred yards to the house.

"Remember," Chris reminded Dolph, "you're to keep to your station here on the porch until you're called to active duty."

He stood at attention, gave Dolph a mock salute, and spun on his heel. Then he quietly knocked on the door, and went inside without waiting for a response.

Dolph heard voices—Chris's and that of a woman—but he couldn't make out what was being said. Soon the voices stopped, and after a brief silence he made out a series of groans and creaking sounds, almost as if a physical struggle were taking place. Then sudden quiet as the noises stopped, and the talking resumed. A moment later, the door swung open.

"Ready to serve your cause?" asked Chris.

Dolph was eager to come in from the chill night wind, but he stood nervously in the doorway until Chris reached out, grabbed him by the elbow, and all but dragged him into the room.

Dolph sniffed the musty animal-like odor that permeated the room. The flickering fire provided only faint light, so that Dolph could barely make out the heavy woman stretched on a sofa in the far corner. She lay panting hoarsely, as if she'd been running and was out of breath.

"Madame Arlette," said Chris in French, "allow me to introduce an apprentice I believe will prove worthy of your tutelage. Though inexperienced, he is a man of warmth and spirit."

"Chris!" Dolph whispered desperately, "what do I do?"

"Don't worry, pal. Madame Arlette will show you."

Christopher urged him forward in the semi-darkness.

"Bon soir, cheri," grunted Madame Arlette. *"C'est ta premiere fois, n'est-ce pas? N'inquietes pas."*

It was all very well for her to tell him not to worry the first time he made love, but Dolph had only the vaguest idea what to expect. Madame Arlette grabbed his hand and pressed it against the wet, curly hair between her legs. Her other hand grasped the back of his thigh, just below the buttock, her fingers circling inward, closer to his groin than any hand but his own had ever been.

Murmuring inarticulately, she drew closer, rhythmically rubbing his hand over the slippery, moist folds of her vagina. Her body stiffened each time his trembling fingers touched the tiny knob of flesh at the head of her vaginal lips.

Suddenly, Madame Arlette touched the front of his trousers and gently clutched at the bulge between his legs. As his knees gave way, he fell forward onto the couch. He put out his hand to steady himself, and encountered her ample breast, partly covered by the thin fabric of her robe. Arlette's fingers worked urgently to undo his trousers, quickly unfastening the buttons and cupping his genitals in the palm of her hand. She lightly traced the shape of his testicles, then slowly moved her fingers to encircle his still flaccid penis.

"Eh, cheri," she whispered, *"n'as pas peur!"*

Dolph moaned as her warm mouth closed over his penis. The pressure of her soft lips, moving all the way down to the root, lit a fire in his loins. He felt himself beginning to swell as her tongue caressed his shaft, sucking as if she might actually swallow him.

His hips took over now, moving tentatively at first, then with increasing urgency, pressing his claim of awakening passion. Dolph almost cried out when she pushed him away and reached up to squeeze his now fully erect penis.

Leaning back against the couch, she declared, *"Bien, maintenant tu es pret."*

Dolph had never felt so ready.

He could hardly breathe, waiting for her to spread her thighs and guide him inside her.

His throbbing penis slid into her silky smooth cavity, expanding, swelling to fill her welcoming wetness. Almost at once, he exploded with a violent, sweet pleasure that engulfed his senses.

"So this is what all the fuss is about," he thought, resting his head on Madame Arlette's enormous bosom. "No wonder . . ."

Madame Arlette fed Dolph and Chris ripe Brie, a crispy fresh bread, and red wine. Just as dawn was breaking, she shooed them on their way with a broad smile of thanks for the pile of francs Chris pressed into her hand.

"Come other time," she shouted after them in her broken English. "You are welcome always."

Returning to camp mildly drunk and in a state of exhausted euphoria, Dolph and Chris were promptly snapped back to reality. The site was alive with activity.

"So much for slipping behind the lines unnoticed," Dolph laughed. But he was immediately silenced by the worried look on Chris's face.

"Ah, there you are, you two idiots!"

Constantine's voice was loud and angry.

"Nice of you schoolboys to take time out from your fun and games to join us here this morning. If this were the military, you'd be facing a court-martial. If I had time, I'd personally kick both your irresponsible asses."

Chris and Dolph hurriedly joined the rest of the men gathered in the farmhouse.

Constantine glared at them briefly, then addressed the

curious group.

"Word came over the shortwave a couple of hours ago that things have heated up faster than we figured in Austria and Germany. It seems a crazy Jewish kid took it into his head to shoot someone at the German Embassy in Paris. That pig Goebbels has been on the radio all night, screaming about 'reprisals.' His patriotic followers have been busy. We don't have many details yet, but we're getting reports of heavy looting, synagogues that have been torched, Jews being hauled into the street and beaten . . ."

Constantine paused briefly.

"It's probably much worse than we know, than we can even guess at. There's been a change in plans. We're speeding up graduation day to give you geniuses the chance to show how much you've managed to pick up. We'll be handing out your assignments today, but," he said sternly, "there's no first, second, or third choice. If you don't like what we have you in mind for, you're welcome to hand me your resignation. Understood?"

He gave them one of his piercing glances.

"Some of you will be moving out in the next few days, the rest by the end of next week. You better have your gear ready."

Constantine turned and headed for his office.

He had no time for questions. They were dismissed.

Dolph could hardly swallow his disappointment when he got his assignment. "Escort refugees sailing on the *Conte Biancamano*. Destination Shanghai. Take up staff position with the IC."

The IC! Constantine had chosen him to babysit for the refugees, then to stay on in Shanghai to shuffle papers for the International Committee, the local relief committee organized by the moneyed Shanghai-Jewish establishment.

Characteristically, Chris had lucked out. He would be escorting a group of handpicked men and women overland to Palestine. They'd spend months in training at a camp in Belgium and would be risking their lives to sneak over the Lebanese border.

Mindful of Constantine's warning, Dolph shared his

disappointment with no one but Chris.

"It's important work," Chris said to console him. "Those poor people are bound to be shellshocked from all they've been through. Besides, look at it this way—no more suffering through cold nights with not enough blankets. Pity me, having to sleep on the ground. Unless you suffer seasickness?"

He raised an eyebrow, trying to humor Dolph into better spirits.

Dolph shook his head. Constantine had been very clear: Accept the assignment—or get out.

Exactly one week later Dolph found himself leaning over the rail of the Italian liner *Conte Biancamano,* watching the French coast disappear. Chris was already headed for Palestine, encountering Lord knew what hardships. How he wished he were with him, instead of here, staring miserably into the inky waters of the Atlantic, regretting the day he'd ever admitted he spoke German.

The comforts of his second-class cabin held surprisingly little appeal. After weeks of slogging through the mud with a pack on his back, hours spent on the rifle range, the lectures he'd sat through on how to infiltrate enemy lines, he wasn't prepared to be a glorified tour guide for the German refugees he'd escorted aboard the *Conte Biancamano.* And once he arrived at his final destination, things would get even worse. He'd be stuck shuffling papers and listening to endless complaints about housing or who knows what else.

What a muddle he seemed to have made of his life. He'd certainly never dreamed, just five short weeks ago, that he would be heading for Shanghai!

Chapter Two

His first few days at sea, aboard the Conte Biancamano, Dolph was desperately lonely. But he soon began to adjust to the altogether pleasant life aboard ship.

The man from the International Committee had handed

him a duffel bag bulging with informational pamphlets
about Shanghai. These he devoured avidly, and in spite of
himself, found that he was looking forward to his arrival in
the strange land. He'd also been given an outline of items to
discuss with his captive audience while they slowly made
their way east.

A program had been mapped out for Dolph to follow.
The IC representative had told him to hold meetings with
the refugees. They were to discuss arrangements that had to
be made once they reached Shanghai: housing, jobs,
language study, adjusting to a city and culture so different
from what they were used to. So many emotional and
economic adjustments lay ahead for them.

Some of the refugees had spent months in concentration
camps and were physically ill or depressed from their har-
rowing ordeal. They stared angrily—or worse,
apathetically—at Dolph when he suggested they give some
thought to how they could earn a living in Shanghai. None
of Constantine's lessons had prepared him to solve the problems of these poor tormented souls.

But most of the group welcomed his efforts. Those who
had single daughters were particularly attentive to the nice,
young Englishman who spoke such good German and
worked so hard to prepare them for the future. *A sheine
bucher*, a lovely boy.

Perhaps, he thought, breathing a sigh of relief after the
third meeting, he might be doing some good after all.

The dust-covered piano in a corner of the second-class
lounge had caught his eye. He flexed his fingers, wondering
how it would feel to play again after all this time. He
fiddled with a simple chord. The instrument had a nice
tone. Most of the passengers were resting in their cabins or
relaxing on the sundeck, so there wasn't much chance he'd
disturb anyone with his playing.

Tentatively at first, he let his fingers slide across the keys.
More easily than he would have thought possible, the familiar notes and chords came tumbling back.

How could he ever have thought he could give up his
music? It was his life, what he had been born to do. An aching guilt swept through him as he remembered the months

of silence following his parents' death when he hadn't played so much as a single note. Music was in his blood, he could never forsake it.

As his mind raced, his fingers kept pace in a wild crescendo of Rachmaninoff. Engrossed in the music, he struck the last note.

The sound of clapping and a soft "bravo" penetrated his trance.

"What gorgeous music you play."

The young woman addressing him in German was about his own age. She wore her auburn hair wound around her head in thick braids, framing her lovely oval face. Serious blue eyes smiled at him from beneath dark lashes.

"I didn't realize anyone was listening," Dolph stammered.

"You'd be surprised," laughed the girl. "Half the ship's passengers are listening outside the door. But I was the only one rude enough to barge inside."

"I'm glad you did." Dolph stood up and introduced himself. "I'm Dolph Robicheck."

"I know who you are. I've been at your meetings. I'm Hannah Stein. But please, don't let me interrupt you. It's wonderful to enjoy a piano again."

"You like music, do you?"

"I've studied piano since I was nine years old. In Berlin, before the Nazis took our home away." A flicker of pain crossed her face. "But I don't have your talent. Where did you learn?"

"I've been playing almost from the time I could walk. My parents were both professional musicians."

" 'Were'? They don't play anymore?"

Dolph's expression darkened. "No, they were killed in a car accident, on the way home from a performance."

Hannah squeezed his hand. "So you've had your share of suffering, too, haven't you?"

Dolph had worked hard to push the memory of his loss to the back of his mind—and he didn't want to trigger that pain by responding to the sympathy in her dark blue eyes.

He quickly shifted the conversation away from himself. "At least I have some understanding of what you and your family have been through—losing your loved ones, having to leave your homes . . ." He beckoned to Hannah to sit next to him on the piano bench. "Since you also play, won't you join me, Hannah? What will it be? A little Brahms perhaps?"

They took turns choosing their favorite pieces from childhood and got so caught up in the pleasure of the music that they lost track of the time until, finally, Dolph threw up his hands in mock surrender. "Enough, Hannah. You've fed my starving soul, but my stomach cries out for food. It must be teatime already."

"My goodness, you're absolutely right. I *am* hungry. Let's go see what they're serving today."

As they entered the dining room, an older man rose to greet them.

"I'm Hannah's father, Friedrich Stein, and this is my wife, Rachel," he said, turning to the small woman next to him. "What a fine concert you two gave us this afternoon."

"How do you do," Dolph said shyly. "Your daughter plays beautifully."

Herr Stein motioned to the empty chair at his table. "We have an extra seat here. Join us."

Dolph would have preferred to be alone with Hannah, though she was so pretty he wasn't sure he could talk to her without stumbling over his words. Besides, it felt good to be with a family, even if the sight of Hannah together with her parents aroused feelings he didn't want to think about.

The *Conte Biancamano* steamed through the Strait of Gibraltar into the Mediterranean, headed for the port of Alexandria. Hannah and Dolph looked for any excuse to be together. She appointed herself his personal assistant for his IC activities and faithfully attended every one of the meetings. Each afternoon the two of them headed for the lounge and spent several hours playing the piano. Word of their impromptu concerts spread quickly and they often drew an enthusiastic audience.

Dolph's undesirable assignment had developed into a thoroughly delightful adventure. The German refugees, grateful for his concern, responded to his helpful suggestions and made no secret of their affection and admiration.

But Hannah was the bright light in his day. He had only to think of her sweet voice, her blue eyes, her delicate fingers poised at the keyboard or curled around the stem of a wineglass, and he ached with desire. His brief introduction to sex had whet his appetite, igniting a passion that was becoming hard to live with.

If only he dared make love to Hannah . . . would she be angry and end their friendship? Or did she share some of his feelings? He sensed that perhaps she might. . . .

The trouble was, he was hardly ever alone with her. The Steins hospitably insisted he join them for every meal, but they kept a protective watch over their daughter. Besides, even if he and Hannah had been able to sneak away, there wasn't much privacy to be found on the crowded ship.

The voyage was more than half over. They had already passed Bombay, en route to Singapore, Hong Kong, and their final destination. Not much time left to overcome his hesitations and make a move.

Except for the nights that Herr Stein played pinochle with his cronies, he and his wife went to their cabin at ten o'clock sharp. Hannah would smile her goodnight and dutifully follow her parents, leaving Dolph to pace the deck for hours before he could fall asleep.

One evening she lingered outside the lounge with Dolph.

"Aren't your parents waiting for you?" he asked.

"It's all right," she said. "I told them I wasn't sleepy yet. The stars are so beautiful."

"They're even better on the top deck where there isn't as much light. Would you like to go up there?"

"Oh, yes," Hannah said quickly. "Let's."

He led her up the stairs to the spot where he'd spent so many hours staring into the night, thinking about what it would be like to make love to her.

"Dolph." Hannah whispered, gazing at the velvet sky, "this is heaven."

She trembled, and Dolph reached his arm around her shoulders to draw her into a protective circle. He could feel the delicate bones beneath the thin fabric of her sweater. Just the touch of her body sparked a fire in him.

"You must be cold, Hannah. Forgive me for dragging you

up here."

"I'm glad you brought me, Dolph," Hannah said, looking into his eyes. "We never get a chance to be alone. I think about you so much . . . all the time. . . ."

"Oh, Hannah." He hugged her slender body. "I've wanted to hold you in my arms for such a long time."

"I feel the same way." She turned her mouth to meet his lips.

A shiver of pent-up passion flickered through both their bodies. Dolph had a momentary vision of the things he had done with Madame Arlette. He touched Hannah's full breasts above her sweater. How soft she was.

He felt the fabric in the crotch of his trousers tightening against his swollen flesh.

"I've wanted so much for you to touch me," Hannah moaned. "Every night since we met I've dreamt of being in your arms. I've imagined us together in Shanghai, married."

She leaned up to kiss him again, then went on with her fantasy.

"We have so much in common, and with the money my father managed to smuggle out of Germany, he could help you start a business in Shanghai. Once we get settled . . ."

A warning sounded inside Dolph's head. He yearned to push his tongue between her sweet lips, to pull back her sweater and kiss her breasts until she opened her legs to him the way Madame Arlette had. But he remembered Constantine's often-repeated warning: Nothing is without a price.

A serious involvement with Hannah would be tantamount in her and her parents' eyes to a permanent liaison. He knew he wasn't yet ready for that. "I have my work with the International Committee," he began.

"Oh, Dolph, I'm sure they can get along without you."

"And there's my music."

"Ah, darling let's not speak of it now. We have better things to do with our evening." Hannah nestled closer to Dolph, fitting the curves of her body closer to his.

It took every ounce of Dolph's self-control to tell Hannah they should be getting back.

She smiled her agreement, but in her eyes he read disappointment.

Their last night aboard the *Conte Biancamano*, most of the passengers attended the traditional Captain's party. Dolph and Hannah performed two pieces for the passengers. Then Dolph announced that he had composed a new piece, entitled "Hannah's Song." Hannah sat next to him on the piano bench, blinking back her tears, as he played a haunting melody.

They spent the rest of the evening dancing. All too soon the lights flickered on and off, signalling that the orchestra was about to play the last song.

Dolph wanted to hold Hannah in his arms forever. He'd thought long and hard about whether he was ready to marry. She was so kind and pretty, and they did share so much—their music, the losses they'd both suffered at such a young age, this long, event-filled journey. But try as he did, he couldn't imagine himself the husband of Hannah Stein. He couldn't imagine himself the husband of *anyone*, for that matter!

Neither of them said a word about the fact that this would be their last evening together. Dolph walked Hannah to the door of her cabin and kissed her goodnight. Her sadness hung between them, palpable in the cold night air.

The next morning, as the *Conte Biancamano* slowly maneuvered its way into port, the confusion was so great that there was little time for farewells. Dolph gave Hannah a chaste kiss on the cheek and shook hands with her parents.

Herr Stein thrust a note in his hand and said, "Dolph, here's our address. Please come visit. I consider you a member of our family."

There was an aching lump in Dolph's throat as the Steins disappeared into the crowd of people who had come to welcome the *Conte Biancamano* and its passengers.

A member of Herr Stein's family! He appreciated their friendship, but he was seventeen years old, on his own in a new and exotic country, and the last thing he had in mind was to become a member of Herr Stein's family.

Chapter Three

Shanghai!

The sprawling metropolis had flourished largely because of its geography. It was the only port in China not cut off from the interior by high mountains. Shanghai was China's financial heart, the center of its import and export trade, the headquarters for the stock exchange and bank system. It was the seventh largest port in the world, and the tall buildings reminded Dolph of the European cities he had visited on tour with his parents.

The local head of the International Committee, Wolfe Kalmanowitz, had briefed the refugees before they debarked, welcoming them on behalf of the Jews of Shanghai. He explained that IC representatives were waiting to interview them, guide them through customs, then escort them to their new homes.

Dolph joined the stream of passengers moving toward the Customs House.

The passengers who had baggage went to claim it, trying to fight off the Chinese coolies with rickshaws who descended on them like a grasshopper plague, eager to make a few cents. Amidst the confusion, merchants were conducting business as usual right on the piers. Harried customs officials who understood neither German nor Yiddish searched for a common language. Dolph got through the process quickly and spent the next several hours working alongside the other IC agents to help the dazed refugees negotiate their way through the maze of questions and forms.

Buses were waiting to take the refugees to their new homes. Most of them, including Dolph, had been assigned to the Hongkew section. Kalmanowitz sat next to him at the front of the bus and gave him a running commentary as they passed through the different neighborhoods.

Hongkew had traditionally been the industrial area, but the Chinese army, retreating the previous year before the advancing Japanese forces, had laid waste to vast stretches of it. Dolph was shocked to see enormous piles of rubble, the result of the recent struggle. But the human spirit being what it was, new homes had already been hastily erected—evidence of the refugees' confidence in the promise of their new lives.

Dolph had been allotted a room the size of a closet in a lane house on a gloomy alley off one of Hongkew's main streets. The rent was low, and he could buy food for pennies in the open-air markets and primitive cafes, so he was able to manage on the meager salary the IC paid him.

In his free time, he explored the Hongkew Gardens and watched the barges, houseboats, and Chinese junks that passed under the Garden Bridge on their way up the Whangpoo River. But mostly, he worked long, full days at the International Committee offices. Each week hundreds of new refugees poured into the already crowded city, as stacks of German documents appeared on Dolph's desk to be read and translated into English.

Many of the escapees arrived with barely a cent in their pocket, in desperate need of medical attention. Dolph and his IC colleagues performed near-miracles to find them room and board, jobs or other sources of income. The least fortunate were those so impoverished that they were placed in the refugee camps, whose pathetic living conditions were infamous throughout Shanghai.

Dolph celebrated his eighteenth birthday, alone, exploring the bazaars where the odor of Chinese food competed with that of animal carcasses hanging in plain view in the front of the butchers' stalls. Brilliantly colored jade and ivory pieces, stacks of silk and cotton and linen—there seemed to be nothing that money could not buy in Shanghai.

He wandered through the elegant public rooms of the Majestic Hotel, wishing he had someone with him in order to share the day. To mark his birthday properly, he treated himself to a gin fizz at the famous Horse and Hounds bar in the lobby of the Cathay Hotel. The slim, beautiful Chinese girls in brocaded satin cheongsams made him think of Hannah.

Of course he could have gone to visit the Steins, who were now the proprietors of one of Hongkew's newest restaurants. But he worried that they would misinterpret his attentions,

born of loneliness, for more serious ones in the future. Especially now that his intelligence and energy had made him
into a minor celebrity in the closely-knit Jewish neighborhoods, where gossip seemed to travel faster than the speed of
sound.

Salah Shawak was the undisputed patriarch of the Jewish
community. Nothing happened in Shanghai that escaped his
notice. And for several months now his many sources had
been reporting to him about the young Dolph Robicheck.
Salah was curious. He always pursued interesting rumors.

Salah Shawak was sixty years old and a bachelor,
although he had had many mistresses. His younger brother,
David, had fortunately fulfilled the family's matrimonial
responsibilities and fathered two daughters and two sons,
both of whom were strategically placed with Shawak Limited. Shawak nephews, cousins, and brothers-in-law held
key managerial positions throughout the company, and
through them, Salah kept a tight rein over his holdings.

The major portion of Salah Shawak's time was devoted to
the day-to-day operations of his farflung business empire.
Local wags liked to tell visitors who were meeting Salah for
the first time that the sun never set on the British Empire—
or on Salah Shawak's.

His interests included the export of tea and silk from
China, textile mills in Bombay and northern England, arbitrage and foreign exchange, breeding racehorses in England
and India, and developing synthetic fibers in America. He
was a major player on the Shanghai and London stock
markets, and owned much of Shanghai's choicest real estate.
Rumor had it that he had a hand in the Turkish opium trade
as well.

In the early nineteenth century, the Shawaks had been a
well-known Baghdadi merchant family. But when the
Turkish Pashas gained control and life became uncomfortable for the Jews, the Shawaks relocated to India. Under the
protection of the British, the family became leaders in
Bombay's merchant and banking industries, and before long
their personal and professional tentacles reached across the
Orient and into England. By the beginning of the twentieth

century, they had established themselves as one of the most powerful families in the Far East.

Stories of Salah Shawak's opulent lifestyle were famous throughout the Far East. He was a connoisseur of the many fine things in life that his wealth afforded him, not the least of which was his collection of beautiful women. Salah usually supported two or three concubines in elegant apartments discreet distances from one another. He took pains to give each of them enough attention and money to ensure their happiness.

The role of distinguished patron was one that Salah relished. A devotee of the Shanghai Symphony, he was one of its major benefactors and rarely missed a performance. He had amassed a distinguished art and antique collection, and his exquisitely appointed home was the perfect setting for his lavish parties. His collection of ancient and contemporary erotic art was among the finest of its kind.

As head of the Shawak dynasty, he took seriously his philanthropic responsibilities. Preoccupation with Jewish survival was a matter of family pride: Each generation had increased and diversified the family fortunes, but wherever the Shawaks settled, they contributed significantly to Jewish community life. Hospitals, libraries, schools, and synagogues throughout the world had been donated by the Shawak family.

As survival grew increasingly precarious for the Jews of Nazi-occupied Europe, escape became imperative. They poured by the thousands into Shanghai, one of the only ports willing to accept them without a visa. Salah Shawak had naturally taken charge of the Jewish community's efforts to feed and house the new arrivals. The additional load of responsibilities created new demands on his time. He had decided to hire a personal assistant.

One rainy morning in March, Dolph was so buried beneath a mountain of forms that he didn't notice Mr. Kalmanowitz standing in front of his cluttered desk. The plump, little man shifted his weight from one foot to another, like a small child with a secret.

"Dolph, I wonder if you realize the reputation you've made for yourself in such a short time."

"I don't understand, Mr. Kalmanowitz. Did I do something wrong?'

"I'm sure you've heard of the Shawak family."

"Of course. Who hasn't?"

"You've received an extraordinary invitation. Salah
Shawak's secretary phoned to ask you to dinner at the
Shawak home."

"What on earth would Salah Shawak want of me?" Dolph
said, mentally reviewing the files he'd handled in the last
few weeks. He couldn't think of anything that should merit
the attention of one of Shanghai's most famous citizens.

"I can't imagine," said Mr. Kalmanowitz, clearly miffed
that his young deputy had been chosen for this occasion
instead of himself. He handed Dolph a slip of paper. "The
secretary would like you to call this number. She needs your
shirt and trouser size."

"My shirt size?" Was Kalmanowitz joking?

"So they can send over a set of dinner clothes. You can't
appear at Shawak's home dressed like that. His car will pick
you up at six forty-five tomorrow . . . unless you're not
free."

Of course, he was free. And if he hadn't been, he would
have cancelled his plans.

Dinner with the famous Salah Shawak was not an every-
day occurrence for ordinary folk. The invitation was more
like a command performance that could not be refused.

At six forty-five the following evening the Shawak
chauffeur, dressed in dovegrey livery, stood at attention in
front of Dolph's lane house. Not ten minutes later, the grey
Daimler glided through the imposing iron gates, emblazoned
with the Shawak coat of arms; a gold, black and red crest
divided into three sections, announcing to the world the
family's vows of industry, creativity, and charity.

Dolph's hand trembled slightly as he lifted the heavy
bronze door knocker. A white-jacketed servant ushered him
into the reception room. Despite all he'd heard about the
Shawak fortune, Dolph was unprepared for the luxury that
awaited him. The gleaming domed ceiling was covered with
silver leaf, and a pair of inlaid-wood Bombay chests flanked

both sides of a coromandel screen.

The servant led him down an apricot-colored marble corridor lined with ornately framed Shawak family portraits. He tapped on the padded leather door studded with brass nailheads.

"Enter," came the response.

Salah Shawak rose and extended his hand to greet Dolph. He looked to be about sixty, and his dark olive-colored complexion spoke of Shawak's Oriental origins.

"Welcome to my home. I am Salah Shawak," he said warmly.

Dolph shook the rough, firm hand, marvelling at the confidence the man exuded. Slim and not very tall, he was clearly a presence to be reckoned with. He was almost completely bald, except for the fringe of gray hair at the back of his head, allowing his wide forehead, large nose, and hooded brown eyes to protrude prominently.

Salah motioned towards a pair of English leather high-backed chairs in front of the fire. "Won't you please join me in a drink, Mr. Robicheck? Since you are English, would you like scotch?"

"Yes, thank you, scotch would be fine."

Dolph surreptiously glanced around the room. Most of the furniture, a blend of English colonial and Chinese, was upholstered in leather the color of persimmon. Elaborately patterned oriental rugs were stacked everywhere two or three deep. The teak-panelled walls were lined with floor-to-ceiling bookshelves that held row upon row of books bound in red, gold and green tooled leather.

Next to an enormous globe of the world was a large, mahogany stand on which lay open an illuminated Hebrew manuscript, similar to one Dolph had seen in the British Museum. An ivory chess set sat on a small table near the fireplace.

"Do you play, Mr. Robicheck?"

"Please, call me Dolph, sir."

"Do you play, Dolph?"

"Yes, sir, but not terribly well."

"I understand that your parents were killed in a motor crash."

"Yes, sir . . . afterwards I went to live in Cambridge with my uncle. I used to play chess with him."

"A lovely town, Cambridge. I attended university in England, at Oxford."

"Do you like England?"

"Very much. We have family there."

"Really?" said Dolph. "I thought the Shawaks were based in Shanghai and India."

Salah smiled. "We're a peripatetic tribe, fortunately scattered all over the globe. We even have cotton mills in Birmingham. Is that scotch all right?"

"Yes, sir, it's perfect."

"Do call me Salah, I feel as if I age five years each time you say 'sir.'"

There was a knock on the door.

"Excuse me, Mr. Shawak," said the butler, "the family has arrived."

"Very well, tell them we'll be right in."

Shawak rose, and motioned to Dolph to follow. "I imagine it's been some time since you've had a Sabbath Eve meal."

Dolph had forgotten that it was Friday night. Salah was right. He hadn't sat down to a traditional Sabbath dinner since before his parents were killed. Although they hadn't been religious, his mother had liked to light the Sabbath candles and serve a special meal whenever the three of them were together in London.

Now he glanced with awe at the Shawak table. The white silk damask cloth was embroidered with flowers of gold thread. Behind every other black lacquered chair stood a white-gloved footman eager to be of service. A massive crystal chandelier hung so low above the middle of the long table that the tear-shaped prisms almost touched the towering centerpiece of fresh fruit.

A small girl ran up to Salah and took his hand. "Good Sabbath, Uncle Salah," she said. Her long hair was slicked back from her pixie face with a giant white hairbow that bobbed when she spoke.

"Amy, this is Mr. Robicheck. He's visiting from England," said Salah. "My niece, Amy Bloom." He introduced the rest of the family, including Amy's mother, his younger sisters, Sophia and Victoria, and his younger brother, David.

Sophia covered her eyes with her hands and recited the blessing on the Sabbath candles. The tall tapers in the seven-branched gold vermeil candelabra flickered at first, then blazed brightly. Salah chanted the *Kiddush* over the wine and invited everyone to be seated.

The Shawaks struck Dolph as friendly and unpretentious in spite of their wealth. There seemed to be quite a few years age difference between Salah and Sophia. David and Victoria were younger still.

"We're rather a large group," Salah explained, "but some of the older children are away at school or working in our factories."

Sophia was seated at Dolph's right, Amy at his left. She was clearly an inquisitive little creature who could hardly wait until the first course was served before she turned to him.

"Mr. Robicheck, I'm going to boarding school in England next year."

"Are you, Amy? What school will you be attending?"

"I don't know. My father's in England now, choosing one for me."

"Now, Amy, remember your father explained that with the war in Europe you might be sent instead to India," her uncle David interjected.

Dolph had heard snatches of gossip about David. He commuted between Shanghai and London, preferring to play golf with the Windsor Castle set than to apply himself to Shawak Limited affairs. With his sandy-colored hair and fair skin, he looked nothing like Salah.

"What's a war?" asked four-year-old Lucy.

"Everybody gets killed. Boom boom." Her young cousin, Samuel, screeched so loudly that Lucy began to cry.

"Children." Sophia's voice was quiet but firm. "This is no way to behave with our guest. In fact, this is no way to behave at all at the table."

The children exchanged sly grins as they peeked at one another around the three epergnes, overlowing with fruit, that divided the table in thirds.

"I have friends who arrived on the *Conte Biancamano*," said Victoria Raben, Salah's youngest sister. "They told me your piano concerts were the pleasantest part of their voyage."

"Perhaps we could impose on Mr. Robicheck for an after-dinner concert," Salah said.

"Of course, though I have a feeling my reputation exceeds my talents," said Dolph, nervously flexing his fingers under cover of the long tablecloth.

The servants set out porcelain platters of honey-soaked rice cakes and passed around chocolates. Finally, Sophia gave the signal for coffee to be served in the drawing room. Dolph helped Amy with her chair.

"Are you going to play for us now?" she asked. "I hope you'll do some of the new dance music."

"Don't let her influence you, Mr. Robicheck. Play whatever you'd like," said Victoria.

Dolph began hesitantly, shy in front of such a knowledgeable audience. But as usual, once his fingers struck the keys, the music took him over. "Here's one I think you'll like Amy," he said, smiling at the little girl.

Amy clapped her hands with delight as soon as she recognized the opening chords of "The Music Goes Round and Round."

After several ragtime hits he switched to Mozart and even felt comfortable enough to play one of his own compositions.

"Brahms' Lullaby might be appropriate," Sophia said at last, pointedly glancing at the restless children.

"Yes," agreed Salah, "let's end with something tranquil. And then, Dolph, perhaps you'll indulge me with a game of chess."

"Thank you so much," said Victoria, "the music was marvelous."

"Please come next week and play more for us," begged the irrepressible Amy. "This is the most fun I've ever had at Uncle Salah's."

"Amy!" chided her mother. "What a terribly rude thing to say."

Salah smiled indulgently. "I'll see that Mr. Robicheck

comes again, Amy. Now off you go, before you wound me even more deeply."

Cognac and cigars had been laid out in the library.

"I'm hardpressed to find worthy opponents," Salah said as he and Dolph settled themselves in front of the chessboard. "If your game is even half as accomplished as your playing, I'm in luck."

"It's been quite a while," Dolph said dubiously.

"Then I'll give you the advantage. You take the white."

Salah watched from beneath hooded eyes as Dolph deftly countered his moves. The young man had piqued his interest. It was time to discuss the real reason for the dinner invitation.

"I've always admired the giraffe," said Salah. "You know about the giraffe, don't you?"

"I'm not sure what you mean," Dolph replied.

"The giraffe has a very long neck and it's not afraid to stick it out. That particular trait fascinates me. So I'm going to emulate my friend the giraffe and stick out my neck. Dolph, I'd like to offer you the position as my personal assistant."

Dolph looked blank. "I don't understand, sir."

"I'm asking you to leave the International Committee and come to work for me at Shawak Limited."

"But I have a commitment to the IC."

"We can find someone to replace you. Probably not as clever and quick as you, but anyone who is reasonably bright and willing to work will be able to get the job done. Although at the rate that we are trying to settle refugees in Shanghai, it *is* rather like trying to empty the ocean with a teaspoon."

"Mr. Shawak . . . Salah, I've absolutely no financial training. Why on earth would you want me?"

"For one thing. I need a man who is multilingual. Besides, you're bright, well-mannered, and personable. I prefer someone who is untrained, with no preconceived ideas. I have a gut feeling about you. And I always trust my instincts."

"I'm terribly flattered, Salah. It sounds like a great opportunity, but I couldn't possibly accept."

"Don't be flattered. Say yes."

Dolph couldn't read the older man's expression.

"But you said yourself, the refugee situation is becoming more impossible each day."

"Quite true." Salah Shawak moved his knight, pinning Dolph's queen. "All the same, I think we need to get to know each other better. Could you dine with me on Sunday evening? It would be my pleasure to introduce you to the night life of Shanghai."

"I'd enjoy that, sir." Dolph hesitated, then slid his remaining bishop towards Salah's king.

Salah quickly advanced his rook and smiled.

"Checkmate."

Two nights later Dolph accompanied Salah to a white stucco house at the far end of Hongkew. He watched as Salah opened his wallet and displayed a card to the pair of eyes peering through the small square opening in the unobtrusive wooden door. The door immediately swung open. A dark-skinned man in dinner clothes said, "Good evening, Mr. Shawak."

They stepped into a courtyard fragrant with the scent of jasmine. In the glow of the full moon, Dolph could see the beautifully tended flowerbeds.

"Where are we?" he asked.

"Patience, my young friend," Salah smiled. "The first lesson."

They handed their coats to the pretty coatcheck girl and walked into a black and silver carpeted vestibule, then down three marble steps into a dining room dimly lit with hundreds of candles that glimmered in the mirrored ceiling.

The tuxedo-clad *maître d'* led them to a corner booth, upholstered in soft, black leather. An unopened bottle of Dom Perignon chilling in a crystal ice bucket awaited their arrival.

Salah waved away the menus and turned to Dolph.

"May I order for both of us?"

Barely pausing for Dolph's nod of approval, he instructed the waiter to bring them caviar blinis—"but be sure it's mal'asol—with sour cream." For the main course he chose hot *fois gras* and broiled lobster.

Dolph tried not to stare at all the beautiful women, elegantly dressed in long gowns and sparkling jewelry, seated next to men who almost without exception appeared to be much older. At the far end of the room was a door that was drawing a great deal of traffic.

"What's the attraction over there?" he asked Salah.

"Dessert," Salah replied with a smile. "Do you see the dark-haired woman at the next booth? Her husband, that slightly stooped gentleman, is a banker here in Shanghai. And one booth over, with his back to us, is a high-ranking government official. I can't seem to place his lady friend."

"I've never seen so many beautiful women in one room," said Dolph, "but why are so few of them Chinese?"

"Ah, you like our Oriental ladies, do you?" Salah leaned back in the booth. "Lesson number two, Dolph. There are a great many caste systems in the East. And La Maison Français is a private club, primarily catering to Western tastes."

"And you," Dolph said, "are a blend of Oriental and European."

Salah laughed. "I guess you might say I combine the best of both worlds."

They lingered over their coffee and cigars. Dolph watched the banker and his wife walk through the door at the far end.

"Shall we follow them?" suggested Salah. "I think we're ready for the next course."

But rather than the elaborate buffet Dolph had been expecting, around the perimeter of the room were a row of cubicles about the size of railroad sleeping compartments. The door to each cubicle was fitted with a silver handle and, at about eye-level, a series of round glass peepholes.

At Salah's suggestion, Dolph glanced through one of the holes and gasped aloud. There was the dark-haired lady from the next booth, seated on a black leather couch. Her maroon lace gown was pulled all the way up to her waist and her legs were spread wide as she slowly caressed her inner thighs.

Several other men wandered over and gazed

appreciatively through the adjoining peepholes. As the crowd began to gather, the woman leaned back, raised her knees, and pulled aside her maroon lace underwear, revealing her clean-shaven vagina.

A bearded man turned the handle on the door and entered the cubicle. He knelt between her open legs and began licking her thighs with long, deliberate motions. After a few moments he unzipped his pants, pulled out his penis, and slid inside her, gently rocking back and forth.

As the bearded man continued his thrusts, a second man walked in and took over stroking the woman's legs. With perfect timing, the two men switched positions, and the newcomer pushed himself inside the woman's well-lubricated passage.

The older man pushed down the front of her dress and fondled her exposed breasts. Lazily, she reached over and stroked his erection, occasionally leaning forward to lick the tip, until, at last, he exploded all over her stiff pink nipples.

The other man continued his delicious, slow rhythm but Dolph tore himself away to find Salah. Searching the room, he saw a fully clothed man, staring into a cubicle with a glazed expression, masturbating violently.

In yet another cubicle, Dolph was shocked to see a naked young woman, her arms and legs spread-eagled on a leather couch, bound by her wrists and ankles with silver cord. Her squirming buttocks rested just at the edge of the couch, and a group of men were taking turns entering her gyrating body. Two other women, stilled dressed in their long gowns, were tongueing her, concentrating on her neck, breasts and arms, Through the glass peephole, Dolph could hear the woman's moans of passion as she shook with repeated orgasms.

He jumped when Salah tapped him on the shoulder. "And how are you enjoying this phase of your education?"

"I never imagined . . ." Dolph was so overwhelmed by the erotic power of the scenes he had witnessed that he could hardly get the words out. "This is the most incredible experience . . ." he stammered.

"Well, it's only the first step for you, Dolph Robicheck. Now you are beginning to understand that Shanghai offers untold delights."

Dolph stared in amazement at his self-appointed mentor.

"This evening's experiences are only one of many pleasures I can introduce you to. Speaking of pleasures, the evening is young. What delights of the flesh have you sampled here?"

"None," Dolph replied. "I'm feeling rather out of my league."

"Let's move on then. I have someone I'm quite sure is more to your taste."

Salah signalled for the bill and signed it with a flourish. Then he announced to the restaurant's captain, "Mr. Robicheck is thinking of becoming my new associate. In the future, I'd like all the club privileges extended to him. Have his charges billed to my office."

"Certainly, Monsieur Shawak," the captain replied. "I will have a member's card made out in his name and sent to your office immediately."

"But Salah, I couldn't possibly . . ."

Salah held up a hand to silence his protests. "Memberships here are not easy to come by. Whether or not you decide to use it, at least you know the facilities of La Maison Français are at your disposal."

Salah's car was waiting outside the courtyard. Salah murmured a few words in Chinese to the chauffeur and the car headed out of the lane.

"Now," said Salah, settling back against the gray silk foulard cushions, "we will savor a more personal touch."

The drive took them up and down many of Shanghai's narrow streets until they came to a halt in front of a brick wall. The chauffeur stepped out, pressed a button in one of the stones, then turned into the driveway, cutting the headlights before he came to a stop. Salah and Dolph stepped out of the car just as a wand of light shone from an open doorway.

A young Chinese houseboy greeted the two men and ushered them inside the house that from the outside looked much like Dolph's own. But as soon as they were inside, Dolph could see that clearly this was not a typical lane house. The dimly lit lamps cast a seductive, pink glow over the rooms, and the Oriental-styled sofas and armchairs were upholstered in sapphire, garnet, and emerald velvet, and trimmed with gold embroidery.

"You give honor to our household, Mr Shawak," said the houseboy. "Madame Soung will be downstairs immediately. In the meantime, may we offer you some refreshment?"

"That would be splendid, Fong," said Salah. "I would like a cognac, and you, Dolph?"

"The same," replied Dolph, wondering what the unpredictable Salah Shawak had in store for him now.

A rustling sound drew Dolph's attention to the top of the staircase. Gracefully descending the stairs was a beautiful Chinese woman, dressed in a traditional, high-necked Chinese gown of scarlet brocade. Her jet black hair was swept upwards in a tight French knot, secured by a diamond clasp, and her diamond earrings glittered brightly as she extended a slender, bejeweled hand to greet them.

Salah stepped forward to take her hand.

"Meilee, this is Dolph Robicheck, a recent arrival from England. Dolph, my dear friend, Madame Soung. I've asked Mr. Robicheck to become my personal assistant, and I'm trying to persuade him to make Shanghai his home."

"I hope you'll accept Salah's offer," said Madame Soung, smiling warmly. "Our young ladies could certainly use an attractive Englishman to brighten their lives."

"Speaking of young ladies, Meilee," Salah interrupted, "whom would you suggest for our young friend here? His imagination has just been piqued by a visit to La Maison Française. But I don't think such a public situation was quite to his liking."

Meilee thought for a moment and then nodded knowingly. "Yes, I think we can provide someone very special. Our sweet Ohna, don't you think, Salah?"

She tugged a silken cord near the fireplace and summoned Fong.

"Please ask Ohna to come down and welcome our visitors," she told him.

Dolph sipped his cognac as Meilee and Salah exchanged local gossip like the two old friends Dolph guessed they were. He already knew Salah well enough to realize that the upcoming experience would be a far cry from the hasty gropings in the darkness of Madame Arlette's cottage, and his heart was pounding with excitement. But the sharp warmth of the cognac soothed his nervousness, and moments later, when a light knock sounded at the parlor door, he felt ready for anything.

Nevertheless, he had to catch his breath at the sight of the slim Chinese girl who stood in the doorway. She looked to be no more than seventeen or eighteen, but unlike many of the Chinese girls he had observed in Shanghai, she held her head erect and didn't seem shy. Her long dark hair was parted down the middle and fell in two shining curtains framing her huge almond eyes. When she smiled, as she did now at the sight of Salah, she exposed tiny, twin dimples.

Salah responded with a kiss on each dimpled cheek. "Ohna, my dear, I would like you to meet a friend of mine from London, Mr. Robicheck. He has heard much about our Oriental hospitality. Meilee and I felt sure that you were the very one to introduce him to our ways."

"That's so kind of you, Salah. I would be delighted. Shall we leave you alone with Meilee," Ohna said, turning her smile on Dolph, "and I will take care of Mr. Robicheck?"

"Please," Dolph said, unable to take his eyes off this beautiful young girl. "Please, call me Dolph."

"Dolph." Ohna savored the sound of his name. "Yes, Dolph. Come, let's go upstairs so I can make your acquaintance."

Ohna took his hand and led him up the circular staircase to the landing on the second floor where the musky aroma of incense wafted through her suite of rooms. She smiled as she slowly began removing his jacket and tie. Without a word, she slipped off the rest of his clothes and helped him into a black brocade dressing gown, her hands brushing against his erection as she deftly tied the obi around his waist.

Unable to wait another moment to kiss her, Dolph reached over to pull her close, but Ohna smiled demurely and said, "Not yet, Dolph. Do not be impatient."

She put a pair of black velvet slippers on his feet, and then excused herself and disappeared through a doorway. Dolph could hear the sound of running water and then Ohna reappeared and led him into the next room, in the middle of which was a round, sunken tub made of black marble.

She waited a moment or two, then tested the water with her fingertips, carefully adjusting the temperature with the two gold-swanshaped handles on either side of the gold faucet. Finally, she seemed satisfied.

She helped him remove the dressing gown, and when he stood naked, she let the satin obi around her thin waist to fall to the floor so that her pink silk gown fell open.

Dolph stared unabashedly at the perfection of Ohna's olive-skinned body. Her high pointed breasts swelled above a taut, flat stomach. The archway between her upper thighs led to a trimmed thatch of dark pubic hair. He longed to touched her, but he understood that she was to set the pace for this evening's activities.

Ohna took his hand and drew him into the fragrant water, scented with gardenias.

"Is this comfortable for you?" she asked.

Dolph nodded, too hungry for her to trust himself to speak.

"Please, sit down, Dolph," she said, motioning to the side of the tub, and beginning to lather the back of his neck with gardenia-scented soap. She continued down the length of his body, stopping occasionally to gaze up at him through her long, dark lashes, as if to make sure she was pleasing him. As she knelt to do his legs, Dolph watched the perfumed water slide in waves over her pert little breasts.

With the grace of a dancer, Ohna perched herself on the edge of the tub. Now she proceeded to lather her own body with a fine layer of soap so that tiny bubbles collected in her pubic hairs and under her breasts. Then she helped Dolph out of the tub and led him over to what looked like a huge, glass-enclosed, oversized shower stall, with space enough for the two of them to stretch out on the soft, sponge-like material that covered the floor.

Ohna gently pushed him down and raised herself above his still soapy body, playfully biting his ear and rubbing herself up and down the length of his squirming body. Her hair tickled his chest as she brushed her breasts back and forth over his face, and massaged his fully erect penis between her finely molded thighs.

Finally, as if sensing that Doph could barely hold back his orgasm, Ohna positioned herself above him so that her buttocks wrapped around his penis and, pressing him between the cheeks of her behind, rode him gently until he was groaning and pleading with her for relief.

She seemed absolutely attuned to his sensations, for at the precise moment when he felt he could not control himself a moment longer, Ohna slowly stood up.

"I see you are enjoying my lessons tonight," she said mischievously. "Now I must ask you to close your eyes, for there is still more to come and the surprise enhances the pleasure."

Too drugged from the prolonged lovemaking to protest, Dolph closed his eyes and lay still, awaiting whatever Ohna had planned for him. Suddenly, he felt a warm trickle of water play across his feet and ankles. Opening his eyes, he saw that Ohna was lightly spraying him with thin jets of tepid water, methodically rinsing the soap off his body.

"Ohna. . . ," he began, but she placed her forefinger over his lips and slowly rubbed him dry with an oversized, thick Turkish towel, pausing occasionally to stroke his nipples and belly with her lips and tongue.

Dropping again to her knees, she allowed her tongue to explore Dolph's engorged penis, blowing softly on his testicles, as Dolph moaned and shuddered with desire.

He was ready to explode.

"Now," she said, smiling so that her dimples deepened. "Now you are ready."

She lowered herself onto his body and guided him into her warm wetness.

There was no holding him back. He came almost immediately, in a torrential explosion that felt as if it had begun at the deepest core of his being. The spasms seemed to continue forever.

Finally, he was done and lay gasping for breath, weak with spent passion.

Ohna kissed him gently.

"Did I please you, Dolph? Will you return here to learn more about our ways?" she asked him with an impish grin.

Dolph pulled her down on top of him and wrapped his arms around her.

"Yes, Ohna, you pleased me very much," he said, hugging her tightly against his body.

It was a moment that neither of them would ever forget.

Chapter Four

The day was unseasonably warm and sunny, ideal for walking and thinking. Dolph threw down his pen, stuck his sandwich in his pocket, and headed for the park.

His thoughts of the previous week's experiences with Salah—particularly the hours he had spent with Ohna—were disturbed by a familiar female voice.

"Dolph Robicheck, where have you been?"

Dolph turned and waited for Hannah Stein who was hurrying to catch up to him. In her left hand Hannah was carrying a basket loaded with groceries, which now she rested on the ground. Her auburn hair glistened in the bright sunlight, and she looked prettier even then he remembered.

"Hannah!" Dolph exclaimed, glad to see her after all this time. "What a nice surprise!"

"Is it?" she said reproachfully. "You knew where to find me."

Dolph searched his mind for an excuse, but the truth was he hadn't wanted to call her. He was all too aware of the Steins' plans, and he had been so absorbed in his new life that he hadn't thought much about Hannah and the pleasant times they had shared on the *Conte Biancamano*. He quickly changed the subject.

"You're looking very well. How are your parents?"

"They miss you, Dolph, and so do I." A flicker of reproach crossed her blue eyes.

"I've thought of all of you often," Dolph lied, "but I've been so busy, Hannah. The work at the IC is very time-consuming."

Hannah glanced around the park. "I can see how full your days are."

There was a long silence. Neither of them could think of anything more to say.

Finally Hannah took the initiative. "Goodbye, Dolph."

"Could I help you carry those groceries?" he offered guiltily.

"I can manage it, thank you." Hannah picked up the grocery basket and walked away briskly.

If only Hannah didn't have to attach so many obvious strings to their friendship. . . . Dolph suddenly had no appetite for his sandwich. He turned back towards his office at the rear of the Sephardic Synagogue.

His office . . . where more forms, more refugees with problems awaited him. The minute he answered one of their questions, they had ten more. The challenge no longer lay in providing solutions, but in getting through the stack of papers before the end of the day. Perhaps Salah was right—anybody with half a brain could do his job.

For once he was too preoccupied to be diverted by the still fascinating sights and sounds of Shanghai. His head was filled with questions and conflicting answers. But by the time he got back to his desk, he had made up his mind. He picked up the phone and called Salah Shawak.

Life changed radically for Dolph from the very first morning he reported for work at Shawak Limited. Never in his life had he even imagined the luxury that was suddenly thrust upon him. Salah demanded that his top executives maintain a successful aura about them: well-tailored suits, beautifully furnished offices and homes. He liked to remind them, "You don't work this hard to live poor!"

Salah insisted that Dolph move into a small bungalow, not far from his own home in Frenchtown, one of Shanghai's most affluent sections. The house, owned by Shawak Limited, which rented it to Dolph for a nominal fee, was a huge step up from the broom closet in Hongkew. It was elegantly furnished and came complete with an English-style garden and a houseboy named Ling. Dolph shopped the city for the one item he felt the house was missing to make it his home. In an old furniture shop he found a grand piano in perfect condition, save for a tuning. High time, he decided, that he return to his music.

He was given an office in Salah's home, where a constant
stream of visitors appeared at the door, wanting to transact
business with Salah Shawak. Most of them had appointments, but others did not, and it fell to Dolph to decide who
should be allowed to take up Salah's valuable time. Salah
also insisted that Dolph attend all the meetings.

Eventually, once he had mastered the nuances of the commodities market, Salah told him, his primary responsibility
would be to trade commodities on behalf of the Shawak
family. But in the meantime, Dolph was to listen and take
notes—and to make sure that the terms of the agreements
were carried out according to Salah's specifications.

"Don't take anything for granted," Salah warned him.
"Don't believe anyone unless you see the evidence with your
own eyes. Many years ago," he continued, his dark eyes
twinkling, "before I had grown wise with age, I agreed to
buy a twenty-story building in the heart of Bombay, for
what appeared to be an extremely reasonable price. I was
very proud of the excellent deal I had transacted for the
Shawak family, until my uncle pointed out to me that the
contractors had neglected to install any plumbing. There
wasn't a single toilet in the entire building!"

Salah often reminded Dolph that "In this world, what's
important is not merely what you know, but whom you
know." One day about a month after he had begun working
for Shawak Limited, Salah suggested that Dolph join him at
the Sephardic Synagogue for Sabbath morning services.

The following Saturday, Dolph put on his new blue suit
and joined Salah in the Shawak pew directly in front of the
rabbi. He watched the men quietly wandering in and out of
the elaborately decorated sanctuary, initiating deals and
exchanging information about real estate and the commodities market. At the close of the Musaf portion of the service,
over the kiddush of sweet wine and raisin challah, Dolph
was introduced to the wealthiest, most influential members
of the Jewish business community.

Salah invited him home for lunch, and afterwards, over a
game of chess, Dolph thanked him again for the introduc-
tions. Salah smiled with secret delight. Dolph was as eager

and astute a pupil as Salah had expected. He knew when to listen, and when to ask questions, and he was curious about every aspect of Salah's many business interests.

Their chess games were a shared pleasure that both men looked forward to greatly. Salah was the more accomplished player, and usually he won. But Dolph's agile mind was doggedly narrowing the gap between them. The games often led to conversation, with Salah taking the opportunity to informally expound on his philosophies about business and life in general.

"You've heard of the risk-reward ratio?" Salah asked Dolph, who was perusing the chessboard for an opportune opening.

Dolph nodded.

"Well, business works the same way," Salah explained. "Those that take the greatest risk, reap the greatest rewards. And well they should. I've never had any use for the man who sits by the wayside watching life go by. For the same reason, spectator sports have no appeal for me. There is a far greater satisfaction to be had in doing for oneself.

"You will learn that the mind is a far better weapon than the body when it comes to manipulating others. I'll show you how many more of our people we can save with proper amounts of well-placed money than with muscle."

Their discussions shaped Dolph's attitude toward his work. He was beginning to sense that, in some way, Salah was as nurtured by their relationship as he was. Perhaps it was the fact that he was an orphan, and Salah had no children of his own. Or perhaps it had something to do with the hideous reality of what was happening to their Jewish brethren in Europe. No doubt it helped that Dolph was a willing pupil, and Salah had the soul of a teacher. In a very short span of time, they were developing a remarkable friendship.

There were many nights that the young Englishman and the Oriental patriarch dined together in Shanghai's elegant restaurants, and they often ended their evenings at Meilee's house. Dolph was smitten with Ohna, and, try as he might, Salah could not persuade his protégé to sample the pleasures offered by the other young ladies.

"Dolph, it's not better, just different," Salah told him again and again, shaking his head in amusement at Dolph's stubborn loyalty.

But Dolph, for once, disagreed with his mentor.

"Salah, I don't need to spend time with any other women. Ohna keeps me perfectly happy and satisfied."

"Very well," said Salah. "Then she is yours."

"Mine?"

"I am giving her to you. As a present. To keep you company when you're at home."

Dolph was aghast.

"Salah, she isn't a horse to be traded," he said. "She's a human being. You can't simply order her to pack her bags and move into my home. How do you know she wants to come live with me? Besides, what will Meilee say?"

"Nothing, of course," Salah replied, his eyes more inscrutable than ever.

"You can't mean that. I'm sure you . . ."

Salah cut him off impatiently. "Dolph, Meilee's house is flourishing because of Shawak investments. We own her business and she runs it for us. Extremely well, I might add. I can do as I like with Ohna. As it happens, she has always been a special favorite of mine, and this is a great honor for her, especially because it's my decision. The East and the West have different ways, Dolph. Don't try to change us. You must accept us for what we are and take my gift graciously."

Just as Salah had predicted, Ohna was thrilled to hear that she was to move into Dolph's house. But she knew to keep her excitement in check, because Meilee insisted that her girls always appear serene and tranquil. And Meilee's orders were law.

Nevertheless, she danced silently in front of the mirror in her room, imagining how wonderful it would be to answer only to Dolph. From the moment she had set eyes on him in Meilee's parlor, she had felt a special spark of excitement for the young Englishman. And she knew he had felt it, too.

Ohna stood still for a moment and stared critically at her reflection in the mirror. She was truly fortunate—few of the other girls in Meilee's house would ever have an opportunity such as this. Picking up her hairbrush, she began pulling it rhythmically through her long, black hair, just as Meilee had taught her to do. One hundred fifty strokes, every morning after she bathed. She smiled at herself in the mirror and watched the deep dimples appear in her cheeks.

She must thank Salah the next time she was alone with him. He had always been so good to her. Better by far than her own father who cared only about Ohna's two younger brothers. Her father had never valued her more than when Meilee had handed him the money they had agreed upon as a fair price for eleven-year-old Ohna.

From the very first day, Meilee had treated her as if she were her own daughter. She had taught her so much, about how to care for herself, and a household, and about the ancient, intricate art of pleasing men.

Ohna hoped that when she was older, she would be as wise as Meilee. Sometimes she even dared to think that one day she, too, would have her own house, where rich men would come to be pampered and loved. All that was a long way off, but certainly within the realm of possibility since, even now, she was already succeeding beyond her and her family's wildest dreams.

Ohna finished dressing, looked around her room one last time, and picked up her small suitcase and the few bundles in which she had bound together her possessions. She wanted to be ready to leave as soon as Salah's driver arrived to take her to Dolph. Giggles of pleasure bubbled up in her as she imagined the look on Dolph's face when he arrived home to find her waiting for him.

How she loved Salah and Meilee for granting her this privilege. And most of all, how she loved Dolph.

Like most couples, Dolph and Ohna soon fell into a comfortable routine. Dolph often wondered how he had ever managed without her. She was both a docile Chinese concubine and spirited, knowledgeable companion who could make him laugh at the oddest moments and thoughts.

She immediately took charge of running their household and seeing to all his needs. By nature Ohna was a playful kitten, but Meilee had set an excellent example, and she could be a hellcat with the butcher or fishmonger if she suspected they were cheating on their deliveries. Ling quickly became her devoted ally and adoring slave, and together they terrorized the merchants at the marketplace as they poked about for the freshest fruits, vegetables, and spices.

Ohna insisted on personally preparing Dolph's dinner whenever he was at home, though Dolph often still spent three or four evenings a week with Salah. He was pleased to discover that none of the same restraints that Hannah might have imposed existed with Ohna. Rather than a stern or sulky face to greet him at the door when he came home late, Ohna would be waiting patiently for him, no matter what the hour, eternally grateful for his arrival.

But when he did spend an evening at home, he and Ohna usually retired early to their bedroom. Ohna's beauty and winning character, her ardent desire to please him, and the contrast between her greater sexual expertise and her deferential manner were irresistible lures. He was happy to spend many long hours with her as they explored each other's bodies and sexual appetites.

Meilee saw the danger signals. Her heart ached as she listened to Ohna's glowing reports of the magical nights and days she shared with Dolph. Again and again she tried to warn Ohna of the problems she was bringing upon herself by falling in love with her master.

"Enjoy your present together," Meilee told her, "for you cannot guess what the future may bring."

Ohna knew that large parts of Dolph's life would forever remain closed to her. Dolph was Salah Shawak's protégé and he moved through a world that she could never even hope to be a part of. But Ohna assured Meilee that she was well aware of the boundaries that divided their lives and she promised that she had no thoughts of crossing those boundaries.

For his part, Dolph never questioned her about her family or her background, nor did he ever suggest that she join him and Salah for dinner. Their arrangement, which according to Salah was quite commonplace in Shanghai, suited him perfectly. More and more, Dolph was discovering how much the Oriental culture and tradition had to offer as a way of life.

No matter how busy he was with the affairs of Shawak Industries, Dolph tried to spend at least an hour each day playing the piano. He had no idea that Ohna regularly listened in on his practice sessions. But one day, when she could no longer contain her curiosity, she gathered up her courage and crept into his study. Silently positioning herself just behind his right shoulder, she stood mesmerized by the sight of his hands gracefully drawing the sounds from the keyboard.

"How long did it take you to be able to do that?" she asked when he had stopped playing.

Dolph looked up in surprise. He had been so absorbed in the music that he hadn't heard her come in to the room, or sensed her standing behind him.

"I don't know," he said after a moment's thought. Music had always been such an essential part of his life that he couldn't remember a time when he hadn't played the piano.

"I think my mother put something in my milk," he joked. "Playing the piano is simply something I've always done— like walking or talking."

"But is it difficult to learn?" Ohna asked.

Dolph shrugged. "Not very, if you put your mind to it. Come, sit here next to me and I'll show you the basics."

Dolph slid over on the piano bench to make room for Ohna and positioned her hands on the keys and showed her the rudimentary fingering and some of the basic chords. For once, she was noticeably reluctant to suggest that they go to bed.

But eventually Dolph had his fill for one night of playing piano teacher. "Enough," he said. Then seeing the thinly disguised disappointment in Ohna's face, he added, "Perhaps I'll show you more tomorrow."

He came home the next day with a package wrapped in brown paper.

"Close your eyes, Ohna," he said, "and hold out your hand. I have a surprise for you."

Ohna quickly ripped off the wrapping paper, then looked

up questionably at Dolph.

"It's a piano instruction book. If you like, I'd be happy to give you lessons. We can work together in the evening when I have time, and you can practice during the day. Would you like that?"

"Oh, Dolph!" Ohna threw her slim arms around Dolph's neck and hugged him happily. "You're so good to me. When can we begin?"

"Why not right now?" said Dolph, enjoying her excitement.

Ohna eagerly nodded her head. "And I must think of a present for you," she said.

Dolph brushed a strand of Ohna's black hair away from her eyes. "Sweet Ohna," he said. "You've already given me so much happiness. You mustn't feel as if you have to match me gift for gift."

The deep dimples on either side of Ohna's mouth creased her cheeks, and she promised herself that she would make the evenings Dolph spent in her company memorable ones. For all her wisdom and experience, Meilee might be wrong, she decided. Perhaps Dolph did love her and wanted her always to be a part of his life.

From time to time, when he had a rare free moment, Dolph would stop to reflect on the extraordinary turns of events since the day he and Christopher Brooke had left England. He was no longer the wide-eyed, ignorant schoolboy who had to be led by the hand to new adventures, but rather, a sophisticated lover and apprentice businessman who was personal assistant to one of the wealthiest and most powerful men in the Orient.

With Salah's encouragement and guidance, Dolph had begun to speculate in real estate and had already turned a profit on three of his deals. The money he earned from his investments he immediately reinvested in more real estate, or in the futures market, where modest sums could be swiftly pyramided. He was learning to gamble, albeit in an educated way—and to like it.

Occasionally, he lost money, which troubled him. He wasn't quite comfortable with the philosophical attitude that

Salah displayed on the rare occasions when they made investment mistakes. But, he consoled himself, a man of Salah's enormous wealth could afford to be philosophical. But Dolph had only his small savings to fall back on. There might come a day when he, too, would be rich, but for now, he keenly felt each loss.

Not that the money itself was the point. He was young, not even nineteen, smart and ambitious. And he was receiving an education that not even a million pounds could have bought him in England.

Dolph kept long hours, so when he appeared at home just after noon one day, Ohna was alarmed even before she felt his clammy, hot forehead. His eyes were glazed with fever. His skin looked pale as moonlight.

"I've a terrible headache," he told her, "so I thought I might just lie down for a while and go back to Salah's later on when I feel better."

Ohna hurried after him to the bedroom and helped him undress, worriedly noticing that his hands trembled as he tried to unbutton his shirt.

He shook his head to her offers of tea or soup. "Just need some sleep," he mumbled, as she covered him with an extra quilt.

When Ohna put her hand on his burning forehead, he grabbed her fingers and cried, "Mother, stay here, with me."

"He doesn't recognize me," Ohna said to Ling. "He thinks I'm his English mother who died long ago."

Ohna sat up with Dolph through the night, anxiously watching his fitful, fever-induced sleep. When he cried out, "I'm so thirsty!" she applied ice chips to his parched lips and bit her own lips raw with worry.

The fever persisted into the next morning. Dolph seemed to be growing weaker by the minute. Ohna was about to send Ling to fetch Meilee when Salah suddenly appeared in the doorway of the bedroom.

"Oh, Salah!" she exclaimed anxiously. "Dolph came home sick yesterday and now he's worse. I'm so worried."

"Child, why haven't you called the doctor?" Salah asked

brusquely, alarmed at the sight of Dolph, ashen-faced, drawing sharp, shallow breaths.

Bowing her head to avoid his glare, Ohna replied, "I was going to go to Meilee's medicine man for herbs to cure his fever."

Salah's face clouded with anger. "Ohna," he berated her. "You should have called the European physician."

"Chinese man is better."

"Let's not argue," Salah whistled through his teeth and went to telephone.

The doctor examined Dolph and reported to Salah, "It's the spotted fever, all right. And a particularly nasty case of it. We've got to get his temperature down or there's a chance he may not survive. As it is, I can't predict what the lasting effects may be."

Ohna wanted to rip out her heart. She turned away from Salah and the European doctor so that they wouldn't see the tears spilling down her cheeks. If Dolph died, it would be her fault for not getting help right away. And now the doctor was saying it might be too late. . . .

"What can we do for him?" Salah asked.

"Keep him cool and rested. Try to get him to drink some tea. If we're lucky, the liquid will arrest the fever. Also, give him a sponge alcohol bath every hour. Beyond that, there's nothing we can do but pray."

Ohna's face revealed her misery.

"Now, young lady," said the doctor, patting her on the cheek, "he's a strong, young man, so don't you despair. I'll be back tomorrow morning, but you can reach me at this number if his condition seems to be worsening. And stop blaming yourself, Ohna. You need to stay strong and healthy to take care of him."

Salah made a phone call and arrange for two nurses to help Ohna take care of Dolph.

Although the nurses urged her to get some sleep and promised to wake her if Dolph's condition changed, Ohna wouldn't listen. Salah stopped by every afternoon and he, too, tried to persuade her to lie down in the other bedroom, but for three days Ohna slept and ate in the chair next to Dolph's bed.

Towards evening on the third day, Ohna suddenly left the house and hurried off to the old part of the city. There were times, she had decided, when only Chinese medicine men could cure Chinese sickness. She would seek advice from the same medicine man whom Meilee's girls consulted whenever they had problems.

"Ohna, how nice to see you," the old man greeted her. "I ask after you each time I visit with Meilee. But have you pain? You are too young and pretty to look so troubled." He squinted at her, as if he could find the source of trouble merely by examining her through his ancient eyes.

"It's my master, Honorable One," Ohna said, still gasping for breath after her trek across the city. "He suffers from a swift fever that has quickly taken his strength."

"Will he eat or drink?"

"No, Honorable One, not for three days already," she said, her eyes filling with tears.

The old man grunted and slowly walked over to a long shelf on which were arranged a row of squat porcelain jars. He squinted at the assortment, grunted again, and carefully emptied three different powders into a small drawstring bag.

"Here you are, my pretty little friend," he said, handing the bag to Ohna. "This mix of herbs should help your master. Make a paste of it with water and rub it on his chest at sunrise, noon, and sunset. It will help his circulation and rid him of the fever. And be sure he drinks strong tea. Do you understand?"

Ohna nodded. She thanked the medicine man, quickly paid him, and hurried back to Frenchtown with the remedy.

The nurse on duty shrugged her shoulders when Ohna repeated the medicine man's instructions. The herbs probably wouldn't do any good, she told Ohna, but neither would they do any harm. She went off to the kitchen to prepare the tea.

Dolph looked only half alive as he lay listlessly in his feverish coma, recognizing no one. As Ohna rubbed his chest with the paste and replaced the covers, she prayed silently for his recovery.

Anguish alternated with anger. She thought of the last six

months they'd spent together, enjoying each other's company, making love, playing the piano, talking and laughing. In her wildest dreams she had never imagined she could be so happy. How could Dolph get so sick and desert her like this? She so much needed him to be well again.

She reached into the ice bucket for another cold towel for Dolph's forehead and realized that there was something else she could do for him. Her father's great-uncle was a renowned fortuneteller. She would go to him for advice.

For the second time that day, Ohna left the house and quickly made her way to the ancient heart of Shanghai. Her stomach churned as she walked down a rickety flight of stairs at the back of the damp, musty building. Behind a bamboo curtain, in a small room lit only with dim candlelight, Ohna found her great-uncle, meditating in front of a low shrine.

His wrinkled face turned slowly towards her as she entered.

"Wise one, I have a question," she said, standing to one side of him.

"Yes, my child," he said in a low monotone.

Her voice trembled. "I must know something about the future . . . about my master."

With a claw-like hand, the fortuneteller beckoned her to move closer. "My child, it is not always pleasant to know what tomorrow brings us. The future may hold unpleasant secrets."

"Tomorrow is very important to me," Ohna said in a rush. "I will pay you much money to know my tomorrow."

"You will pay in more than money," he warned softly.

"I must know," Ohna said, her voice pleading but firm.

After a moment's consideration, the old man shrugged his shoulders and dumped the contents of a worn, cloth bag onto the dirt floor. Ohna held her breath as the man studied what appeared to be a pile of animal bones.

After what felt like an interminable length of time, he raised his head to meet her frightened gaze. "Impudent one, what can be so important that you tempt God's wrath?"

"I love someone very much. He is terribly sick. Will he live and come back to me?"

The wizened old man turned his attention back to his bones. Tears trickled down Ohna's cheeks. In spite of all Meilee's careful teaching, she had allowed herself to fall in love with Dolph. To lose him now would be unbearable.

Finally Ohna stepped forward. "Please, tell me," she said anxiously.

The fortuneteller sat up and spoke in a hushed voice. "Yes, he will recover. But he will not come back to you as fully as you would wish. There will be an ocean between you. An ocean and a bridge."

"A bridge?" Ohna asked. "What kind of bridge?"

"A bridge to eternity," the fortuneteller replied. "The signs say you will always share the boundaries of its span."

Dismissing her with a wave of his hand, the fortuneteller returned to his meditation. Ohna took out a pile of coins and put them down on the table in front of the old man. As she trudged up the wooden staircase, she heard him mutter, "Foolish, foolish."

When the sun rose the next morning, Ohna was greeted by the sight of Dolph, sitting up in bed. His cheeks were still flushed, but he was smiling.

Weakly, he held out his arms to her. Ohna hugged him gently, weeping tears of relief. When the doctor arrived for his daily visit, he confirmed that now that the fever had broken, Dolph was indeed on the road to recovery.

"We were quite lucky with you, Mr. Robicheck. We've had several deaths of late from this fever," he said, shaking down the thermometer. He coughed nervously before he went on. "Unfortunately, we've had some evidence of a rather disturbing side effect of the illness. There is a very strong possibility that the fever causes sterility."

"Sterility!" Dolph exclaimed weakly.

"But your other sexual functions should be quite normal," the doctor added quickly. "Well, then, I shall stop by tomorrow to see how you're feeling. But we should have you up and about in another week."

"How long have I been ill?" Dolph asked Ohna when she returned.

"It's been four days. Oh, Dolph," she said, suddenly feeling weak herself with relief and joy, "I'm so grateful you're feeling better."

"And starving. I feel as if I haven't eaten in days. I haven't, have I?" he said cheerfully. "Do you suppose Ling could bring me some soup or . . . why Ohna, whatever is the matter?"

Ohna covered her face with her hands to hide her tears. She shook her head, her long hair swinging from side to side as she struggled for control so that she could speak.

"I'm sorry," she said at last, "I've been so terribly worried and frightened. All of us have been . . . Salah and . . . Salah! I must call him immediately to tell him that your fever has broken. He's been here every afternoon."

"You've taken very good care of me, haven't you, my Ohna? I'm sorry to have worried you so."

Dolph took Ohna's hand and briefly held it to his lips, then leaned back against the pillow, as though the slight effort had tired him out. "Now," he said, closing his eyes, "go tell Ling I'm starving. Then call Salah and inform him that his assistant is back among the living and ready to work. We'll show that doctor that it takes more than a fever to keep me in bed for a week, won't we?"

"Yes, Dolph," Ohna nodded, ready to agree to anything he said, now that he was better.

She wondered whether the doctor's words about possible sterility had registered, but knew better than to ask. They had never discussed the subject of children, but occasionally, while she sat alone practicing the piano, she had day-dreamed about bearing Dolph's son—or even his daughter. Of having a child who would irrevocably cement the bond between herself and the man she loved so much.

Chapter Five

Salah insisted that Dolph take time off before returning to work. "I'll have you dismissed immediately if you appear at my house," he said with an imperious smile. "You've been quite ill, and you're no use to me if you're not fully recovered. I trust you'll take good care of him, my dear," he said, turning to Ohna. "Let me know if you need anything."

The next week, which Dolph and Ohna spent together, was made that much more precious because of Dolph's near-miss with death. Ohna particularly felt the presence of what she had almost lost. She happily pampered him, preparing all his favorite foods and begging him to tell her what else she might do to amuse him while he was regaining his strength.

"I'm not an invalid," Dolph protested when Ohna tried to persuade him to stay in bed. "And you must stop treating me like one, no matter what Salah says. Now, how would you like a piano lesson? After that, if you insist on my being in bed, you can give me a massage. And I've a wonderful idea about just what we can do after *that*!"

By the time the doctor declared him fit enough to return to work, Dolph had had enough of playing house with Ohna, as pleasant as that might be. Besides, he'd been following the war news in the daily papers. The English and French positions were rapidly deteriorating.

Salah had stopped by several times during the week for a chess game, but if he had any inside information, he was keeping it close to his chest. It felt wonderful to be back at his desk down the hall from Salah's office. The Shawaks had long since transferred most of their capital to banks outside Shanghai. But the market was fluctuating wildly because of the war escalating in Europe. Dolph was kept busy monitoring the supply and demand of goods that were needed for the war effort.

Now he stretched and went over to the long window that fronted on Salah's well-tended gardens. The skies were pearl-gray, and a light rain was falling. At the border of Salah's property, a unit of Japanese soldiers, part of the joint American-Japanese force that patrolled the British sector, was marching in neat lockstep formation.

Dolph watched them until they passed out of sight. They want us to take notice, he decided. It's a show of strength. And again he wondered what secrets Salah was holding that he wasn't yet choosing to share.

His questions were answered less than three weeks later. Late one evening, he and Ohna had just began to get ready for bed when Ling summoned Dolph to the door, where Salah's driver stood waiting for him.

"Mr. Salah apologizes for the intrusion, but he asks that you come back to the house with me. He needs to see you at once."

"I'll be right there," Dolph said and ran to get his jacket. "Don't wait up," he told Ohna. He wasn't surprised by the late-night summons and felt sure it would be a lengthy meeting.

Salah was seated in the large chair by the fireplace in his study. "Close the door," he said, dispensing with his customary civilities. "I've just received some very bad news. News that requires immediate action."

He paused a moment and then went on. "I've had word that the Japanese are planning a massive airstrike. One that is sure to bring the Americans into the war."

"But that's ridiculous," Dolph said. "I thought they were negotiating with the Americans for support."

Salah shook his head. "A clever cover. No, I'm certain my information is accurate. And apparently, the attack is scheduled to occur sometime before the end of the year."

"That's only two months away!"

"Precisely," Salah said grimly. "Which is why we must act immediately. There is no time to waste. We must prepare to leave Shanghai as quickly as possible."

"Leave Shanghai!" Dolph was incredulous. "But we've been living with a Japanese military presence here for some time. Why turn and run now?"

"This will be just the beginning. The Japanese will declare war on America and England. The word is that they'll intern all of us as alien nationals. As executives of a well-known company such as Shawak Limited, we would be particularly vulnerable."

Dolph sat down heavily. "Will you go to England?" he asked.

"No. India. As you know, we have a large branch of our family there already."

"Of course," murmured Dolph, slowly beginning to absorb the implications of Salah's imminent departure.

Salah rubbed his chin thoughtfully before speaking.

"Dolph, I'm hoping you'll come to India with me and the rest of my family. I think you know how much I value not only your business acumen, but your friendship as well. I'd like to see our association continue for a very long time. I realize all this comes as great shock, but fortunately, you don't have much time to give it any thought."

Dolph was silent for a moment. "I appreciate your offer, Salah," he said at last with a sigh. "But the time has come to go home. I would never forgive myself if I sat out the war in India, instead of fighting for my country. I need to go back to England."

"There are many ways to win wars," Salah said, smiling slightly, as if he had already known Dolph's response.

Dolph returned the smile. The two men were so finely tuned to each other's thoughts by now that there was no further need for words.

"In any event," Salah said, "we've a great many plans to make. We've got to liquidate as many of our remaining assets as we can. Once the news leaks out—and you may be sure it will—everything will deflate in value." Salah reached over and rang the bell on his desk to summon one of the servants. "This is going to be a long night. Would you like coffee or tea?"

"Tea," said Dolph. He stood up and began to pace the length of the room. "Salah, how will you move all your remaining cash out of the country? The Japanese are sure to be keeping a close watch on you."

Salah laughed with pleasure at the thought of outwitting the enemy. He slipped a ruby ring off his finger and held it up to the light. "We will convert all our cash into precious stones. Gem stones are a sure thing in any market, in any part of the world. They're small, easily hidden, and can be quickly converted to cash. My family discovered this solution centuries ago. Unfortunately, we've had to use it often in the past. Ah, good, here comes our tea," he said.

A servant appeared with a silver tray laden with a pot of tea, plates of sandwiches and fruit.

"Let's get on with it, shall we?" said Salah.

By eight the next morning, after countless cups of tea, they had outlined the work to be done in the coming weeks and divided up the responsibilities among the top Shawak Limited executives.

"A good night's work," Salah said, escorting Dolph to the door. "I'll see you back here at noon?"

"Right," nodded Dolph wearily, his thoughts on a shower and a few hours of sleep.

Certainly, India was the logical place for Salah to relocate, he reflected as Salah's chauffeur drove him home. But he had to return to England. Nevertheless, the prospect of uprooting himself again depressed him. He had hated the thought of coming to Shanghai, and now, ironically, he hated the thought of leaving.

He would have to say goodbye to so much. The city itself, which still seemed so exotic and endlessly fascinating. Salah, who had become not only his mentor, but also his substitute father. The work that he loved. And of course Ohna.

For the first time since Ohna had arrived to live with him, he was reluctant to return home. For try as he would to picture a life together with her in England, he couldn't imagine it. Dolph was all too aware of how important class and race differences were in England. Their relationship, so commonplace in Shanghai, would be totally unacceptable in England. As a Chinese girl living with an Englishman, Ohna would be an outcast.

Besides, he would probably be sent to the continent. Ohna would be obliged to stay in London. She would be completely alone, left to cope by herself with the food shortages and nightly air raids that had become a routine part of life in London.

No, there really was no choice. He only hoped she would understand.

Ohna knew better than to ask questions, but when she greeted him at the door, Dolph could read the concern in her dark eyes. Since his illness, she had fussed over him a great deal and worried about his health. He hated the thought that he would again be responsible for disrupting the serenity of her life.

"Thank you," he said gratefully, as she pulled back the covers and helped him into bed. "Wake me at eleven. We'll talk then."

He fell asleep instantly.

Sunlight was filtering through the curtains when Dolph woke up to Ohna's hand gently stroking the back of his neck. He rolled over and kissed her, enveloped in the sweet fragrance of jasmine, Ohna's favorite scent. And then he remembered with a jolt the decisions of the previous night. He dreaded the news he was about to give her. Sadness wrapped around him like a shroud.

"What's wrong, Dolph? Your sleep was restless."

Dolph sat up and groaned. "I have to be back at Salah's in an hour. Let's talk over breakfast."

As usual, the table was set with delicately arranged fresh flowers. Ohna waited until Dolph was seated before pouring the cup of steaming hot tea which she herself had prepared. Not until he had helped himself to toast and fresh fruit did she take her own seat.

Staring at her across the table, Dolph realized how much he would miss her and the quiet grace she brought to his life.

"Ohna, I'm afraid we have some serious problems. Salah has received information that the Japanese will soon be in the war," he said. "It's not common knowledge yet, and we must try to keep the news a secret while we prepare to leave."

Ohna's eyes widened with fear. "Leave? Where are we going?"

"Salah and his family are going to Bombay. He's asked me to go with him, but I told him I must go back to England. My country is fighting for its life, and I should be there. . . ." He felt as if a lump had lodged itself in his throat.

"I could take you back with me, and I will, if you like. But I'm planning to enlist, and the army is sure to send me at once for basic training. Unfortunately, you'd be all alone in a strange city—a city that is being bombed nightly, where there are food shortages, where you would know no one. London, for someone like you . . ." The lump in his throat grew harder, nearly choking off the words. "It couldn't be as it is here, Ohna. English ways are very different."

Ohna sat immobile as a statue. She hardly seemed to be

breathing.

"Ohna, Salah wants to take you to India with him. You'll feel far more comfortable with his household in Bombay. As soon as the war is over, I promise we'll be together again. The Nazis are sure to fall soon, we'll see to it, and then I'll be on the first boat out. . . ."

Ohna stood up, bending her head to hide her tears, and said, "Of course, Dolph. Of course you are right. Please, excuse me a moment, I must get a handkerchief."

Meilee had taught her that tears of grief were to be cried in private. Dolph's brave words were empty reassurance. Now she finally understood some of what the fortuneteller had told her.

Dolph worked feverishly to settle all pending matters and ensure that the transition period for Shawak Limited be as smooth as possible. He also had several of his own personal matters to resolve. One involved a visit to the Steins, who received him coolly at first. Dolph understood their hurt. He'd not been in touch for months, and no doubt they knew he was now working for Salah Shawak.

But he wanted to warn these people who had been so kind to him aboard the *Conte Biancamano*. Was there anything he could do to help them, he asked. Perhaps he could use what influence he had to get them papers for India or even England.

Herr Stein shook his head ruefully. He and his family had established themselves here. The strain of yet another flight, of being brand-new emigrants again . . . Hannah was especially distressed because the date had already been set for her marriage to a wealthy Jewish merchant. Fleeing Shanghai would ruin her plans. Dolph shrugged his shoulders. At least he had tried.

Though Dolph spent even more hours than usual with Salah preparing for their departures, his good friend did not try to persuade Dolph to change his plans. But in the midst of the whirlwind preparations for their departures, Salah insisted they find time for one last game of chess. Capturing Dolph's queen, he took a sip of cognac and said, "I've an idea about how we can make this work out."

"Pardon me?" Dolph asked, his mind intent on the strategy of the game.

"I respect your feelings of patriotism and loyalty to England," Salah said, "but I've a notion you'd do your country a lot more good behind a desk than on the battlefield. I don't think you're cut out for carrying a gun. That's meant as a compliment," he added quickly, noting Dolph's look of dismay. "You can save as many lives by using your head as you can by using your rifle. I think you'd do well to offer your services to the intelligence chaps. And I know some people who'd be happy to talk to you."

"I feel as if I should go wherever they need me most," said Dolph. "But it's certainly an interesting suggestion."

Salah laughed. "And not an altogether unselfish one, I should add. If you could arrange to be based in London, I have a plan. We would establish a special trading account there. I will advance you the money. You could continue to do in your spare time exactly what you've been doing for me here. You could also keep your eye out for real estate opportunities. In wartime, good properties are always available."

"I'm enormously complimented, Salah. But my plans are so up in the air. Besides, you're talking about a great deal of money, and I imagine that communication between London and Bombay will be no easy matter."

"Indeed," said Salah, "but I've taught you well, and I trust your judgment." He studied the board a moment. "And your instincts," he said with a smile. "I see you've trapped my king and I must concede defeat."

"Think it over, Dolph," were his final words as Dolph left that evening.

"I will," promised Dolph, laughing at himself. Agreeing to think over one of Salah's propositions was almost tantamount to saying yes.

"I'm delighted," Salah declared when Dolph told him he would consider the proposition—depending upon what the army chaps had to say about his enlistment. If he ended up in intelligence and that allowed him to continue his association with Salah, so be it.

He and Salah shook hands on their proposed partnership. Salah would send a cable to Clive Kabasis, his London solicitor, giving Dolph permission to trade on his behalf. The profits would be split, seventy percent to Salah, thirty percent to Dolph.

As usual, the Shawak name was powerful enough to slash through the red tape and secure Dolph a rare free berth on a Portuguese freighter to Lisbon. From there, he would have to try to get passage on a London-bound ship. As the date of his departure approached, he found himself daydreaming about England, suddenly impatient to be there, to proceed with his life.

If Ohna sensed his eagerness to depart, she made no mention of it. She kept busy packing their belongings. Saying her goodbyes to her family and the other girls, she took comfort in the fact that Meilee would also be going to Bombay. Whatever Ohna was feeling in her heart, it was kept well-hidden, so that even her brown eyes reflected none of her sadness. She offered to sew the gems that Dolph had purchased with his savings into the seams of a rather cumbersome scarf. This he was to wear around his neck for the entire trip. And she patiently waited for him to return in the evenings, always ready to give him a soothing massage.

Their last evening together they didn't speak of their separation. In fact, they hardly spoke at all. Each word skirted the pain that sooner or later they would have to face. Dolph gave Ohna a piano lesson and then played her favorite Beethoven sonata.

"Enough music," he said finally. He wanted to make love to her. He wanted to memorize every inch of her, so that he could carry her image with him until they could be together again.

They caressed each other gently, making love slowly and tenderly, then with greater abandon as the hour of their leavetaking grew near. He stroked her eyes and lips and kissed her nipples until she whimpered with pleasure. "I'll miss you, my sweet, sweet Ohna," he whispered.

Ohna stared at him in the moonlit darkness with her soft brown eyes, not daring to speak. She had been trained never to talk of love to a man—and tonight those were the only words that wanted to come to her lips.

They fell asleep in each other's arms when it was close to

dawn. In the morning there was hardly enough time for Dolph to shower and shave before they had to leave.

Salah was waiting for them at the pier. Though he had told him it wasn't necessary, Salah had insisted on taking time from his crowded schedule to say goodbye. Dolph nervously tried to lessen the tension he and Ohna were feeling, while Salah filled the gap with small talk.

"Are you sure that scarf is sewn tightly enough?" she fussed.

"Yes." Dolph made a face. "And it's already irritating my neck. But as long as it's bothering me, I won't lose it."

"When it annoys you, remember who made it for you," Ohna said with a sad smile.

Dolph brushed the back of his hand against her soft cheeks. "You never annoy me, Ohna," he said, tracing her dimples.

He turned to Salah. "I owe you so much, dear friend. You've changed my whole life."

Salah shrugged. "You were receptive to change. It had to happen."

"There's no way I can ever thank you," Dolph struggled to find the words to express the gratitude and love he felt for Salah.

"One day I'll find a way," joked Salah.

"Anything you could ask would not be payment enough."

At that moment, the stack on the freighter roared, an angry admonishment rather than a beckoning call.

Dolph took Ohna in his arms. They held each other tightly, kissing for the last time. Suddenly, Ohna released him and ran swiftly up the pier to the main road. Dolph's gaze followed her until she was out of sight. Then he turned to Salah and silently shook hands.

The passage to Portugal was markedly different from the one he had taken on the *Conte Biancamano* three years earlier. Dolph spoke to few of his fellow passengers aboard the freighter. He knew to be wary, and besides, he had no heart for conversation. His mind was filled with thoughts of the people he had left behind—and the unknown adventures that lay ahead of him.

The dangers of the voyage, coupled with the lack of companionship, made the trip thoroughly unpleasant. Dolph almost welcomed the discomfort, as a way to ease his heartache and distract him from his misery.

Lisbon was full of refugees and rumors about the war. On the morning of December 8, the newspaper headlines screamed of the bombing of Pearl Harbor. Dolph had already arranged passage on a ship bound for Southampton that was set to sail at the end of the week. But on this December day, as he sat drinking coffee in a portside cafe, his mind was on Shanghai, not England.

He prayed that Salah, Ohna, Meilee, and the rest of the Shawak family had left safely and were well on their way to India. They'd become his family, and now he wondered whether he had made the right choice. The memory of his reassuring words to Ohna echoed in his head. The war would be over in no time, and they would soon all be reunited. In the meantime, he had work to do for England.

Chapter Six

As the familiar shoreline of Southampton came into view, Dolph was filled with emotion.

Here was England. His home. Except that in actuality it was no longer home.

Home was Shanghai. Home meant days spent in his office, evenings playing chess and talking to Salah, nights making passionate love with Ohna, waking up next to her in bed as the morning sun peeked through the curtains.

And England?

England was the past—his birthplace, the memories of his parents and their shocking deaths, the few months he had spent with Uncle Maurice in Cambridge. Now he wasn't sure whether he could make a life for himself that would mean as much to him as the full and happy one he had left behind.

The customs agent stamped his passport and said, "Been away, have you? Come back to fight the Krauts? Welcome home, then. We could sure use you, lad.''

Everywhere were men in uniforms—Englishmen, as well as Americans and Canadians who hadn't wanted to wait until their own countries decided to get into the war. The train to London was packed full of soldiers, RAF men, and sailors, all of whom seemed to want to do nothing but sleep. Not even the pretty girls in the short skirts—shockingly short, to Dolph's eye—were diverting enough to keep them awake.

Dolph remembered the miserable weeks he'd spent at the training camp in France. After a day of waking up before dawn, slogging through the mud with his rifle and a heavy pack on his back, trying to cram his head full of Constantine's lessons about how to survive behind enemy lines, more than anything else, even food, he had craved sleep.

He wondered guiltily how many of these poor fellows had already seen action. And all the while he had been sitting pretty in Shanghai, making money and living the good life. Well, just as soon as he'd seen Uncle Maurice in Cambridge, he would get himself back to London and find out where he fit in.

He'd hoped to spend an hour or two in London before continuing on to Cambridge, but the ticket-seller warned him to run for the train that was just about to leave, for there wouldn't be another one for hours. Walking up the path to the old cottage in the chilly darkness of early evening, he was assaulted with memories. Suddenly he was glad that he'd come straight through. He couldn't wait to see Uncle Maurice.

Dolph's knock was answered by Maurice himself, who blinked in pleased astonishment at the sight of his long absent nephew.

"Uncle Maurice," Dolph said, taking a step forward.

The old man stared in disbelief for another instant and then threw his arms around Dolph and drew him into the vestibule.

"My word, nephew, I never thought I'd see you again!" he exclaimed. "What a marvelous surprise!"

In the light, Dolph saw how much his uncle had aged. He

was very thin, and above his blue shirt collar, his neck was
wrinkled with old age. But his blue eyes still twinkled and a
grin lit up his gaunt cheeks.

"Were you on your way out?" Dolph asked, noticing his
uncle's overcoat.

"I was just getting ready to assume my nightly post," said
Maurice. He proudly displayed the crest of the air raid war-
den insignia and laughed. "I get to blow the whistle on the
Nazis. Why don't you come on patrol with me tonight? It
will give us a chance to get reacquainted."

Dolph begged off. The long day of travelling had caught
up with him.

"Of course," Maurice said at once. "Scrounge around in
the cupboard and help yourself to whatever's there. You
know where to find everything, don't you?"

Dolph nodded. It was home after all, and it felt good to
be here again.

Later they sat in front of the fire with a bottle of brandy
and talked into the early hours of the morning.

"Certainly, I know the name Shawak," said Maurice.
"They've got family here." He shook his head in amazement,
as if he could hardly believe this was his nephew. Imagine
young Dolph, telling him these stories about the life he had
led as the protégé of Salah Shawak.

"And what about you?" Dolph asked.

Maurice shrugged. "Life as usual . . . except for the war,
of course. I've had to say goodbye to a great many of my
students. Some of them have already been reported as
casualties." He fell silent for a moment and stared into the
fire.

"What about Chris, Uncle? I've not had a word from him
since he saw me off on the *Conte Biancamano*."

"The last I heard of Chris, he was still in Palestine. I had
a letter from him just after he arrived there. He'd visited a
couple of the collective farms—they call them
"kibbutzim"—and wanted me to know that socialism *can*
work. And do you remember Ian Wallingford?"

"I think so, yes. Tall chap with dark hair?"

"Right. That's the one. Well, he's up in London with the
Special Operations unit of the Foreign Office. In fact, now

that I think of it, he phoned me just last week and asked if I could recommend anyone for his department. They're looking for people who are clever, not merely bright. Might you be interested?"

"I certainly would be."

Maurice beamed. "We'll ring him up straightaway in the morning, then. And speaking of morning," he said, checking his watch, "look at the time. You can sleep in, but I've an early class to teach."

Dolph underwent a battery of intelligence tests and a physical. He answered what seemed like hundreds of questions about his family, friends, and everything he'd done since the age of five.

Ian Wallingford bought him a drink at the Palm Court and told him not to worry. Ian knew that the fellows over in decoding were desperate for people who understood and spoke fluent German. It was just a matter of waiting until he got security clearance.

Sure enough, within a month of his return to England, Dolph was issued housing in Chelsea and assigned to a tiny, windowless office in the basement of a building on Baker Street. There he and seven other men and women spent eight hours at a stretch decoding German messages between Berlin and the war fronts.

Compared to what his life would have been like at the front or even in the barracks, his present living situation was absolutely luxurious. The work was relatively uncomplicated once he got the hang of the codes, and his colleagues were good company. But he missed Shanghai. Damn it, he thought, leaving the office at the end of the first week, he knew he had it good, but he couldn't get either Ohna or Salah out of his mind.

Once or twice, looking up from a long, intricately coded message that he had just deciphered, he momentarily imagined he was back in Salah's house, about to be summoned to a meeting. Or waking up before dawn, still half-asleep and disoriented, he thought he was in bed in the little bungalow in Frenchtown with Ohna at his side.

Had they arrived safely in India? Was Ohna happy? Was

Salah well? How were the Shawak fortunes faring now that the Americans had finally jumped with both feet into the war? He wrote a letter to Salah, enclosing a short note for Ohna as well, and dropped it into the post box at the post office, wondering whether it would ever reach them.

Homesick and yearning for the sounds and smells of the Orient, he followed the West India Dock Road to the old docks of Limehouse where police patrolled the enormous walls, on the lookout for smugglers trying to carry stolen goods through the tall gates. The sailors coming in from Hong Kong and Singapore and Shanghai frequented Charley Brown's Tavern, on West India Road. Occasionally, Dolph went by there to drink weak, wartime beer and eavesdrop on their talk of foreign ports and how the war was affecting the shipping routes.

Weekends he often went up to Cambridge to visit with Uncle Maurice. The students were still riding their bicycles to class and stopping in for a pint at the Anchor Pub, right on the Cam. But the atmosphere at the university was different from what he remembered. The talk, of course, was about war, about enlisting, about friends who had already left school to sign up. They seemed so much more serious than the young men who had sat for hours in Maurice's livingroom, philosophizing about the Spanish Civil War and the merits of socialism versus communism.

"They're growing up quickly, these chaps," Maurice commented. "Dolph," he said, suddenly changing the subject, "it's good to have you back in England. I can't help thinking that you very much resemble your father."

"Do I?" Dolph smiled at Maurice. "It's good to be back here, Uncle."

He hadn't realized how much he enjoyed his uncle's company. His dry wit and humorous insights were valuable diversions at the end of a long, sometimes tension-filled week of listening to and decoding German messages.

He gradually made friends at work and soon discovered that he was a rare and valuable commodity in wartime London—a young, able bodied, attractive single man. His male colleagues all had sisters or cousins, and the women, many of whom had fiancés in France and Africa, all had friends who were eager to go out dancing or drinking with him. As the spring turned into summer, he spent less and less time at Charley Brown's, and found himself instead escorting lovely young ladies to the cinema and the theater, to dinner parties and makeshift balls.

The girls he was meeting, especially the Americans, were breezy and independent and perfectly able to take care of themselves. Though they seemed to want to please him, they didn't worry about his every whim and desire. No doubt, he mused, they would have been shocked by Ohna's submissive manner and quiet obedience.

But there was a distinct advantage to their Western attitudes about men and life in general. He was responsible only for making interesting conversation and seeing that their cigarettes (for they all smoked) were lit and that they got home safely.

And to his surprise, he realized that he had stopped thinking about how he and Ohna made love and how she would look up at him through her long lashes as she poured him a cup of her perfectly brewed tea. The first time he slept with another woman—a young American freelance journalist—he felt a quick pang of guilt, as if he had betrayed Ohna.

Ridiculous, he told himself. And he knew that Salah would have been the first to agree. How many times had he encouraged Dolph to spend an evening with one of the other girls at Meilee's house? Certainly Dolph had made no promises to Ohna, nor would she have expected him to remain faithful. And he craved the physical contact, hungered for sex.

A letter arrived from Salah. He was delighted to hear that Dolph had found a place for himself in Intelligence, and that he knew he'd made the right decision about returning to England. Property was sure to be undervalued, Salah wrote, and he'd told Clive Kabasis to cooperate with Dolph in any way he could.

Salah also suggested that Dolph look into an interesting situation one of his contacts had put him on to. It seemed there was money to be made at the end of the war—if the Allies were victorious. And if they weren't, Salah noted with a shrug so eloquent Dolph could read it between the lines, they might as well all hang it up anyway, eh?

Salah's information was this: In the years before the war, in some cases as far back as 1907, British government-backed bonds had been issued by Germany and Japan. Now, of course, these "Enemy Alien Bonds" were being traded very cheaply. Salah had heard of one, for example, the "Jap 5% of '07" (issued by the Japanese government in 1907 at a five percent interest rate), which normally sold for one thousand pounds. Now it could be bought at a deep discount of fifty to sixty pounds.

If the Axis Powers lost the war, and Salah was fully confident they would, one could fairly safely assume that they would honor their debts. The bonds would appreciate considerably in value and would eventually pay off at their issue price.

"Buy as many as you can for me," Salah wrote to Dolph, "and if you're smart, you'll do similarly for yourself. It's a gamble, but it's an educated gamble, and thus a risk worth taking."

And, oh yes, Ohna was fine and adjusting to her new life in Bombay. She said to tell Dolph she missed him very much, especially missed their piano lessons and their nights together. But she felt well and Bombay was an interesting city and Salah and his family were very kind to her.

Dolph chuckled to himself. A continent away, Salah was still guiding his career and financial fortunes. He tried to imagine Salah's Bombay home—no doubt it was as sumptuous as the one in Shanghai, and he wondered how Ohna spent her days.

And her nights. For after all, she had been trained to be a concubine . . . but he pushed away the thought. No ties bound them. He was free—and she was no longer his. Until they were reunited, as he had promised her, after the war.

In the meantime, on days when the brass at German headquarters were quiet, and he got bored with his colleagues' endless talk of the war and the lack of decent coffee, Dolph spent his lunch hours in Threadneedle Street, talking to the commodity traders and investment bankers and stockbrokers, gathering information, soaking up the atmosphere, as Salah would say.

Sure that Salah's instincts were right, he sold one of the diamonds he'd bought in Shanghai with his savings, and purchased as many of the Enemy Alien Bonds as he could find. A tip from a broker persuaded him to buy into a gold mine in South Africa, and an insurance chap he met at a pub two doors down from the Royal Exchange told him about some decent real estate in Hampstead that was going begging.

"Just you watch," said the fellow, taking a long sip of beer, "that's where they'll all want to be building when the boys come home after the war."

After the war . . . Everyone he knew was playing the same waiting game, putting their lives on hold until they'd licked the bloody Germans and the bombs stopped dropping and they could pick up where they'd left off in 1939 and 1940.

Sometimes Dolph wondered whether such a thing were really possible. He knew he'd changed in the months and years since he'd left Shanghai. Despite the power of Salah's long-distance influence, he was no longer the naíve youngster, eager to learn and grateful for Salah Shawak's attention and advice. He'd come to know his own mind, to trust his own judgment and instincts.

By the war's end in 1945, Dolph had done very well for himself as well as for Shawak Industries. The sale of two more of the four Shanghai diamonds helped him pay for the parcels of cheap properties and abandoned bomb sites that were going begging all over London. All over England, for that matter.

"The provinces," the insurance company chap had said beerily, "that's where you'll want to be buying, if you're smart. That's where our fellows are looking."

As hopes for an Allied victory soared in England, so did the value of real estate. In the last year and a half of the war, Dolph often felt as if he were working two jobs. After his eight-hour shift at the Ministry Building, he would hurry home to return calls from commercial property agents, solicitors, and government officials who knew that Dolph Robicheck had money to invest in property development.

Months before he was mustered out of the army, he'd

found himself a tiny office, hired a secretary, and ordered stationery.

"The British-Orient Limited" was the name of the company printed at the top of each page.

"Dolph Robicheck, President and Managing Director," read the next line.

While all of England took to the streets in noisy celebration of Armistice Day in November, 1945, Dolph sat as he had so many times before, staring into the fire behind the grate in Uncle Maurice's cozy sitting room. The news that peace had been declared had spread like wildfire across the Cambridge campus, and through the closed window Dolph could hear the students' "hip, hip, hurrah's" and cheers of triumph.

If only, he thought morosely, Uncle Maurice were here to share in the excitement. Even now, a full month after Maurice had died suddenly of a massive heart attack, Dolph couldn't quite believe that his uncle was dead. They had spent so many hours talking about the war, analyzing its philosophical, economic, and moral implications, planning the trip they would make to the Far East as soon as it was safe again to travel.

Committed socialist though he was, Maurice had nevertheless taken great delight in his nephew's entrepreneurial activities, applauding Dolph's stories about the properties he'd bought up for a song, including a country estate in Devonshire that had gone begging.

"A businessman," he would say, shaking his head ruefully. "Your father would never have believed it."

On Saturday mornings, when Dolph came up to Cambridge, Maurice would greet him at the door and ask, "And which London suburb have you taken over this week, Mr. Rockefeller?" But the twinkle in his eyes had signalled his love and approval.

Once again, Dolph reflected bitterly, someone he loved had been taken from him. It was nobody's fault, but the loss nevertheless cut deeply. For a man of not quite sixty, Maurice had seemed in good health. There'd been no warning— just a brief phone call: "You'd best come up to Cambridge as quickly as possible. Your uncle's very ill."

Dolph had stood by Maurice's hospital bed, trying to hide his worry and fear. "Sleep well, Uncle," he'd said.

"I will," Maurice had answered with a weak smile.

He had died very early the next morning.

Now it fell to Dolph, as Maurice's only living relative, to sort out his uncle's affairs. He had inherited the Cambridge cottage and had decided to rent it out through the university. Beyond that, he still didn't have the heart to make any but the most pressing decisions about his uncle's modest estate. One thing he had resolved, however: Never again to allow himself to be hurt by loving—and then losing—someone who was dear to him.

Chapter Seven

Salah arrived in England on January 1st, Boxing Day, 1945, impatient as ever to get a first-hand fix on what was happening to his cotton mills and property investments.

Feeling unaccountably nervous, Dolph waited for him in the suite at the Ritz that was reserved permanently for Salah. Telephone calls had been completely out of the question during the war. Aside from infrequent letters, communication between them for the past four years had consisted of terse cables devoted to business matters. And yet so much of their past relationship had revolved around their close personal connection.

Then, of course, there was the question of Ohna. He remembered his promise to her.

"As soon as the war is over, we'll be together again. . . . I'll be on the first boat out."

It had never occurred to him—and now he could not imagine why not—that he might choose to stay on in England. But he had made a place for himself in London—friends, business and professional acquaintances, diversions that he would miss in Shanghai. Life promised to be even more exciting and full of interesting opportunities and possibilities once peacetime became a reality.

The truth was, he had no intention of returning to the Far
East. And he knew for certain that there was no place for
Ohna in his present life. He took for granted his absolute
freedom to come and go, to spend time with whatever
woman he chose to whenever he chose to, to be alone for
long periods of time if such was his pleasure.

Not that Ohna would ever have thought to reproach him
even mildly for doing so. But what they had had between
them, as special and wonderful as it was, seemed to belong
to another era. He was twenty-six years old, he owned
pieces of what promised to be some of London's most valuable properties, and he could make whatever he wanted of
his world.

Guiltily he admitted to himself that for the next few years
he wanted nothing to hold him down—not even the fragile
silken ties that ever-so-loosely bound him to Ohna.

But the moment Salah walked through the door and
embraced Dolph, none of that seemed to matter very much.

"Well, well," Salah said, stepping back to take a long look
at Dolph, "I see that you learned my lessons well. You've
made an excellent choice of tailors."

Dolph laughed sheepishly. "Salah, you always said you
paid us well to live well."

"Indeed, I did. And from all the reports I've received, you
deserve the perquisites. I think we both need a drink," he
said, sinking into the wing-back armchair. "I've been bounc-
ing around on a troop transport plane for three days with
only a few hours to stretch my legs in Alexandria and Paris."

Abruptly changing the subject, Salah said, "I was sorry to
hear about your uncle's death, Dolph. I had been looking
forward to meeting him."

"Thank you." Dolph once again marvelled at Salah's
highly efficient information network. More impressively,
Salah always seemed genuinely to care about what happened to the people who worked for him. "I had told Uncle
Maurice so many stories about you. He very much wanted to
meet you, too. In fact, we talked often about travelling to
the East. . . ." Dolph's voice trailed off. Suddenly, the topic
was too painful to discuss.

Salah tactfully changed the subject. "I suggest," he said,

"that we adjourn this meeting to the dining room. After three days of airplane food, I need a good meal, served to me on a table with a linen cloth, rather than a shaky plastic tray. Dolph, could you call down and reserve us a table while I wash up and change for dinner? And tell them to open a bottle of their best claret. I've not had a decent bottle of wine since I left Shanghai!"

They were seated at the far end of the enormous room, next to one of the floor-to-ceiling windows that faced Green Park. The lights of the city twinkled through the twilight mist. Salah sighed with obvious contentment as he looked around the familiar gilt- and cream-colored room, accented by the pink tablecloths and napkins.

"It's rather comforting to know, is it not, that despite all the horrors and killings and bombings, certain things remain unchanged. I don't suppose that can be said of too much in this world, however."

He gazed at Dolph from beneath his hooded eyelids, as if searching for the changes that Dolph had undergone since leaving Shanghai.

"How is Ohna?" Dolph asked abruptly.

"She's well," Salah replied. "When we first got to India, she had a bit of a hard time of it—so far from home, even with Meilee there to keep her company. She missed Shanghai very much. I should say," he corrected himself with a sly grin, "she missed *you*, although, of course, she never said a word to that effect. But my household in Bombay is large and lively, and she's quite a favorite, as you can imagine. She sends you her love and said to tell you she's still playing the pieces you taught her. She was so eager to continue her lessons that we even found a teacher for her."

Dolph couldn't bring himself to ask whether Ohna shared a bed with one of the members of Salah's household. Instead he asked, "Does she feel at home in Bombay now, or does she want to come to England?"

"Well, that's rather up to you, isn't it?" said Salah, peering over the rim of his crystal wine goblet. "I suppose you've given some thought to whether or not you want to resume your life with her?"

"Salah, you know, don't you, that I would not have

traded those years in Shanghai for anything? I learned so much from you—whatever I know today about business, and human nature as well. And from Ohna . . ." Dolph smiled, remembering the lessons he had learned from her about lovemaking.

"But I've realized that England is where I belong, for the time being, anyway. There are such wonderful opportunities here for me—and for you, too, Salah," Dolph said, leaning forward with excitement. "But I see," he continued more slowly, "that there's no place in my life now for Ohna. I know I led her to expect to rejoin me after the war, and I'm still terribly, terribly fond of her, but it simply wouldn't work out there."

"I understand," Salah said. "And Ohna will, too. Now, let's order dinner. We've much to discuss."

Salah was concerned about the growing strength of the independence movement in India. He had decided, he told Dolph, to move his headquarters to Hong Kong and had hoped Dolph would join him there. But after listening to Dolph's description of the opportunities in England, he agreed that Dolph was right to stay on in London. And he also understood Dolph's desire to branch out on his own and head up his own small company.

But he also hoped that the two of them could continue their extremely profitable business relationship—and remain close friends as well.

"I'd like to toast to that," he said, lifting a glass of the famous Ritz pink champaign he had ordered to celebrate their reunion. "To your future happiness and to the success of British-Orient Limited. And to many successful joint ventures with Shawak International."

Their glasses clicked across the table. Salah smiled with the satisfaction of a teacher who is well-pleased by the brightest student in his class.

Salah spent a month in England, meeting with his lawyer and broker and accountants, inspecting his family's mills in Birmingham, visiting with family members whom he hadn't seen since before the war. He took one look at Dolph's tiny flat and said, "I think it's time you found yourself a proper place to live, don't you agree? A suite of rooms at the Ritz would do nicely if you don't want to be bothered setting up a household."

As he had done in Shanghai, he invited Dolph to the theater, and made sure to introduce him to some of the most influential members of the London financial community. He also hosted several dinner parties at the Ritz and nodded approvingly at the women who accompanied Dolph. "I see you've finally discovered the pleasures of playing the field," he said, after Dolph appeared with yet another pretty, young woman.

Dolph grinned and shrugged his shoulders helplessly. He knew that women enjoyed his company, enough to accept the unspoken ground rules: Nothing serious. Nothing exclusive.

Certainly all the girls agreed that Dolph Robicheck was terribly interesting and oh-so-attractive. Not precisely handsome, but he had something else they found irresistibly appealing—a quiet self-assurance. He was so very attractive, kind and amusing. And so *rich*, besides. And he dressed so very well. If he wasn't ready to settle down, well, that was all right, because at least that meant he was available (if one called early enough) as an escort.

Indeed, as one of the most eligible bachelors in London, he had to refuse more invitations than he could accept. The Carlton Club in St. James and the Travellers at Pall Mall were happy to accept him as a member. And an invitation to one of his small dinner parties was highly coveted. In a very short time, Dolph Robicheck had made a place for himself in the upper echelons of London's business and social sets.

If, after a week of too many late-night meetings and parties, he momentarily longed for the serenity of his bungalow in Frenchtown and Ohna's gentle presence, he quickly dismissed such thoughts. Why waste time being nostalgic for what had been?

Living for the moment was what mattered to him now. He'd learned his lesson—life was too chancy to permit oneself to become seriously committed to one idea, to one woman. He was riding a colorful carousel that he hoped would never stop. After all, he reasoned, as long as he was enjoying himself, why bother jumping off?

The Jazz Club in St. John's Wood was one of his favorite spots to hear American jazz, and he often arranged to meet friends there. He'd been waiting a long time to hear Duke Ellington, so he was happy when he was handed a message that his date would be late. He settled himself comfortably at the bar to wait for her and lost himself in the music.

At the end of the first set, he shook his head in admiration and signalled the bartender.

"Can I buy you a drink?" asked the man sitting next to him.

Dolph turned and looked up at a tall black man with an engaging grin and an American accent.

"I saw you at the London Symphony concert last night. You were with a redhead, I believe."

Dolph nodded, puzzled.

The black man grinned ruefully. "I have to admit that it was the redhead I noticed."

Dolph laughed, enjoying the fellow's honesty. He was a good six feet, slightly stooped, and very handsome. When he smiled, which he seemed to do easily, his teeth showed white above a thick beard, but his dark brown eyes were hard to read.

"Allow me to introduce myself," the man said, extending his hand. "Jeff Gotley."

Dolph grasped the man's hand. "Dolph Robicheck."

"What did you think of the symphony last night, Mr. Robicheck?"

"It wasn't too bad."

"My reaction precisely. I've heard better."

He glanced towards the entrance. "There's my lady," he said. "Why don't we join forces and spend the evening together? I'm intrigued by a man who obviously shares my taste in music."

"Thanks very much, Mr. Gotley, but I'm waiting for someone myself." Dolph felt a pang of regret as he declined the offer. The man had a certain magnetism that he found intriguing.

"Well, at least share our table until your friend arrives,"

Jeff Gotley suggested.

"I'd be delighted," Dolph said.

"*Bon soir*, Madeleine," Jeff said as she leaned over to kiss him. "Dolph Robicheck, Madeleine Laval."

Madeleine Laval could have been a model. She was tall, with large blue-green eyes, and her ash-blond hair was perfectly coiffed in a shiny pageboy. She looked to be in her thirties and carried herself with the proud posture of a woman who took her beauty for granted.

"*Enchantee*," she said to Dolph. "Robicheck . . . I know that name." She smiled and turned to Jeff. "Are we three for dinner this evening?"

"Mr. Robicheck is waiting for someone, but he's ours in the meantime."

"Please, call me Dolph," he interjected, following Jeff and Madeleine to their table, one of the best in the house. The table captain obviously knew Jeff Gotley and addressed him in rapid French.

"You seem to be a regular here," Dolph said after they had given their orders.

"I drop by whenever I'm in town. Their music suits me."

"Where is home?" Dolph asked, curious about this cosmopolitan American.

"To use an old chiché, anywhere I hang my hat. Actually, I guess I'd have to say Los Angeles. I'm a lyricist, movie songs mostly. And since movie moguls move it in L.A., that's where I spend a lot of my time."

"What brings you to London, then?" asked Dolph.

"I'm here on business," Jeff said. "I'm working on a minor epic called *Sing a Song of Sixpence*. A catchy title if I ever heard one," he grimaced. "But why complain if it puts a little caviar on the table. And what about you, Dolph Robicheck?"

Dolph laughed. He liked the American's candor, so different from his polite and guarded compatriots. He was about to reply when Denise Mark, his redheaded friend from the night before, appeared at the table.

"So sorry I'm late, darling," she said, flashing the brilliant smile for which she was famous, "but I've had a frightful day."

"No problem," said Dolph and quickly introduced her to Jeff Gotley and Madeleine Laval.

Jeff winked almost imperceptibly at Dolph as he rose to greet Denise. "I was just telling Mr. Robicheck . . . Dolph . . . that he seems to share my taste in good music— and interesting women as well."

Denise smiled again as she took her seat and said, "And what other interests do you and Dolph have in common?"

Dolph noticed the look of amusement on Madeleine Laval's face. He immediately decided he wanted to know more about this woman who was apparently secure enough not to be threatened by Jeff's obvious flirtation. "What brings you to London, Mademoiselle Laval?" he asked.

She had a lovely, throaty laugh. "It's Madame Laval, actually," she said, "but please, you must call me Madeleine or I shall feel like your nanny."

"I'm sorry. You're divorced, are you?"

Madeleine laughed again. "Not at all. Quite happily married, in fact. And, Monsieur le Prosecutor, to anticipate your further questions, my husband is Pierre Laval."

"Ah, yes, Parfums Laval. And what have you done with Monsieur Laval this evening?" Dolph asked, sensing that this intriguing woman wouldn't object to his blunt question.

"I presume he has found his own diversion. He usually does." Waiting for Dolph to consider the implications of her statement, she looked up at him and lightly bit her lip.

Their drinks arrived just as the second set began. He couldn't help but be distracted by Madeleine Laval's presence and found himself stealing glances at her, as she listened and nodded her head appreciatively.

There was something about her . . . something he couldn't define, but she intrigued him in a way no other woman had for a very long time. And, he noted with some amusement, she looked utterly unperturbed by the fact that Jeff was clearly mesmerized by Denise.

Now here was an interesting idea, he thought. Denise was sweet and great fun, but she lacked a sharp wit and her conversational abilities were limited. Madeleine, he had already gathered, had no such deficiencies.

"Would you all join me for a nightcap at my flat?" he suggested when the musicians began gathering up their instruments.

"Oh, Dolph, it's early," pouted Denise. "I'm dying to go dancing."

"Well, that's a coincidence," grinned Jeff, "because so am I. How about you, Madeleine?"

"Another night, I promise, Jeff. But this evening I should be getting home. So if you agree, Denise, I will lend you Jeff and perhaps you, Monsieur Robicheck, will be so kind as to escort me home."

Dolph could not help but admire the grace with which Madeleine Laval had handled the situation. He waited with her as Jeff and Denise found a taxi.

"Here's my number," said Jeff, handing him a card. "Give me a call if you feel like it. We could discuss music appreciation—or whatever." He grinned and clapped Dolph on the back. Kissing Madeleine, he said, "Good night, sweetheart. Don't forget to call."

"I won't, and thanks so much, Jeff. *Bon soir*, darling."

Dolph wondered about the nature of their relationship but as they settled into the backseat of his limousine, he said, "You know, I have no intention of taking you home."

"And I have no intention of going home," Madeleine replied, her hand brushing the back of his neck, a promise of things to come.

During the short drive to the Ritz, Madeleine asked him about himself. Unlike many of the girls he escorted around town, she seemed genuinely interested in his responses, as if she really wanted to know who he was and what was important to him.

But she fell silent as soon as they entered the lift at the Ritz and didn't say a word until they reached his suite. And she was silent even after they had shut the door behind them.

After removing her cloak, Dolph tried to take her in his arms. But Madeleine ever so gently disengaged herself.

"*Mon cheri*, we shall do lovely things together, you and I, yes?" she said.

"Yes!" Dolph quickly replied, moving once again to

embrace her.

"Ah, but time is our friend, *cheri*. I am in no hurry, and
I presume, neither are you."

Madeleine walked into his bedroom and immediately
noticed the enormous mirror above the fireplace. As if
oblivious to Dolph who was watching her curiously from
across the room, she slowly reached for the satin snaps at the
shoulders of her white gown. The dress slithered over her
waist and down her legs, revealing the fact that she wore
nothing underneath.

With Dolph as a rapt witness, she stared at her image in
the mirror and silently fondled herself, concentrating on her
nipples until they stood hard and erect. Her hands caressed
her belly, briefly brushing her pubic mound, then moved
downwards to her thighs, which she massaged with gentle
concentration.

Madeleine's lips were parted and her breathing became
more audible as she continued to play with the tender flesh
of her inner thighs, touching her budding clitoris. She
seemed to have no need of him, so totally involved was she
in her own responses.

Dolph could not tear his eyes away from the sight of her
exquisite body reflected in the gilt mirror. Although he had
learned from Ohna the value of postponing pleasure, he was
already so aroused that he couldn't keep from touching himself. Eagerly he waited for a signal from Madeleine.

When, at last, she stretched herself across the bed with a
groan, he moved to reach for her. But the gentle pressure of
her foot against his groin stopped him. For the present, she
would permit him to be a voyeur—nothing more.

Stroking his erection, Dolph watched as Madeleine
rhythemically teased herself with wet and glistening fingers
until she was writhing with passion. Dolph groaned, barely
able to hold himself back, his hand working almost
automatically to achieve the relief he so desperately yearned
for.

Just when he thought he could no longer contain himself,
Madeleine reached up and pulled him onto the bed. Her
tongue searched for his, hungrily probing. She seemed to be
sucking him deep within her hot, moist cavities.

"Now, *cheri*, now," she whispered urgently, tickling his ear with her tongue.

"Yes, yes, yes," he heard himself cry, as if from a distance, and then he came in a breathless violent explosion.

As he sank back against the pillow, Madeleine slithered down and licked his stomach clean. Then her lips met his and she shared with him the salty traces of his sperm.

Chapter Eight

Before long, the London gossips were busy spreading the word that Dolph Robicheck had at last been tamed. And by no less a temptress than Madeleine Laval, who was herself an estimable catch. The eldest daughter of a wealthy family that owned considerable land and a chateau in the Loire Valley, Madeleine De Martigny Laval was a born aristocrat who never, ever doubted her rightful place in French society.

Madeleine had never been able to decide where she felt more at home—whether in her family's chateau or in an artist's studio in Montmartre. But early on she had realized there was no need to make that choice. She was free to cultivate friendships with whomever she pleased, whether it be a dustman or a duchess. Among her good friends she counted a former racing car driver who had guided her party on a thrilling expedition through the deserts of Morocco and Algeria; the Duchess of Westminster; the homosexual author of a current bestseller; and a parish priest whom she had grown up with in the country.

Five foot nine and mannequin-thin, she was a naturally glamorous standard-bearer for Parfums Laval. Her natural élan created excitement whenever she entered a room, and she lavished her warm smile an anyone willing to be its recipient. Her photograph regularly appeared in *Elle*, French *Vogue*, and the *Tattler*. Most people thought she was beautiful, though in fact she was not. But she had a serene bearing and chic elegance that served her better than beauty.

Madeleine was clever rather than brilliant, and

adventurous rather than merely curious. She could hold her
own in the Paris fashion ateliers as easily as she could ski the
slopes of St. Moritz or spend a day riding her horse through
the countryside.

She made no attempt to hide the fact that she and Dolph
were frequent companions, and Dolph quickly surmised that
Monsieur Laval evidently had no objections to his wife's
infidelity. The Lavals, it seemed, had long since arranged
their lives to suit themselves. If they met in public, it was
quite by accident, and each greeted the other lovingly. In
each other's company, they had a marvelous time.
Separately, they could enjoy themselves just as well. And
one never asked questions of the other.

Pierre and Madeleine had grown up together. Their
betrothal was arranged by their parents when Madeleine
was thirteen, and they were married five years later. Both of
them were relieved that the difficult choice of a marriage
partner had been made for them. Someday they would
have children, they told each other, but somehow Madeleine
never became pregnant, which left them free to come and
go as they pleased.

Pierre Laval's perfume business took him all over the
world. They maintained homes in London and Paris, as
well as a ski house in St. Moritz. The Lavals were great
favorites, either individually or as a couple, wherever they
happened to be. They knew what was expected of them—
appearances at certain family functions, bright smiles for the
photographers, the fulfillment of social and charitable
responsibilities.

Madeleine Laval was not only a woman of rare style and
intelligence, but she also was remarkably well-organized and
efficient. Her dinner parties were triumphs. She knew what
to serve, as well as how to arrange the flowers, and whom to
invite. The conversation at her tables flowed brilliantly.
Dolph found himself depending on her more and more as a
hostess.

Madeleine picked up Dolph's education where Salah
Shawak had left off. Without seeming to instruct, she
taught him how to buy furniture and fine art. Tactfully, she
suggested that it was time to leave the Ritz. Hotel living was

efficient, but it had its limitations. She had seen a divine townhouse for sale on Eaton Square. In short order, she had introduced him to one of London's best interior designers. The man's talent, Madeleine's taste, and Dolph's bank account combined to create a gracious setting.

Overlooking a small private park open only to residents of the Square, the cream-colored house with its pillars trimmed in black and black iron gates was soon the talk of London. Dolph and Madeleine had searched the city for the finest Chinese and English antiques—black lacquered coromandel screens with mother of pearl insets, a prize set of jade stemmed cups, a pair of Chinese hardwood throne chairs.

The polished wood floors were covered with Chinese silk rugs in muted pastels. On the wall that led from the foyer to the living room were hung a priceless collection of folded silk Chinese dressing gowns.

"You've created for yourself a little bit of the Orient," Madeleine said, surveying the rooms. "But my favorite touch is still the swimming pool that overlooks the garden. What a clever idea to have had it enclosed. Did you have the mirrored ceiling put in especially for me?"

Dolph was pleased with his new home, the first one he had ever owned. In the library stood a grand piano that he had seen in a store window and bought on an impulse. He hadn't played since leaving Shanghai. Suddenly, he needed to rediscover the music within him. It was as if he had succeeded in blending his Shanghai past with his English present. And who knew where his future might take him?

He flew to Paris to accompany Madeleine to the courture shows and fell in love with a charming flat on the Avenue Foch. Its east-facing windows let in the early morning sun and warmed their love-making, which was both inventive and passionate. In the evenings, beneath a seventeenth-century crystal chandelier that lit the dining room with one hundred twinkling candles, he and Madeleine entertained her Paris friends, an eclectic mix of artists, politicians, and businessmen.

Although she was very sure of her appearance, she often asked Dolph his opinions about her makeup, hairstyle, or choice of gown. "A man's touch is important, *cheri*," she told him, "for you may see what I have missed."

But there was one area of her life about which she did not consult him. Madeleine saw no reason why she and Dolph should not have other lovers. She made no secret of the fact that when they were apart, and even occasionally when they found themselves in the same city, she followed her own inclinations.

At first, Dolph felt wounded whenever Madeleine casually made reference to a romantic liaison. But gradually, he learned to accept and enjoy her attitude, appreciating the freedom that they were both able to enjoy.

Madeleine Laval was everything Dolph would ever have dreamed of in a wife. And more—for she had one superb advantage. She was already married. "Yes, indeed, she's something else, that lady," was how Jeff Gotley summed up Madeleine's many virtues. He had met her at a weekend house party in Deauville. Originally, they had been lovers, but neither one was willing to devote the time required of a romance. Soon they drifted into an affectionate friendship.

Madeleine was one of the few people who knew Jeff's true background. Not that he tried to conceal it, but he amused himself by maintaining an air of mystery that allowed people to concoct the most outrageous stories about him. In reality, he was the son of a doctor from the Portuguese-black community of Fall River, Massachusetts, and his upbringing had been thoroughly middle-class. He'd married his high-school sweetheart, fathered two children, and moved to Los Angeles, where he'd had some success as a songwriter.

The day after Pearl Harbor he enlisted in the Army—and fell in love at first sight with Europe. Languages came easily to him, and life for a black man overseas was less difficult than it was even in enlightened Hollywood. But his wife was a hometown girl who missed Massachusetts and when he suggested a divorce, she sighed with happy relief.

Now, in the era of the Hollywood musical, Jeff was in great demand as a lyricist. He found that he could name his own price. He was able to spend more than a few months of the year amusing himself in high style in London, Paris, or wherever. One columnist had dubbed him the "expatriate celebrity," and he liked the phrase well enough that he joked about having it printed on his business card.

He and Dolph were becoming fast friends. At his urging, Dolph had even begun composing again, with lyrics supplied by Jeff. "Nothing serious, man," as Jeff would put it, but their musical collaboration was developing into a strong bond between the two men.

Music wasn't their only common interest. With Madeleine as their guide, they spent hours in London wandering through the British Museum, in Paris at the Louvre and the Jeu de Paume across the Tuileries Garden. They visited the galleries in Montparnasse and Montmartre and drove south to picnic along the Loire.

It was an exciting time for Dolph. His world had suddenly widened to offer him tantalizing financial and social vistas. He had no family to hold him back, no responsibilities except to himself and the British-Orient Limited. Like a child with an intriguing new toy, he explored every new opportunity. The freespirited, freespending way of life to which Madeleine and Jeff were accustomed precisely suited his state of mind.

The three friends, blessed with unlimited funds, could just as easily wake up in Madrid as Milan. It made no difference, as long as the party looked promising and the guest list amusing. If the evening turned out to be a disappointment, they invented their own games and stunts to liven things up.

On one memorable trip to the south of France, their three-person act was declared "the rage of the Riviera" by a Paris tabloid. Headquartered at the Hotel Carlton in Cannes, they sat on the terrace, drenched by the warmth of the Riviera sun, laughing over the description of their escapades.

"Lady, don't you have any selectivity at all?" exclaimed Jeff. "Or do you sweep up the people of the world like a vacuum cleaner?"

"Darling, whom are you picking apart now?" smiled Madeleine, accustomed to Jeff's acerbity.

"I'm not picking, but that guy last night was a real creep," said Jeff stubbornly.

"As a matter of fact, I thought he was rather attractive."

"Attractive! Aggressive is more like it," he protested.

"Well, I suppose that anyone forced to go through school as Norbert Mandelstein—and nicknamed Norbie, no less—is bound to turn out either tough as leather or a milksop. But what is true about him is that he runs like a madman after every pretty young thing that won't have him. And when he finally conquers her, he just as quickly runs in the opposite direction, blindly seeking the next one who catches his fancy. You can always spot him bobbing blissfully in a sea of women."

"Personally," Jeff said, "I prefer the Princess. Now that is a body to have and to hold."

Dolph leaned back, silently enjoying the typical exchange between his lover and his friend.

"I understand that she is one to have, but definitely not to hold," Madeleine said. "She plays for pay."

Jeff was aghast. "With that rich daddy of hers? No shit!"

"Her daddy may be royal, but he's not rich. Don't confuse the two," admonished Madeleine. "Besides, her spending habits could break the Bank of England. So if you are thinking of sharing her bed for the night, be prepared to go shopping in the morning."

"Well, I'll be!" Jeff exclaimed.

"Also, stay away from Roy," Madeleine went on. "You know who he is . . . that very proper-looking American lawyer. Edna says he gets his thrills reading dirty magazines in the closet while he masturbates."

"I won't ask," Dolph said, laughing so hard he almost choked on an ice cube. "How she happened to come by that particular piece of information. But don't we know any normal people?"

"Depends on what you call normal," said Jeff.

"How about Magu, that sculptor we met in Aix?"

"Ugh," Madeleine said. "Did you see him the other night at the Maugham party? He tried to draw on all the women's gowns with crayon. He said it would increase the value of their clothes."

"Did you let him draw on yours?" asked Dolph.

"On my Balenciaga? I should say not! I gave him a doily from under the chocolates and he drew my picture on that."

"Smart lady."

"You don't know how smart." Madeleine winked. "Someone offered me a hundred pounds for it."

"I hoped you grabbed it," laughed Jeff.

"*Mais absolutement non!* I'm worth a great deal more than a hundred pounds, don't you agree?"

"Definitely," Dolph said.

Jeff nodded his agreement. "Let's look over the broads on the beach. I still can't get over that scene in the men's toilet," he said.

"You mean in that department store in Milan?" Dolph replied.

"Whatever possessed us?" Madeleine shook her head in amusement.

"Don't you remember?" said Dolph. "It was a dare from Freddy McNichol, that photographer for *Life*. And good Lord, I'm certain he got the whole thing on film."

"I had so much to drink that weekend I'm a little fuzzy about the details. But I do recall that you dressed me up as a man and the six of us invaded the men's room."

Jeff chuckled ruefully. "Oh, Lord, it's beginning to come back to me. That guy Hopkins was bragging about how big he was. All I remember is him standing in front of the pissoir, playing with himself, while the customers were walking in and out."

"And the shocked expressions on their faces!" Dolph said.

"But do you remember that fellow who finally took the initiative after just one look at the size of him? The poor old soul offered money if he could take him home. And we were laughing so hard that we fell out of the two stalls we were hiding in. That old geezer was so startled he ran out of there without even zipping up his fly."

"Why did we start drinking so early in the day?" asked Madeleine.

"We started the night before, actually," Dolph said. "The party simply lasted two days. It was just before we left for Munich. They had to pour us onto the train. You remember . . . I had to go meet that automobile manufacturer."

"Now that guy," Jeff declared enviously, "knows how to pick his women. Not a one over sixteen. A habit like that could kill you."

"Not you, my good man." Dolph smiled at Jeff. "Personally, I prefer my women like my wine. The older vintages
are the best."

Madeleine laughed as she tucked an arm through each of
theirs. "And a good thing, too. But, *mes cheris*, we must go
back to the hotel. I need a nap before dinner."

"Dinner . . . where to this evening?" asked Jeff.

"You recall those two American movie stars? They rented
a villa at Juan-des-Pins. And dinner is at nine-thirty."

By nature rather a private person, Dolph wasn't altogether comfortable with the celebrity status he was
acquiring—his photo in the tabloids, items about him in the
gossip columns. "The mystery man who came riding out of
the Far East," wrote one society chronicler. Dolph shook his
head in amusement. How Uncle Maurice would have
enjoyed that juicy tidbit.

Nevertheless, it was an exciting time for Dolph. With the
backing of Shawak Industries as well as his own money to
invest, he was finding growth opportunities everywhere he
turned: Real estate in London, a winery in France whose
owner had gone into receivership, consumer goods from the
States that were desperately needed to shore up the ailing
English economy. Salah had also asked him to serve as a
director of the private banking company that had been
formed in part to service Salah's Bahamian corporation.

The truth was that the notoriety didn't hurt. Increasingly,
he was becoming a financial force to be reckoned with—the
man to know in London.

Chapter Nine

On a gloomy autumn afternoon in 1947 Dolph hurried down
St. James Place, late for a meeting. He turned his collar up
against the rain that had been falling steadily for three days
straight. A man brushed past him, then swiftly turned and
grabbed his arm.

"Is that you, Dolph?"

Dolph stopped and peered through the mist of a familiar face.

"My God, Chris, I can't believe it's you!" Dolph exclaimed, stunned to see his long-lost friend.

"None other," said Christopher Brooke.

"I've thought about you often all these years," Dolph declared, taking a closer look at him. Chris's blond hair was streaked with gray, and the lines on his deeply tanned face, which spoke of the outdoor life, only made him even more handsome. He had the same twinkling eyes, and Dolph immediately noticed that Chris had lost none of his charisma.

"Well, I certainly didn't have to wonder about you. I bet a day hasn't gone by that I've not seen your name in the columns."

"Well, where in hell have you been, man? And what are you doing in London? Don't tell me you live here?"

"No." Chris smiled. "You aren't the only one who gets around, you know. I'm a foreign correspondent with Reuters. New York is home, but wherever they send me, I go. This is the first time I'm back in England since you and I left. It feels like a hundred years ago. What luck to run into you! I've only just arrived and one of my first orders of business was to hunt you up."

Checking his watch, Dolph said, "Damn! I'm running a little late for a meeting, but tell me where you're staying. I want to move you to my place right away."

"That's really not necessary, Dolph."

"The hell it's not," Dolph replied. "We have years of catching up to do. I'll send a car to pick up your things. Do you have any special baggage?"

"Like what?"

"Like a wife or kids."

Chris grinned. "I was married, but it didn't work out. I don't think I was meant to settle down."

"It's not for me, either. Well, it's settled then. What's the hotel? The car will pick you and your gear up around 5:30 this afternoon."

"Claridges."

"All right. I'll be home by six and I'll have my man set us up with some food and a bottle of wine. See you later, Chris."

"This is quite a setup," Christopher said, after the two men had settled themselves in front of the fireplace at Eaton Square.

His handsome face as animated as Dolph remembered, Christ listened eagerly as Dolph described the voyage on the *Conte Biancamano* and the years in Shanghai. He described his meeting with Salah and how he had decided to become his assistant. And he told him about Ohna.

Chris shook his head in admiration. "And to think you were the shy one!" he said. "Whenever I read about you I wondered what had caused the transformation."

"Now it's your turn, Chris," said Dolph, eager to hear about his friend's experiences as a foreign correspondent. "I imagine that you finally saw all the action you had always wanted."

"I'll save the trip to Palestine for another time," Chris said. "That's a whole evening's story in itself. But when the war broke out I signed on and shuttled between Egypt and North Africa. Afterwards, I found that I rather missed all the action and excitement. I suppose there were a lot of us who felt that way. So I managed to nab myself a job as a correspondent and then, as luck would have it, they posted me to Washington. Lots of intrigue, but not much danger there. Except, of course, for the women.

"Before long I married a senator's daughter. I should have known better, I suppose, and, predictably, it didn't work out. I don't think I'd stopped to consider what being married was all about. After a while the arguing got to be too much and I bolted. I finally convinced them to send me back to Palestine. The situation is heating up over there, and I want to be in the right place when the story breaks. Which it certainly will before very long," he said with the air of a man who knew he could spot a good story.

"What are you doing in London?" Dolph asked.

"Using up some vacation time on my way over. I thought it was about time I looked up some of my family and old friends. You were near the top of the list. Just behind your Uncle Maurice."

"Ah, of course, you wouldn't know," Dolph said slowly. "Maurice died just before Armistice Day."

"Damn, I'm sorry to hear that. What a shame, Dolph. He was all the family you had. He was a tremendous influence on me, you know. I mentally wrote him many letters over the past few years, but I never seemed to get them on paper. I was so anxious to tell him about what the Jews have been accomplishing in Palestine, and what I think is going to happen there next."

"He told me you'd written him when you first arrived. He was very pleased. You were a great favorite of his."

A silence fell between them.

After several moments Christopher stood up and walked over to the piano. "Do you ever play, Dolph? As I recall, you'd given it up after your parents died."

Dolph brightened. "Once in a while. One of these days I may even begin composing full time."

"*Eh, bien*, you will, will you?" Madeleine's voice preceded her entrance. As always she looked stunning in a deep blue gown with a dramatic decolletage. "Ito let me in. I hope you don't mind, Dolph. I've just come from the Langfords' annual 'Boozy-Doo.' What a dreadful party! Lots of punch and cucumber sandwiches. Ugh," she grimaced. "You were clever to have turned it down. But now I see why. You have company, and I am being so rude, chattering on like a monkey."

"Not at all, my sweet. Madeleine Laval, I'd like you to meet an old friend of mine, Christopher Brooke."

"Pleased to meet you," said Christopher, and Dolph suddenly remembered how easily Chris had wooed and won the girls at Cambridge.

"*Enchantee*," Madeleine said.

They shook hands, and Dolph sat back and silently watched his lover and his oldest friend take each other's measure. Strangely, instead of being jealous, he was experiencing a sense of relief. Despite how much he cared for Madeleine, lately he had begun to feel hemmed in by her frequent presence. Even a part-time mistress, he had decided just the other night, seemed too much for him.

Perhaps, he mused, she might enjoy getting to know Chris. Besides, he thought, chuckling to himself at the memory, he owed Christopher one.

Madeleine Laval was accustomed to getting whatever she wanted. And for some time now, what she had been wanting was the excitement of a new affair. Besides, knowing men as well as she did, she sensed that Dolph, too, was chafing at the intensity of their relationship. So several days later, when Dolph suggested that she give Chris a tour of London's latest nightspots, she happily said yes.

Chris had been expecting her call. Dolph had told him that Madeleine had offered to show him post-war London.

"I wouldn't want to poach on your turf," Chris had said, "but she is very lovely."

Dolph chuckled. "Be my guest, Chris. Madeleine and I have an unusual and marvelous friendship. We both enjoy an open arrangement."

Chris raised an eyebrow. "Indeed? I'd no idea the British had become so progressive."

"Only an elite minority—tutored by our French allies, if you must know the truth," said Dolph. "Quite seriously, she is a wonderful woman and she pays both of us a compliment by her interest in you."

"Very well, then. I never decline an invitation from a lady who knows her mind."

The next afternoon promptly at one o'clock, Madeleine collected Christopher in her bright new M.G. convertible. As he slid into the passenger seat, she smiled sweetly and declared, "You are now my captive."

"Sounds marvelous. And where are you whisking me off to?"

"A lovely suburb of London," she said slyly. "It's called Paris."

"Paris? You do have pizazz, as they say in America."

"Pizazz? Yes, I like that. Now that I have you in my power, I shall steal you away."

"Well, this is one robbery I'm going to enjoy. Take me, as they say in the films. I'm yours."

"Just as I'd hoped," Madeleine replied.

They drove out to a private airfield. The company plane owned by Parfums Laval was fueled and ready to take off.

Buckling herself into her seatbelt, Madeleine turned to Christopher and said, "*Cheri*, I have taken the liberty of organizing your day. You don't mind, do you?"

"I'm on holiday for the first time since I came down from Cambridge. My last visit to Paris consisted of five hours at Orly in transit to America. I've nowhere to go until I leave for the Middle East three weeks last Tuesday, and I can't imagine a more delightful tour guide than you. So, my director general, what's the schedule of the day?"

"It's a surprise! You like surprises, *n'est-ce pas?*"

"As long as they don't involve bombings or men pointing rifles at me. But I have the feeling that's not what you have in mind."

"No rifles, but I hope an explosion or two," she replied with a teasing laugh.

The chief steward emerged from the cockpit and walked down the aisle to their seats. "I'm sorry, Madame Laval, the pilot has asked me to tell you that we will be coming into some turbulence shortly. He would like you to please be sure your seatbelts are properly fastened."

Madeleine smiled shakily at Chris.

"Chris, we both have a surprise today. And I will tell you a great, dark secret of mine. As much as I fly, I am still scared of it. And in bad weather?" She shuddered. "So you must help me get through the storm."

The sight of this sophisticated, self-assured woman suddenly turned into quivering jelly was totally unexpected. Chris reached over and squeezed her cold-as-ice hand.

"I'm an old hand at comforting damsels in distress. What can I do? Ask me anything."

"Let's talk so I don't have to think about the bad weather."

"Of course. Actually, there's something I've been wondering about ever since we met. How is it that you and Dolph seem to have such a nonpossessive affair?"

"Did Dolph also tell you that I am married?"

"He called you Madame Laval, but I assumed you were a

widow."

"*Non, non,* not at all. My husband is very much alive, thank the good Lord."

Chris looked at her quizzically. "Forgive me, Madeleine, but I don't understand."

"Pierre and I, we both believe that personal freedom is a very precious commodity. Much too precious to waste by limiting a relationship with provincial and self-indulgent restrictions. It is perfectly acceptable to have more than one very close friend. Why not more than one lover? I do not compare, nor do I use one to make another jealous. I am secure within myself, so I can be secure about Pierre or Dolph or you, if you and I choose to become lovers."

Chris stared at Madeleine in frank amazement. Here, at last, was a woman whose philosophy completely agreed with his own. Warm, amusing companionship—but without lies, guilt, or tears. Fate had delivered to him the woman of his dreams in the person of Madeleine Laval.

"Chris? You have nothing to say?" asked Madeleine.

"It's an absolutely first-rate concept, but one I've never heard stated so eloquently. Madeleine," he declared with a broad smile, "you are a woman after my own heart."

"*Bien,* for if we are to become good friends—and I suspect we are—we must agree on two counts. The first is, never to put demands on each other. And the second is that you must promise to keep me distracted during bad flights. Agreed?"

Chris offered her his right hand to seal the bargain. "Agreed!"

The next several years were a period of rapid growth for the British-Orient Limited. With the small fortune he had already amassed, and the frequent participation of Shawak Industries, Dolph was making a name for himself as the man who knew the right business to acquire at the right moment.

After the austerity and rationing of the war years, the English were demanding quality consumer goods. Unemployment was way down, and people had money to spend. They wanted to be offered a wide choice of products when they shopped. Dolph took the pulse of the times and moved quickly.

He bought a highly-regarded but cash-poor textile manufacturer—to Salah's chagrin. "I must be slipping," Salah told him during one of their static-ridden phone calls. "I should have spotted that one before you did." Noticing that all his friends were busy refurbishing their homes, Dolph acquired a large upholstery and drapery company, then introduced a discount line of fabrics that eighteen months later was outselling the more expensive ones.

"Might as well make money for myself as for someone else," he decided, and took over a moribund chain of small department stores in the north of England. The ceremony celebrating the dedication of the brand-new flagship store in London was attended by the Lord Mayor and a raft of royalty.

And guessing correctly that air travel was on the verge of becoming the standard mode of transportation, he bought into a newly-formed commuter airline that promised to turn the London-Paris connection into a daytrip.

He and Madeleine remained dear friends, but they saw each other infrequently. Madeleine had taken charge of the advertising and artwork for Parfums Laval. Much of her free time was spent with Chris in the picturesque ports and beaches of the Mediterranean.

Occasionally, a woman came into Dolph's life and captured his interest for a week or two. But for the most part, he was too involved with the expansion of his business empire to devote himself to a love affair. He didn't mind being alone, he told himself, but dreams of Ohna came to him in the night.

Often he awoke with a with a feeling of regret. He would remind himself how difficult it had been to keep in touch during the war. And after the war, when Salah had moved his family to Hong Kong and communication was easier, there had seemed nothing to say.

Their two worlds were so different. Dolph was a man with driving goals, while Ohna seemed to skim along the surface, like a bird ready to land wherever the wind might take her.

Partly out of curiosity and more from a sense of

obligation, Dolph regularly inquired about Ohna each time he and Salah spoke. But Salah gave him little news of her, and from his reticence, Dolph deduced that she had found a new lover, probably one of Salah's friends or relatives. Gradually, almost with a sense of relief, he stopped asking about her.

He was too busy to look back.

Nevertheless, he had always told himself that one day, "soon, when the time was right," he would fly out to Hong Kong and . . . what? resume his quasi-marriage with Ohna? The fantasy blurred after the image of her welcoming embrace. But in the very early morning hours, or when the moon was full and he felt his aloneness, he thought of Ohna as she had looked the day he had said goodbye to her in 1941.

Thus, when he got Salah's phone call, the words he heard Salah saying made no sense. Dolph's knuckles tightened around the telephone receiver.

"I'm sorry," he said stiffly. "I don't understand, Salah."

"She's dead, Dolph." Salah's voice was tight and ragged, as though he were barely holding back tears. "She took ill with meningitis last week."

His words faded, and all Dolph could hear was the crackle of the overseas connection.

"Wasn't there something that could be done to save her?" he shouted into the receiver.

"Believe me, Dolph, we tried everything. I know how you must feel. We are all feeling the pain of her loss. She was a lovely gift that God had loaned us."

Dolph hung up the phone without saying goodbye. Slumped in his chair, he broke into loud, wracking sobs that echoed the anguish in his heart. He suddenly thought of his parents and the shock of their tragic death. Now he seemed to be crying for all the people he had lost—his mother and father, and Uncle Maurice, and sweet, lovely Ohna who had given herself to him so generously.

In all the years since then, he had never met a woman quite like her, nor anyone who had touched him in that special, deep way that she had. "When the time was right," he had promised himself. But how could he have believed that she would wait for him until he was ready to take her back into his life? Why had he never troubled to let her know what she had meant to him?

And now it was too late. The chance to say "I love you, Ohna. You taught me so well," was lost for eternity.

He locked the door to the library—against whom, he didn't stop to think, since the servants were all in the country—and stumbled over to the piano. His fingers crashed down on the keys, relentlessly pounding out his anguish, filling the room with his grief. Finally, exhausted, he slumped down on the sofa and fell into a deep sleep.

His dreams of Shanghai and Ohna dressed in silken veils were disturbed by an unpleasantly loud, insistent ring. He struggled to hold onto the dream, not to let her go, but the sound didn't stop. Stirring to consciousness, he said, "Turn it off. I hate it."

But he was talking to an empty room. And the noise he realized, more awake now, was the ringing of the telephone. There was not a soul in the world he cared to talk to at this moment, but someone obviously very much wanted to speak to him. Angry at the intrusion, he picked up the phone and said, "Yes?"

"Hey, man, doesn't anyone over there answer your phone?" It was Jeff. "How's it going? I just got back into town and I wanted to call you right away. You've got to hear some great lyrics that I wrote while I was in L.A. I remembered a composition you played for me a couple of weeks ago that would fit like a glove. Wait until you hear this. Doing anything tonight?"

"No . . . tonight's not good."

"Shit, I can barely hear you. You got a hot date over there?" Jeff pressed.

Dolph hung up the phone.

It rang again almost immediately.

"Look, Jeff," he began, but Jeff cut him off.

"Never mind that shit. Something's wrong. I can hear it in your voice. I'm coming over right now." He rang off before Dolph could protest.

He was at Eaton Square within minutes.

After listening to the incessant noise of the doorbell,

Dolph finally roused himself to open the front door.

Jeff strode inside. "Christ, where are the servants? What the hell is going on here?"

"They've already gone off to East Grinstead, I think. They've gone to open the house for the weekend," Dolph said.

"How about a drink?" Jeff made his way over to the bar.

"Don't mind if I do," he answered himself mockingly when he got no response. He stared at Dolph and shook his head. "If you don't mind my saying so, buddy, you look awful. What's up?"

Ignoring the question, Dolph walked back to the library, sat down again at the piano, and resumed playing.

Jeff listened in silence for a long time. Finally, he cleared his throat loudly. "Sounds like you're trying to exorcise a devil. That's torture music you're playing there. Soul torture, I mean."

Dolph didn't reply. He felt as if he had no words left in him.

"Listen, Dolph, if you're going to let it all out in your music, at least let's accomplish something," Jeff said, walking over to look his friend in the eye. "I just happen to have here some of the greatest lyrics ever written. I know my modesty is overwhelming, but these words of a genius are crying out for exactly the right score. And I have good reason to believe you can deliver it. So let's get to work, man!"

Jeff stuck several sheets of music on the piano rack.

"Leave me alone," Dolph mumbled.

"I damn well will not. You look as if you've just seen a ghost. Who died, man?"

The words hit Dolph like a brick. When he met Jeff's gaze, the pain was clearly etched in his eyes.

"My God, I'm sorry," Jeff said quickly. "You got some bad news, didn't you? Was it Salah?"

Dolph shook his head. He had never told Jeff about Ohna and he couldn't begin now to explain what she had meant to him.

"Look, man," Jeff said, "you don't have to talk, though it might help if you did. But you need a friend right now and I guess I'm the logical candidate, whether or not you want me. And you *know* what a pain in the butt I can be. So if you want me to keep my big mouth shut, you better take a peek at those lyrics."

"You're relentless, do you know that, Gotley?" said Dolph, managing a thin smile. "You'll do anything for a hit." He smiled again to show his appreciation.

"That's right, Robicheck. I've been down and out. And I'm not planning to be there again. So are you ready to work?" He looked uncharacteristically serious for a moment. "Or would you rather talk?"

"Thanks, Jeff, maybe later on I'll sing the blues. Right now I think I'd rather write them."

"All right then!" Jeff made himself comfortable next to Dolph and flexed his fingers. "Let's get to it, man. I see this as the beginning of a long-term collaboration."

"Sure, why not?" Dolph agreed, suddenly grateful for Jeff's affection.

He struck a chord and the memory of Ohna, solemnly practicing the piano, flashed through his mind. Perhaps, someday, he would write a song about her.

But that would come later. In the meantime, Jeff was waiting for him. "Jefferson Gotley," he said, picking up the sheets of lyrics, "I think Rogers and Hammerstein had better watch their backs."

BOOK II

Chapter One

1964.

Alahna stepped out of the white porcelain tub and stood
naked in the middle of her bathroom. Her arms stretched
above her head, she did a slow pirouette, carefully examining her dripping wet body, reflected in the floor-to-ceiling
mirrors that covered all four walls of the room.

This was one of the rare moments Alahna had to be alone,
when she could give some worried thought to her father and
the future he had planned for her. A future in which she
had very little say.

Certainly she should have been used to that by now. For
as long as she could remember, her father had overseen
every facet of her life as carefully as he oversaw every aspect
of his business. And she had been taught always to obey
him.

But now, for the first time, Alahna wished she could say
to her father. "No! I'm too young to be married!"

And worse, to a man she had never even met. Her father's
business partner, who would make her leave home and all
that was familiar to her.

Her father was very ill, he had explained, and he wanted
everything settled before he died. All the more reason, as far
as Alahna was concerned, for her to stay in Hong Kong, to
take care of him while he was sick. Maybe even to keep him
from dying.

How could he bear to send her away, she wondered
bitterly, toweling herself dry. She loved him so much. In
many ways he had been both father and mother to her. In
return, she had attended to his needs with the careful concern of a much older woman.

"You remind me so much of your mother," her father
often said. This pleased her, though she hardly remembered
her mother, who had died when she was only four years old.

She treasured the one photograph she had of her mother,
which she kept hidden in one of her drawers, along with a
photo she had discovered of the man her father had chosen
for her. Though the picture was blurry, she could make out
a young man, standing on the deck of a ship, smiling and
squinting into the camera. But that had been many years
ago, before the man had even met her father. And her
father hadn't seen him in a very long time, although they
talked on the phone almost every day.

Already she had decided she probably wouldn't like him.
He was so *old*, and he was so involved with her family and
their affairs. Which left her at a disadvantage. She felt as
though everyone but she had a hand in her future.

Deep down, Alahna knew she had no choice. If it was
true that her father was dying, she had to marry someone
appropriate in order to safeguard the family fortune. It was
a financial transaction, pure and simple, necessary for the
sake of her father's business empire. Like the marriages she
had read about that had been arranged for the kings and
queens of Europe.

Running her hands down the front of her boyish figure,
she wondered what the man would think of her body.
Would she have to undress in front of him? Make love with
him?

From what she had heard from her cousins about sex, and
from her frequent, secret explorations of her body, she
suspected she would like making love. But she wasn't sure
her husband-to-be would be pleased with her skinny arms
and legs.

She sighed nervously, evaluating for the umpteenth time
the rest of her features. Her black hair was closely cropped
to frame her fine-boned face. Her strong chin and wide

forehead were her father's. But her almond-shaped black eyes were most definitely her mother's, and so were the dimples.

She had also inherited her mother's delicate frame, although her mother had not been as tall as she was. Alahna circled her waist with her two hands. Her mother's waist had been tiny. Alahna knew this because ever since she was a little girl she had asked her father endless questions about her mother's appearance. "Your mother was very beautiful," he had told her again and again. "Small, but very womanly."

Womanly . . . If only she had been born a boy. The men in her life held all the power. Though she would never have dared to say so aloud, that seemed unfair. She was as smart as any of her male cousins and she could do much of what they did. Given the opportunity, she could do it all.

Her clothes had been laid out for her on her bed. Looking around, she realized that her room, with its pink ballerina wallpaper, gauzy pink curtains, and row of stuffed animals perched on the window sill, was right for a young girl, wrong now for her.

If she were going to stay here, she would redecorate it. But this was not to be her room for very much longer.

Her father was intent on sending her away. . . .

She swallowed a hard knot of tears. In her darkest moments, when she couldn't hide the truth from herself, she knew he was dying. And she would be left entirely alone. More alone even than when her mother had died.

She had only the haziest memories of that time. Crying herself to sleep, dreaming of being left all alone, waking up and calling out for her mother, who never came. For months afterward, Alahna was terrified of being left alone in the dark, convinced that the nightmare would recur, that she would be left alone again.

Ever since her father had told her he was sick, she had been having nightmares again. She dreamt that he had disappeared, abandoning her the way her mother had, without any warning.

The old wound brought quick tears to Alahna's eyes. Before they could roll down her cheeks, she grabbed a tissue and blotted them away, anxious to rid herself of that memory as quickly as possible. It wasn't a good idea to dwell on the past, to feel sorry for herself.

Her mother would have suffered silently, privately, without any public scenes. Alahna had been brought up to do the same. Mostly she was adept at concealing her feelings. But inside she ached with unspent emotion. And she felt guilty, because she knew her mother never had these bad, angry feelings. Her mother, she was sure, had simply done whatever had been expected of her, willingly, gladly, without argument.

That was how they differed, Alahna decided, slipping into her red silk dress. Her mother had never wanted to be a part of her father's world outside their home. She had had no interest in learning his business, or in having any say in her own future.

Her mother, according to her father, had been content with her very pleasant but totally sheltered existence. Alahna, on the other hand, couldn't bear to be left out of anything. Her father's office, with its familiar, comforting smells of leather and ink and cigar smoke, spoke to her of power and action. It was her father's world, and so it had became her world.

When nothing else seemed to help, her father had brought her with him to the office where she happily played with his pens and pencils and papers. But she had such a quick mind that he couldn't ignore her intelligence. Born teacher that he was, he couldn't resist teaching her the letters and sums— using whatever balance sheets or memoranda that happened to be lying on his desk.

Alahna had been thrilled. She loved spending her days with Papa, and the games he played with her were such fun. But she was impatient, too. Papa sometimes scolded her. She must learn patience and obedience. There was so much to learn, and never enough time.

Now they had run out of time, and there were no more lessons. Her father was dying. And who would love her and take as good care of her as Papa did?

Surely, not this stranger, as blurred in her mind's eye as he was in his photograph. Except for her aunt, she had no one else who understood her. She occasionally played with her cousins, but none of them was her close, close friend.

What she shared with her father was different. Out of the ordinary. His world was special and exciting. It was what she loved and knew best. It was all she knew. And she knew very little about this man to whom her father was intending to give her.

"He has been like a son to me," he had explained to Alahna.

Streaks of jealousy had flashed through her. No doubt her father wished he had had a son. Probably he thought this man would have been perfect for the role. She felt as though she were being asked to move over to make room for the newcomer, to welcome him graciously without ever having been asked her opinion or her heart's desire.

And yet her father would never have chosen anyone in whom he didn't have full confidence. She supposed she could see the logic of it all, but that did nothing to dampen her fury at this man whom she couldn't help but think of as an intruder.

It was all too horrible.

She studied her olive complexion for flaws and nodded with satisfaction. Her breasts did not quite fill out the top of the dress, but her jet-black hair contrasted nicely with the red silk. All that was left was to choose a piece of jewelry. Experimenting with the various pieces that were neatly displayed against the black velvet of her ebony jewel box, she settled on an ivory pendant that had belonged to her mother.

Then she settled herself in a chair to wait.

The sound of the door knocker echoed ominously through the three-story house. It seemed to be signalling the end of her childhood. Alahna jumped up and quietly slid open the door to her room at the top of the stairs, hoping to catch a glimpse of the man who stood in the entrance foyer.

In the dim light, she couldn't quite make out his features or his expression, but he stood straight and firm, as if he were accustomed to getting his own way. Watching him confidently follow the houseboy into the library, she suddenly thought, *just like Papa.*

Chapter Two

Dolph noticed the change in Salah immediately. It wasn't
simply that too many years had passed since they had seen
each other. The last time Salah had been in England, he'd
maintained his usual dawn-to-late-night schedule of
appointments, luncheons, and social engagements. But now
Salah seemed not only to have aged, but to have shrunk. As
always, he held himself erect, but it was as if there were less
of him, and his hands shook slightly as he reached to
embrace Dolph.

Dolph glanced about the oak-paneled library. The inter-
vening years immediately fell away. There on a low wooden
mahogany table sat the chessboard over which he and Salah
had had so many engrossing conversations. Dolph smiled,
realizing that he half expected Salah to challenge him to a
game.

But first they had a great deal of catching up to do. For
one thing, Dolph was very anxious to hear why Salah had so
abruptly summoned him to Hong Kong. Not that he
minded. Midway between London and his destination, as
the hum of the jet's engines were lulling him to sleep, a
thought had flashed through his mind.

"I would do anything for Salah Shawak."

"You are looking very well, my friend," Salah said, settling himself into his chair.

"As are you, Salah," Dolph lied.

Salah blinked his eyes like an old turtle who has seen too
many winters to accept anything but the truth. "Thank you
for your diplomacy. How was the flight? I understand these
new jets have transformed the London-Orient route into a
rather pleasant journey."

"The trip was actually quite enjoyable. I'd been thinking,
in fact, that we're foolish not to take advantage of the
improved connections and see each other more often."

Salah nodded absent-mindedly, caught up in his own

train of thought. "Dolph," he said, "you're probably wondering why I invited you out to Hong Kong. Besides the obvious pleasure of your company."

"I'm happy to be here, Salah. I should have come sooner."

"Nonsense. You're a busy man. I would not have made this request had I not had a very good reason to take up so much of your time."

"Salah. . . ." Dolph began.

"Yes, yes, I know what you're going to say. But we're long past the point in our friendship when expressions of gratitude are appropriate."

"Salah," Dolph said firmly, "with all due respect, I disagree. It's time I said thank you for all you've given me. I wish there were some way I could begin to repay my debt."

"Indeed." Salah smiled contentedly.

The expression on his face was one that Dolph recognized. It meant that Salah had already planned the agenda for this meeting.

"But how rude of me. I've not offered you any refreshments." Salah pulled on the thick cord to signal one of the servants.

"Please ask Alahna to join us," he said to the houseboy who appeared almost instantly.

"Are you hungry, Dolph?" Salah asked.

"Actually . . ."

But he cut himself off to stare at the young girl who appeared in the doorway of the library. She hesitated for a moment before she walked into the room and bent to kiss Salah's forehead. Then she turned to Dolph and smiled gravely.

Her eyes . . . the smile . . . those dimples!

But it wasn't possible.

"Allow me to introduce my daughter," Salah said. "Alahna Shawak."

The girl stared at him, solemn-faced.

"Alahna, this is my very dear friend, Dolph Robicheck, of whom I've spoken so often."

"How do you do, Mr. Robicheck." She dipped slightly to greet him.

"Could you arrange for our tea, my dear? I suspect that

Dolph could do with some nourishment."

"Of course, Papa," she said. "Excuse me, please."

She smiled again, a slim, graceful porcelain doll figure dressed in red silk that rustled softly as she left the room.

Dolph sat in silent astonishment, waiting for Salah to offer an explanation.

"You know, of course," Salah said, "that I have always been meticulous to a fault. I'm like a housewife who can't leave the room without running her finger across the bookcase to check for dust. I'm not comfortable unless I'm sure that I've crossed all the T's and dotted every I."

"Well, you've evidently trained me in your image. I hear the same comments and complaints about my work habits," laughed Dolph.

"You did turn out to be rather a lot like me, didn't you? Interesting. I wonder whether that was coincidence or by design."

He paused and stared into the shadows of the room, lost in his thoughts. Then, clearing his throat, he continued. "You're surprised, aren't you, to discover I have a daughter, that I kept this a secret from you all these years."

"Surprised is rather an understatement. She's lovely. How old is she?"

"Sixteen. Yes, she is very lovely. She gives me great joy. And in fact, it's because of Alahna that I asked you to visit me in Hong Kong. Dolph," Salah said, "there is something I want you to do for me and my daughter."

"Anything."

"I'm glad you feel that way, because I assure you that I appreciate the magnitude of my request. I want you to marry Alahna this week and take her back to London with you."

Dolph's face drained of color. Had Salah lost his mind? He had seemed perfectly sane and coherent only seconds earlier.

"You want me to marry your sixteen-year-old daughter?"

"That's right," Salah answered calmly.

"But that's absolutely ridiculous. She's just a young girl. I couldn't possibly. I'm almost thirty years her senior. We don't even know each other. Besides," he added, trying to

toss logic into his argument, "you know as well as I do,
Salah, that I can never give her a child. Why would you
want to do such a thing to your own flesh and blood?"

"For several very good reasons. When I die, Alahna will
be an enormously wealthy young woman. And as clever and
precocious as she is, she's not yet prepared to manage her
fortune. No matter how diligent her guardians might be, she
would be a prime target for unscrupulous predators who
would jump at the chance to take advantage of a beautiful
young heiress. I want her looked after from close up, not at
a distance."

"But what about your brother and sister? Surely you could
depend on them to safeguard Alahna and her fortune. And
why are you talking as if you're about to disappear off the
face of the earth? I'm sure you'll be here to take care of your
daughter and Shawak Industries for many years to come."

"In fact not, I'm sorry to say. I'm dying, Dolph." Salah
held up a hand to prevent Dolph from interrupting.
"There's no use my pretending it's not so. The doctors and I
agree I've not much time left, and I've never believed in
fighting the inevitable. But as far as Alahna is concerned, I
cannot leave anything to chance. It's not merely the money,
Dolph. It's her happiness as well. You're the only person I
can trust to protect her and watch over her affairs."

"But what about her mother?"

Dolph waited for Salah to say, "Yes, Alahna is Ohna's
daughter."

But instead Salah said, "She passed away some years ago.
Meilee and I have raised Alahna together, but now I must
turn her over to you. Besides," he chuckled, "it's time you
were married."

"Salah, I owe you everything in the world, but you can't
ask me to marry your child."

"Can't I?"

Dolph stood up and began to pace the room. "Look, I'd
be happy to bring her back to England with me after
you . . . when it's necessary. I could adopt her if you think
that would safeguard her fortune. Or" he said, frantically
searching for a compromise that would satisfy Salah, "we
could make it a marriage in name only and later, when she's

old enough to choose a husband, an annulment could be arranged."

"Adoption isn't good enough. I wouldn't want to risk your marrying someone else and bringing home a stepmother for my daughter. No, Dolph. I've made up my mind. I want you to be a husband to her in every sense of the word. Alahna is a child of two heritages, one of which believes in marrying its daughters at a young age. As you will quickly discover, she is very different from the average sixteen-year-old. She needs both a father and a husband. You, my dear friend, are the only man I know who can fill both those roles."

"You can't be dying. Surely there's something to be done."

Salah shrugged. "It is God's will. My time has come. I accept that, as you must some day."

Dolph's world suddenly seemed to be crumbling about him. Salah dying? Was it possible? The man was invincible. If anyone was going to live forever, it would be Salah Shawak.

And yet Salah was not a man who indulged in melodramatic fantasies. He never flinched from the truth. Dolph had long ago recognized and admired that quality in him.

But surely Salah knew that Dolph couldn't simply nod his head in agreement and then go on to discuss business matters. What Salah was proposing was merely the greatest change he could possibly imagine. There was too much here to absorb, too many factors to consider.

"I need time to think. I don't mean to be rude, but if you don't mind, I'll be back in an hour or two."

"Of course," Salah said amiably. "My driver can drop you wherever you wish. I'll tell Alahna we'll have our tea when you return."

The car took him along the hilly road from Repulse Bay towards the center of downtown Hong Kong. "Here," Dolph said to the driver, "I'll get out here. Don't wait. I'll find my way back."

He walked down Queens Road Central, elbowing through the passersby who were windowshopping on the crowded street. Chinese and Indian merchants stood in the doorways, inviting would-be customers to stop and browse their wares.

It was his first visit to the Orient since 1941. If he closed his eyes, he could imagine himself back in Shanghai, a boy not much older than Alahna, thrilled to be discovering the mysteries of the East. The smells and sounds felt the same— a hybrid recipe of Chinese and European, barely stirring so that the blend retained the flavor of both cultures.

Like Alahna. He felt a sharp stab of sympathy for her. Orphaned when he was still a boy, certainly he knew what it was like to be alone in the world, to lose the people he loved best.

Finally, after hours of aimless wandering, he realized with a jolt that the choice had already been made for him. There was no way out that he could fathom. Salah had foreseen all the moves.

Just like the old days.

Checkmate!

Salah's house was dark and quiet by the time Dolph returned. A sleepy servant answered his knock and let him in.

"Mr. Salah said to tell you there is food in your room and I'm to make your tea, if you wish it. He said to tell you he looks forward to chess in the morning."

"Crafty old bastard," Dolph said to himself. "He knows he's won."

The servant showed him to his room on the third floor, where a tray of fresh fruit, cold chicken, and Chinese vegetables had been laid out, along with a vase of artfully arranged flowers.

Alahna's handiwork? He stared thoughtfully at the bouquet as he hungrily ate his long-delayed dinner and washed it down with hot tea such as he hadn't tasted since he had left Shanghai. Then he quickly undressed and dropped into bed.

Questions raced through his mind. What had Salah meant when he'd said that Alahna was different from most sixteen-year-olds? Did she know that her father meant for her to be married? And how would she feel about being paired off with a man old enough to be her father? And her mother . . . Ohna? Could it have been Ohna?

"Ohna," he mumbled into the pillow, remembering the scent of jasmine, her favorite fragrance. "Ohna," he said again, and then he was asleep.

Salah and Alahna were already seated in the breakfast room, engrossed in a discussion about "buys" and "sells" and "puts." Not the sort of thing Dolph would have imagined most teenagers cared about. This morning Alahna was dressed in a Chinese-style black silk shirt and a simple skirt. When she greeted him politely, he was struck by her poise and self-assured manner.

The silver coffee service stood in front of her at the foot of the table. Alahna poured Dolph a cup of coffee.

"Do you take cream or sugar, Mr. Robicheck?" she asked.

"Just some cream, thank you." He couldn't tear his eyes away from her. What an intriguing blend of East and West she was.

"Did you have enough to eat last evening?" Alahna said.

"Yes, certainly, and the flowers were lovely."

"My aunt Meilee taught me how to arrange them," said Alahna, color flushing her cheeks.

"Meilee! How is she? I'd love to see her."

"You will," Salah promised. "She's eager to see you, too. In fact, she not only insisted on planning the menu for tonight's dinner, she went to the market herself to make sure that the ingredients were the freshest."

He shook his head ruefully. "Meilee is almost sixty, though she'd never admit it, but she has the energy of a forty-five-year-old. However, we have more pressing matters to discuss. Alahna," he said, smiling across the table at his daughter, "you should be a part of this conversation."

"Yes, Papa, of course," Alahna said demurely.

"I take it, Dolph, you gave my request all due consideration and you've come to the table with an answer?" Salah asked.

"I have to trust that you know what you're doing, Salah. I only hope I can live up to the faith you've put in me."

Salah smiled broadly. "You always have. Why should this particular venture be different from any other? Well then, excellent! I congratulate the both of you. We shall celebrate this evening. Alahna, I hope you don't mind if Dolph and I spend the day talking business?"

Alahna set her lips tightly. Of course she minded. Not because she cared a bit to be alone with Dolph—in fact, the thought made her cringe—but why was she to be excluded? It took all of Meilee's years of training to keep her from throwing down her serviette and running away from the table. How unfair all of this was! No romance, no love match, not even a proper proposal. And now she was being dismissed as if she were a small child who would disturb the grownups' conversation.

Amazingly, Dolph seemed to read her thoughts. "Alahna," he said kindly, "I must be perfectly honest with you. This is as difficult for me as I suspect it is for you." He stood up and walked over to her chair. Reaching for her hand, he said, "Alahna, will you do me the honor of being my bride?"

Alahna swallowed hard and blinked back the tears that stood in her dark eyes. She glanced briefly at her father before meeting Dolph's gaze, and her voice was low but steady when she spoke.

"Yes, Dolph," she said, stumbling slightly over his name. "Yes, I'll be pleased to marry you."

She hurried out of the room without another word.

For once, Dolph could read the sorrow on Salah's face.

But all Salah said was, "Now, let's discuss the wedding."

In spite of the difficult emotions of the moment, Dolph was amused, though not altogether surprised, to learn that the wedding arrangements were almost complete. The ceremony was to take place on Saturday evening, ten days following. It would be a small, private affair. Only the very closest members of the Shawak family had been invited.

Salah, as usual, had correctly guessed that Dolph would not refuse him, and he was determined that Alahna leave for England as quickly as possible. He wanted to spare her from having to witness his deterioration. He also wanted to know that she was comfortably settled in London before he died.

Alahna stayed close to Meilee, taking refuge in the

preparations, and even allowing herself occasionally to get excited about her wedding dress. A traditional ivory satin gown and veil had been ordered, and two of Hong Kong's finest seamstresses were working almost around the clock to finish the gown in time.

Meilee had decreed that Alahna must have a proper trousseau and several other seamstresses were kept busy sewing lacy lingerie and silk blouses and skirts and dresses.

"I'm sure they sell clothes in London," Alahna giggled, watching Meilee pack her suitcase with layer upon layer of new clothes.

But she quickly stopped laughing and thought, London! She was actually leaving Hong Kong. This was not a theatre piece for which she had been chosen to play the starring role. This was real life—her life.

Chapter Three

As her wedding day drew closer, Alahna's moods became increasingly mercurial.

In the evenings, she joined her father and Dolph for dinner, sitting silently while they continued their day's discussion about the myriad details of their joint business interests. Dolph tried to include her in the conversation, but Alahna answered his questions with nothing more than politeness, staring at him with her luminous eyes.

Thus, he was surprised to discover how conversant she was with the affairs of Shawak Industries. Salah frequently turned to her with technical questions. He seemed to expect of her the same competency that he would of a much older, educated associate. When Dolph commented on this, Salah explained that Alahna had been coming to his office since she was a small girl.

"She's almost as quick a pupil as you were," said Salah. "Full of questions, eager to know it all. I've often had to tell her what I used to tell you—be patient, move slowly, take only educated risks. But you'll find her an apt and interesting companion."

Salah appeared to be ignoring his own best advice. He never seemed to sleep these days and burned with a feverish impatience to make sure that every detail of the wedding was properly taken care of. He insisted on a Jewish ceremony ("Alahna was converted when she was an infant. She must have a Jewish wedding beneath the traditional *chuppah*,") with a rabbi to officiate.

Dolph had no objection. In fact, he rather liked the idea of being married beneath a wedding canopy of a prayer shawl held up by four members of the family. Alahna said nothing.

The service was held on Saturday evening just after sunset. Alahna's face was as pale as her ivory gown. She barely heard what the rabbi was saying. In her mind, she was replaying the conversation she had had that morning with her father.

"Alahna," he had reminded her yet again, "I believe that a wife should always be honest with her husband. But there is one secret you must keep from Dolph."

"I know, Papa," she had said impatiently. "You made me promise not to tell him that Ohna was my mother. Though just because they were once friends, I don't see why he shouldn't know."

Her father looked uncomfortable. "In fact, they were more than friends. They shared something very special."

"They were in love, weren't they?" she said, hearing the accusation in her tone. "Papa, Dolph and you both loved the same woman, didn't you?"

"It was a different sort of love than the one I pray you and Dolph will develop for each other. My dear, for all your intelligence, there are some matters you cannot yet fathom. Someday I hope you will understand—and then you will also understand why you must not speak to Dolph of your mother."

"Are you telling me to lie to him, Papa?" Alahna had never dared speak this sharply to her father.

"There will be no need for lies. I am quite sure he will never ask you about her."

She burst into tears. "I don't want to get married," she wept. "I don't want to leave you."

Salah put his arms around her and held her until she
stopped sobbing. "You must promise to heed my words,
child, and your life will be long and happy."

"Yes, Papa," she said numbly. "I promise to be a good
wife to Dolph, and to be a good mother to our children."

For a moment she thought she saw tears in her father's
eyes. But that was impossible. Her papa didn't cry. But she
would never forget his next words.

"Alahna," he said, "it tears me apart to tell you this, and
how I wish it were otherwise. But many years ago in
Shanghai, Dolph was stricken with the spotted fever. Unfortunately, the illness left him sterile. He will never be able to
give you children."

She had stared at him, too shocked to say a word. Finally
she had said, "You mean you're marrying me off to a
stranger who is not only thirty years older than I am, but
who is sterile?"

He hadn't taken his eyes off her stricken face. "As you
know, you are the heiress to a great fortune. Your personal
safety is my first concern. Something often happens to people when they catch the scent of great wealth. Dolph is
honest beyond question. I wish I could say as much for my
own family, but I sense in them jealousy and greed. I must
be absolutely sure of your happiness and safety. I would
trust my life with Dolph. That is why I am trusting him
with yours."

Salah went on. "Listen carefully, my darling. You must let
Dolph make you as happy as I know he can. Do not use
your strong will against him. You were meant to do many
things with your life besides raise children. You can continue
to learn the workings of Shawak Industries. With the money
that will be yours, you can carry on our family's tradition of
supporting hospitals, universities, and cultural institutions.
Remember, Alahna, kindness and charity are embroidered
on the Shawak crest."

The living room, heavy with the odor of spring flowers,
had an air of funereal sadness. Through her lacy tulle veil
Alahna glanced sideways at her father, standing just to her
right. Salah's expression seemed to have been carved from

stone. Was he happy or sad, she wondered, watching his closest friend claim his daughter in marriage? And Dolph, standing on her other side—how did he really feel about all of this?

As the rabbi chanted the seven blessings, Salah watched the faces of those present—his brother and sister-in-law, his youngest sister and her husband, their assorted offspring. He had navigated the family through the Japanese domination and a world war, but he knew they whispered amongst themselves that he had turned into an eccentric.

Would Alahna be safe were she to remain in Hong Kong after his death? Who could foretell the future? This was no time for mistakes or hindsight. Yes, he assured himself, he had made the right decision. Marriage to Dolph was the only sensible answer.

Dolph, too, was anxious for this ordeal to be finished. The responsibility of Alahna's future felt like a heavy boulder that was punishing his shoulders with its weight. Alahna had blushed when he tried to talk to her about a honeymoon, so he had decided that they were best off returning as quickly as possible to London.

Salah had intended that the marriage be consummated under his roof, but on this one point Dolph had been adamant. He and Alahna were to leave after tonight's wedding dinner on the BOAC midnight flight.

Dolph dreaded watching Alahna say goodbye to Salah. The girl looked so solemn and unhappy in her wedding gown. Was Salah being wise and prudent—or was he being cruel? Nor would it be easy for him to say goodbye to Salah. Not with the threat of Salah's death hanging over them like a hungry vulture.

"Please lift the bride's veil, Mr. Robicheck," said the rabbi. "It's time for the wine."

Dolph did as he was told. Alahna's lips quivered as she bent to sip from the silver wine goblet. Her hand trembled when he slipped the plain gold band over her forefinger and recited the words that would make her his wife.

"With this ring you are sanctified to me according to the laws of Moses and Israel. . . ."

A crystal glass wrapped in a piece of linen was placed

under his foot. He stepped down on it, and at the sound of the glass being smashed, a satisfied sigh went through the room.

"Mazal tov!" declared the rabbi.

"Mazal tov, mazal tov!" pronounced the guests.

Alahna turned to him dutifully so that he could kiss his new wife.

When all the guests had left, Meilee hurried Alahna upstairs to change into her travelling suit. Her bags were already packed and in the trunk of the car. There was time only for a brief private moment with her father. She walked stiffly into his study, and no longer able to hold back the torrent of tears, she reached blindly for the familiar shelter of her father's arms.

"Alahna," Salah said, hardly able to hold back his tears, "you and I won't really be apart. It's true that before too long my physical being will cease to exist, but according to the beliefs of your maternal ancestors, my spirit will always remain with you."

"Oh, Papa, my mother's spirit has always guided me, and I know yours will, too. I'll make you so proud of me, Papa, I promise I will."

"I'm sure of that, Alahna. Remember, my precious, that each Sabbath Eve I will take joy as you light the candles for intelligence, taste the spices for love, and sip the wine for life. And now you must stop crying. Here, take my handkerchief, and smile at me before you leave this room."

Salah waited until she had obeyed, and then, with grim resolution, he gently propelled his daughter towards the new life that awaited her.

Dolph tried to distract Alahna by talking about the wedding dinner that neither of them had eaten and the guests who had been present. "I knew your cousins when they were much younger than you," he remarked, and immediately regretted having made a point about their age difference.

Alahna listened in silence. Finally Dolph gave up and moodily contemplated the strain of the nineteen-hour flight with his reluctant bride. He'd reserved three seats in the

first-class cabin in case Alahna wanted to stretch out and fall
asleep. A wise precaution, he thought to himself, noticing
her exhaustion.

"Have you flown before?" he asked her.

"Yes," she said. "Once Meilee and I flew to Bombay to
visit my family. This isn't my first time."

She flushed red and looked flustered.

She's thinking about having to make love for the first time
with me, thought Dolph.

"Good, so you know what to expect then. Though the
flight to London is a good deal longer than to India, even on
this new 707 jet. We should be landing in England at seven
in the evening. Hong Kong time. That's eleven A.M. in London."

Alahna yawned. "Oh, I'm sorry," she said, "I'm just so
tired." She propped a pillow up against the windowpane
and snuggled into it. "You don't mind if I rest for a bit, do
you?"

She fell instantly asleep. After they were well into the air,
Dolph undid her seatbelt, lifted the armrest, and gently
shifted her so that she was lying across the two seats. He
covered her with a blanket and rearranged the pillow.

Alahna sighed deeply. Asleep, she looked much younger
than sixteen—a sweet, innocent child.

Suddenly, he had grave misgivings about whether he'd
ever be able to consummate his marriage. "Salah, what have
you done to us?" He sent the question into the darkened
cabin. Then he, too, fell asleep, worrying about how he
would ever make a life for himself and Alahna.

Early the next morning, they began the descent into Karachi for the first refueling stop. The stewardess came by to
offer them breakfast and request that they refasten their
belts.

Alahna awoke with a start. "It's morning," she said.

"Yes," said Dolph. "We're about to land in Pakistan. Did
you sleep well?"

"Yes." She stretched her arms and legs. "I'm stiff, though."

"We'll get out and walk around a bit while they're refueling. Care for some coffee in the meantime?"

"Yes, please," she said, reverting to her polite child tone.

Strolling through the transit lounge at the Karachi Airport, they passed a newspaper and sweets kiosk.

"May I buy a newspaper?" Alahna asked. "At home I read one every morning."

"Of course." Dolph was delighted not to have to try to entertain her. They bought the *London Times* and *International Heral Tribune* and kept themselves occupied until they were once again airborne.

By the time they were approaching the Leonardo da Vinci Airport in Rome to take on more fuel and passengers, Alahna had wolfed down her lunch of poached chicken and wheedled a second helping out of the obliging stewardess.

"I was famished," she said contentedly after she cleaned off the second tray. "I didn't eat a thing at dinner last evening."

"Neither did I," Dolph said. "Nerves, I suppose."

"Are you nervous?" Alahna asked with surprise. "Why should you be? I'm the one who's being sent away from home to a place I've never been before."

"You're right. You've much more to adjust to, but I've never been married before, you know," smiled Dolph.

"Yes, I see," she said thoughtfully. "But I'm so terribly worried about my father."

"I know, Alahna, so am I. Salah probably told you that my own father died when I was just seventeen. I met your father shortly after that. He's been both friend and parent to me ever since."

"Oh, Dolph," she said, addressing him by name for the first time, "I love Papa so much. I can't bear not to be there to take care of him." She looked up at Dolph with tear-filled, anguished eyes.

"Your father is the wisest man I know, Alahna. If he thinks it's best that you come with me to London, we must accept his decision. But I know how you feel. I wish we could have stayed longer in Hong Kong."

He squeezed her hand encouragingly and didn't let go until they had touched down in Rome.

The last leg of the long trip passed quickly. Alahna slept again. When she woke up, she turned to Dolph and asked him whether or not he thought the Americans would elect President Johnson to a full term.

Ah, thought Dolph, beginning to realize what Salah had meant when he'd said his daughter was different from most sixteen-year-olds.

"Ladies and gentlemen, welcome to Heathrow Airport," the stewardess announced. "Local London time is precisely eleven-thirty A.M. The weather, as you can see, is rainy and twelve degress centrigade."

Alahna wrinkled her nose. "Is it always like this in London?"

"Too often, I'm afraid," Dolph said. "But you'll get used to it."

Poor child, he thought. There was so much she had to get used to.

Ito, Dolph's houseman, was waiting at the gate to help them claim their bags and clear customs. Whatever his reaction when Dolph introduced Alahna as Mrs. Robicheck, he gave not a clue.

"How do you do, madam," he said, his face expressionless.

Dolph's Rolls was parked in front of the terminal. Her face as impassive as Ito's, Alahna took silent refuge in the corner of the spacious back seat. Suddenly, Dolph had a thought.

"Alahna, would you like a short tour of London? Perhaps we can show you some of the sights on our way home."

"If you wish, Dolph," she said unenthusiastically.

Dolph was tired from the flight. All he wanted was a bath and a change of clothes. Alahna's gloomy mood was depressing him. Still, he thought, patience. I must be patient.

He picked up the speaker phone and said, "Ito, this is Mrs. Robicheck's first time in London. I'd like her to see some of the city on our way to Eaton Square. Go across the London Bridge and over to Threadneedle Street."

After they had crossed the Thames, Dolph said, "Look, Alahna, there's the Bank of England, and that's the Royal Exchange."

"My father used to go to the Royal Exchange when he was

in London, didn't he?" said Alahna.

"Yes, that's right. And here's the Lord Mayor of London's mansion house on Queen Victoria Street. I believe Salah's been to visit there as well. Now we're turning onto Fleet Street. Those two obelisks are marked with the emblem of St. George and the Dragon. You'll find a pair just like that at each of the entrances to the Old City of London."

Ito drove them past the Covent Garden flowermarket, where at this hour, the vendors were vying with one another to attract customers.

"Do you see that building just across the way, Alahna? That's the Covent Garden Opera House. We could go to the ballet there. Would you like that?"

"If you wish," Alahna said sullenly.

Evidently, all that mattered to her was her father's London.

"Down Picadilly, please, Ito," Dolph said into the phone. "Drive past the Ritz."

"That enormous building facing Green Park is the Ritz Hotel where your father used to stay whenever he was in London. In fact, he persuaded me to move in there. I lived in one of their suites until I bought the house I live in now. I remember sitting in the hotel dining room with your father, at a table that had a window view of the park. It was just after the war ended and I hadn't seen Salah in four years. What a wonderful reunion that was! Would you like to have dinner there some evening?"

"Yes, Dolph, I think I should like that very much," Alahna said, staring out the window at the hotel, as if she half-expected her father to walk through the door and down the steps to their car.

"And here we are, at last," Dolph said, as they drove down Grosvenor Place. "This very pretty part of London is called Belgravia. This is Eaton Place and this," he said as Ito pulled up in front of the house, "is my home. Our home," he corrected himself. "I think you'll like it. I suspect it may remind you a bit of Hong Kong."

Alahna rewarded him with a shy smile. "Thank you, Dolph," she said as he helped her out of the car.

Dolph smiled back. He would never have chosen of his

own free will to take responsibility for a child, but Alahna had the maturity and knowledge of someone much older. She was at once sophisticated and reserved. Dolph wondered how much of an education she had been given in the area of sex.

A child of two cultures, Salah had said. Meilee had helped raise her. Well, we shall soon see, he thought, and followed his bride into her new home.

Chapter Four

Salah had seen to it that his daughter was brought up to recognize and appreciate quality. Now she found herself surrounded by pieces of Chinese furniture and artifacts which she knew to be rare and priceless. She gasped with pleasure when she saw the silk dressing gowns displayed all along the wall leading into the living room.

"Jade stemcups," she said softly. "How beautiful. Wherever did you find them? And what exquisite rugs!" She granted him another of her shy smiles. "This does feel almost like Hong Kong. I almost forget for a moment that we're in London."

"There's a swimming pool downstairs, overlooking the back garden, but let me show you your room. You probably want to freshen up," Dolph said. He took her arm, noticing that she didn't pull away, and led her up two flights to the room adjoining his.

"If I'd known in advance that I was bringing home a wife, I would have had the room redone for you. Tomorrow I'll ring up my interior designer and set up a meeting. Together with him, you can choose exactly what suits you," he told her.

"The room is lovely just the way it is," Alahna murmured.

Dolph turned to her and took both her hands in his. "Alahna, I want you to be happy, but for now, you must rely on what I think is best for you. In time, I know you will learn to hold the reins yourself. Until then, you must allow me to direct you."

"I only meant," Alahna said with a quiver in her voice, "that you don't have to be troubled because of me."

He saw that he had blundered. He would have to remember to be tactful and proceed more delicately. "Tomorrow we'll also see about hiring you a personal maid. In the meantime, I'll send someone up to help you unpack. When you're ready, come downstairs and we'll have a bite to eat."

"Dolph," Alahna said quickly, "where's your room? Is it on this floor?"

He turned to look at her. "Yes, Alahna, it is. I'm right next door. Will that bother you?"

Alahna matched his stare. "No, I'm very glad."

Dolph hesitated only a moment. The realization was dawning on him that he had, after all, married a woman. For the first time since they had met, he took Alahna gently in his arms and kissed her.

Dolph had chosen with utmost care their first dinner at home, which they ate in the library where the atmosphere was more intimate than in his imposing dining room. He had told his cook to serve a first course of the Malassol caviar to which Salah had introduced him. They drank Dom Perignon, the same champagne Salah had ordered for their first dinner at La Maison Française. The next course was a simple breast of chicken with truffles and, for dessert, a fruit sorbet.

They drank their coffee in front of the fireplace.

"That was a lovely meal, Dolph," Alahna said.

"Would you like some brandy?" he asked.

Alahna nodded. She had hardly spoken during dinner, merely answering his questions and making the minimum of polite chitchat. Dolph wondered what was going on behind her dark eyes.

"Would you like me to fix your cigar for you, Dolph?" she asked solicitously.

"I don't smoke cigars, Alahna."

But of course Salah did. Would his presence haunt them everywhere?

"I see. A cigarette then?"

"No, thank you."

Again, silence.

Finally, Alahna spoke. "I know that you are supposed to take me into your bed and make love with me. Don't you want to do that? Don't I please you?"

Her directness caught him unawares. All through dinner he had been remembering his promise to Salah to consummate the marriage as soon as possible. But he felt guilty each time he thought about how young she was.

"Alahna, do you know what going to bed with a man entails?" he asked.

"Yes, Dolph. Meilee talked to me about it. She said I would like making love. Especially with you," she added, blushing bright red.

"I see." Dolph choose his words carefully. "Alahna, I don't want you to be afraid. I promise that I won't hurt you. I want you always to feel safe with me. Do you trust me?"

"Papa says I must trust you."

"This is one decision your father cannot make for you. But I suppose that's the best we can do for now." Noticing that she had finished her brandy, he stood up, took her hand, and led her up the marble staircase to the third floor.

Dolph's bedroom was dominated by a huge antique Chinese bed, covered with a black silk canopy that was held up by four pillars. The black silk draperies were drawn back in front, revealing a black silk coverlet and masses of colorful cushions.

Alahna was immediately reminded of similar beds she had seen in the Hong Kong marketplace where she and her father had shopped for antiques.

"It's a nineteenth-century opium bed, isn't it?" she said, smiling at the carved gold dragons that were winding their way up the pillars. Her dimples deepened, and suddenly she could have been Ohna, standing there in the middle of the room.

My God, thought Dolph, this was very nearly incest. He was furious with Salah, as well as himself for being an accomplice. He dropped her hand and turned away.

Alahna stared at his back, hurt by his rejection. "What's

the matter, Dolph? Did I say the wrong thing?"

"Alahna, it was nothing you said or did. It was just—"

The intimacy of the moment was gone. He couldn't make love with her now. He drew her to him and brushed the hair from her forehead.

"Lord in heaven, Alahna, I can't go through with this," he began.

But how could he possibly explain?

He turned on his heels and retreated to his library, where he spent an uncomfortable night tossing on the leather couch.

Forlorn and bewildered, Alahna crawled onto Dolph's bed and cried herself to sleep.

She didn't appear at breakfast the next morning, even after Dolph sent one of the servants to wake her.

"She called through the door that she wasn't hungry, sir," the servant reported.

Dolph picked up a piece of toast to butter it and instead flung it angrily across the breakfast room. "Damn it," he muttered, and hurried upstairs to her room.

"Alahna, are you all right?" he said, knocking softly on the door.

"Yes."

"Do you feel unwell?"

"No."

"Do you want breakfast."

"No."

Having exhausted his repertoire of solicitious questions, Dolph rattled the doorhandle. It was unlocked, and the door swung open. Alahna was huddled in a ball on top of the covers, fully dressed in the clothes she had worn the evening before.

"I missed you at breakfast," he said. "Why didn't you come down?"

Her words were muffled by the pillow. "If I don't please you, why don't you send me back to Hong Kong?"

"Not please me. Is that what you think?"

"Yes. Why else would you have left me alone last night?"

"Alahna, I'll be right back," Dolph said.

He wet a cloth with cold water and returned to her side.

Cradling her in one arm, he gently wiped her face, washing off the tear stains.

"You've been lying here like this all night, haven't you?"

Alahna burrowed deeper into the shelter of his shoulder and shook with sobs she couldn't suppress. He hugged her closer to him, stroking her cheeks which were wet with her tears. Suddenly, unexpectedly, he was kissing her. The shock of her warm, moist lips against his made him forget the emotional torment of the past ten days.

They were simply a man and a woman, alone, together.

"You are so lovely, Alahna, like a beautiful untouched flower," he whispered.

With unsteady fingers, he undid the buttons of her high-necked gown, and reached for the two small mounds of flesh concealed beneath her silk chemise.

Alahna pulled away to look at him, her eyes begging him to continue.

"Sweet Alahna," he said. He removed the rest of her clothes and stroked her nude body until she was purring like a kitten. Quickly undressing himself, he drew the bed curtains and stretched out next to her in the darkness.

They lay perfectly still, silent except for the sound of their ragged breathing. After a while he could feel her begin to relax in his arms. He moved his hands across her body, feeling the desire within her rising to the surface.

She sighed and moved closer to him, pushing against him, her body asking for more.

Dolph reached down and traced the triangle between her legs, then carefully moved the tip of his forefinger back and forth across the lips.

"Alahna," he said, "open your eyes and look at me."

She moaned as his fingers reached deeper inside her.

"Alahna," he whispered, "I shall be as gentle as I can with you. But I must take you with me. Together we can climb the magic mountain. I promise that heaven awaits us on the other side."

She moaned again and he entered her.

Alahna whispered, but pinned to him as she was, she couldn't pull away. Now he began to slide deeper inside her, and her sighs rose to groans of passion as he brought her closer and closer to the edge.

There was a quick sharp pain, and then feelings beyond anything she had ever imagined swept through her body. She clung to his shoulder and buried her face in his neck, shaking with tumultuous waves of pleasure.

She knew they were one. She never need be afraid of him. For as long as they were together, she was safe.

Alahna opened her eyes and looked at her sleeping lover. It was just as Meilee had promised. Except for a brief moment of pain, making love with Dolph had felt wonderful. Warm and thrilling and beautiful. She could hardly wait to do it again, she thought, reaching over to touch her husband's hand.

Dolph stirred and opened his eyes. "Sweet Alahna," he said. "How do you feel?"

"Fantastic," she said, a satisfied smile turning up the corners of her mouth. "But I'm longing for a hot bath."

He threw back the covers, jumped out of bed, and scooped her up in his arms.

Alahna giggled nervously as he carried her into the bathroom.

Dolph leaned over the marble tub and turned on the taps to draw the bath. Then he poured a handful of scented bath oil and beckoned Alahna to join him in the steaming water.

"It's been years since I've had company in the bath," giggled Alahna. "I think I shall like being a married lady."

Dolph soaped her body, reaching down to wash away a fleck of caked blood from between her legs.

"That tickles," she laughed, her dimples flashing. "Just for that . . ." She knelt in front of him and played her tongue over his lips, forcing her way into his mouth.

"Mmm," Dolph grinned, "I see that my young wife is ready to continue her education. I suggest that we dry off, ring for breakfast, and then discuss how to spend the rest of the morning."

Alahna followed him into the bedroom. Suddenly her hand flew up to her mouth. "Oh, no," she gasped.

"What's the matter, Alahna?" Dolph asked.

"Look at the bed. It's ruined."

She pointed to the blood-stained sheet and looked puzzled when Dolph began to laugh.

"I think we should make a package of the sheets and post them to your father. That's what was done in the old days as proof of the bride's virginity. In this case, of course, we would be offering proof positive of my having kept my promise."

"Your promise? What on earth are you talking about?" Alahna asked. "What promise?"

"Ah, never mind, sweet Alahna. Look, the sun is shining and I'm ready for breakfast. This is much too fine a morning for such serious talk. We have the rest of our lives ahead of us for that."

Chapter Five

The days that followed were a time of learning for Dolph and Alahna. Dolph was learning to be both husband and parent. He was discovering that his bride was not only an enchanting companion and lover, but also the child he would never be able to father. Her quick mind and thorough grasp of financial matters, particularly when they pertained to Shawak Industries, continued to amaze him. At last he had found someone to mold to his measure.

Alahna also had much to learn. The role of Mrs. Dolph Robicheck demanded a high degree of maturity and sophistication. Dolph wanted her to be comfortable no matter what the social setting or situation. Within the first month of her arrival in London, she and Dolph flew to Paris. They spent a whirlwind three days, choosing a new wardrobe, more suited to Alahna's life as Mrs. Robicheck.

Dolph called ahead to consult with Madeleine.

"Congratulations, *cheri*," she said, amused and delighted to hear that her old friend was now a married man. "I would love to meet your wife, but I am flying to Egypt. Christopher and I are going to climb the pyramids. But yes, from your description of Alahna, I would suggest Givenchy."

Alahna fell in love with Paris—and Paris fell in love with
her. Her mannequin-slim frame showed off her new clothes
to perfection. She had her hair styled and cut by Alexandre,
hairdresser to some of the world's most beautiful women.
She and Dolph spent an afternoon carefully choosing elegant
high-heeled shoes from Helene Arpels' collection.

Salah had insisted that Alahna speak fluent French. The
shopkeepers and headwaiters, impressed by her mastery of
their language, fawned over the lovely Madame Robicheck.
On their last evening in Paris, Dolph proudly escorted
Alahna to dinner at Tour d'Argent. All eyes were upon her
as the maître d' led them to their table. Who *was* that
exquisite *jeune fille?* the patrons whispered among themselves. Such interesting eyes. Could she be one of Givenchy's
new girls?

Alahna was having to grow up in a hurry, but she had little time to dwell on the many changes. As he had suggested,
Dolph hired a lady's maid whose job it was to take charge of
Alahna's personal needs. An appointment was arranged with
his interior designer. Their home, Dolph told Alahna,
should reflect her taste as well as his own. Before long their
bedroom as well as the private sitting room next door had
been transformed into the colors of a summer sunset. Pinks,
mulberrys, and peach tones were the perfect backdrop for
her jet black hair and white skin.

Dolph put so much energy into taking care of every facet
of her new life that sometimes Alahna felt guilty. She knew
he only meant to make her happy, but his concern could be
almost suffocating. He worried about how she spent every
moment of her day, what clothes she wore, what cosmetics
she used.

In spite of all he did for her, Alahna missed her father and
Meilee. She longed to see Salah . . . she even missed having
Meilee fuss over her.

No, she scolded herself. She could not permit herself to
look back at what once had been. She was a married woman
now, with a husband and a household to attend to.

And as a married woman, she had no intention of going to
school! She wished she could make Dolph understand how

much she preferred to go to the office with him. That felt familiar to her, almost as though she were sitting at her father's side, the way she always had.

But Dolph doggedly explained that she needed more schooling. For once Alahna refused to let him have his way.

"Ridiculous!" she declared.

She had ten times the education of most girls her age. How many other girls of sixteen could read a balance sheet, or understand the delicate connection between world politics and the fluctuations of the marketplace? She could converse in three languages and was already a voracious reader.

Dolph worried that she would be lonely. He thought it was important for her to develop friendships with girls her own age, girls she could talk to.

"Talk about what?" Alahna asked him "About how wonderful it feels to make love with you? About how you touch me—here and here and here? Dolph," she said, her chin assuming the same stubborn set as Salah's, "I had no girlfriends in Hong Kong—not even my cousins. I had my father—and Meilee. Did you have many friends when you were young?"

"No I didn't, but my parents and I were so involved with music. I wasn't much encouraged to participate in sports or games like other boys my age. I don't suppose Salah pushed you much in that direction either."

"Actually," Alahna said, "I do play rather a good game of tennis. We belonged to the Ladies' Recreation Club. Did you know that when my father was young he played on his college team?"

Dolph shook his head and laughed. "Your father has always been full of surprises."

Alahna blushed. "But look how good this one turned out. You're not sorry, are you?"

"Not the least bit," Dolph said. "And speaking of sports, would you care to go for a swim?"

Alahna had taken instantly to the luxury of swimming in Dolph's indoor pool. When the servants were not about, she loved to dive in nude. Now she threw off her clothes and beckoned to Dolph to follow her. Her black hair glistened as she slithered through the crystal blue water and bobbed to the surface like an exotic mermaid.

With one quick lunge, Dolph captured her in his strong grasp. Together they swam to the steps at the shallow end and lay staring up at their reflection which shone in the mirrored ceiling of the dimly lit room.

"Oh, Dolph, I love you."

"I love you, Alahna," Dolph said. "And if you're so opposed to being sent off to school, we'll find another solution."

The solution, of course, was to hire private tutors. Alahna would have lessons in British and world history, English and French literature, and chemistry.

She turned up her nose at the idea of chemistry. "Well, if you say I must, but then I should like economics as well."

Amused, Dolph readily agreed. He also insisted that she have ballet and piano lessons, and promised to teach her to ski and sail as soon as they could find the time to travel.

Dolph spoke to Salah almost daily, but Salah had deliberately specified that Alahna was to telephone him no more than once a week. Brought up to obey, Alahna lived from phone call to phone call and through the week worried constantly about her father. Her fear that she might never see him again was the only flaw in her new life.

She was so happy with Dolph. But she couldn't stop thinking about her father and his illness.

Dolph had taken note of the shadows that fell across Alahna's eyes whenever he told her that he and Salah had spoken, and that Salah sent her his love. Poor Alahna. She was having to adjust to so much, and she was trying so hard not to show her concern.

It was hard to believe he had met her—married her!— only four months ago. Already she seemed such a part of his existence. He loved coming home to her at the end of the day, analyzing with her the ins and outs of business situations, introducing her to his favorite wines and foods, the theater, showing her London and the surrounding countryside.

Watching her dress for dinner one evening, fastening the diamond necklace Salah had given her as a wedding gift, Dolph realized he had never bought his wife a wedding present. And then he knew just what she would love best.

"Alahna," he said, coming forward to take her hand, "you look beautiful in that dress."

"Thank you. I'm so glad we decided on it. It's one of my favorites."

"I'd love for Salah to see how his daughter had changed into a young woman," Dolph said.

"Oh, Dolph, so would I. If only . . ." Her voice trailed off wistfully.

"Perhaps we could arrange it," Dolph said. "I've some things to discuss with him that would be better taken care of in person anyway. Would you like that?"

She didn't have to speak. The look on her face was answer enough. She threw her arms around him and buried her head in his chest, trying to hide her tears.

Sometimes he forgot that she was just a child of sixteen. It was ironic to think that when he was seventeen, all alone in a foreign land, Salah Shawak had taken him under his wing and changed his life . . . and now here he was, doing just that for Salah Shawak's daughter.

Alahna stared out the window, straining to catch the first sight of Hong Kong's skyline. This time the trip had seemed much longer than nineteen hours. Perhaps that was because she had been too excited to sleep much. All she could think about was seeing her father again, talking to Meilee, showing off all her pretty new clothes.

She felt so different from the girl who had left Hong Kong four months earlier, who had sat silently next to Dolph for much of the flight to England. Glancing at him, she sighed with contentment. Her father had been so right. Here was the man she could always trust and love.

Dolph reached over and took her hand. "Nervous?" he asked.

"I suppose I am a bit, though I don't know why. Nervous and excited."

The stewardess walked briskly down the aisle, collecting pillows and blankets.

She smiled at Dolph and Alahna and said, "Is this the first visit to Hong Kong for you and your daughter?"

"My wife," Dolph said.

"Pardon me?" The stewardess looked at him blankly.

"This young lady is my wife."

"Oh, I'm so sorry." She blushed bright red and retreated quickly.

"I'm sure she thinks we're quite odd," Alahna giggled. " 'Your wife,' Yes, I do like the sound of that. I shall have to remind my cousins if they try to tease me as they used to."

The stewardess still looked embarrassed when they deplaned.

"Thank you for the delightful trip, Alahna said politely.

"You're quite welcome, ma'am," replied the stewardess, her eyes fixed on Alahna's gold wedding band.

Salah's gray limousine was waiting for them in front of the terminal building. And inside was Salah, noticeably thinner than when they had last seen him, his legs covered with a carriage robe.

Alahna flew into the backseat and hugged him tightly. "Oh, Papa, my darling papa, I've missed you so," she cried.

"And I you, my dear," Salah said, his voice shaky with emotion. "How was the trip?"

"Long," said Alahna. "I was impatient to see you."

"You're lucky this wasn't ten years ago." Salah chuckled. "Before the jets began flying, it took days. But look at you, you're even more beautiful than when you left. I can see you are enjoying being a wife."

"Being Dolph's wife," Alahna said with a smile. "Papa, I love him so much. He's a wonderful man."

"And here he is," her father said, as Dolph approached with the chauffeur and the porter. "Dolph, I was just telling my daughter that her happiness is showing—and so is yours."

Dolph was shocked to see how much Salah had aged with his illness. He seemed to be shrinking into himself. Suddenly he was very grateful they had made this trip.

Alahna was equally unprepared for the change in Salah. He would never complain or tell her how he really was. She would have to get the truth from Meilee. Funny, she thought. Now that she was here in Hong Kong, being driven through the streets she knew so well, she realized that

London already felt like home.

But home had meant her father—the safety and security of knowing he would always be there to protect her. For the first time since he had told her he was ill, she began to accept the fact that Salah was dying.

Meilee was standing in the doorway as the car pulled to a stop beneath the porte-cochère. Without waiting for the driver to open her door, Alahna jumped out and ran into Meilee's arms.

Meilee, usually not so demonstrative, embraced Alahna, as the tears slowly trickled down her cheeks. "My little girl, my baby," she crooned, "let me look at you."

Alahna stepped back and proudly modeled her new dress and high heels.

"Well, Meilee, what do you think?"

Meilee shook her head. "You're all grown up. And so beautiful. Come, come," she fussed, "you must be tired and thirsty. Let's not stand about outside. Your father and Dolph can find us in the salon."

Dolph matched his pace to Salah's slow step.

"You are taking excellent care of my daughter, just as I knew you would," Salah said in a low voice. "She looks well and happy."

"But how are you?" Dolph asked. "You've lost weight."

Salah grinned. "You never did mince words. As a matter of fact, I am rather well at the moment, notwithstanding my appearnace. I've been feeling better ever since you told me you were coming. I'm glad you decided Alahna needed to see me. I needed to see the two of you as well."

He nodded at Alahna and Meilee who were seated on the sofa. "Let's let the ladies have a few minutes together. There's something I wanted to discuss in private with you. I've understood from our telephone conversations that Alahna has been staying at home while you are at the office."

Dolph hesitated. Salah had immediately hit upon the one source of conflict in his marriage. "She says she wants to come with me. But Salah, I hardly think it's appropriate."

"Appropriate?" Salah's eyes twinkled with amusement. "You know, Dolph, from the time she was five years old, I frequently took her to work."

"I know that, Salah. But she's busy with her lessons. Besides, I think that as my wife, she should be at home, taking care of things."

Salah couldn't contain his laughter. "Things? What sort of things? No doubt you have servants whose job is to take care of things. Dolph," he said, more somberly, "I have no intention of interfering in your marriage, and I'm pleased that you are seeing fit to continue her education. But I want my daughter someday to be able to manage her own affairs. She's already extremely knowledgeable, and I expect her to become even more astute as she matures."

"What are you two talking about over there?" Alahna asked.

"Your father has just been reminding me how little it pays to disagree with him. What I can't figure out, Salah, is how it is that you're always right. Had I been clever enough to guess what a treasure you were giving me, I would have grabbed her straight out of the cradle."

Salah nodded his head, satisfied that Dolph had taken his point. "I imagine that you'd both like a bath and a change of clothing. I suggest we continue this conversation in one hour's time. Alahna, I'm looking forward to a long chat with you before dinner. And Dolph, you and I shall play chess afterwards."

Meilee had brought Alahna up to date on the events of the past months. Salah's physical condition had seemed to be deteriorating rapidly. But in the last several weeks, he had begun to improve.

"The doctors called it 'remission,'" she explained. "Of course, seeing you and Dolph is the best medicine he could possibly have. You know your father is far too proud to say so, but he has been missing you dreadfully. Though certainly it's for the best that you be with your husband. Tell me, child, are you truly as happy as you appear to be?"

"Oh, Meilee, I never dreamed I could be this happy. Dolph is so good to me. Demanding, yes, but I suppose I'm used to that because of Papa. In many ways he reminds me of Papa. So kind and attentive."

Meilee smiled. "He had excellent early training, you know."

Her words stayed with Alahna as she and Salah strolled through the garden before dinner. The early summer flowers were in full bloom, and they mocked Alahna's melancholy mood. Salah was dying, but she had to console herself that she would not be alone. She was married to a man who could and would give her everything she had come to expect from her father.

All of the Shawak family had been invited for dinner. Salah's niece, Amy, whom Dolph still remembered from Shanghai as a delightful eight-year-old, now had her own daughter of six. Raquela was every bit as outgoing as her mother had been.

"Tell me what it looks like in London," she begged Alahna. "Did you see London Bridge? Were you frightened? Was it really falling down?"

Dolph watched Alahna patiently answer her cousin's questions. For the first time that he could recall, he regretted his inability to have children. Not now perhaps, but on some future morning, Alahna would surely wake up and wish she could have a child of her own. It seemed unnecessarily cruel to deny her the opportunity. Salah had taken into account everything but that. Ah well, Dolph thought, why regret the future? There was too much to deal with in the present.

The two weeks passed quickly. Salah had proposed to Dolph that they merge Shawak Industries and the British-Orient Limited.

"Won't your nephews have something to say about that?" Dolph asked.

Salah raised one eyebrow and spoke with the authority of an Oriental potentate. "They have other interests to occupy them. But just in case they object, we can set aside one or two companies to remain exclusively within the Shawak family."

With Alahna present at their meetings, they spent each morning working out a strategy for future expansion. The name of the new corporation was to be Shawak

International. Dolph had already given some consideration to expanding into the American markets. Now, backed by the capital of Shawak Industries, he could begin to make his financial presence felt in North America.

One afternoon he and Alahna stole away to confer with Salah's doctor. The man offered them little hope. "Yes, he's in remission now, but your father isn't a young man. It's hard to say how long this good period will last. He could have two months or two years."

Alahna clutched at Dolph's hand. "Doctor," said Dolph, "is there nothing more to be done? Perhaps we should take him back to England with us. With all due respect . . ."

The doctor shrugged. "If I thought that would help, I would certainly encourage you. But I assure you, we are giving him the best possible treatment here. Besides, Salah is not a man to be easily persuaded to leave his home. As I understand, it took the bombing of Pearl Harbor to get him to quit Shanghai."

Dolph nodded grimly. "I see you know your patient. Well, we thank you for your time. And if there are any changes . . . if there's anything we can possibly do for him in London, please call me immediately."

He handed the doctor his card and led Alahna out into the summer sunshine.

"Oh, Dolph," she said, her voice thick with anguish. "But he looks so much better."

They walked for a while hand in hand, trying to console each other, then hailed a cab.

Salah refused to concede to his illness, and they followed his lead. Nothing was said to acknowledge the possibility that they might never see him again after this visit. They took walks, played chess, toasted one another gaily at dinner, and talked endlessly about the past.

Alahna learned more that week than she had ever known about her husband and her father. She loved the story of their first meeting when Dolph had come dressed in the dinner clothes provided by Salah.

"But what finally persuaded you to leave the IC?" she wanted to know.

"Let's just say," Dolph cleared his throat, "that your

father made me a very tempting offer."

Despite the doctor's discouraging words, they were convinced that they were seeing a marked improvement in Salah.

"Papa, you look wonderful," Alahna declared. "Don't you think so, Meilee?"

"Yes, certainly he does. You and Dolph have brought wonderful medicine for your father."

"We'll come back in two months," Dolph said. "I promise. I've lost too many games this visit not to want a rematch."

Meilee had suggested that it might be easier if Salah not accompany them to the airport, and Dolph agreed immediately. Surprisingly, so did Salah.

"Quite right," he said gruffly. "I've some papers to go over before I go to sleep tonight, and you don't need me there. Meilee, you go along with them to make sure they get off properly."

But all through their last dinner together, he couldn't seem to tear his eyes away from Alahna. They lingered over the coffee until the last moment.

Alahna continued to wave through the back window of the limousine long after she had lost sight of her father.

Even after the car had disappeared through the grove of trees at the end of the road, Salah, too, kept watch. He stood for a long time in the open doorway, breathing in the cool night air. He had completed the necessary arrangements, done what had to be done. It was all as it should be.

Chapter Six

Dolph would be forever grateful that they had made the trip to Hong Kong. Just two weeks after they returned to London, he received the telephone call he had been dreading. Salah had passed away in his sleep. He had left strict instructions with Meilee and his oldest nephew that the funeral was to be held the very next day, according to Jewish custom.

"He wanted to spare Alahna the ordeal of his funeral," Meilee said sadly. "My poor Alahna. This will be so hard for her. Help her through this, Dolph."

"I'll do my best," Dolph said.

He rushed home to tell Alahna.

"But he looked so well when we said goodbye," Alahna protested, as if to deny his words. "He was getting better, Dolph. You saw it yourself."

Dolph led her over to the sofa and gently put his arms around her. "Darling, we both heard what the doctors said. We were very fortunate that he was feeling so well, that we had that time with him. We can be comforted that he was spared any pain and suffering. Meilee said he died peacefully. He had thoroughly prepared himself for this moment. He was ready, Alahna. It was God's mercy that he didn't have to suffer."

Alahna sat stiffly, hardly able to breathe. "Oh, Dolph," she said, "I hurt so. I don't think I can bear the pain. Please, I have to go to bed. I need to be alone for a while."

Dolph led her upstairs to their bedroom and removed the clothing from her shaking body. Alahna sat quietly, obedient as a tired child, on the side of the bed.

Dolph pulled back the covers and helped her lie down. "Can I bring you something to drink—a cup of warm milk, or perhaps something stronger?"

"No, thank you. I want to sleep."

He paced the floor of his study for hours, remembering Salah's many kindnesses, his lessons, all that they had shared. Salah had had a full and happy life—but he had had many years left in him. And could he now find the words to comfort Salah's daughter—his wife?

Alahna was wide awake, gazing blankly into the shadows of the darkened room. She didn't move or speak when Dolph sat down beside her on the bed and took her hand.

"Alahna, do you need anything?" he asked.

He could hardly make out her response.

"I've spent the last few hours thinking about your father. I'm so glad you're here with me, Alahna. At least we have each other."

"Dolph . . ."

"Yes, darling?"

"Do you think . . . I . . . would you mind if I slept alone here tonight? I . . . I need to be alone . . . to think."

"Well . . ." He was taken aback for an instant, but then he chided himself. His grief, deep as it was, couldn't compare to what Alahna must be feeling. If she needed to mourn in her own way, he must accommodate her. "Of course, Alahna, of course, I understand. Do you want me to stay with you until you fall asleep?"

She nodded slowly and closed her eyes.

Dolph pulled the covers around her and clicked off the lamp.

"Goodnight, my dear," he whispered. "I promise never to leave you."

What a cruel world this was, he thought. That we should so easily lose the people we love. He sighed heavily as he lost himself in his memories.

Alahna lay staring up at a spot on the ceiling, still caught in the dream from which she had awakened.

"He's mine, mama," she had scolded her mother. "You can't have him. He's mine."

But what was it her mother had tried to take from her? Her little furry rabbit that she had slept with until the day she had married Dolph—or had it been Dolph himself?

"Married women don't sleep with stuffed animals," Meilee had said. "You may not take that with you. Absolutely not."

But now—oh! how she wished she had sneaked the rabbit into one of her suitcases. Just to have something familiar. Something to hold tight next to her, to protect her. Life held too many dangers. It was safer to stay here in bed. She could pull the covers up above her head and sleep and sleep and sleep. She didn't care what Dolph said. She was never going to leave her bed.

Nor did she want to eat any of the breakfast he brought her on a tray.

"No, thank you, Dolph," she said, turning her head away from the sight of the eggs and kippers. She was sure she would choke if she tried to swallow even a bite.

"Alahna, I want you to eat some of this, and then get

dressed. We've a lot to discuss."

"I can't, Dolph. I really can't. Not today. Maybe tomorrow I'll get up. I'm not feeling very well this morning."

It was true. Her head ached and the bright light was hurting her eyes, which were swollen and puffy from crying. Her arms and legs felt numb, almost paralyzed.

"Alahna," Dolph said gently, "I remember how I felt when my uncle told me my parents were dead. At first I thought I must have misunderstood, or that he was playing a terrible joke on me. But I knew that, of course, Uncle Maurice wouldn't do such a thing. So if it was true, I decided, maybe if I closed my eyes, his words—and the truth behind them—would simply go away. And when that didn't work, I thought my world had ended. I knew I would never laugh or feel anything good, ever again."

Alahna lay absolutely still, her eyes shut tight. For a moment he wondered whether she had heard a word of what he was telling her.

"I can imagine what you must be feeling," he went on. "But I love you and I am here with you. Let me help you, Alahna. Please, listen to me. Let's spend this day talking about Salah. Meilee said the funeral service was being held this afternoon. Probably right about now. If we can't be there, let us—the two people he loved so very much—at least think about him together."

Tears spilled out of Alahna's eyes and splashed down her pale cheeks. "No," she said. "I can't."

"All right. I understand. But I'll be downstairs all this morning if you want to talk or have me sit with you. If I go to the office this afternoon, I'll tell Wilma to bring you a tray at lunchtime. Otherwise, I will see you this evening at dinner."

She was, after all, just a child, he told himself. For all her sophistication and grownup ways, just sixteen years old. And she had been so carefully sheltered from pain by Salah and Meilee. She'll be fine. She simply needed some time alone, to mourn, to grieve for her father and the end of her childhood.

Wilma greeted him at the front door that evening, a look

of concern on her normally placid face.

"Mr. Robicheck," she said, helping him with his raincoat, "I brought Mrs. Robicheck a tray at noon, just as you told me to. But she wouldn't touch a bite of it. And I made her such lovely eggs, just the way she likes them. I suggested she get up so I could straighten up the bed a bit and I laid out the light blue dress she loves so. But she just stared straight ahead and then she closed her eyes and wouldn't say a word to me. It almost seemed as if she wasn't hearing me."

"Thank you, Wilma, I'm sure you did your best."

Dolph hurried up the stairs and into the bedroom. He found Alahna just as he had left her nine hours earlier, flat on her back, her eyes closed, her face pale and tear-stained.

"Alahna," he said, "I thought surely you would have been up and dressed. You know, darling, you must eventually leave your bed. And you must be almost weak with hunger by now. Please, let me help you get dressed and we can eat in the library and talk."

She opened her eyes and cleared her throat several times before the words came out in a low voice. "No, Dolph, not this evening. I'm not feeling too well. I'm so tired."

"If you're ill, Alahna, I shall call the doctor."

"No. No, I don't need a doctor. I need to sleep."

Dolph went into the bathroom and wet a facecloth.

"Here," he said, returning to her side, "let me at least wipe your face. I can't bear to see your eyes so red and swollen. Now listen to me, darling. You've had a deep, deep loss, and I appreciate your sorrow. I, too, am grieving. But the last thing your father would want is for you to retreat from life. He believed in facing all of life's evils and disappointments, and conquering them as best we can. Now you must let me help you put your anguish behind you."

Alahna turned over and buried her face in the pillow.

"Alahna . . ." He tried once more. But he could see that his word would do no good.

Dolph spent another restless night in the guest room, worrying about Alahna. What would Salah have done, he wondered. Well, he consoled himself, perhaps by tomorrow she will have had the time she needs. Yes, he was quite sure of it. In the morning she would certainly feel much better.

But to his chagrin, the next day Alahna seemed no more ready to get up and face the world.

"I just want to lie here and remember how things used to be," she told him plaintively. "If I close my eyes and try hard enough, I can see Papa's face. I can even hear him talking to me, telling me what to do."

"Darling, don't you think your father would tell you to get up and carry on your life? Unless you are feeling ill—in which case, I shall call the doctor—I would like you to get up and join me for breakfast."

"I can't." She stared at him, her mouth set defiantly.

"I'm sure that if you try, you will find that you can. Wilma has laid out your clothes. And I'll help you bathe, if you'd like."

She shook her head and closed her eyes.

He waited to see whether she might change her mind. But after several minutes of silence he said, not unkindly, "Very well. Just as you wish. I'll see you this evening then."

Three days went by and still Alahna couldn't bring herself to leave her bed. Wilma brought her trays of tea and soup and crackers, which she at last consented to eat. But she could summon neither the will nor the desire to get up and come downstairs.

Dolph seemed to have disappeared. She hadn't seen him or even heard his voice outside her door since the morning he had urged her to get up and join him for breakfast. Finally she swallowed her pride and asked Wilma whether Mr. Robicheck had been called out of town.

"No, ma'am," her maid replied. "But I believe he's dined out the last two evenings. He had on his dinner jacket last night. But he seemed pleased when I told him you'd eaten this lovely soup."

"Thank you, Wilma," Alahna said. "You can go now."

Whom, she wondered, had Dolph seen last night? Was his friend Madeleine Laval in town? She had told herself again and again that it was silly to be jealous of Madeleine. Dolph had mentioned that she was very lovely and elegant. But she and Dolph were very good, old friends—nothing more.

Nevertheless, the fact that he had gone out infuriated her. While she lay here, disconsolate, mourning her father, her husband had no doubt been sitting across from another woman, laughing and enjoying himself. Didn't he, too, feel the need to mourn Salah, whom he'd said time and again had been like a father to him?

Why wasn't he here, by her side, mourning with her?

Because she had sent him away, that was why. Because she had closed her eyes and shut him out and refused to allow him into her grief.

Suddenly the thought struck her that probably Dolph, too, needed comforting. And she had forced him to go seek it elsewhere.

"Oh, Dolph," she whispered. "I'm sorry."

Wilma had opened the drapes, and the sun was shining brightly. It appeared to be a lovely summer morning. The sort of morning when her father would have said, "Come, Alahna, it's much too fine to take the car. Let's walk this morning."

It was time to get up and begin to live again.

She was sitting in the library, wearing Dolph's favorite dress, when he returned home from the office late in the afternoon, looking wearier than she had ever seen him. But his face lit up as soon as he saw her and he quickly came over to give her a kiss.

"I'm sorry, Dolph," Alahna said, her voice faltering.

Dolph silenced her with another kiss. "No," he said, "don't apologize. I'm so glad you came back to me, Alahna. We need each other now—more than ever."

Again, Dolph was reminded of Salah's wisdom. In the weeks that followed, Alahna was more subdued than usual. But there was little time for her to brood or dwell on Salah's death. Her mornings were spent at the office with Dolph, and her afternoons were filled with lessons. Now, instead of calling Salah once a week, she telephoned Meilee, who had sent her a long letter describing Salah's last hours and his funeral, which had been attended by half of Hong Kong.

As if by unspoken agreement, she and Dolph curtailed

their social life. Neither of them had much heart for restaurants or the theater. For the time being, they both preferred to dine at home, informally in the library. After dinner, Dolph played the piano or they listened to music and talked quietly, often about Salah and what each of them knew of his remarkable life.

Then, suddenly, it was December, and the Christmas season brought Jeff back to London.

"Christmas in Los Angeles? Man, that's a travesty," he told Dolph. "So here I am. Am I invited for dinner?"

When Dolph said, "Yes, I want you to meet my wife," Jeff was momentarily speechless. But he quickly recovered. "Can't wait, pal," he declared. "I'll bring the champagne."

The next day, by happy coincidence, Madeleine telephoned from Paris. Chris would be joining her in London the following week. Now they could finally get to meet Alahna. And, oh, yes, she had someone she wanted Dolph to meet, as well.

"Come for dinner next Wednesday," Dolph said. "Bring your friend. We'll have a grand reunion with Jeff, too."

"My dear," he told Alahna, "it's time I introduced you to some of my friends. They're all quite amused that an old buzzard like me has finally taken himself a wife. I've invited some people for next week. I'd like to discuss the menu with you."

Up until now, Dolph had always planned the meals with Ito and the cook. Alahna was delighted to be trusted with the new responsibility.

"Who are the guests to be?" she asked.

"My friend, Maleleine Laval, of whom you've heard me speak so often. As you know, she and I have known each other for many, many years."

"Were you lovers?" Alahna asked. There—it was out in the open. The question she had wanted to ask him whenever he spoke of Madeleine.

"At one time we were, Alahna, but now we are simply very good friends. In fact, I introduced her to her present lover, Christopher Brooke, one of my oldest friends. He'll be here, too. Madeleine is bringing someone she wants me to meet. I know nothing about him except that if he's a friend of hers, he's certain to be interesting and probably odd. The fourth guest is another old friend, Jeff Gotley, through whom I met Madeleine. Jeff writes music for films. He also happens to be one of the most fascinating, charming characters you'll ever meet."

"Tell me more about Chris," said Alahna, wondering what kind of man would interest Madeleine Laval, whom she pictured as the epitome of chic and sophistication.

"I've known Chris since I was just your age. In fact, in a roundabout way, he's responsible for my getting to Shanghai. He's a correspondent for Reuters, and he's been in the Middle East so long he speaks Arabic and Hebrew like a native. Whenever there's a war in that part of the world, he's there to cover it. He was also a great friend of my uncle Maurice. So that's the guest list. Now, what shall we serve for dinner?"

"Well, I've rather an interesting idea, if you think your friends might like it," Alahna said with increasing excitement. "What about a traditional ten-course Chinese banquet?"

"You're wonderful, Alahna. That's the very thing. Do you know that after all my years in the Orient, I've never thought of that? I don't suppose our cook is familiar with Chinese cuisine. But perhaps Ito knows someone whom he could hire for the evening."

Ito, in fact, had a friend whose meals, he assured them, were fit for an emperor. Did Mr. Robicheck know what he wanted to serve his guests?

"I shall leave that to you and Mrs. Robicheck," Dolph said, "if that's all right with you, of course?"

"Of course," Alahna said. "Just leave it to us. And I know just how I want to do the table and the flowers. Ito can take me to the flower market and we'll surprise you."

The table was a study in black, accented with lavendar. Alahna had bought chopsticks and black china vases in Chinatown. These she filled with delicate sprays of baby orchids, purchased at a Covent Market flower stall and arranged in the spare Oriental manner that Meilee had taught her.

To mark the occasion of Alahna's first dinner party, Dolph had bought Alahna a three-carat, heart-shaped diamond suspended from a thin gold chain. The glittering stone fell just to the hollow of her throat, the perfect complement to her red silk gown, one of her trousseau dresses. Her hair was combed straight back from her face, and her high cheekbones gleamed not with makeup but with excitement.

"You grow lovelier each day," Dolph told her. "And the table looks elegant. I'm so proud of you, darling."

"Thank you, Dolph," Alahna said primly. The palms of her hands were wet with nervousness. What if his friends didn't like her? What if she had nothing to say to them? The tablesetting had been easy. It was the next several hours looming ahead of her that were the real test.

Jeff Gotley was the first to arrive. *"Ni hao ma?"* he said, instantly putting Alahna at her ease by greeting her in Chinese.

"How do you happen to speak Chinese?" she said. "Few Westerners do, it's such a difficult language."

"Actually, sweetheart, I collected just those few words in order to impress you. Did Dolph tell you that one of these days he and I are going to write a musical together?"

"No, really? He's never said a word, though I've no doubt he could do it," Alahna replied, already charmed by the attractive black man.

Dolph laughed good-humoredly. "We've been cultivating that fantasy for years, Alahna. But some day maybe we'll get serious and do something together. Probably when we're both too old to do much else."

"Mais non, neither one of you will ever be that old," Madeleine declared, overhearing his last comment as she and Christopher were ushered into the library. They were accompanied by a short slim man who looked like an oddly styled elf. He wore a one-piece suit, and with his dark, curly hair hanging down to his shoulders, he stood out among the other guests. He hadn't bothered, even on this cold, wet December night, to put on socks, and his leather shoes, turned up at the toes, looked like a genie's. Staring at the apparition in front of them, Dolph and Alahna were momentarily speechless.

"Dolph, I'd like you to meet a friend of mine from New York. Dolph Robicheck, Ace Taylor," Madeleine said.

"How do you do." Ace Taylor's voice was high and squeaky.

"And you must be Alahna," Madeleine said, kissing Alahna on both cheeks in the continental manner. "I am so very pleased to meet you at last. Dolph, you didn't do her justice," she scolded. "And this gentleman who is probably falling madly in love with you is Christopher Brooke."

"As your husband's oldest friend, I'm delighted to meet you, Alahna. He's outdone himself this time," Chris said, gallant as always.

Jeff insisted that they straightaway uncork one of the bottles of Cristal champagne he'd brought to celebrate his friend's marriage. As Ito passed the glasses, Dolph chatted with Ace Taylor. After the initial shock of Ace's outrageous appearance, Dolph soon realized that the man had an exceptionally keen mind. A witty rancounteur, he seemed to have friends and associates all over the world.

For some time now, Dolph had been quietly looking for a man to head up the soon-to-be-established New York office. He'd mentioned the matter to Madeleine. Obviously, she'd brought Ace along so that Dolph could size him up for the position. A financial wizard with contacts in America and elsewhere might nicely fit the bill.

As they gathered at the table, Dolph's announcement that they were about to partake of an authentic Chinese feast drew an enthusiastic response.

"How very clever of you, Alahna," declared Madeleine.

Alahna smiled shyly and listened wide-eyed to their banter, feeling too tongue-tied to say more than a word or two. She was uncomfortably aware of the great age difference between herself and Dolph. She glanced at her husband, wondering what he was thinking. But Dolph was too engrossed in the conversation to notice her discomfort.

Ace Taylor could well turn out to be his man, he mused. Dolph was growing more and more bored with being the front man in his corporation. He needed someone who liked to be in the public eye. Certainly Ace would never get lost in a crowd. And he appeared to have the right business background, not to mention some interesting connections.

"Dolph . . . Dolph!" Madeleine waved her hand in front of his face to capture his attention. "I hope I can count on all of you to join me in St. Moritz next month. Alahna, do you ski?"

"No, but I'd like to learn. Dolph's promised me lessons as soon as we have time."

"I thought I might rent a house there for the month of February," said Dolph.

"Wonderful. Would you like me to make the arrangements for you?"

"Absolutely, Madeleine. That would be marvelous."

Alahna looked up, surprised at how easily Dolph had agreed to Madeleine's suggestion. Would he ever trust her, Alahna, to take care of such an important matter as renting a house for the two of them?

The last course was a dessert of mandarin oranges and lichee nuts with lemon sherbet, followed by coffee and tea in the library.

"Please, *cheri*, you must play for us," coaxed Madeleine.

"Yeah, man, play that song we wrote together," said Jeff.

"Well," said Ace when Dolph had finished his impromptu concert, "I hate to leave this delightful party, but I've a yoga lesson at five-thirty in the A.M. Thank you, beautiful lady, I hope to have the pleasure again soon." He bent and kissed the back of Alahna's hand. "And thank you, Dolph. You were most kind to include me. My psychic predicted an important meeting for me. Perhaps this was the one she meant."

Jeff left soon after with a promise to see them again very soon.

Madeleine and Chris lingered for a nightcap and some gossip.

"Tell me about this Ace, Madeleine," Dolph said.

"Well, for one thing, I'm sure he knows we're discussing him and he doesn't mind a bit," Madeleine began. "In fact, that's probably the real reason he left early."

"He's a fascinating fellow, though definitely a bit of an odd bird," chuckled Dolph.

Oh, *absolutement*," smiled Madeleine in agreement. "I

met him last June in Monaco. He was the talk of the
glamour set there. They were all sure he was either a con
man or a madman—or possibly both. He claimed to have
made sixteen million dollars in a matter of a couple of years
as the biggest individual trader on the New York Stock
Exchange. Before that he'd spent years travelling in India,
Nepal, and Tibet. He also says he has an agreement with a
group of monks at a monestery in Tibet. If he takes a fancy
to you, he'll have them chanting prayers on your behalf."

Dolph was laughing so hard he could only shake his head
in amazement.

"Wait," said Madeleine, "there's more. As I heard it, Ace
was once upon a time a highly respected attorney in Los
Angeles with a wife and a young child. But he got bored
with the law and all the materialism in L.A. He divorced his
wife and went up to San Francisco where he fell in with
some of the beat poets. They sent him to the East in search
of truth. Most recently, he discovered he had a great talent
for playing the arbitrage game on the stock market. Somewhere along the way, he married Jana. She's a ballerina
who also happens to be a full-blooded American Indian. I
understand they're very happy. But she's quite involved with
her career, so Ace is often left to amuse himself in various
corners of the world."

"Madeleine, this is whom you're suggesting to run my
New York office? You must be daft!"

"No, no, Dolph, *pas du tout!* Ace is exceptionally bright
and innovative, and I think ready to settle down. He has
friends everywhere, but he's let me know that he's rather
bored and ready for a challenge. Think about it. Get to
know him better. The man quite grows on you."

"I'm looking for an executive, not an ivy plant," Dolph
laughed. "But I've learned to trust your instincts,
Madeleine. I shall have to give it some thought."

"*Bien!* And now we must go," Madeleine said. "Chris, am
I interrupting your conversation or are you ready to leave?"

Chris stood up from the sofa he was sharing with Alahna.
"Yes, you are interrupting, but it's been a long evening for
our hostess. I'm afraid I must be boring you, Alahna."

"Not at all," Alahna protested. "Your stories are

fascinating. I hope we'll have a chance to get to know each other better."

Dolph beamed, pleased that she had hit it off so well with his friends. "We must make a point of it, either here during the holidays or in St. Moritz. And thank you, Madeleine, for all your help."

"Good night, Alahna," said Madeleine, hugging the younger woman. "You are lovely. Wonderful for Dolph. I can see that. *A bientot, mes cheris.*"

Alahna was flushed with pleasure from her triumph as a hostess. But she had trouble falling asleep. Over and over again she heard Dolph saying, "That would be marvelous, Madeleine."

She remembered the look on his face as he bent closer to Madeleine, talking quietly, while she and Chris had chatted across the room. The more she thought about her husband's close relationship with Madeleine, the more unhappy she felt about it.

The French woman was so beautiful, Alahna agonized. But she was even older than Dolph, maybe even over fifty. Fifty! Still, Madeleine's clothes were stunning, and the way she walked into the room made all the men stop talking and look at her. Perhaps Dolph thought she was silly and immature and preferred to talk over his important decisions with his former girlfriend. Well, Madeleine would have to let go.

Yes, Alahna decided, she would speak to Dolph about her.

After a few days of quiet sulking, Alahna finally brought up the subject with Dolph. They were driving to their country house in East Grinstead in the green Jaguar convertible Dolph had bought for her. She was only just learning to drive, but already she loved the feel of being in command of the sleek machine.

"Dolph," she said, summoning her courage, "why do you still depend so much on Madeleine? I really don't see the need for it."

Dolph looked at her, annoyed. "Madeleine is a close friend. If I 'depend' on her, as you put it, it's because I value her judgment. Just as I value Jeff's or Chris's. I think you're jealous, Alahna, because she's a woman. But I certainly wouldn't expect you to give up a close male friend if you had one."

Alahna squirmed but continued, convinced she was right. "Dolph, I think she feels something for you that is more than friendship."

Dolph laughed. "All that was finished between us long before I ever met you. I owe Madeleine a lot. She has been very good to me and I love her very much. But I assure you, Alahna, we no longer have a physical relationship. Though if we did, I would expect you to accept it with good grace."

"What?" Alahna said angrily. "Dolph, that's ridiculous. I could never accept any such thing!"

"Indeed?" said Dolph. "Ah, there's the turnoff. Let's continue this discussion when we get to the house."

They were settled in front of the fireplace, watching the flames spread through the stack of logs, when Dolph reopened the conversation.

"Alahna," he said, "I'm rather disturbed by what you said earlier in the car."

"Do you mean about you and Madeleine?"

"More than that. You told me you would never accept my having a sexual relationship with another woman. I think that you're confusing sex with love, my dear. I don't believe that we humans were meant to be monogamous. I also refuse to lie to you about my whereabouts. I have always made love with whomever I wish, and I will continue to do so. By the same token, I certainly don't expect you to make love to me alone. I want you to explore and develop your own sexual appetite, so that you will be able to savor and enjoy the best."

"But Dolph," Alahna said, tears filling her eyes, "I don't need any other man."

"It's not a question of 'need,' Alahna. I believe that sexual intimacy is merely another way of getting to know someone better. You and I share a special love and understanding. I care for you. I respect you. But because I'm your husband doesn't mean I own you. Love to me means feeling secure, sharing an honest friendship, with uninhibited desire and open communication. That is something you will have with very few people. You may sleep with many men. But I hope and trust that the pleasure you have in my company you will find with no one else."

"Well, what a fine speech that was," Alahna said. She stood up abruptly. "Excuse me. I'd like a few minutes alone to digest it all."

Daylight was fast fading. Alahna shivered in the dampness of the twilight air. She walked briskly along the garden path. After the heat of the fire and the stuffy room, the mist felt clean and refreshing against her skin.

She had hated hearing what he had said. She didn't even want to consider the merit of his points. No, that wasn't right, she told herself. "Listen to the other person and consider his arguments," her father had always said.

Very well, she decided, staring at the stream that bordered on their property. She picked up a handful of pebbles and tossed them into the lightly rippling water. She must at least consider his ideas, even if in the end she didn't agree with him. Besides, he'd brought so much into her life. Perhaps someday, somehow, she'd come to see that he was right. In the meantime, she would force herself to ignore her jealousy. For there was really no other choice. He'd made himself quite clear. Whatever her feelings might be, Dolph was not about to change his philosophy or his lifestyle.

Accustomed to coming and going as he pleased, whether for business or social reasons, Dolph thought nothing of leaving London for several days at a time without telling anyone. After his chat with Alahna, he expected that she would manage to keep herself busy and ask no questions when he returned.

But all Alahna's good resolves flew out the window when Dolph disappeared one very long, dull weekend in January. Sunday evening he found her in the library, furious that she'd not been included in his plans.

"How could you do this to me?" she said, almost screaming in as angry a tone as he'd ever heard from her. "How could you leave me all alone when I don't know a soul in London! And I was so worried about you, Dolph."

She crossed her arms against her chest and stared angrily

at the carpeted floor, refusing to meet his eyes.

"I'm sorry, Alahna. That was rude of me. I should have realized you'd worry. But you told me you had no need of girlfriends your own age. We can't be Siamese twins, my dear, forever attached, unable to move one without the other."

Eventually, she relented and came to bed with him. But it took several days before she smiled again. He hadn't meant to cause her pain, he reflected, and he'd already put her on notice that he wasn't about to give up his freedom. But it pained him to think she'd been lonely. She needed companionship.

Precisely! He snapped his fingers, delighted to have hit upon the ideal solution. The answer was so simple that he couldn't imagine how he had not thought of it before.

The pile of luggage stacked in the front foyer immediately caught Alahna's eye.

"Do we have visitors?" she asked.

"Yes, but I wanted to surprise you. Come, let's see who's waiting for us in the drawing room," Dolph replied.

He pulled open the double doors.

There sat Meilee, her wrinkled face alit with a broad smile. Alahna rushed straight into her arms, almost capsizing the woman's chair. "What a wonderful surprise! How did this happen? Oh, Meilee, I've missed you so much."

"And I've missed you." Meilee said, her eyes filled with tears of joy. "But Dolph arranged all this."

"Dolph, thank you . . . thank you so much. Can you stay for a very long time, Meilee?" Alahna was dancing with glee.

"For as long as you'd like. Dolph has invited me to join your household. With you here and your father gone, there's very little left for me in Hong Kong."

"I imagine the two of you have quite a lot to talk about," Dolph said. "And I've a lot to ask you myself, Meilee. But Alahna probably wants you all to herself for a bit. I shall see you both at dinner." He kissed both women and grinned. "Welcome to London, Meilee. I can't tell you how happy I am to have you with us."

"Thank you, Dolph," Meilee said with a smile of pleasure. "I'm very happy to be here."

There was no need for Alahna to say a word. The look on her face said it all. She hadn't realized until this moment how much she had been missing Meilee. Now London truly felt like home.

Chapter Seven

Alahna had made herself a promise not to mention Madeleine again to Dolph, but she felt sharp stabs of jealousy whenever she saw Dolph looking fondly at his former lover. That Madeleine was obviously very much in love with Chris didn't console her a bit.

Finally, Alahna confessed her feelings to Meilee.

"Poor Alahna," said Meilee. "I had to teach your mother the same lesson. In fact," she hesitated for a moment, "your father believed as Dolph does. It was from Salah that Dolph learned this philosophy. You must accept his lifestyle. He will always be true to you, even when he takes other women into his bed."

Alahna shook her head stubbornly. "But he says I must sleep with other men, too. I shan't, Meilee. Not ever."

Meilee laughed knowingly. "I don't think Dolph Robi-check is a man who likes to hear 'shan't' or 'never.'"

Dolph was aware of Alahna's unhappiness, but he knew to be patient. "One thing at a time," he told himself, watching her schuss down the beginner's ski trail. She had taken to the sport with great enthusiasm and even her instructor, not given to easy compliments, had commented on her natural abilities as a skier.

They had a wonderful three weeks in St. Moritz. They spent their days on the slopes, stopping to eat lunch at one of the many charming cafes. At night, they often met their friends at Madeleine's chalet, warming their feet in front of the fire, drinking wine and eating great quantities of pasta cooked to perfection by Madeleine's Italian chef.

Alahna was more subdued than usual in Madeleine's

presence. But Chris had won her over. He could usually get her laughing at his tales of his adventures in the Middle East. Then Jeff showed up and insisted on music every night. He flattered Alahna shamelessly and soon she was relaxed enough to enjoy his crazy banter.

There were several evenings when Alahna preferred to stay home with Meilee, who had joined them for the last week before they all went on to Paris.

"You don't mind, do you, Dolph?" asked Alahna.

"Of course not, my dear. I'm sure Meilee would enjoy your company."

But on one such night, when Dolph didn't come home until the morning, Alahna's bad mood was all too evident.

"Let's not ski this morning," Dolph suggested. "We'll walk a bit instead."

Without a word, Alahna put on her warm pants and boots and parka, and they set off briskly towards the base of the mountain.

"Are you angry because you think I spent last evening with Madeleine?" Dolph asked her.

She kicked at the powdered snow and nodded yes.

"Well, my pet, it wasn't Madeleine with whom I shared a bed, though even if I had, you'd still have no cause to be angry. I will never lie to you, Alahna. I will never call you from the bed of another woman and tell you I am at my club. That is certainly cheating. But I see how hard it is for you to accept my absences. Perhaps I've been remiss by not helping you find an opportunity to expand your own sexual experience. We must improve the situation."

"You can improve the situation by staying home," Alahna said tartly.

"That I will not do. But I want you to partake of all life's bounty. And by the same token, you need never have a desire or a fantasy, and be denied its fulfillment. You will enjoy the same freedom as I. What's sauce for the goose will be caviar for the gander. And I think I know just the man to further your education."

"I prefer not to have any additional instruction, thank you," Alahna said vehemently. "I'm quite content as I am."

"Ah, but you're not, you see. For if you were, you

wouldn't pout and sulk because I'm absent from our bed for a night. Now what about Christopher?"

"Christopher? I'm certain Madeleine would have something to say about that!"

"Indeed she would. I imagine she'd think it was an excellent idea. Certainly he did very well himself by introducing me to some of the pleasures of sex."

"What do you mean?" Alahna was intrigued in spite of herself.

Dolph described in hilarious detail his experience with Madame Arlette, not omitting to mention how nervous and fearful he had been. "If it hadn't been for Chris, I might still be a virgin today," he joked.

"Well, I'm certainly grateful to Chris for that," said Alahna. "But that doesn't mean I want to make love with him—or with any other man besides you, for that matter."

Dolph smiled. "I'm starving," he said. "And I've heard that there's a tiny restaurant just down that road that has delicious raclette and mulled cider. Do you think you're sufficiently recovered from your sulk that you can let me buy you lunch?"

"Oh, all right," Alahna conceded. She couldn't stay angry at him for long. Especially since he wasn't about to change, no matter what she might feel or say. It was all too apparent that, as far as Dolph was concerned, she must be the one to make the change. And that would bear more thinking about.

From St. Moritz they drove to Paris. Alahna and Meilee oohed and aahed at the passing winter landscape, so different from anything either of them had ever seen.

"Just wait 'til you see Dolph's flat, Meilee."

"Our flat, darling," Dolph corrected Alahna.

"Our flat."

When Meilee fell asleep in the back seat, Alahna grew silent and stared out the window at the snow-covered villages that flashed by them, thinking about what it would be like to make love with Christopher Brooke. If Dolph was so insistent that she make love with another man, she liked the idea of Chris. At least that would even the score between

Madeleine and herself. Madeleine might have a few years experience on her—more than a few years, she giggled. But Alahna was willing to bet half of her inheritance that her breasts and stomach were firmer, her legs more muscular.

Yes, she decided, she just might like the idea of showing Chris what it was like to sleep with a younger woman.

But she would wait to see whether Dolph brought the subject up again.

Their fourth night in Paris they dined out, alone, at a small bistro overlooking the Seine. Alahna was wearing a new Balenciaga. As usual, her entrance caused heads to turn.

"You're the most beautiful woman here," Dolph whispered, kissing the nape of her neck. "I love you, Alahna."

High on his adoration and the champagne they were drinking, Alahna felt as if tonight she might well be the most beautiful woman in Paris. Tonight all her fears and insecurities about Dolph seemed unnecessary and silly.

She took another sip of the champagne. Perhaps he was right. Perhaps she should sample other pleasures.

"Are Madeleine and Chris back in Paris yet?" she asked with a teasing smile.

"Why, yes, they've just returned," Dolph replied. "Why do you ask?"

"I was just thinking that it might be nice to see them."

Dolph leaned over and took her hand. "You read my mind, Alahna. In fact, I spoke to Chris this afternoon. I took the liberty of suggesting that he call to make arrangements for an evening alone with you."

"And he agreed?" Alahna said, not sure what she wanted the answer to be.

"Yes, he did, once he understood why I was asking him. I told him that I've already made other plans for tomorrow evening and that you're free. Alahna, I very much want you to enjoy your evening with Chris, but you won't, you know, unless you put effort into it."

"I don't understand."

"All I mean is that you will receive from any relationship

only what you put into it. You're very fond of Chris—and he of you. I want you to look as beautiful for him as you do for me tonight."

"I suppose," Alahna teased, "you've already picked out the dress I'm to wear."

"Ah, darling, how well you know me. I think you should wear your turquoise silk gown—the one with the deep butterfly sleeves."

"And for my accessories?"

"Your jade and ivory necklace. And your new jade earrings."

"Anything else?" Alahna asked, laughing at Dolph's typically thorough analysis of the situation.

"That's all, except for your white lace garter belt and stockings."

"No underwear?"

"For a romantic tryst?" Dolph said, pretending shock. "Certainly not!"

"Very well," Alahna said lightly. "I shall sample the gander's caviar and see whether it's truly as tasty as you say it is."

Dolph had already left the flat when Chris appeared at eight-thirty. That had been Chris's suggestion.

"Look, Dolph, it could be a bit of an awkward situation, don't you think?" he'd said. "Are you really sure you want to go through with this? She is rather young, you know."

"I suppose she is, but no younger, really, than I when you so generously introduced me to the inimitable Madame Arlette. No, it's time Alahna began to appreciate the freedom that she is entitled to. As you know yourself, there is nothing so delicious as a little variety in your sex life."

Chris laughed. "I can't argue with that, old chap."

"And I can't think of anyone I'd rather she have that variety with than you."

So Chris had telephoned Alahna and invited her to dinner. Now, in the foyer of her flat, as he helped her on with her coat, he wondered whether he'd made a mistake.

"You're looking particularly lovely this evening," he said.

Alahna smiled shakily.

"Thank you. Dolph said I should wear this dress."

She bit her lip, annoyed by her own comment. Don't talk about Dolph all evening, she chided herself.

"I've booked us a table at the Ritz. Have you been there?"

"Oh, yes," Alahna said stiffly. "That would be very nice, Chris."

Chris helped her into his car, feeling suddenly awkward. "Good. Off we go then."

Alahna sat quietly, her hands primly folded in her lap, trying not to think about the cold air blowing between her bare thighs where the garters reached the tops of her stockings.

Chris paused at a red light. "Penny, Alahna," he said.

"Pardon me?"

"Don't you know the old expression—a penny for your thoughts? I'm wondering what's on your mind . . . though I suspect I have a fair idea."

"I suspect you do, Chris. Look," she said nervously, "we both know why we're together tonight. Maybe instead of going to dinner we ought to get it over with."

Chris laughed at her candor. "Alahna, that's not exactly a romantic way to turn a man on. But I know how nervous you must be, and I must confess that I'm feeling rather tentative myself."

"You are?" Alahna looked him straight in the eye for the first time since he'd arrived at the flat. "Don't you *want* to make love to me? Don't you think I'm sexy? Or are you simply doing this as a favor to Dolph? Because if so . . ."

"No, no, no," Chris interrupted her. "Not at all. I think you're an extremely attractive, sexy young woman. I only meant . . . hell, I don't know what I meant. The truth is, I've been having every sort of lascivious fantasy about you ever since Dolph first brought up the subject."

"Fantasies?" Alahna couldn't help but giggle. "What sort of fantasies?"

"Oho, you don't really want me to get into them right now, do you? We could have a traffic accident. At the very least, we'd never get to dinner. And I did reserve that table for two."

"Actually," Alahna said, meaning it, "all of a sudden I'm

not hungry. Are you?"

"Not for food." He reached over and squeezed her hand.

"Chris," she said, "Chris, if I'm to be with anyone in this situation, I'm so glad it's you."

Chris's flat on Rue Jacobe on the Left Bank was a small bachelor's *pied-a-terre.* He'd bought it some years earlier, having decided he needed his own place to retreat to when he visited Madeleine in Paris.

"Well, what do you think?" he said. "Small, but it does me quite well."

"It's adorable. Do you often entertain ladies here?"

"Ah, but I'm not the sort to kiss and tell," Chris said. "I'm going to open a bottle of wine. The bathroom is to your left."

She examined herself in the mirror. Large, nervous eyes stared back. Excited eyes. Chris would never do anything to hurt her. She trusted Dolph, and she trusted Chris. Yes, it would be all right. It might possibly be more than all right. It most probably would be a great deal of fun.

"To us, Alahna—and to our friendship." Chris handed her a glass of white wine.

"This is delicious. Sweet, but also spicy."

"Do you know what I would very much like to do?"

"What?" she said, her heart beating rapidly.

He took the glass from her and placed it on the table. Then, slowly, with the tip of his index finger, he carefully sketched the line of her cheekbones and her lips, trailing downward to stroke the soft skin that was exposed above her breasts.

She could feel the rising tension in his body, and her own growing desire for him.

Then his hands were stroking her bare shoulders, and then they were resting on her breasts, and she knew he could feel, through the thin silk, her already erect nipples.

"Oh, Alahna, Alahna," he murmured and bent his mouth to hers, gently nibbling at her full lips.

Her arms were around him and he was holding her so close that she could hear his heart beating quickly and feel, against her leg, how hard he was.

"Wait," he said huskily. "This is what I dreamt of doing."

He held her at arms' length and with one hand unfastened her dress, pulling away the top and exposing her breasts.

And then his hands were on her breasts, touching them, holding them, teasing her with his tongue and his fingers. Impatiently now, he pushed the dress down over her hips and let it fall to the floor in a silky heap. She stood still, nude except for her garter belt and stockings.

Chris carefully slid his hands along her stockinged legs, moving in circles toward the naked flesh framed by the lace of the garter until he reached the soft mound of hair. Then he knelt and put his mouth to her, probing gently with his tongue.

She went weak beneath his touch—all molten liquid and burning desire.

His tongue licked at her thighs and then she was on her knees, next to him, needed to feel his body against hers.

She was so ready for him. He lowered himself to the floor, his hands encircling her waist, and positioned her atop him. Again and again he caressed the cheeks of her buttocks, his fingers seeking her most sensitive, hidden places. And then she was lying on her back, her legs spread, hungry to feel him inside her, as he gently lowered himself into her.

Alahna reached her crest first, and Chris quickly followed. Afterwards they lay quietly, holding each other close, entirely spent, until Chris broke the silence. "Alahna, you make me feel like Lucifer Lust," he said.

She rolled over to look at him, her dimples showing as she smiled. "Who ever is Lucifer Lust?"

"He's a fellow I knew in Washington. We gave him that name because he had a legendary appetite for screwing. That's how I feel about you. I could go on with you end-lessly."

"Lucifer Lust. I like that very much. It suits you, Chris."

"Alahna, this was wonderful," Chris said, more serious now. "I think that we shall be friends for the rest of our lives. I've sensed that ever since we first met. If you should ever need me—for whatever reason—know that you can call. In fact, we'll use Lucifer as our private signal. If it's Lucifer you want, I'll come running."

"You're a very special person, Chris. I shall hold you to that promise." She kissed him, and he pulled her to him, feeling the stirrings of desire again.

"Again?"

"Unless you'd rather go eat dinner."

"Well, the night is young—and I wouldn't want to disappoint Lucifer Lust," Alahna giggled.

Chris began to touch her again so that she felt swollen with pleasure. For an instant she had a fleeting thought of Madeleine and Dolph and her desire for revenge.

But this had nothing to do with either of them. This had only to do with Chris and herself and something they could share. Dolph had said, "Not better, just different."

Different . . . Then she wasn't thinking about anything except the touch of Chris' fingers on her breast and belly and between her legs.

BOOK III

Chapter One

1980.

"With all good wishes, Yours sincerely, Alahna Robicheck, Vice-Chairman, Shawak International."

Alahna Robicheck paused, stared out the window of her corner office at the view of Central Park twenty stories below, and then continued talking into the dictating machine, "That's it, Meg. I'll need the report by tomorrow afternoon, so get that done first. And the letter should go out by the end of the day. I'm coming in late tomorrow, but I'll give you a call to see what's going on."

She clicked off the machine, pushed back her chair, and wriggled her stockinged feet. Her high heels were somewhere under the desk, discarded hours earlier when she had settled down for the afternoon to answer her correspondence and finish the report on Pretty Face.

Well done, she congratulated herself. It was exactly twenty-five minutes after six. She had promised herself she'd be out of the building by six-thirty. That gave her just enough time to rush home, bathe, and get dressed.

Dolph's plane was due to have landed half an hour ago. She was surprised he hadn't called yet.

As if on cue, her private phone rang. Alahna smiled and picked it up.

"Hello, darling, welcome back," she said.

"I hope that's not your standard telephone greeting,"

Dolph teased. "Though I must admit, it's a lot more effective than a simple 'Hello.'"

"I knew it must be you. I've been expecting your call for the last half hour," Alahna said.

"Same old story. Air traffic jam at Kennedy. But here I am, in the car. I'm waiting for George to bring the bags. How are you doing?"

"Terrific, now that you've landed safely. Your timing couldn't be better. I've just finished for the day and I'm about to leave. I should be dressed and ready by the time you get home."

"How about undressed and ready?" Dolph's voice caressed her ear. "I've missed you desperately this whole week."

"If that's your pleasure, it could be arranged, my love. I'll call Le Cirque and cancel the reservation. Let's skip dinner. There's plenty of champagne on ice, and I'm sure we can scare up something to nibble on. We can celebrate in bed."

"What a marvelous mind you have, darling. That must have been why I married you."

"As I recall," Alahna laughed, "my mind had nothing to do with it. You married me because my father told you to. But I won't hold that against you. Especially not on our sixteenth anniversary."

"Sixteen years! It's hard to believe, isn't it?"

"I've loved every minute of it, Dolph," Alahna said. "And I can't wait to see you."

"I love you, Alahna." He hung up abruptly. How typically Dolph. He didn't believe in wasting words. She admired him for that—and for so many other reasons.

Sixteen years . . .

May it be sixty more, she offered a silent prayer to whatever gods were watching over her. If she wasn't the luckiest woman alive, she was certainly a close second.

Married to a man she adored—who returned that adoration.

Alahna loved her life as vice-chairman of the board of Shawak International, responsible for seeking out and developing new business opportunities in the United States. She was so successful that she had to turn down more speaking engagements than she could possibly fulfill.

Her New York home was a showpiece—a Fifth Avenue tri-plex penthouse that was both elegant and welcoming.

"Alahna," Madeleine had told her, after taking the grand tour, "you've created the apartment of my dreams. You never cease to amaze me."

Thank goodness she had long ago gotten over her jealousy of Madeleine, whom she now considered one of her few close women friends. Not that she blamed herself for having been unhappy about Dolph's friendship with Madeleine Laval. She had been all of sixteen years old, newly married and frightened, trying to hold on for dear life to her husband. As if keeping him close by would ensure his love.

But that was all in the past. She had long since learned that what Dolph did in his spare time had nothing whatsoever do with his feelings for her.

Not that Dolph—or she, for that matter—had much spare time. Though they still maintained their homes in London and Paris, the demands of the company meant that too many of their days were taken up with business concerns. Even with Ace Taylor doing a brilliant job as president. Ace was primarily responsible for overseeing the day-to-day operational aspects of running a major, multinational corporation.

They had done themselves a great favor when they hired Ace Taylor. The eccentric genius had gradually adopted a less flamboyant style of dress. But his unconventional mindset hadn't changed over the years. They both valued his intelligence and enjoyed his companionship as well.

Jeff had dubbed Ace and his ballerina-turned-choreographer wife, Jana, "the long and the short of it," for Jana towered above her diminutive husband. Otherwise they were well matched—outgoing, amusing, blessed with the ability to feel comfortable in any situation. The Taylors' social expertise provided a much needed relief for Dolph and Alahna, who were so much sought after, so much in the public eye, that they sometimes joked about hiring a public relations firm to keep their names *out* of the newspapers and magazines.

The Robichecks were constantly in demand. Each day's mail brought a new stack of invitations to social, charitable, and business functions. It was not an unusual occurrence for them to receive a letter engraved with the stamp of the White House or Buckingham Palace, asking for the pleasure of their company.

Sometimes they were pleased to attend. More frequently, it seemed they had no choice. In the early years of their marriage, Alahna had loved getting dressed up for the endless, glittering charity balls and dinner parties. And Dolph had enjoyed showing her off.

But they had since grown tired of seeing the same faces on the New York-Washington-London circuit. After a long day's work, neither of them wanted much more than a quiet dinner in front of the fireplace or on their rooftop terrace with its three-sided views of Manhattan. Often Meilee joined them. Jeff, Chris, and Madeleine all had standing invitations, though, busy people that they all were, they only rarely happened to be in New York.

But tonight, in celebration of their anniversary, Dolph and Alahna preferred to dine alone. Alahna was determined that they not talk business, though she could hardly wait to tell Dolph about their last quarter figures. Her project had shown a thirty-five percent increase in profits.

Another Pretty Face was the fourth largest modeling agency in the United States—and rapidly catching up with the other three. It specialized in models whose faces were interesting and attractive, though not necessarily beautiful. Faces with which the average woman—"though we believe there is no average woman," according to the Pretty Face brochure—could identify.

The fifth annual Pretty Face Beauty Pageant was two months away but every minute of the television commercial airtime had already been bought up by advertisers. The participants, bright, attractive young women between the ages of twenty-two and twenty-nine, all had careers and professions. Some of them were married. A few of them were even mothers. The resounding success of the pageant had spurred Alahna to set up a cosmetics company, a retail clothes company, and a magazine, all targeted at the professional woman.

Alahna had discovered the company when it was a small

chain of modeling schools, struggling to turn a profit. It was her idea to refocus the company's direction. She was intrigued with the possibilities offered by the professional women's market. Being a business woman herself, she felt a kindship with women who were achievers.

Dolph thought she'd gone mad when she gave him the numbers on Pretty Face. But convinced she could turn the losing company around, she stuck to her guns. Finally, Dolph had agreed to the acquisition. It was hard not to trust Alahna's shrewd instincts in these matters, even when she seemed to be playing a wild card. When her instincts proved to be accurate, Dolph was especially intrigued that Alahna, who could rarely relate personally to other women, had such a thorough understanding of the women's market.

Now the modeling schools were only one small part of the very profitable Pretty Face Division, Alahna's "baby." She would give him the good news tomorrow morning when she and Dolph were scheduled to meet with the architect who was helping them redesign their recently purchased twenty-two story Madison Avenue office building. Alahna was surprised but pleased that Dolph was so actively involved in the remodeling project. More and more in the past couple of years, he had tended to let Alahna and Ace make all but the most important business decisions.

He was getting bored with the corporate world, he'd admitted to Alahna. Bored with the endless succession of mergers and acquisitions that were its lifeblood. He already had far more money, influence, and power than he could ever need or want. By anyone's accounting he had achieved enormous success. But there was still one area in which he hadn't yet attained his goal.

Music.

Dolph's first great love.

Deep in his heart he still nursed his dream of composing music that people could enjoy and remember. Lately he had been making fewer trips to Europe and the Orient, spending less time at the office, choosing instead to sit for hours at the piano, working and reworking compositions.

Alahna wasn't even sure whether this last trip had been for business or pleasure. But Dolph had never been a man who answered for every minute of his time. Alahna had learned not to question him. He seemed to need that affirmation of his freedom, both sexually and spiritually.

Of course, she, too, could exercise her option of sexual freedom, but she rarely chose to. Whenever Dolph brought up the subject, she would laugh and remind him that freedom meant she also had the freedom to decide what she wanted out of life.

And she had all she wanted.

Much later that evening, after they had made love—and then made love again—and shared a bottle of champagne, she told him just that.

"I'm so happy, Dolph," she said. "I wouldn't want to trade places with anyone in the world. I have you and I have my work. I can't imagine that I would ever need anything else to make my life more perfect or complete."

Dolph stared at her silently. She couldn't read the expression on his face.

"What is it?" she asked, unnerved by his long silence. "Is something wrong?"

"Alahna, there's something more you need out of life. I want you to have a child."

"A child? What are you talking about?"

"Just what I said." Dolph smiled and stroked her cheek. "To make your life—our lives—even more perfect than they already are."

"But Dolph, I just finished telling you that you're all I need or want."

"Alahna, although we choose to ignore it, the fact is that I am much older than you. In all probability you will outlive me by many years. You will still be a young and vital woman after I'm gone. Your father was very careful to leave nothing to chance in arranging your future, and I would like to do the same for you. I can't bear the possibility that you might be left all alone, with no family of your own."

"You're being ridiculous, Dolph," Alahna said angrily, not wanting to hear what he was telling her. "Besides, we both know perfectly well it's not possible for me to get pregnant."

"Correction, Alahna. *You* can become pregnant. It's I who

have the problem."

"Stop it," she pleaded. "I can't bear to hear you talking like this."

"I'm sorry, my darling. I know this is difficult. But trust me. It's important and necessary. Of course, I can't be the actual blood father of our child, but in every other sense, he or she will be my child."

Alahna shook her head, bewildered. "Do you mean that we should adopt a baby?"

"And deprive you of the experience of giving birth? No, I have something else in mind," Dolph said. "We shall carry out this project with the same careful planning that we bring to all our ventures. We want as perfect a child as possible, so we must look for several candidates from whom we will select the perfect man to provide the seed for our child. No one but you and I will ever know. Think of it as a game, Alahna—a wonderful secret for us to share."

A game! Alahna was shocked. Having a child was far from a game to be taken lightly. Not that she had ever given the idea much thought. A bride at sixteen, she had been hardly more than a child herself. And of course, she had known from the very beginning that Dolph was sterile. Over the years, she occasionally wondered what their life would be like if they had children. But her love for Dolph and her responsibilities at Shawak International had never made her feel deprived.

Except for Ace and Jana, and Jeff's faraway, long ago family, whom she had vaguely heard of, none of the people closest to her had children. She couldn't even begin to imagine how different her life would be if she agreed to Dolph's crazy plan. She would have to find the time . . . but that was silly. Didn't her own magazine assure women that they could be mothers *and* continue to work? Just yesterday, as she was flipping through the latest issue, she had noticed an article on how to hire the right mother's helper.

"I need to think about this more," she said slowly. "To get used to the idea."

"I understand," Dolph said cheerfully. "But don't think too long. We've lots of work ahead of us, finding the right men, setting up dinners and parties so that you can get to know them, outfitting you with a properly seductive wardrobe."

"Dolph, if I do agree, why can't we simply do artificial insemination? Isn't that less complicated and less time consuming?"

"Ah, but artificial insemination is totally anonymous. We'd have no idea who the donors were. I don't want to leave something like that to chance. It's not immodest of me to describe myself as brighter than average, musically talented, athletically capable. And you, of course, are beautiful, extraordinarily intelligent, with a heritage that goes back thousands of years. Naturally, I want to know exactly whose genes have been transmitted to our son or daughter, so that we can be assured he or she will have the same intellectual and physical advantages we enjoy."

"But can you really plan these things?" Alahna asked dubiously.

"Trust me, Alahna. You and I have proven ourselves to be a great team once we put our heads together. Why should this be any different?"

Gradually, the idea began to appeal to Alahna. A child of her own, to love and to nurture. Born of her own body. A child to whom Dolph could be a doting father. That alone was reason enough for her to agree. To deny him such an opportunity seemed selfish and cruel.

"Trust me," he'd said. She had trusted him before—always to her benefit. Now she would trust him again with this, the strangest of all their projects.

"Thank you, darling," Dolph said when she told him yes. He hugged her tightly, and suddenly she realized how much this meant to him. "We'll begin right away. Now, I know I promised that only you and I would share this secret. But I'd like to take Ace into our confidence. He's not only very discreet, but his rolodex is a veritable who's who."

"But Dolph, why? It's such an intimate subject. Do we want anyone else to know about it?"

"Darling, we need someone to help us set up the means to meet these men. Ace is perfect. He's charming enough to convince even the busiest person to make time in his schedule for a lunch or dinner. So with your permission, I'd like to talk to him as soon as possible."

"Could that possibly mean tomorrow morning?"

"It could and does, my dear. Salah always counselled me to be patient, but that's never been my strong suit. Certainly not with something like this."

At eight A.M. the next morning, Ace settled himself comfortably in Dolph's office. He'd brought with him a mug full of herb tea for which he was famous. A dedicated vegetarian, he prided himself on the fact that he never drank caffeine or used other stimulants.

"I'm high on life," he liked to say. "The best drug of all."

Dolph wasted no time in getting to the point.

"Ace, Alahna and I are about to embark on a rather ambitious program and we'd like your help."

Ace leaned back in the chair. "You know," he said in his squeaky voice, "I've often thought that the reason I married Jana is because she so calmly accepts whatever comes across her path. Perhaps that has to do with her Indian heritage. I, on the other hand, have a little antenna that starts to wiggle at the first sign of trouble. Like right now, for instance. It's vibrating wildly. What's up, folks?"

"Your antenna needs a tuneup, Ace. Something exciting, yes, but not trouble. Alahna is going to have a baby."

Ace's eyes lit up like a pinball machine that had just hit tilt.

"Hey, congratulations, you two. This is the most fantastic news! I can't wait to tell Jana. When can we expect baby Robicheck?"

"Whooa, slow down," Dolph laughed. "I didn't say Alahna was pregnant yet."

"Huh?"

"We need to swear you to utter secrecy, Ace. You can't tell a soul, not even Jana. Do you mind having such a burden placed on you?" asked Dolph.

"You're not planning to do anything illegal, are you?" Ace asked, sqirming with curiosity.

"I think you'd better hear the whole story. If you want to

say no, you can still back out," said Alahna, breaking into the conversation for the first time. "What we have in mind isn't illegal; it's simply a bit . . . out of the ordinary."

"But then, so are both of you." Ace leaned forward with excitement, almost spilling his herb tea.

Ace's mouth fell open as Dolph unfolded the proposed scenario. He was amazed at the scope of the plan.

"Well," he said, after Dolph had finished, "you two certainly have your own peculiar style. And I like it!" he announced, banging his fist for emphasis on the arm of the chair. "So, when do we get moving?"

"As soon as possible. Have your spies get me a list of the top ten candidates. Alahna and I will narrow that down to four and then you can figure out some clever ruses so that we can meet these fellows. All right?"

"Righto," Ace declared. "But just one question. Does this plan have a name? I'd hate to see 'Project Pregnant' at the top of an interoffice memo."

"Good point," laughed Dolph. "Any ideas, Alahna?"

"Actually, yes. What about 'Project Ultimate Secret'? For short, we can call it "Project US.'"

There was one other person with whom Dolph and Alahna had to share their secret. Alahna realized she must include Meilee in their plans. Too much would be happening, too much changing. She could never lie to Meilee, but she dreaded her reaction.

She had underestimated the older woman's adaptability.

"How wonderful of Dolph to think of such a clever idea," Meilee exulted.

"I suppose," teased Alahna, "that if Dolph had turned out to be a rapist, you would have said he merely had a healthy sexual appetite."

"Not true," Meilee protested. "It's simply that, aside from your father, there's no other man I love and respect as much as Dolph."

Alahna gave the older woman a big hug. "I'm so glad you feel that way, and that you approve. We have so much to do. Dolph wants us to go to Paris in the fall. I'm to buy a new wardrobe, have my hair styled. I feel quite like a beauty queen."

"But you're already absolutely perfect," Meilee said. "What do you need, besides a few new dresses?"

"Think about it, Meilee," Alahna said. "When I meet the man who's to make me pregnant, I have neither the time nor the desire for a long, gentle courtship. We want him to be immediately smitten. I need a new look, so that I can play the mysterious seductress."

"Ah, I see," nodded Meilee. "But Alahna, I'm sure you realize that women rarely get pregnant on the first try."

"We thought of that. I'll be taking my temperature over the next few months, charting my cycle so that I know precisely when I'm most fertile."

"What can I do to help you?"

"Give us your blessing and moral support, for one thing."

"That you have a hundredfold," said Meilee. "What else?"

"Come to Paris with us. There will be thousands of details to attend to, and your wisdom and advice has always been the best. Oh, Meilee," Alahna said, kissing the woman's hand, "I'm so glad you're sharing this with us. You know, I'd never thought about having a baby. It never seemed possible. Now that I'm more used to the idea, I'm very excited. I've been thinking a lot lately about Papa. How much he would have loved a grandchild. But you shall be the child's grandmother, yes?"

"Yes," Meilee said, her voice soft and teary. "Yes, my dear, I shall very much enjoy being a grandmother to your child."

No more than two months had passed before Ace presented Dolph with a file folder bulging with dossiers on the ten most outstanding men in America and Europe. Dolph carefully read the material and put together his own short list. Finally, he was ready to present the men to Alahna.

They were sunbathing by the pool over the Memorial Day weekend at their home near Cornwall, in northwestern Connecticut. Alahna lay on her back, covered only with sunscreen.

"What a life," she sighed contentedly. "A cloudless sky, a hot sun, and a long weekend alone with you. What more could a woman want?"

"I can't imagine," Dolph chuckled. He stripped off his bathing trunks and lay down next to her on the queensized foam mattress. "I must admit, darling, I've no regrets that Ace and Jana couldn't join us this weekend."

"Oh, Dolph, I was just feeling guilty for having that very same thought. They're wonderful company, but we so rarely have long stretches of time to ourselves."

"It will be rarer yet as soon as Project US gets underway. And once we have a baby, such a luxury will be a thing of the past."

Alahna sat up and peered at him. "You're not having second thoughts, are you?" she asked. "We can still change our minds."

"Quite the opposite. In fact, I think I've narrowed the field down to four candidates whom I want to discuss with you."

"Really? Dolph, that's very exciting! Who are they?"

"Well, first we have Doctor Gerard DeGrosveld. He's forty-seven years old, divorced, with one daughter, and quite handsome from what I can see of his photograph. If his name sounds familiar, it's because he recently won the Nobel Prize for chemistry. Next on the list is an American, Anthony Reed Johnson."

"Our Secretary of State?" Alahna asked.

"That's right. He's fifty-three, married, the devoted father of two boys, and a former partner in one of Boston's leading law firms. A brilliant mind, by all accounts. I met the man briefly the last time I was in Washington and found him a refreshing change from the usual Washington bureaucrats. Any questions?"

"Not yet," Alahna smiled. "So far, very interesting."

"Good. Number three, then, is the journalist and athlete, Dwayne Smith. You've heard of his South Carolina newspaper empire and his heroic climb last spring up Mount Everest. He's forty-two and married to a fellow journalist who seems always to be at the opposite end of the earth from her husband. They've an odd sort of marriage, but he's supposed to be quite charming, and no one can quite fathom why they spend so little time together. They have one daughter.

"Now, I think you'll rather fancy number four, Emilio Amati. He designed the Amati racing car, the one that won the Grand Prix de Monte Carlo several seasons back. He's brilliant, movie star handsome, and from what I understand, quite a charmer with women. He's only thirty-seven years old, married, father of four."

"They all sound excellent. How do you suggest we choose the right man?"

"Easy. You'll try all four of them."

"All of them?" Alahna gasped, sitting bolt upright. "Surely you don't mean that."

"Oh, but I do. I want you to have sex with each of them. That way you can decide for yourself."

"But what if they don't like me or they're just not interested?"

"My darling, you underestimate yourself. If you feel seductive, the feeling will be communicated. I don't foresee that being a problem. But don't worry, if necessary, we'll select four more men. Sooner or later we will find the perfect solution to our problem."

Alahna stood up. "Time for a swim," she said. "I need a cool splash of water to clear my head. Care to join me?"

"Love to. And after that I think you should practice your seduction techniques on me, though I admit it won't take much effort on your part to get me to succumb."

Alahna gazed up at her husband, standing at the edge of the pool. "Dolph, tell me again we're doing the right thing."

"I know we are, Alahna. You'll see, the end result will more than justify the means. And I suspect you'll have some fun in the process."

By the middle of September, Ace had already begun working his magic, calling friends and friends of friends.

"I thought we could have you host a formal dinner in Paris to honor this year's Nobel Laureates. The guest of honor would be, of course, Gerard DeGrosveld. How's that for a setup?" Ace asked proudly.

"Yes, I like that very much," said Dolph. "Could you arrange it for some time in November, if possible? That should give us enough time to take care of all the preparation."

They flew to Paris. Their lavish flat on Avenue Foch was to be the official headquarters for Project US.

The first order of business was to properly outfit Alahna. Her clothes had to be a perfect blend of subtle seduction and elegance. Clothes dramatic enough to draw attention to her, but tasteful enough so that if she chose to say "no" the next time, the man would believe her.

Over the years Dolph had given her many beautiful and unique gifts of jewelry. She adored the pieces, because of the love that had come with the giving, but she wore them only infrequently. Now her entire collection was pressed into service.

"We should hire an armed guard to bring them over safely," Alahna had joked nervously.

"I intend to do just that," said Dolph. "Otherwise we'll be looking over our shoulders all the way across the Atlantic."

From the earliest days of their marriage, Dolph had taken the utmost care and concern in choosing Alahna's wardrobe. He loved to see her tall, slim figure shown off to the best possible advantage. But now he was absolutely obsessed with finding exactly the right clothes to suit her.

"What I have in mind," he said thoughtfully, "is someone young, possibly a new designer. A talent who hasn't yet been discovered by *tout* Paris. Someone with fresh ideas and an unjaded eye."

Typically, it was Madeleine who provided the answer. "A new image for Alahna? *Mais oui.* I know the very person."

She sent them to a small workshop in Les Halles, owned by a young American designer married to a Frenchman. From the moment Alahna saw her creations, she knew Bettina would be the perfect choice. The ideas were fresh and imaginative, slightly reminiscent of the clothes worn by the movie queens of the 1930's.

Dolph, Alahna, and Bettina spent days huddled in Bettina's tiny attic atelier, planning outfits for every possible occasion. For daytime wear, Alahna would need two- or three-piece suits of several different weights of wool, as well as softer, less formal dresses and sportswear. For the evenings, she would have to have gowns of several lengths.

Bettina also designed all the accessories, including Alahna's hats and scarves, but for shoes Alahna remained faithful to her favorite, Helene Arpels. A perfume was specially blended for her at an essence factory in Grasse. Alahna was entranced by the fragrance and wanted to market it through the Pretty Face Division. But Dolph was adamant in his refusal.

"This scent was created just for you, Alahna. I love the idea that no one else but you will ever wear it."

She didn't bother to press the issue. She was having too much fun being launched as a "femme fatale." Dolph had always been an attentive husband, but now he was outdoing himself. They were co-conspirators, about to embark on a delicious adventure, the result of which would change their lives forever in ways too wonderful and radical to imagine.

Chapter Two

The dinner in honor of the Nobel Prize winners was a formal, black-tie affair. Dolph wanted Alahna to focus her attentions and energy only on Gerard DeGrosveld, the guest of honor.

"No sense your having to worry about the flowers or the food," he told her. "You'll have more important things on your mind that night. I'm sure Meilee would be only too happy to take charge of the arrangements."

At Dolph's orders, Paris's preeminent caterer had brought in white simbidium orchids, spilling out of towering glass vases. Scattered along the lace cloth were white votive candles which provided the perfect backdrop for Alahna, who was dressed in a gown of shimmering ivory peau de soie. Around her neck she wore a necklace designed for her by Van Cleef and Arpels—an emerald and diamond pendant in the shape of a four-leaf clover.

Forty-two of the invitees had said yes, they would be delighted to attend on the evening of November fifth. The caterer had set up eight small, round tables in the dining room and library. The apartment glowed with candlelight. Animated conversation flowed in French, English, and German.

Doctor DeGrosveld was seated to Alahna's right. As his photograph had indicated, he was quite handsome, with a full head of slightly graying black, curly hair, and large green eyes. But Alahna was most fascinated by how thin he was. Perhaps, she thought, DeGrosveld spent so much time in his laboratory that he didn't have time to eat.

Even now, as the servants brought to the table platter after platter of elegantly cooked fresh fish, followed by a main course of pheasant, the man only picked at his food and drank only a sip or two of his wine. He must be a vegetarian, she decided. Why hadn't Ace mentioned that in his report.

Finally she said, "Are you not enjoying your meal, Doctor DeGrosveld? Would you like something else instead?"

"Please, do call me Gerard," DeGrosveld replied, his eyes boring into hers. "And this is fine. I never eat very much. I'm not interested in food except as sustenance."

"Really? But how very unFrench," Alahna said. "Is that for health reasons?"

"Only secondarily," DeGrosveld said, still staring at her as if they were discussing a matter of intense importance to both of them. "I'm a man in a hurry. I like to direct my attention to the more important things in life. Food does not rank highly on my list. What I would really like to discover," he continued, leaning closer to her, "is a pill that I could swallow three times a day that would not only supply all the necessary nutrients, but also satisfy my cravings for particular food tastes. Clever idea, isn't it?"

"I suppose," Alahna said politely. "Rather like manna, you mean?"

"Manna? Oh yes, what the Hebrews were supposed to have eaten in the desert all those forty years. Yes, precisely so. I see we think alike." He beamed with pleasure.

Alahna returned his smile although she was certain that at least as far as food was concerned, she and DeGrosveld were far apart in their thinking. She wondered what besides chemistry ranked high on his list of importance. Sex, she hoped.

"Your father was Salah Shawak, I understand," DeGrosveld said.

Alahna brightened. "You've heard of him?"

"Certainly. I even shook his hand once. My parents and I were refugees from Belgium. We spent the war years in Shanghai. It was partly because of your father's generosity that we managed to survive, Madame Robicheck."

"Please, call me Alahna. And thank you for telling me that about my father. It always touches me greatly to talk to people who had any kind of contact with him."

"Very well then, Alahna. What a beautiful name. It suits you quite well."

He waved away the waiter who was standing with a tray laden with five varieties of perfectly ripened French and Italian cheeses.

"Not even a slice of cheese, Gerard?" asked Alahna.

"Our conversation is rich enough to sustain me," DeGrosveld said, moving still closer.

So much for needing to be a seductress. Doctor DeGrosveld seemed ready for whatever she might suggest. His left knee, bony even through his trousers, was twitching against her leg.

"Do you come often to Paris, Alahna?" he asked.

"Less often than I used to. When Dolph and I were first married, we lived in London and frequently travelled back and forth. Now I'm here only two or three times a year. I buy my clothes here, of course. But I'm sure you're not interested in women's fashions."

"Only to the extent that I admire what you are wearing this evening."

"Why, thank you. I had it made especially for tonight's dinner."

"I'm flattered," DeGrosveld smirked. "It's been some time since a woman dressed for me."

"But that can't be," Alahna said, smiling flirtatiously. "Such a charming, handsome man . . . surely you have many female admirers."

"You forget that I'm locked away most of the time in my laboratory. I was looking forward to this evening, though,

not only because of the honor, but also to enjoy the pleasure
of meeting Salah Shawak's daughter. I'm not disappointed.
You do your family great justice, my dear."

"You don't find it lonely, there among your test tubes?"

"My former wife used to ask me the same question. But
I'm a scientist, Alahna. With a mission. Though from time
to time, I admit it, I have had my lonely moments."

Dr. DeGrosveld proceeded to rearrange the food on his
plate. Alahna noticed that very little of the dinner had actually reached his mouth.

"Do you ever have an appetite for anything more than
chemistry?" Alahna asked with a flirtatious smile, hoping to
make the man aware of her interest in him.

Rather startled, DeGrosveld looked around to see whether
they were being overheard.

Alahna offered more bait. "I'd love to hear all about your
work," she said.

Delighted with her flattery, Dr. DeGrosveld gently
squeezed her knee.

"Do you really want to talk about my work?" DeGrosveld
murmured in a low voice, pleased with his conquest.

Across the room, Alahna caught sight of Dolph who nodded slightly.

"Ladies and gentlemen," Dolph said loudly, "I suggest we
adjourn to the ballroom for coffee and musical entertainment. Please, this way through the double doors."

Alahna understood his signal. She was to linger behind
with DeGrosveld, so that they might have more time alone
together.

"Gerard," she said, "I don't care for any coffee, do you?
I'd much rather give you a tour of our art collection, if
you're interested."

"That interests me greatly, my dear lady. If you're sure
your husband won't miss us . . ."

"He asked me to be sure you enjoyed yourself. After all,
this is your evening," Alahna said, leading DeGrosveld to
the gallery beyond the library where her favorite paintings
were displayed.

"Gerard," she said, "You are a most attractive man.

Perhaps we could meet some afternoon—if you're not too busy at the lab, of course?"

"Tomorrow," DeGrosveld suggested immediately.

That was impossible. She wasn't due to ovulate until the end of the week.

"Oh, I wish I could," Alahna sais. "But I've meetings and appointments every day but Friday. Where and when shall we meet?"

"It would be lovely to be alone with you. How is lunch on Friday, one o'clock at my apartment?" He pulled his card case out of his pocket. "Here's my card with the address."

"Friday it is, then," Alahna smiled. "Shall we rejoin the guests?"

She could hardly wait to tell Dolph.

Dolph was delighted to hear about DeGrosveld's enthusiasm. "I told you no man could resist you," he said proudly.

"I don't know," Alahna said dubiously.

"He's a healthy, energetic man. All the better for our purposes," Dolph assured her. "Well done, my dear. The next act sounds very promising."

Alahna rang the doorbell to Dr. DeGrosveld's apartment promptly at one o'clock. There was a knot in the pit of her stomach that she was trying to ignore. This is a game, she told herself again and again, only a game. One which could bring something marvelous into her life with Dolph.

Gerard himself opened the door. "My dear, my dear," he greeted her, "I have been looking forward to this day. So much so that I have given the servants the day off, and we are quite alone. There is champagne chilling for you, Alahna."

Alahna gratefully took the ice cold glass and sipped the champagne, noticing that although Gerard was also holding a glass, he drank very little. What a cautious man he seemed to be. Did he make love the same way? Well, she would soon find out.

"Let me show you the apartment," he said. "It doesn't compare to yours, of course, but it's nevertheless quite comfortable."

Alahna followed him through the foyer, noticing how absolutely neat and orderly each room was. The large apartment must be the same one he had shared with his ex-wife, for the decor had a woman's touch. Not a thing was out of place. It looked as if he hardly lived there. Even the spacious, beautifully equipped kitchen was spotless, not a dish or a pot in sight.

Sipping their champagne, they settled themselves on the couch in the living room and began with small talk. Alahna, ever mindful of the purpose of her visit, put down her glass and said, "Gerard, isn't there another room in your apartment that you haven't shown me?"

"Oh, you mean the bedroom," DeGrosveld answered, opening the door

Alahna reached up and drew his mouth to hers, softly licking his lips with her tongue. Gerard kissed her back and she began to relax, as a gentle wave of desire washed through her. He was a good-looking man—and he knew how to kiss. This afternoon could turn out to be very pleasant, indeed.

"Shall we get undressed?" Gerard whispered. "I've thought about nothing but you since last Monday evening."

He watched her as she stepped out of her silk blouse and skirt and began to unhook her garters.

"*Merde,* you are lovely," he said. "Let me do that."

But instead of helping her off with her stockings, he pulled her to him and began to stroke her passionately.

"Wait, Gerard, let me take everything off."

"No, no," he said urgently. "There's no time."

He kissed her breasts and with his tongue he circled her nipples, all the while rubbing himself against her groin. Suddenly, he shifted positions.

"Please, suck me," he begged, positioning himself above her head.

She liked the taste and feel of him in her mouth, and concentrated on kissing and licking him until the perfect moment, when he would be ready to push himself between her legs.

"Good, good, good," he moaned again and again, in

rhythm with her lips and tongue. And then suddenly, he groaned deeply and threw back his head and she could feel him coming, filling her mouth with his warm, salty semen.

After several shuddering seconds, he pulled his limp penis from between her lips and kissed her forehead. Too startled to speak, Alahna lay still, waiting for him to continue. But he merely got up, handed her a tissue, and said, "You are such a beautiful woman. What a privilege to make love to such a work of art. Please, excuse me a moment."

Alahna could not believe the position in which she now found herself. Flat on her back, yes—but frustrated and angered beyond words by this man who seemed to have not the least desire to satisfy her now that he himself was satisfied.

Gerard reappeared in the doorway, rubbing his groin with a towel.

"Well, my dear," he declared cheerfully, "that was wonderful, wasn't it? I could tell how much you were enjoying yourself. If you'd like to use the bathroom, feel free. When you are ready, come join me in the dining room for a light lunch. It will take just a minute for me to prepare it."

Alahna was livid with anger. The man was absolutely ridiculous. Did he think she was a prostitute, to be paid off with a meal? Well, he could damn well eat alone!

She quickly pulled on her clothes, rinsed her mouth and washed her face. Quietly, so as not to alert her host, she tiptoed down the hallway.

"Almost ready, Alahna?" Gerard called. "You must be starving!"

But Alahna was already halfway out the door, pulling it shut behind her.

"Eat it yourself, Dr. DeGrosveld" she thought, as she hailed a cab.

Dolph was waiting for her in the music room.

"How did it go?" he asked. "And why do you look so unhappy?"

Alahna stood in the doorway and shook her head in disgust. "Doctor Gerard DeGrosveld may be a Nobel Prize winner, but he's an awful man, just awful."

"Good heavens, Alahna, what happened?"

Angry tears in her eyes, Alahna grimly described her experiences of the afternoon.

"Oh, Alahna, I know that must have been a shock. You're used to much better. Come to bed and let me make you happy. You know how I can do that, don't you?"

They flew back to New York in time to spend Thanksgiving as they always did in Connecticut, with Ace and his family. Watching Jana with the children made Alahna realize how much she had embraced the idea of being a mother. It was obviously a demanding job, perhaps far more demanding than anything she'd ever done. But the rewards seemed well worth the effort.

All right, she decided. She wasn't in the habit of surrendering simply because the first try had been a bust. She'd soon be ready to try again.

Several more weeks went by and neither she nor Dolph mentioned Project US. And then it was Christmas, which they spent alone, except for Meilee, hiking in the snowy woods behind their house. They made love at dusk in front of the fireplace in their bedroom and drank wine as they soaked in the jacuzzi, admiring the stars in the winter sky as night settled in.

"A perfect day," Alahna said dreamily. "I love you, Dolph."

Over dinner they discussed the second candidate, Anthony Reed Johnson, whose distinguished family were among the first settlers in the United States. They had made their fortune in railroads, and Johnson, like all the other men in his family, had attended Harvard University, where he had majored in political science. He'd gone on to Harvard Law School, and from there to a partnership in one of Boston's leading firms. This was his third year serving as Secretary of State. Known for his diplomacy and gentlemanly manner, he enjoyed the admiration of both political parties.

"Very impressive," Alahna said. "But it also says here that he's the happily married father of two. What makes you think he's interested in an extramarital adventure?"

"Ace has done his homework. Apparently, this wouldn't be the first time."

"That settles it," Alahna decided as she put down the dossier. "How is it to be arranged?"

"Easily enough. I think I mentioned to you that I've already met Johnson briefly. He indicated that he would enjoy another opportunity to chat, I suppose. I'll have Ace set up a lunch for us in Washington. How about—"

"Third week in January would be perfect, but that doesn't give Ace much time, does it?"

"Ace has already complained to me, half in jest, that Project US isn't enough of a challenge. Let's see if he can pull this off," Dolph said, reaching for the telephone.

They were not disappointed. On January fourth, Ace triumphantly marched into Dolph's office and pointed to his calendar. "Schedule yourself a trip to Washington for Wednesday, the twentieth. You and Alahna are lunching with Secretary Johnson."

"Nice work, Ace. I won't ask you how you managed it."

"My little secret," Ace said smugly. "The rest is up to you two."

Alahna dressed carefully for the occasion. A chic amber wool dress, with a narrow skirt slit to below her thigh. With it she wore a gold and topaz pin and matching earrings.

"Mrs. Robicheck, it's a pleasure to meet a well-known female industrialist, for a change," he said, shaking her hand. "No offense to you gentlemen," he laughed, "but this is indeed an auspicious occasion."

Alahna smiled at the compliment.

The Secretary was an attractive man whose trim, athletic body made him look younger than fifty-three. Prominently displayed on his desk was a photograph of a woman, handsome rather than pretty, and two teen-aged boys. "My family," Johnson said, noticing her interest. "Do you have children, Mrs. Robicheck?"

Alahna blushed. "No, we don't. But I hope to someday. Your sons look like fine boys."

"Can't complain. Ellen—my wife—and I feel very blessed."

His telephone buzzed. "Excuse me, please," he said. "Yes? Good. We'll be right there."

"The car's outside," he announced. "I thought we'd lunch at my club. I hope you're hungry. I'm starving."

Behind the Secretary's back, Dolph and Alahna exchanged relieved glances. At least Anthony Reed Johnson had more of an appetite than Dr. DeGrosveld.

Secretary Johnson's club was of the sort that never failed to amuse Alahna. Very masculine. Very somber color scheme of burgundy and navy blue. The majority of the diners, dressed in three-piece, pin-striped suits, were eating salads and fish. After glancing at the menu, Alahna understood why. Instead of prices next to the entrees, the calorie count was listed.

"I'll have the broiled chicken," Alahna decided.

"Good choice," Johnson said approvingly. "I try not to eat too much red meat. My wife and I watch our diets carefully. We're both in better shape than when we were college students."

"Did you meet Mrs. Johnson while you were at Harvard?" asked Alahna.

"Before that. We've known each other almost from childhood, but there was no romance between us until we were in high school. I like to believe that Ellen and I have a very special marriage. We share everything."

That didn't seem to fit Ace's research, Alahna thought. Could there have been a slipup somewhere?

Johnson was a bright, witty conversationalist. By the time they finished their meal, Alahna was feeling very comfortable with him. Now all she had to do was arrange to see him again, alone.

"Are you staying on in Washington?" he asked.

"I have to get back tonight," Dolph said quickly, "but my wife has a meeting here tomorrow morning."

It was the first Alahna had heard of the meeting. She glanced sharply at Dolph, realizing instantly what he had in mind.

"Yes," she said. "And I thought I might stay over tomorrow evening and go to the National Gallery. I haven't been there in such a long while."

"A lovely idea, Mrs. Robicheck," said Johnson. "Would you care to drop by for drinks and an early dinner? I would hate to think of you dining alone."

If it hadn't been for the little extra pressure of his hand, Alahna might have thought that this was simply a dinner invitation. But his fingers were expressing a far different message than his words. Perhaps Mrs. Johnson was out of town with the boys. She was willing to bet that what Secretary Johnson had planned was probably banned in Boston. The man was certainly a cool customer.

"Why, how kind of you, Secretary Johnson," Alahna said warmly, meaning it. "I think I should like that very much."

Standing in front of the Johnson's red brick Georgetown townhouse, Alahna struggled to keep a straight face, thinking of what Dolph had said when he'd phoned her earlier.

"I do hope that the two of you are on a first names basis before you get into bed. And they say that we English are a prim and proper bunch. We've nothing on the Boston Brahmins!"

"Ah, Mrs. Robicheck," the butler greeted her. "You're expected. May I take you coat, and follow me this way, please."

"Good afternoon, Mrs. Robicheck. How nice to see you again."

The Secretary rose and shook her hand. "You're very prompt. But of course, you are a business woman. We'll have cocktails shortly. Tell me, how did you enjoy your day?"

As Alahna described the paintings she'd seen that afternoon at the National Gallery, she wondered whether perhaps she and Dolph had misread Johnson's intentions. Perhaps she had imagined the touch of his hand. And where in the world was Mrs. Johnson?

"Would you like sherry or something stronger, Mrs. Robicheck?"

"Sherry would be lovely, thank you. My father and I always had a glass before dinner. It was a habit I learned in the Orient. I grew up in Hong Kong, you know."

"What else did you learn in the Orient?"

"All sorts of interesting things," Alahna said meaningfully, hoping that Ace's information was correct. "I have a taste for the unusual."

"Mrs. Robicheck, you interest me greatly. From the moment you walked into my office yesterday, I wanted to know you better. I hope you're not offended by my straightforward approach."

"Uh, no, not at all, Mr. Secretary," Alahna stammered.

"Reed. Call me Reed. And if you don't mind, I shall call you Alahna."

"What a magnifcent room this is," Alahna said, admiring the museum-quality furniture.

"Would you like a tour of our collection? It has rather a good reputation."

Johnson leaned over and took her hand. "Does that sound agreeable to you?"

"Yes, it does, Reed," Alahna said, taking his arm.

"I promise," Reed said, leading her up the stairs, "you won't be disappointed."

"And this is the bed in which I and my father before me was born."

Alahna had never seen a bed as large as the one that sat in the middle of Johnson's enormous bedroom. The covers were already turned back, the drapes drawn across the windows.

He moved closer to her. Spurred on by her encouraging look, he took her in his arms. "You are an extremely attractive, alluring woman," he said. Leaning down, he kissed her for a very long time.

Alahna liked the way he held her, and how his lips felt against hers. And she very much liked the touch of his hand against the back of her neck. Reed was a gentleman in every sense of the word.

"Reed," she whispered, "this is lovely."

"Would you excuse me for a moment? Please, make yourself comfortable. I'll return shortly."

Alahna took off everything but her full-length slip and neatly placed her clothes on a chair. A moment later, Johnson was back, dimming the overhead lights, taking off his tie

and unbuttoning his starched white shirt before he was even
inside the room.

"Lovely, lovely," he said quietly. "Alahna, I can't believe
you're here with me."

He sat down next to her on the bed and kissed her again
and again on her lips and eyes and neck and arms.

His fingers felt her body through the crepe de chine of her
chemise. The thin slip increased the electricity of his touch.

Alahna lay down and closed her eyes, giving herself over
to Reed's tender ministrations.

"Lovely, lovely," he whispered again and again. "Ah, yes,
let me touch you there."

Her eyes still closed, she shuddered as his lips brushed
against her nipples, and his tongue lit a flame that snaked
across her belly to her groin.

For all his proper Boston manners, Anthony Reed Johnson
certainly knew how to make love to a woman.

"Alahna," he whispered, "Alahna, open your eyes. I want
to ask you something."

He held up a black silk scarf.

"Alahna, I'd like you to allow me to cover your eyes. I
want you only to feel the wonderful sensations of my mouth
and hands upon your beautiful body. No thoughts—pure
feelings, unhampered by visual stimulation. May I do this to
you?"

His left hand played over her nipples. His right hand
pulled softly at the tangle of her pubic hair and lightly massaged her clitoris.

"Yes, yes," she murmured. "Yes, just don't stop."

"Tell me if I tie it too tightly," he said, carefully putting
the scarf in place. "Is that all right?"

"Oh, yes," she groaned as Johnson's lips brushed against
her vagina. She arched her hips upwards to meet his mouth
and was rewarded by his tongue, thrusting between her lips
to explore her further.

Alahna reached blindly to find Reed's thigh, then his
groin. He was already hard, and he moaned as her fingers
tightened about him.

"Good, good, yes," he encouraged her, shifting around so
that their heads fit between each other's legs. His hand

gently massaged the small of her back and the cheeks of her behind and the sensitive skin on the inside of her thighs.

"Oh, Reed!" she cried out breathlessly.

And then he was playing with her breasts again, his teeth biting at the nipples ever so gently, his tongue licking her between the legs.

How wonderful it all felt . . . so absolutely wonderful . . . so impossibly wonderful. . . .

Because, she was realizing, what was happening to her really was impossible.

There had to be someone else in bed with them, she thought dreamily.

She knew she should reach up and tear away the scarf. But drugged with pleasure, the effort seemed too great. There were so many hands fondling her body. To resist these marvelous sensations would be folly.

A woman's voice whispered in her ear. "Do you mind, Alahna?"

"My dear," Reed Johnson whispered softly, "this is my wife, Ellen. I knew from the moment I first met you that the two of you could be marvelous friends."

His hands—or were they Ellen's hands?—continued to play over her neck and breasts.

Alahna knew she should tell them to stop, that she had every right to be furious. But she was too far gone to leave, too aroused even to protest. One of Dolph's favorite business maxims popped, unbidden, into her thoughts.

"When rape is inevitable," he had said more than once, "lie back, spread your legs, and enjoy it."

In this case, she was sure she had some choice in the matter. After all, the Johnsons could hardly keep her prisoner. But perhaps the better choice—the more exciting choice—would be to take the path of least resistance.

Dolph was not amused when she called him, much later that evening, from her hotel room.

"You mean he didn't do anything but watch?"

"They're very close, Dolph. I got the distinct impression that he saves himself for her alone. Not our style, perhaps, and it does put him out of the running for Project US, but it was a delightful evening. I stayed for dinner."

For once, Dolph was left speechless.

But only temporarily.

The very next day, he brought home a folder marked "Number Three."

"Take a look at this photo," he said, handing her the file.

"Who is he?"

"Dwayne Smith. You know of his worldwide media empire, of course. We know for a fact that his wife's never around, and the man's been photographed with pretty girls from here to the Himalayas. I think he may be just what we're looking for."

Alahna studied the photograph more carefully. "Wasn't he the one who climbed Mt. Everest? How old is he?"

"Now, my dear, age is a number," Dolph joked.

"Yes, but there aren't many in the world like you."

"Flattery will get you everywhere, my sweet. But Mr. Smith is only forty-four. Ace tells me that Smith has a town-house just a few blocks away from here. He spends more time in New York than at home in South Carolina. Why don't we arrange a dinner party and invite him?"

But as it turned out, the day that Dwayne Smith was invited to dinner, Dolph received an urgent call from Greg Andrews, his project director in Indonesia. Shawak International held the land leases for several thousand acres of teak-wood forests. But now there was trouble—talk of rebellious tribesmen who claimed they owned the land, that the trees were sacred, and that anyone who put an axe to them risked incurring the wrath of their gods. A foreman and two workers from a forestry camp deep in the Borneo jungle had been found dead.

"Murdered, they were, Dolph, I'm quite sure of it. And these government chaps aren't being a bit helpful. Do you think you could send me over some help?"

"I'll do better than that," Dolph said. He'd worked with the project director for fifteen years, and knew that the fellow didn't make calls to the boss unless there was a damn good reason. "I'll fly out this afternoon. Meet me tomorrow night in Jakarta, and together we'll find out what's what."

Andrew's grateful "Thanks, Dolph," assured him he'd made the right decision, even if it meant leaving Alahna to host the dinner herself.

It was one of those rare, magical evenings. Dolph's presence was missed, but the wine and talk flowed, and Alahna relaxed in the warmth of the party. She had asked Dwayne Smith to sit in Dolph's seat. But now, as he dominated the conversation, she felt uneasy.

She knew from the look in Dwayne Smith's eyes that she looked particularly beautiful this evening. She was sure she would not have to work hard to manage a liaison between the two of them.

He lingered behind as the other guests said their goodbyes.

"Another brandy, Dwayne?" Alahna asked, hoping he would stay.

He accepted the snifter, took one sip, then said, "Alahna, when will Dolph be back?"

"Saturday or Sunday, perhaps. Whenever he solves the problem. Thank you for substituting as host for him tonight. I loved your stories about Nepal. As did the rest of my friends."

"You underestimate yourself, Alahna. But I was more than happy to do whatever I could to help you out."

"You're very sweet, Dwayne."

"Sweet—and selfish, Alahna. I had an ulterior motive. I would like to have you for my friend. My close friend. If you agree, I will give you a night that you will never forget."

Alahna laughed. "I've been thinking much the same thing since you walked in. No one would be foolish enough to turn down an offer like that."

She stood up and pointed to the door, saying, "We're both adults. I don't think either of us needs persuading. The bedroom's upstairs."

Dwayne Smith's physique gave evidence of his athletic prowess. There was not an extra ounce of fat on his body—he was all lean muscle and sinew. His right shoulder and the upper part of his chest were marked by three long scars.

"A souvenir from a trip I made to northern Alaska," he grinned. "A bear got in my way."

Alahna leaned over him, tracing the length of the deep gashes with her tongue and lips.

"Mmm, nice," breathed Dwayne, guiding her head towards his flat stomach and legs. "Yes, yes, there," he groaned his approval.

But several moments later he pulled her up and knelt above her.

"What a challenge you present, Alahna Robicheck," he said, his hands fondling her breasts and playing with her nipples.

"Do I?" she whispered, already feeling herself melt under his deft touch.

"But we've all the time in the world and I promise you a night to remember."

His hands and tongue glided, touching her, teasing her, promising her more and more, until she thought surely she would go mad if he didn't come into her quickly. But he took his time, carefully controlling her responses, as if somehow he knew exactly how much of this exquisite torture she could bear, how much would take her beyond the limits of passion.

Finally he entered her and she groaned with anticipation of release. But still he continued to play, effortlessly thrusting back and forth inside her body as she moaned with pleasure.

"Please," Alahna begged, "please, I need you now."

Then, at last, he brought her to a climax, a wave of overwhelming relief. When she opened her eyes, he was still poised above her.

"More?" he asked, and even before she had a chance to nod, he was inside her again, still rock-hard, and she was coming again, the second every bit as intense as the first.

"What about you?" she whispered, but now Dwayne had moved down, between her legs, and his tongue was probing her, urging her to submit once again.

"No, no, I can't," she moaned, even as she began to feel

herself responding, letting go, and then she stopped protesting and allowed the moment to take her over.

"I want you to come again and again and again," Dwayne whispered, kissing her tenderly on the lips.

"Oh, but I have," Alahna laughed weakly. "How can you do this? I've never met a man with such stamina."

"My joy in life is to give women pleasure. That is happiness enough for me."

"Don't you ever have an orgasm?" Alahna asked timidly.

"No. I had an implant operation to give me a permanent erection. I can't ejaculate."

"How . . . amazing," Alahna said faintly. "Then you can't have any more children?"

"Three is enough, don't you think."

Alahna rolled away from Smith, completely exhausted. A little bit of Dwayne Smith, superstud, went a very long way.

Chapter Three

Dolph was fascinated by Alahna's report on her experience with Dwayne Smith, but Alahna was less amused. Project US was beginning to seem less like a game with a marvelous prize to be won at the end, and more like a series of onerous tasks. Obstinate as usual, Dolph was not discouraged.

The late summer greenery grew increasingly more lush as Dolph and Alahna passed the lovely coastal towns of the French Riviera. Combining business with pleasure, they had spent two weeks in Paris and were now behaving like true Parisians, fleeing the heat by heading south.

Alahna's head was filled with thoughts of sunbathing, swimming, slow dancing, and long nights of romance.

"I thought we were finished with all the business," she said lazily, as Dolph pulled a file out of his briefcase.

"Emilio Amati," Dolph announced.

"Pardon me?"

"Emilio Amati. Thirty-seven years old."

BOOK III   207

"Should I know him?"

"Candidate number four, Alahna. We spoke of him last May. You know how it's impossible to travel more than a few kilometers without seeing an advertisement for Amati gasoline. The man has boundless energy, and he's a brilliant engineer. Lucky for us, he happens to be in Monte Carlo for the month."

"Oh, Dolph, you never told me! I was picturing a relaxing time, just the two of us. . . . Dolph," her voice rose plaintively, "how long must this torture go on?"

"Alahna, my darling. I don't understand. This is for us, for our future happiness. And of course we shall have time together. But it's also a splendid opportunity for you to meet Amati. I understand he's terribly handsome," Dolph grinned.

"I don't care," Alahna said sulkily. "I'm tired of these impossible men!"

"Darling, I know we've had a series of failures, but I've saved the best for last. I think you should at least give him a chance. You may be very pleasantly surprised."

"And what if I don't get pregnant? There's no guarantee he'll turn out to be any better than the others. And then this search will go on and on and on."

"It won't take much longer, I promise you. Just relax and bear with me, won't you please?"

Emilio Amati was indeed as handsome as a movie star, Alahna decided, and he attracted as much attention. He came out onto the veranda of the Hermitage Hotel, flanked by two tall blond girls who appeared to be identical twins of no more than seventeen or eighteen years old. The Robichecks had invited Emilio to join them for a drink. He hadn't said anything about bringing along friends.

Alahna raised her eyebrows questioningly.

"I don't know," Dolph shrugged, rising to greet Amati.

"Good evening, good evening," Amati said, flashing a smile. "May I introduce," he pointed to his two friends, "Astrid and Brigida."

Reaching into his pocket, he withdrew a roll of bills.

"A thousand for you and a thousand for you," he said,

patting each of them on the behind. "Buy yourselves something pretty to wear tonight," he instructed them.

"I can make it faster than they can spend it," he said, turning back to Dolph and Alahna. "A glass of water only," he told the waiter.

"Thank you for joining us," Dolph said. "My associate, Mr. Taylor, tells me that you are interested in having our firm underwrite a part of your oil explorations in the Middle East."

"Yes, yes," Amati said animatedly. "We are very optimistic about the project. I was so happy to hear from Mr. Taylor that you would be in Monte Carlo and we could meet in person."

Dolph turned to Alahna. "Do you have the projections with you?"

"Right here."

Amati smiled at Alahna. "It is such a great pleasure to make your acquaintance *Signora* Robicheck. Ace Taylor told me that you are not only a brilliant businesswoman, but also extremely beautiful. But I see he did you an injustice. You are one of the most beautiful women I have ever met."

"Why, thank you, Mr. Amati," Alahna smiled, flashing her dimples.

"Please, you must call me Emilio. Will you both be in Monte Carlo long? Perhaps you will permit me to show you the night life of the city."

"As a matter of fact," Dolph broke in, "nothing would suit us better. My wife was just saying she would love to see the Riviera at night, but I must rest in the evening. Perhaps we could prevail upon you to be Alahna's escort?"

"Nothing, not even the consummation of our business with Shawak International, could possibly please me more," laughed Emilio. "Tonight at nine, Mrs. Robicheck?"

"Alahna," she corrected him. "That would be lovely, Emilio," she said, meaning it.

Dolph's competitive nature asserted itself. He knew Alahna could look more spectacular than the Scandinavian twins. So she didn't need a mirror to know she deserved the reaction in Emilio's eyes when he caught sight of her in her gold and silver gown, covered with shimmering sequins that dipped to a low V in the back. He reached for her hand and brushed it lightly across his lips.

"Dancing," Emilio said decisively. "For that dress, there must be dancing. Yes?"

Alahna loved to dance, but Dolph went dancing only under protest. "Oh, lovely," she said.

Alahna thought that Emilio, with his suntanned face and white linen suit, was possibly the most handsome man she had ever seen. But it was more than good looks. He had an electricity about him as he moved.

He drove as if he were still training for the Grand Prix. Alahna held her breath and closed her eyes as they took the turns at a breakneck speed.

"Care for some?" Emilio waved a joint in her face.

"No, thanks," Alahna shouted above the noise from onrushing wind. Emilio took several long puffs. Alahna wondered what effect the marijauna might have on his already reckless driving.

But they arrived in one piece in front of a large building with a small neon sign that flashed on and off, "Club Ultra Violette."

"Very now," Emilio told her, taking her hand and hurrying her inside.

"Alahna felt as if she had just been catapulted into the twenty-first century. Silver mobiles dangled from the mirrored ceiling, and colored lights darted about the room like technicolor fireflies. Loud music blared from the enormous speakers strategically placed around the room.

The dancers all wore the same look of frozen concentration as they swayed and jumped in the tiny space each had staked out.

"They look as if they've taken a bath in novocaine," Alahna shouted.

"Pardon?" Emilio cupped his ear.

"Never mind," she shook her head. Conversation was impossible. Besides, it was all she could do to keep up with his gyrations. Here, on the dance floor, Emilio commanded every eye with his performance. She was his perfect complement and they smiled obligingly as the photographers' flashbulbs popped.

By eleven, Alahna was starving and ready to sit down. She pulled Emilio close to her and screamed into his ear, "I'm hungry. How about you?"

"Just a few more minutes, okay?" he shouted back.

A half an hour later, he was ready to quit.

"I know the perfect place for dinner," he said.

They drove down the coast about fifteen minutes south of Monte Carlo and pulled up in front of a large white building, overlooking the sea.

"La Mer," Emilio said. "Have you been here before? It was formerly the home of a maharaja. Now it's a restaurant and gambling casino. The lobster diablo is incomparable."

The dining room was an open vista of white marble and glass, with the sea crashing towards them through the wall of windows. But to Alahna's chagrin, Emilio guided her past the open doorway and down the wide marble stairs to the gaming rooms. What looked to be a small fortune in art was hung about the room. Alahna recognized a Utrillo, a Van Gogh, and at least one Seurat. Emilio had said that the heavy hitters never arrived until after one in the morning, and, in fact, at this hour, the atmosphere was quite relaxed. White-gloved waiters passed among the tables with silver trays of champagne, and the croupiers, in white ties and tails, seemed to be taking their time calling in the bets. The only action appeared to be in the corner, where three men were engaged in a game of chemin de fer.

It seemed as if most of the serious players were still upstairs, finishing their dinner. Alahna's stomach cried out for food. How she longed to join them.

"What would you like to play, Alahna?" Emilio asked.

"Oh, nothing, thank you," Alahna replied. "I'll just watch."

"Are you sure? But would you mind putting some money on the black for me? I'll be back in just a moment."

Alahna did as he had asked, while Emilio disappeared into the crowd. Before she knew what had happened, she had lost all but one hundred francs of the ten thousand he had handed her. That was gambling enough for her. She glanced around the room, wishing Emilio would return quickly.

"How do you handle knowing that no matter what room you walk into, you're the most beautiful woman there?"

Alahna whirled around and found herself looking at a red-headed, impish faced American with a gap-toothed grin.

"Forgive me for being forward, but you're so beautiful that I just had to tell you." He shrugged his shoulders. "It's not a pass, honest—merely a declaration of my admiration."

Alahna laughed at his honesty. She was about to reply when Emilio materialized by her side.

"Have you made a friend already, Alahna?"

"Excuse me," he said with obvious annoyance to the America, "but the lady and I were about to leave."

Steering her across the room, he said, "On my way back from the men's room, I bumped into some acquaintances. You don't mind if they join us, do you?"

She did mind, but didn't know how politely to tell Emilio that she would have preferred to have him all to herself. Nor did she get the opportunity. A man and two women immediately bore down on them, screeching a greeting.

"Oh, Emilio, you naughty boy," cried one of the women, who was dressed from head to toe in feathers. "Emilio, we let you out of our sight for one week, and look what you have found for yourself!"

Alahna smiled weakly, wishing she were any place but here. But Emilio caught her look of dismay. Without skipping a beat, he announced, "Wonderful to see you, but I must take my friend home quickly and safely. We will see all of you another time, I hope, yes?"

"Thank you so much, Emilio," Alahna said, as they climbed into his car. "I hope I wasn't rude to your friends, but I had so been looking forward to a quiet dinner, just the two of us."

Emilio's white teeth glistened in his tanned face. "How rude you must think me that I haven't fed you yet. But I have the perfect idea. Shall we return to my hotel and we can order something to be served in the comfort of my suite?"

"Marvelous," said Alahna.

"What time does your husband expect you home?"

Alahna smiled. "I'm on the longest leash you ever saw, Emilio. I make my own hours."

"Ah, it's like that. I thought so, when I saw what an old man you were married to. Not much fun I expect, but of course a great deal of money."

A wave of fury swept over her with such force that she couldn't speak. She felt like shoving her foot in his groin, bolting out of the car, and never again speaking to this Italian Don Juan. But Dolph would tell her that she was acting like a child. Besides, if she didn't consummate something with this preening peacock, what followed might well be far worse.

All right, she gritted her teeth. For the child. For our child.

Emilio had the penthouse suite, overlooking the beach.

"What a lovely view, Emilio," Alahna said, sure he could hear her stomach growling. "I would love to eat our dinner on the balcony."

Emilio moved closer and put his arm around her shoulder. "I bet I know just what my bambina would like."

"Anything would be fine," Alahna said, "some fish, or a cold salad."

"Something else first."

"Oh, I don't need an appetizer. I'll have some fruit and cheese for dessert."

Emilio laughed and pulled out of his pocket a tiny bottle and an equally tiny silver spoon. "I love your English wit. But this is no joke. I have here the best cocaine you will ever snort. Alahna, *cara*, get ready for the ride of your life. This will transport you to paradise."

"Could we call downstairs first?" Alahna coaxed. "I would love some champagne." She gazed into his eyes and tried to convey to him the message, that she hoped to make love with him. "That's close enough to paradise for me."

"We will have it all, Alahna. But first, wouldn't you like a line or two of this? Better than the finest champagne, I assure you."

He bent his nostril to meet the spoon filled with the powdery, white substance.

"Ah," he inhaled, repeating the ritual with the other nostril. "Alahna, I have such a wonderful thought. Let me drive you up into the mountains. In just two hours we could be drinking wine and eating at one of Provence's best kept secrets. Here," he offered her the spoon, "your turn."

"Not for me, thanks. I don't do drugs."

He pushed a button and music blared from the speakers beside the couch. "You can call down and order some food. We will drink champagne. Say, I have a marvelous idea! Let's get the twins up here."

But Alahna had heard enough.

"Goodnight, Emilio," she said.

She hurried out the door and down the elevator, almost running in her haste to put behind her the distastefulness of the experience. She was furious with Emilio, furious with herself for not having escaped earlier—and most of all, furious with Dolph.

Dolph was already in bed, reading, when Alahna stormed into their suite. Crying with rage and frustration, she stood in the middle of the room and shouted, "I will not, I will not, do you hear me, endure another evening like this!"

"What happened? Did he hurt you?"

The tears came in a waterfall. "How could you degrade me this way with that Italian mosquito? He jumped and flitted and pranced about like an insect. If this is the humiliation I have to suffer to bear a child, I don't want any part of it! All I want is to be left alone!"

Suddenly feeling sick to her stomach, she dashed into the bathroom, and released all the tensions of the evening. Afterwards, she lay on the bathroom floor, emotionally and physically spent.

Dolph washed off her face and carried her to their bed, trying all the while to get her to tell him what Amati had done. But Alahna said not a word until he gave up and turned off the lights.

"I want to go home, Dolph," she said quietly. "Take me back to New York. I must go home."

This time Dolph knew not to argue.

Chapter Four

Angry and confused, Alahna threw herself into her work with even greater than usual dedication. She would forget about being a mother, she had decided. Certainly it was not worth the price it seemed she had to pay.

It wasn't just that Amati had been insensitive and cocky. It was the sum total of the experiences she had been through. She felt humiliated, she told Dolph, humiliated and ill-used.

"By whom?" he wanted to know.

At that moment she suddenly realized that she was also angry with Dolph.

All her life, she had been shielded from most of life's grimmer realities. Although she was grateful for all the love and attention Salah and Dolph had given her, she now saw that they had also done her a grave disservice. In some ways she had been cheated by the firm control they had always exercised over her.

She had never so much as had to call a cab, register in a hotel, make her own airline reservations, arrange an appointment with the hairdresser or the manicurist. And all the men she had made love with, up until recently, had been considerate, skilled lovers. She had never had to submit to the indignities of dating men who thought only of themselves and their own pleasures.

Certainly she adored her husband. Making love with him still thrilled her. She felt protected by the sheltering umbrella of his attentions, and reveled in his daily shows of thoughtfulness.

But now, obsessed with the notion of her bearing the perfect child, he no longer seemed to be the same man. Normally, Alahna could reason with him, but on this one subject, he would not listen. He had made up his mind that finding the perfect biological father was the only solution.

In the pursuit of this idea, his obsession had turned to madness. A madness that Alahna had come to fear and resent.

If only they could return to their life as it had been. . . .
But was Dolph willing to do so? Alahna took her worries to
Meilee, who soothed and comforted her. But even Meilee
could offer her no answers. Dolph was a very willful man,
accustomed to always having his way.

The question continued to nag at her, keeping her awake
nights and distracting her from her work. Ever since their
return from France, Dolph had said not one word about
Project US. But that didn't mean he'd put it out of his mind.

She would have to confront him directly. As far as she
was concerned, the project was no longer viable. She had to
be sure he knew how she felt—and could accept her feelings.

One afternoon, at the end of a long senior staff meeting
when she had barely been able to focus on what was being
discussed, Alahna stayed behind after everyone else had filed
out.

"Dolph," she said, "we need to talk seriously."

"What's the matter? Did I miss something just now? I
thought the meeting went very well," Dolph said.

"This isn't about Shawak International. This is about us.
I'm frightened."

"Frightened!" Dolph looked bemused. "Alahna, what on
earth are you talking about?"

Alahna stood up and began to pace back and forth across
the room. "I'm frightened about what could happen
between us if we continue with this ridiculous attempt to
breed the perfect heir."

"Ah, I see," Dolph said thoughtfully. "In fact, I've been
wanting to talk to you about this. But I've hesitated, knowing how distressed you were by what happened with Amati.
I wasn't sure how you were feeling, whether or not you
were ready to try again."

"Dolph, I absolutely refuse to go on with this insanity.
I've had one absurd experience after another—surely you
can see that. And I'm worried and frightened that your
determination will create a rift between us too great to
mend. I love you so, Dolph. Please! Let's not allow that to
happen!"

"Alahna, my darling." Dolph stood up and put his arms
around her, hugging her tightly. "Believe me, I love you too
much to permit that. I tell you what. Let's let things lie

until after the first of the year. We won't even think about Project US. If you've had a change of heart by then, we'll decide what to do next. You must see that we've barely scratched the surface, but of course, ultimately, it's your decision. Agreed?"

Alahna stared at him for a moment. Then she reached for his hand and brought it to her lips. Dolph had never lied to her. She believed him, trusted him.

Yes, she nodded. Yes. They could wait until then to make their final decision.

In early November, another one of the company's Indonesian lumberjacks was found dead not far from the jungle camp, and the rest of the crew walked off the job.

"They're spooked, Dolph," Greg Andrews told him. "They figure that any one of them could be next."

The Indonesian government was sympathetic but uncooperative. "How we wish we could help you, Mr. Robicheck," declared the government representative in New York. "But we have no more information than you do."

"And if you did, would you share it with me?" Dolph asked. The representative looked hurt. "But of course, Mr. Robicheck. We look forward to our continuing relationship. And in the meantime, may I take the liberty of reminding you that your lease obligations are coming due?"

"Dammit," Dolph growled, "I know what's due when. You'll get your money. Don't worry about it."

He'd have to make another trip to Jakarta, to dig around and find out why nothing more was being done to find the murderers. The prospect wasn't altogether uninviting. The jungle interior had a mysterious grandeur that tugged at his imagination. Tracking down some useful clues presented a welcome challenge.

Alahna wanted to come along.

"No," he told her. "I have to do this alone. It could be dangerous—and I don't want you exposed to that. And I'd like to get off on my own for a bit. Besides, there's something that needs organizing, and I'd love for you to get on it right away."

He pointed to the window.

"Look," he said.

"Yes?"

"It's just beginning to snow. We should be thinking about skiing."

Alahna smiled. "I'm beginning to see what's on your mind."

"How about Christmas in St. Moritz? Madeleine will be there, and she could help us find a house. We'll invite Jeff and the Taylors and maybe even lure Chris away from the Middle East. What do you think?"

"Absolutely, darling. I think it's a marvelous idea. Madeleine's in Geneva, right? I'll call her right away and see if she knows of a house we could rent for Christmas through New Year's Eve. Don't worry about a thing. By the time you get back from Borneo, I'll have it all under control. I hope we can get Jeff and Chris to join us. We haven't seen Chris in ages, have we?"

"I'll tell you a little secret," Dolph said. "I have good reason to believe he's got someone special keeping him in Israel. I wonder whether he'll let us meet her."

"Dolph," Alahna said, half-annoyed, "why didn't you tell me? And when did you hear from him?"

"I got a letter this morning. That's what gave me the idea for a reunion in St. Moritz. Here it is," Dolph said, pulling an airform out of his pocket.

"I'm going to write him immediately," Alahna said. "No, better yet, I'll call him. And Madeleine, and Jeff, too. Now all we have to do is pray for snow."

Madeleine knew of just the place. "It's a bit dear," she said, "but so comfortable, Alahna. It comes complete with an indoor swimming pool and a bowling alley. The house is down the hill from my chalet. It belongs to an Arab sheik whose boyfriend prefers palm trees and Beverly Hills. I know he'd be delighted to rent it to you."

"Tell him we'll take it," Alahna said.

Madeleine promised to get back to her as soon as possible, and Alahna hung up the phone. About to put through a call to Jeff, she hesitated a moment, struck by an astonishing realization.

As Alahna Robicheck, an officer of Shawak International, she had made hundreds of decisions over the years and put in motion the steps to implement those decisions. But this was one of the few times she could recall, in all the years she'd been married, that she had been responsible for making social arrangements for herself and Dolph.

It had always been left up to him to decide, to say yes, to make the calls. He had protected her, yes, but with her total cooperation.

Well, she decided, dialing Jeff's number in California, it was about time. She'd allowed herself to be a child for far too long.

Alahna, Dolph, Meilee, and Jeff flew to St. Moritz in the Shawak jet. Ace and Jana had gone ahead, and Chris was due to arrive the following day from Israel. He'd declined to bring his Israeli lover, "but I'll bring a picture," he promised.

He would be staying with Madeleine and her husband. After a lengthy succession of extramarital affairs, Madeleine and Pierre had finally discovered each other as lovers. But she and Chris were still close friends, and Madeleine insisted on hosting him.

The nightlife in St. Moritz was in full swing, but the group had little desire to leave the enclave they had created for themselves. They alternated evenings between the two houses, and a path was soon worn in the snow as the friends shuttled between the Laval's chalet and the Robicheck's much grander rented home.

Madeleine set forth the ground rules. Two different people were in charge each night for the evening's entertainment. One of the more memorable dinners was cooked up by Dolph and Chris—a very English supper of scrambled eggs, smoked salmon, and kippers. But instead of the tea they'd drunk in their nursery days, they offered wine and beer.

"Delicious meal," Alahna said, catching Chris for a rare moment alone. "It's such fun to see you again. But we've had so little time to talk. Are you serious about this woman, Chris? And when do we get to meet her?"

"Very serious, though at the moment we're having a bit of

a rough time. That's why she's not here, actually."

"Care to share your troubles with me?"

"It's funny, Alahna," Chris said pensively. "I've always had such wanderlust. But now I'm thinking about settling down. At long last, I might add. But my lady, who's quite a bit younger than I, says she's not ready. But I suppose this must sound a little mad, especially coming from me, old Lucifer Lust."

"No," Alahna said slowly, "no, Chris, it doesn't."

How ironic, she thought, that Dolph and Chris should both have reached the same conclusion at the same point in their lives.

"Penny, Alahna."

She smiled, remembering the first time Chris had said that to her.

"I can't talk about it now, Chris, but maybe someday."

"All right, but you know that Lucifer Lust is still your best friend, and that I'm ready to listen, whenever or wherever."

"Thanks, Chris, thanks very much," Alahna said. "I can't tell you how much that means to me."

On New Year's Eve they gathered at Madeleine's home, an unpretentious stone and wood chalet whose focal point was a round stone fireplace in the middle of the cozy living room. There was room enough for twenty or more people to arrange themselves comfortably on the huge pillows behind which was a wide, circular ledge that doubled as a buffet.

Madeleine had set out platters of cold meat and cheese, as well as a large pot of melted cheese for fondue. In one corner of the room sat an old washtub filled with bottles of champagne and white wine, kept chilled by fresh snow.

"What absolute heaven this is," said Jana, pulling herself up to retrieve another bottle of champagne. "A perfect way to celebrate the new year, don't you think?"

"Absolutely the best," Alahna agreed.

"You're right, baby, this is the greatest," said Jeff, strumming softly on his guitar. "There's nothing better than spending good times with people you care about. Hey, man," he called to Dolph who was playing the piano, "while I cuddle up with your wife, why don't you play us some of the stuff you and I wrote?"

Dolph laughed and for once did as he was told.

"What wonderful music you two are producing," Alahna murmured. "I wish you could persuade him to take it more seriously."

"All in good time, babe, all in good time. You just leave it to Jefferson Gotley." Jeff struck a chord for emphasis.

"It's almost midnight," Madeleine announced. "My neighbor has put together his annual fireworks show. It's quite spectacular. We shouldn't miss it."

With some mild protests about being taken away from the warmth of the fire, her guests roused themselves and put on their parkas and boots. A burst of colored lights illuminated the black sky just as they took their places on the veranda overlooking the snow, sparkling in the moonlight. Stars, flowers and candles exploded in rapid succession as the designs spread a glow against the silvery night.

"Happy New Year, my darling," Dolph whispered.

Alahna put her arms around her husband. She felt so filled with happiness, so blessed with everything she could possibly want, so sure that she and Dolph could easily resolve all their conflicts.

"Happy New Year," she said. "To our very best year yet."

Soon after their return to New York, Alahna decided to make good on her New Year's resolution. Turning to him in bed she said, "I've given this a lot of thought, Dolph. I know how much you want a child, but perhaps there's another way. I've quite made up my mind. I simply can't go on with Project US."

Dolph put down the book he'd been reading. "Forgive me, Alahna, but it's not like you to be so uncompromising. Don't you realize that I've only your best interests at heart?"

"I'm sorry, Dolph." Alahna's tone was quiet but firm. "You said that ultimately it was my decision. And my decision is to not continue."

"Alahna," Dolph spoke in a voice that was as close to pleading as she'd ever heard him, "I meant what I said. But surely by now you've had a chance to calm down and reconsider. I know you had a couple of unpleasant encounters, and I can only blame myself. You simply weren't prepared for such men. But I promise you, that sort of thing won't happen again."

"No, Dolph. I'm sorry, but there's no way you can guarantee that. We'll have to come up with another solution."

"Alahna, I will not tolerate a no from you in this matter. You must do as I say."

"No," Alahna said.

He continued as if Alahna hadn't spoken. "We've developed a new list. It's much more thoroughly researched than before. I think you'll be pleased."

"I don't want to talk about it now," she said quietly.

Dolph reached over, turned off the light, and went to sleep.

But she lay awake most of the night, her head filled with frantic, contradictory thoughts. She loved and trusted Dolph—for the past sixteen years she had obeyed his every instruction. She could hardly imagine taking a stand against him.

But she couldn't subject herself to the prospect of another humiliating sexual encounter. And living with this man in the throes of an obsession was becoming intolerable.

In the morning, she told Dolph that she needed to spend a few hours at home.

By the time he returned in the evening, she was gone.

Chapter Five

Alahna stared out the window of the small commuter plane that she had boarded in Denver. As the plane jolted its way toward Aspen, she realized that for the first time in her life, she had made a decision all on her own.

She had chosen Aspen almost on a whim, because she'd seen a picture of the fashionable ski resort on the cover of a magazine lying next to her bed. In her hurry to leave New

York, she hadn't even thought to pack her ski clothes. No matter, she told herself, she could buy whatever she needed in Aspen.

Fortunately, she had brought plenty of cash with her—fifty thousand dollars from the bedroom safe, kept there in case of emergency. This was an emergency—her peace of mind was at stake. She'd also brought with her several pieces of jewelry. A legacy from her father, she reflected grimly, who'd told her time and again that the Shawaks had often run for their lives with jewelry sewn into the linings of their clothing. She wasn't sure how long she would stay away. All she knew was that she had to get away, to be alone for a while. The time had come for her to begin to live her own life.

She had left two notes, one for Dolph, the other for Meilee, explaining her abrupt departure.

"My darling Dolph," she said, "I know you want only the very best for me and my future. But I don't think you realize to what degree you dominate my life. I've loved everything you've done for me. But I'm a grown woman, capable of making my own decisions, and I've tried to tell you in every way I know how that I cannot go on with this detestable search. Unfortunately, there seems to be no way to make you understand how I feel. You are not my father, and I am not your child. I think it's best to put some distance between us for a while, until I feel you are open to discuss our future, rationally, with me as two adults.

"I beg you not to try to find me, but rather to let me at last find my own way. Though I may flounder a bit, and possibly fall, that is part of growing up.

"Do not think that I don't love you for I love you more than life itself. But I must be on my own for now."

To Meilee she had written, "Dearest Meilee, I must go away for a time, leaving you to pick up the pieces as you have done so often in the past for the Shawak family. Please take good care of Dolph, for he will need you more than ever now. You needn't worry about me. Thanks to you and my father, I have reserves of strength to draw on. Your teachings will guide me through this difficult time. I love you."

She had waited two and a half hours at LaGuardia Airport for a Denver-bound plane. It had felt strange to be standing on line, hoping for a reservation on a commercial airline. For so many years now, she had flown only on the company plane.

Now, stepping off the prop plane that flew the Denver-Aspen route, she was overcome with panic. It was late afternoon, and a light snow was dusting the runway. All the other passengers seemed to know where they were going. She was sure she was the only one who had no reservation, no idea of what hotel to call.

She tried to shake off her anxiety and hurried to join the other skiers waiting for taxis in front of the terminal. Clutching her cosmetic bag into which she had stuffed her jewels, she jumped when she felt a hand on her shoulder.

"Cab, lady?"

"Uh, yes, please," she stammered.

"Where to?" the driver asked.

Good question, she wanted to tell him. Instead she said, "Which is the best hotel in Aspen?"

"Hey, ma'am, this is high season in Aspen. If you don't already have reservations someplace, I'm afraid you're out of luck. This town is full up."

"That's fine," Alahna said in her most brisk, businesslike voice. "But I asked you for the best hotel in town, and I'd like you to get me there as quickly as possible. Is that quite clear?"

The cabbie eyed her through the rearview mirror. "Yes, ma'am," he nodded. "Here we go," the cabbie announced after a short ride through the charming little town. "The Aspen Inn. The mountain's right next door."

He jumped out and opened the door for her. "Want me to wait for you? You probably won't get a room here."

"Yes, thanks," Alahna said, her depression beginning to lift. She smiled confidently. "I'll be right back."

The cabbie's approving whistle followed her into the hotel.

"I'd like a room, please," she informed the blond young man behind the desk.

The desk clerk eyed her. "Very sorry, ma'am, but if you

don't have a reservation, I've nothing available."

"There's usually something, young man. What about one of your larger suites?" Alahna said pleasantly.

"Well, we do have our presidential suite," the young man said, looking her up and down, "but it rents for six hundred dollars a day."

"That exactly what I had in mind. Here's a two thousand dollar deposit. Could you have someone help me with my bag?"

The cabbie shook his head as Alahna handed him the fare and a tip. "Nice going," he said. "You have yourself a good time, ma'am."

"Thanks, I intend to," Alahna said, sounding braver than she felt. But her spirits improved as soon as she walked into her two-bedroom suite. The rooms were rustic but comfortable, decorated in earth tones of brown, tan, and white. Several paintings, New Mexico landscapes, hung on the walls. Thick white carpeting added to the warmth. Her windows faced west, and the late afternoon sun shone on the skiers on the neighboring mountain slopes.

Alahna unpacked quickly and decided to use what was left of the day to shop for warm clothes and skis. To her surprise, she discovered that most of the boutiques were open late into the evening and business was booming. She had never shopped before without Dolph. It felt strange and lonely to be choosing ski equipment, a jacket similar to the one she'd worn in St. Moritz, furry, après-ski boots, and several brightly colored sweaters and ski outfits.

That taken care of, she strolled the busy streets watching the laughing tourists. Perhaps Aspen had been a mistake, she thought, watching all the couples strolling hand-in-hand. As she reached the end of Galena Street, a group of young people rode by in a haywagon, laughing and waving.

How strange to think that just a month ago in St. Moritz, she and Dolph had been laughing, skiing, enjoying themselves with their friends. And now she was by herself, feeling very lonely and vulnerable.

The circle of white-capped mountains rose like a protective cap above the moonlit town. Although Christmas was long past, the twinkling lights strung across the streets gave the illusion of a holiday spirit.

Alahna couldn't help but think about what Dolph and Meilee were doing at this moment, how they were reacting to her absence.

Well, she decided, gazing up at the mountain that sloped down into the village, she would try to make the best of the situation. For the next seven days she intended to have some fun here by herself, and that's all there was to it.

And after that?

No . . . For the time being, she would simply take it one step at a time.

Newly fallen white powder glistened on the sidewalks and storefronts, promising perfect ski conditions for the next day. Suddenly she felt exhausted by all the turmoil of the previous twenty-four hours. Time to get back to the hotel for a room service dinner and a good night's sleep.

Passing a newsstand, she gave into a life-long habit and stopped for a copy of the *Wall Street Journal*. As she took out her wallet to pay, she heard a chagrined voice.

"Oh, no, you're taking the last one."

Alahna looked up at the man next to her. "I'm sorry. Were you about to buy it?"

"Hey, wait a minute," the man exclaimed. "I know you . . . I can't remember your name, but I know we've met before."

In fact, there was something familiar about the fellow's curly red hair and freckles. But she couldn't put a name to his face, and she had no desire to make small talk with anyone just now.

"I think you're mistaken," she said with a chilly nod.

"Hey, can I at least see the headlines?" the man called after her. but she was already out the door, hurrying towards her hotel and the security of her suite.

The sun was shining brilliantly on Ajax mountain, a quick five-minute walk from the hotel. Alahna was among the first in line for the chairlift up to Ruthie's Run. A fearless skier, she threw caution aside as she gave herself up to the exhilarating twists and turns of the path. By noon she was hungry, tired, and thoroughly refreshed by the morning's exercise.

Midway up the mountain was a restaurant with an open deck that offered splendid views of the area. Alahna carried her tray outside and settled into a chair in the sunshine. A moment later the red-headed man from the night before appeared and took the seat across from her.

"Lady, you are one hell of a skier!" he said cheerfully. "A thousand girls in this town, and I fall madly in love with the one who's trying out for the Olympics. I had a devil of a time keeping up with you on Ruthie's. But I didn't want to let you out of my sight."

Alahna stared at him in amazement.

"And furthermore, I stayed up half the night trying to figure out where I'd met you before. At about two o'clock it came to me. It was in Monte Carlo. You were with an Italian who started breathing fire when he saw me talking to you. Don't you remember? I'm the guy who came up to you and told you how beautiful you were."

Suddenly, Alahna did remember. The painful memory of her night with Emilio Amati jarred her out of the good mood created by the snow and sunshine. But whatever her expression, the man across from her took no notice. He continued speaking as though Alahna had responded enthusiastically to his reminiscence.

"But I still haven't figured out what you're doing with the *Wall Street Journal* instead of *Harper's Bazaar*. Why don't you tell me about it over dinner tonight?"

He extended his right hand. "I'm Kevin Olsen from Los Angeles, good credentials, warmhearted, good to my mother, and extremely eager to make your acquaintance."

Alahna couldn't help but laugh at the man's good-natured banter. Behind the security of her sunglasses, she examined him more closely. He appeared to be in his thirties, with a healthy athlete's tan and the most impish grin she had ever seen on a grownup.

"I'm a movie producer but don't hold that against me," Kevin Olsen went on. "And now that I've almost broken my neck chasing you down the mountain, aren't you dying to keep that date with me? You know, I thought that the women are supposed to chase the producers, not the other way around. Haven't you always wanted to be in the movies?"

"No," Alahna said, still laughing.

"Well, that's a beginning, anyway. What time shall I pick you up tonight?"

"I'm sorry, but I can't."

Kevin Olsen's face fell. "Oh, but you have to. I have a long list of questions to ask you—who you are, where you're from, what you were doing in Monte Carlo, and why you speak with a faint British accent but act so very American. How's eight o'clock? And if you'll slow down a bit, how about another run?"

Alahna was intrigued by the man's irrepressible spirits. And—she had to admit it—she was lonely. "All right," she agreed. "I'll slow down and I'll even have dinner. But no more questions, because I'm not giving out any answers today. Deal?"

"Deal," he said, with a wide grin that had she known him better would have told her they had a lot more negotiating ahead of them.

Chapter Six

Kevin Dane Olsen's charm and enthusiasm had carried him far in the relatively short time since he'd arrived in Hollywood. He swam gracefully through the shark-infested waters of the movie industry, shrugging off the snubs and putdowns with the air of a man who was utterly sure of himself. As the first-born, only son of a wealthy, socially prominent family from the Chicago suburb of Winnetka, Kevin Olsen had learned early in life that all he had to do was make the effort. The rest fell easily into place.

A natural athlete, Kevin learned to ski at Vail, where his family spent a week each winter. He was one of the stars of his country club tennis team, and played hockey in high school well enough to earn a letter. But he also had the brains and the marks to get accepted at Dartmouth College. After that, it would be on to business school, in preparation for his rightful place in his father's company, the Metropolitan Paper Corporation. But in his sophomore year at Dartmouth, Kevin took a course in filmmaking. By the end of the semester, he was hooked on the movie business.

He had no interest in acting, he told his father; he wanted to make movies. But he wanted to make money, too. He could go out west and starve, he supposed, but with a degree from Columbia Film School under his belt, he was sure he could make it in Hollywood.

Though John Olsen was less certain, he knew better than to fight with his son, who had inherited his own determination and obstinance. Convinced that Kevin would eventually give up on the highly competitive film industry, he staked him to two years at graduate school. Afterwards, he even used his connections to help Kevin get a job in Hollywood as junior assistant and general gofer with Diamond Pictures.

The California life suited Kevin very well. The weather was great, the girls were gorgeous, and the work was easy. Kevin's good looks, high spirits, and excellent tennis game were in great demand.

But after a couple of years he knew that his job was a dead end. He needed an "opportunity." In Hollywood that meant a relatively decent script and some cheap financing. His father had the money, but his father had helped him enough, he decided.

And then, opportunity knocked in the person of Elliot Reams, one of his pals from the country club tennis team. Elliot had always had more money than any of the other guys—and now he was looking for an interesting way to spend it.

"Making movies takes a lot of money, Elliot," Kevin said.

"You find me the scripts and make the movies. I'll put up the money. We'll split the profits seventy-thirty."

"Make it sixty-forty and you got yourself a deal," Kevin declared.

"Sixty-forty and get me a date for tomorrow night," was Elliot Reams's counter-offer.

"Okay," said Kevin.

They were in business.

The arrangement suited both of them. Kevin did all the

work. Elliot had the title and the girls. Despite the risk fac-
tor, Kevin was convinced that leaving his job at Diamond
was a chance he had to take. He always played his
hunches—and his hunches were almost never wrong.

This one proved to be better than most. Their first film
was a smash. Kevin and Elliot were the talk of the industry.
They were besieged with offers of scripts, money, deals,
drugs, and girls.

Elliot joined the party circuit.

"Just give me girls and grass," he told his new acquaintances.

Kevin, too, got caught up in the whirl. Eventually, he fell
in love with a beautiful actress, Eileen Emory, who was
starring in his new film. The marriage was doomed from the
beginning. Eileen insisted on buying and redecorating a
house in Beverly Hills. The bills for her clothes, furs, and
makeup fell on his desk like a storm. He vied for time with
her hairdresser, agent, and exercise consultant. When he
came home at night, the house was filled with people he
didn't know, snorting cocaine and drinking champagne.

After six months, he moved out. Eileen let him off the
hook moneywise. The movie had made her a star. That was
enough.

A year after that, Eileen married Elliot Reams. Kevin
laughed when he got the wedding invitation. He sent them a
Steuben crystal bowl (big enough, he figured, to hold all
their cocaine), and called his laywer about dissolving his
partnership. Thanks to Elliot Reams, he'd made enough
money to finance his films himself.

He also decided his lifestyle could bear with some radical
surgery. He bought a small house in Malibu, stopped dating
starlets, and stayed home more than he went out. When he
went for his annual physical, his doctor suggested he get
more exercise.

Aspen, he decided. It would be good to get away, and he
missed the winters of his childhood.

The snow on his face felt great, and the little town reminded him of his boyhood vacations. In a matter of days, he
felt rejuvenated. One stormy afternoon, he wandered into a
real estate office and asked to be shown some properties.

When he saw the house on top of Red Mountain, he knew he was home.

When he saw Alahna at the Primrose Drugstore, he was sure that he'd seen her before. She was a sensational-looking woman—*and* she read the *Wall Street Journal!* Here was someone he wanted to find out about.

Aspen was a small town. Whoever she was, she wouldn't get lost in the crowd.

He spotted her flying down Ruthie's Run as if she were possessed. By the time she stopped for lunch, Kevin was feeling as though he were in a chase scene out of one of his movies. When he finally got her to accept his dinner invitation, he felt as if he'd put on an Oscar-award winning performance.

There was no doubt about it. The lady was a tough sell! And she was one hell of a skier. Driving up the mountain after an afternoon of trying to keep up with her, he considered what else he'd found out.

Her name was Alahna. That's all she would tell him.

"You promised, remember?" she'd said with her slight foreign accent. "No questions."

His Mexican houseman, Charlie, suggested lobster and chocolate mousse.

"Okay, Charlie, but make it extra special. This is top drawer tonight."

She was already outside, waiting for him on the front steps of the Aspen Inn when he pulled up in his yellow Jeep. Dressed in a silver fox jacket over a pair of jeans tucked into red cowboy boots, she looked sensational. As he jumped out of the car to get the door for her, he felt like a kid on a date with the prom queen. This time he had lucked into something out of the ordinary.

"Listen," he said, wheeling the Jeep around to head back up Red Mountain, "don't get the wrong idea, but I thought we'd eat at my place."

"Wait a minute," Alahna began.

"It's not what you think," Kevin assured her. "Charlie, the fellow who works for me, serves the best food in town. I promise, I'm a man of honor. Hey, that was some fantastic skiing we did this afternoon, wasn't it?"

The man was sincere, Alahna decided. With those freckles and that grin, he simply didn't look like someone who would try to rip off her clothes and rape her. He had a certain boyish charm that she was finding very appealing.

"Okay, here we are," Kevin said, pulling in front of a white stucco house at the end of a cul-de-sac. "Modest, but we like it."

"We?" Alahna asked, as he opened the door for her.

"Charlie and I. He takes good care of me and my guests. Right now he's in the kitchen, preparing his sensational lobster and wild rice. Do you like lobster?"

"Mmm, I love it," Alahna said.

"Terrific. Follow me then, please."

Kevin led her into a large room, all windows and skylights. A fire was blazing in the fireplace pit in the middle of the room. With a pang of sadness, Alahna remembered the fireplace in Madeleine's chalet.

As she made herself comfortable among the fur-covered cushions, memories of her recent St. Moritz vacation flashed before her. She leaned forward, pretending to warm her hands, so that Kevin wouldn't see the tears that filled her eyes.

No! She rebuked herself. Today was all that mattered. For the time being, she must put her old life behind her.

"Here you go."

Kevin handed her a glass of wine. "How about some vegetables and Charlie's caviar dip to munch on until dinner's ready?"

He settled himself next to her. "Nice, isn't it? I fell in love with the place as soon as I saw it. So, Alahna, aren't you even going to tell me your last name?"

"You're breaking our deal, Kevin. No questions, remember? I have no yesterday, only a today and possibly tomorrow. But I'd love to hear about you."

"You sure are stubborn, lady. But okay, I stick by my terms. Let's see. I'm single, though I was married a few years back for a very short while to an actress—a mistake I'm never going to repeat."

"Which was the mistake, the marriage or the actress?"

"The actress. She was very pretty, but turned out that was

all she had going for her. After a couple of months the
novelty of staring at her face wore off, and we had nothing
to talk about. The divorce was no big trauma, no hard feelings, not even when she married my former business
partner. As far as that goes, I'm more on the business side of
films than the creative end. I love my work, and I'm damn
good at it. But I like to get away from Hollywood when I
can. Aspen keeps me and my perspective in good shape."

"Tell me about some of the movies you've produced. I
wonder whether I've seen any of them."

"Do you go to a lot of movies? Whoops, sorry, no questions. Well, I started out small—low-budget scripts and
locations. My first one—sure does feel like a long time
ago—was *Moonbaby*. You missed that one? You're lucky. No
Oscars, but it made me a small pile of money. You might
have heard of *Pot of Gold*. It wasn't, but it won all the
awards. My latest, and I'm pretty proud of it, too, is *Living
Arrangements*."

"We saw that," Alahna exclaimed excitedly. "We were
invited to a screening a couple of weeks ago in New York.
We loved it!"

"Oh yeah?" Kevin said casually. "Who'd you go with?"

Alahna blushed. "I feel a bit silly," she said. "Believe me,
Kevin, I'm not trying to play coy. I have my reasons, good
reasons, for wanting to guard my privacy. Nothing shoddy
or criminal, I promise you. Can you accept that?"

"Of course," Kevin replied. "Let me do the talking. All
my friends would tell you I'm a regular motormouth. Just
know that if you do want to tell me anything more, I'm
ready to listen."

"Thanks, I appreciate that."

"Here's dinner," Kevin said, grateful for the distraction as
Charlie rolled in a wagon laden with trays of lobster, wild
rice, and steamed vegetables.

"You weren't exaggerating," Alahna said when Charlie
reappeared to clear away their plates and serve coffee. "I've
loved the dinner. Charlie, that dessert looks sinfully delicious."

Spooning up the last of the mousse, Alahna felt as if she

were caught in a spell. Was this magic a nightly occurrence, because of Kevin's charm and the dramatic setting of his home—something that happened every time he brought a lady back to dinner?

Or was she right in sensing a special connection being forged between the two of them? She half-hoped that Kevin would take her in his arms and make love to her, make her forget everything except the two of them and this night.

Instead he said, "My pretty lady, if you and I are going to burn up a mountain tomorrow, you need to get some sleep. It pains me to call it a night, but I'd better get you back to the hotel."

The disappointment showed momentarily on her face, and Kevin saw it. But his instincts told him he was right not to press her. Whatever was going on with Alahna—if indeed that was really her name—she was worth waiting for. Watching her relaxed and laughing as they rode down the mountain, Kevin ached to touch her. And if he was not mistaken, she felt similarly. But at the door of her room, he gave her nothing more than a warm, friendly kiss on the cheek.

"Tomorrow at the chairlift? Nine o'clock?"

Alahna nodded, her eyes shining. "Thank you, Kevin. Tonight was wonderful."

"For me, too." He kissed her once more, this time very softly on the lips. "Goodnight, Alahna," he said. "Sleep well."

The next few days passed as in a dream. Alahna relaxed in the warmth of Kevin's attentions. They spent the days skiing in the Colorado sunshine, the nights exploring the town or watching the stars through the skylight of Kevin's living-room after another of Charlie's culinary extravaganzas.

Kevin had never in his life been so happy. But he moved carefully. Alahna was like a deer in the forest. A false move or loud noise might scare her away. At night, after he had left her at her hotel, he fantasized about what it would be like to make love to her. What he would do to her and with her. How she would feel.

But he bided his time, sensing that when she was ready,

she would give him a signal. In the meantime, although he kept his promise not to ask her questions, he was learning more about her.

The stories spilled out of her. Stories about her childhood in Hong Kong, the only daughter of a father who obviously doted on her. About her mother, who had died when Alahna was very young.

"I was brought up by my Chinese aunt. And I played with my cousins. But mostly I spent time with my father. He taught me a great deal about business."

"But you speak English so well, like a native really," Kevin said.

"Yes, of course, because my father . . . well, I spent some years in England when I was older."

She smiled in that special way that meant "I'm sorry, I can't say more," and this time he couldn't help himself. He reached over and brushed his lips over her dimples.

"You're enchanting," he said. "No matter who you are."

She felt dizzy with desire for him. Since that first night, when he'd entertained her with his droll tales of Hollywood, she'd wanted to make love with him. He'd made her forget the difficulties of the last few months.

Was this what it was like to fall in love? She wondered. It had been such a long time since she'd learned to love Dolph, she could hardly remember. And why hadn't he invited her into his bed?

She knew he wanted to. Finally, on one of their nightly strolls through town, in the forthright manner that Dolph had taught her, she asked him.

"I guess you've figured out how special you are to me, Alahna," Kevin said, choosing his words carefully. "Almost from the moment I laid eyes on you, I knew you were the woman I've been waiting for. It was love at first sight, no doubt about it. But I sensed that you were easily scared off, so I decided to be patient, because when I take you in my arms, I want you to feel as if you can't wait another second to have me. I want to hold you, Alahna. I want to put my head on your breasts, feel the soft velvet back of your neck, touch and kiss every inch of your body. I've been imagining how it would feel since the first night we spent together, but it can only happen when you're ready."

"Kevin, I owe you an explanation. It's rather a long story, and some of it is rather painful for me. In fact, I hardly know where to begin. I certainly don't know where it will end. Hold my hand and let's walk," she laughed weakly, "and I'll answer all the questions you've been so good about not asking me."

The snow was falling more heavily now as the storm began to intensify. Alahna and Kevin walked in silence, wandering past the boutique windows filled with expensive, one-of-a-kind sweaters, scarves, pieces of pottery, handmade jewelry.

Rather than speak, they pretended to look at the colorful displays, designed to tempt the free-spending tourists who usually thronged the shops. But tonight the streets were quiet. Only their muffled footsteps echoed through the winter snowscape.

They paused in front of a store done up to look like a gingerbread house.

"Gingerbread Jewelers," read the sign on the door. "Gold and silver artisans."

"Say the word and it's yours," Kevin said, squeezing her hand. "What's your pleasure? A silver bracelet? A necklace made of gold and rubies and diamonds?"

"Oh, Kevin," Alahna said, turning to look into his eyes.

And then she stared into another, more familiar pair of eyes.

"I hope you're not planning to buy the lady a ring, because she already owns one," said Dolph, appearing like a spirit in the night.

"Hey, buddy, who the hell are you?" Kevin angrily demanded.

But Alahna quickly responded before Kevin could say anything else.

"I should have known you would hunt me down, Dolph," she was saying. "I'm amazed it took you so long."

"Alahna, who is this guy?" Kevin asked. "Mister, why don't you disappear? The lady's with me."

"I can see that," Dolph said calmly, "but unfortunately for you, the lady belongs to me. Isn't that right, Alahna?"

Alahna nodded faintly, wishing she were any place but right here. She huddled closer to Kevin, as if to protect herself, as Dolph went on, unperturbed.

"I knew you needed a few days rest. I wanted you to have some playtime, and I'm glad to see that you've found yourself an agreeable companion. But there's something we need to discuss, Alahna. My car is parked just up the street. I suggest we get inside, where it's warm and we'll be more comfortable."

"We have other plans for this evening," Kevin objected, reaching for Alahna's arm.

But Alahna, feeling the force of Dolph's fury, weakly shook him off and followed her husband to the waiting rented limousine, so incongruous in the laidback mountain atmosphere.

Kevin also couldn't help but follow, gripped by the strange dream in which he seemed to be playing a featured role.

Dolph opened the back door and motioned Alahna to get in.

"Would you like to join her, Mr. Olsen?" he said. "I'll sit up front."

How did this guy know his name? Kevin wondered. And what game was he playing? And most importantly, what the hell had he meant when he'd said Alahna belonged to him?

The silence in the car hung about them like a heavy velvet curtain as Dolph sat alone in the driver's seat.

Finally, staring at them through the rearview mirror, Dolph began to address Kevin in a tight, controlled voice.

"You have captured a very rare prize, Mr. Olsen. Alahna is like an exotic musical instrument. When properly played by skilled, knowledgeable fingers, she is capable of offering almost limitless pleasures. However, since she's used only to the very best, I would like to share with you some of the knowledge I've acquired over the years about how to bring forth her finest qualities."

Kevin knew he should interrupt, object, open the door and get out. But the scene was strangely compelling, and he stayed where he was, waiting to see what would happen next.

Alahna looked like a figure carved from stone, incapable
of speech. She hardly dared breathe, for fear of unleashing
Dolph's wrath. She knew her crime. For the first time in sixteen years of marriage, she had defied her husband. Had
Dolph selected Kevin as a candidate for Project US it would
have been fine. But this was Alahna's choice and wasn't
within Dolph's control. He had to fight to regain his power
by taking charge of this liaison.

Huddled in the spacious backseat of the limousine as if it
were her refuge, she couldn't even glance at Kevin to see his
reaction.

"Ah, yes," Dolph was saying to him now, "why don't you
reach over and touch her hand? After all, isn't that what a
lover should do? You are her lover, aren't you, Mr. Olsen? I
certainly hope so. My Alahna is not used to being neglected.
Touch her, do you hear me?" Dolph commanded. "Turn her
hand upward and stroke it with yours. Let the heat of your
body flow into hers."

Mesmerized by the force of the man's voice, Kevin
obeyed, and took Alahna's icy cold hand.

"That feels good, doesn't it, Mr. Olsen? Let us continue
with our lesson."

"Dolph, don't do this," Alahna rasped.

"But why not, Alahna? I'm sure Mr. Olsen has no idea of
your potential. I shall show him how to explore and maxim-
ize your abundant talents. But please, relax. Isn't that
always the best way? Let your breath warm Alahna's ear.
Very lightly run your tongue around its softness. Now lick
her lovely neck ever so gently.

"Now kiss her throat. Can you feel her pulse throbbing?
I'm sure you can. And now take your other hand and feel
beneath her sweater for the softness of her beautiful breasts.
So lovely and round, aren't they? Though I'm not touching
them myself, I can feel them in my mind. Once a man has
touched Alahna's breasts, he could never forget them, don't
you think?"

Mechanically following Dolph's instructions, Kevin was
beyond thinking. All he knew was that Alahna, warm
beneath his probing fingers, was allowing him to touch her.

"Yes, unbutton her skirt, but slowly, very slowly, continue

to stroke her breasts. Now move your hand down and caress her belly, until you find the crease between her thighs. There, yes, now move your fingers gently into the little folds. Stroke her, yes, stroke her, so very softly. Do you feel that tender flesh? Touch her there again and again. She likes that, Mr. Olsen, she likes that very much.

"Rub your hand across her curly black patch of hair. She's trembling now, isn't she? You have such power over her. Use that power, Mr. Olsen. Search beneath the hair, explore her with your fingers. Find her greedy little clit. Touch her there softly. Touch her more. She wants more. You feel how much she wants it, don't you? And now bring your face down to suck her. Your tongue loves her wetness."

Utterly seduced by the power of Dolph's voice, Alahna writhed beneath Kevin's hungry touch, her body begging him to continue, to release her, to bring her to completion.

"Now you may enter her," Dolph went on in the same flat tone. "Now, Mr. Olsen . . . right now."

Kevin clumsily pushed his pants to his knees and knelt before Alahna. He thrust himself into her once, twice, then groaned with relief as he brought them both to a violent, shuddering climax.

Alahna's haunting scream hung in the silence that followed, broken only by Kevin's hoarse breathing and the sound of Dolph, striking a match to light a cigarette.

"My God in heaven," Kevin whispered finally, "who are you?"

"Her husband," said Dolph.

Chapter Seven

Alahna had only the dimmest memories of what had happened next that night. A vague recollection of Kevin, humiliated, mumbling an apology and slamming the car door as he left. The even hazier recollection of Dolph, suddenly full of remorse, climbing into the seat next to her, trying to take her in his arms, trying to calm her piteous sobs.

Had she told him then that she wanted to die? That he

had shamed her beyond anything she ever could have imagined? That she didn't know whether she could ever find it
in her heart to forgive him?

Or did those thoughts come together for her only later,
when she was back in New York, calmer, more rational. But
angry, still very, very angry. And absolutely at a loss as to
how she could reconcile Dolph, the man she loved, with the
man who had turned into the bizarre stranger who used his
will against her.

For the first time since her father's death, when she had
needed to be alone to mourn, she slept alone again, locking
the door to their bedroom, incapable of sharing a bed with
her husband.

Perhaps, had she been able to forgive him, the bitterness
might not have developed between them. But accustomed to
being treated with only love and tenderness, Alahna was at
a loss to make sense of his behavior. Her anger fed Dolph's.
Two stubborn, iron-willed people, they felt they had no
choice but to go their separate ways.

Ever disciplined, however, when it came to their work,
they resumed business as usual at Shawak International.
They kept to their old routines. When they needed to
confer, they communicated through Ace. Alahna missed
their nightly conversations, but she couldn't bring herself to
approach Dolph. She wasn't ready to break the invisible
wall that had been erected between them.

Ace knew something was amiss. But he kept his distance,
assuming that Dolph and Alahna would eventually work
things out for themselves. In the meantime, Alahna had
thrown herself into work with an intensity that was unusual
even for her. Most evenings she stayed home with Meilee,
chatting or reading.

Sometimes she could hear Dolph in the library, playing
his piano. More often, he was away for days at a time. She
had no idea where he went. She told herself she didn't care.

When they happened to run into each other at the office
or coming and going at home, they were polite, but distant.
A deep, deep fissure had been torn in the fabric of their
marriage, and neither of them knew how to mend it.

One rainy Sunday evening in April, Jeff appeared at the

door.

"Long time no see, baby," he said, greeting her with his usual bear hug and kiss. "How the hell are you two? I haven't heard a word from Dolph in—yeah, it's months—not since we left St. Moritz. So what's happening?"

"Oh, Jeff, I'm so happy to see you," Alahna said. "I was just this minute wandering around the apartment, trying to decide how to entertain myself tonight. You're the answer to a girl's prayers."

"Where's Dolph? Out of town again? Doesn't that man ever stay home with his gorgeous wife? Hey . . . Alahna, did I say something wrong? Why are you crying?"

"Long story, Jeff. Come on in. I'll give you a drink. Perhaps you can give me a shoulder to cry on and some advice."

"Sure, baby. But what a bummer that Dolph's not here. I had a great idea for the two of us, and I was really hoping to rap with him about it." He grinned mischievously. "That's my alibi, anyway. And now I have you all to myself."

Alahna smiled wanly. "Scotch, isn't it? On the rocks?"

"You got it, sweetheart."

He held up his glass and clicked it against hers.

"To old friends, Alahna."

"To old friends," Alahna echoed him.

"We sure do go back a long way, don't we?" Jeff stared into the fire. "So what's making you look so blue? Tell Uncle Jeff and I'll kiss it better for you."

"I wish it were that simple, Jeff. But some things you simply can't fix with a kiss or a hug."

"Oh, yeah? Name one, and while you're thinking, pour me another drink. I've been freezing ever since I got off the plane. This stuff warms the old bones."

"Why don't you move closer to the fire? Here, share this pillow with me."

They sipped their drinks in comfortable silence, watching the logs burn down. Grateful for Jeff's company, Alahna realized with a jolt how deprived she'd felt without close male companionship.

"Jeff," she said suddenly, "you know that Dolph and I

don't believe that marriage means we can't sleep with anyone else. How is it that you and I have never been lovers?"

Momentarily taken aback, Jeff quickly recovered and
laughed his big, hearty laugh.

"Now, that's a damned good question, isn't it? What are
you getting at, Alahna? Did you and Dolph have a fight and
you want to get back at him by sleeping with his best
friend?"

"Not at all," Alahna lied. "Why, you know very well that
at this very moment he's probably in someone else's bed, and
I don't mind in the least. But of course, if you don't want to
sleep with me. . . ."

"Alahna, stop teasing me. You know I'm one of your
greatest fans. If you want me to make love to you, honey,
all you have to do is snap your fingers and I'll come running."

"I'm not teasing, Jeff." She snapped her fingers. "All right.
Now it's up to you."

Jeff searched her face. "Talk about an offer a man can't
refuse," he said at last, kissing her gently on the lips.
"Mmm, don't you taste good, honey." He put his arm
around her and said, "You know, baby, this has gotta be my
lucky night."

"Come upstairs," Alahna whispered shakily, and Jeff followed her silently to her bedroom.

Locking the door, Alahna unwrapped the sash from her
tiny waist, and slipped off her white silk kimono.

"Oh, baby," Jeff said hoarsely, taking her in his arms,
"you feel like silk."

Alahna tore at the buttons on his shirt, impatient to feel
his skin against hers, and Jeff pulled off his trousers.

"Look what you've done to me," he laughed, pointing to
the bulge that swelled beneath his underpants.

He scooped her up gently and deposited her on the bed,
then cradled her in his arms as he began to kiss her face and
body.

If Jeff sensed her urgency, he ignored it. He was an expert
lover, who knew how to set the pace, tormenting her with
his fingers, tongue and lips, growling his pleasure with her
body and the way she was touching him.

Finally, he gave in to her pleas and entered her, thrusting himself deeper and deeper, bringing her closer and closer to the edge. She clung to him, moving with him, feeling as if bolts of electricity were pulsing between them.

They lost control at the same moment, coming together with loud cries and shuddering gasps and waves of relief that seemed to go on forever.

Afterwards, they clung to each other in silence, neither of them yet ready to let go.

It had felt so good, so right, Alahna thought, to fall into Jeff's arms, to be made love to by him.

What had motivated her? She wondered quietly. A need to be close to a man she cared about? Sheer lust? Or was it revenge?

Jeff brushed away a strand of hair that had fallen across her forehead. "Hey, baby, come back. That was terrific."

"For me, too." Alahna said.

"Alahna, I have to ask you something."

"Yes?"

"How about we raid your refrigerator, open a bottle of champagne, and celebrate another milestone in our friendship?"

Alahna sat up and nodded. She was hungry. And she had no regrets about what she had just done, she told herself. Hadn't Dolph always told her that she was sexually free? But one question echoed repeatedly in her mind: Why?

She never had a moment's doubt about the exact instant her child was conceived. The fact that she missed her period didn't surprise her in the least. What did come as a shock was how she felt about the child she was carrying.

Suddenly she understood the fierce love and devotion that mothers felt for their children. The child might not be the genetically perfect son or daughter of Dolph Robicheck's dreams. But this was her child. And it didn't matter to her in the slightest what its talents or abilities were, or whether it was white or black or brown or any shade in between.

She tossed and turned at night, worrying about Dolph's reaction. He had wanted a child so badly. Now she could give him one. But it was a child conceived by her own design, independent of his well-intentioned plans.

Could Dolph accept that fact?

She hated the cold war that existed between them, hated their chilly formality, their lack of physical and emotional contact. Pregnant, she especially needed his support and comfort. But in the three months since he had tracked her to Aspen, she seemed to have lost the words to tell him that.

One other person knew her secret. Meilee guessed she was pregnant even before her doctor confirmed that it was so. Usually reluctant to interfere between husband and wife, Meilee finally broke her silence.

"So I shall be a grandmother, after all," she said calmly as she and Alahna shared a late afternoon pot of tea. "I am very pleased, my child. Are you happy?"

"How did you know, Meilee?" Alahna asked in amazement.

"Years of experience and observation," Meilee chuckled. "Of you and your mother, and so many other women. Whose baby are you carrying, Alahna? I understood that you and Dolph had given up the search for a suitable natural father."

Alahna studied the leaves at the bottom of her cup, as if hoping to find there the answers to her problems.

"I'll tell you, Meilee, of course. But Dolph mustn't know."

"Don't be foolish, child. You must tell him. He'll see it with his own eyes before too long, anyway. If you take after your mother, you'll be showing by the end of your third month. How do you propose to keep it a secret then?"

Alahna shook her head miserably.

"Listen to me, Alahna," Meilee said sternly. "I've kept my peace long enough, hoping and praying that you two would get over this terrible rift. I don't know what happened to cause such bitterness. But I beg you, for the sake of this child, heal your differences."

"Oh, Meilee," Alahna began, and then burst into tears.

"My sweet baby, don't worry," Meilee crooned, rocking her in her arms as she had done so often when Alahna was a child. "It will all work out, have faith, my darling, it will all work out."

When she had calmed down enough to speak, Alahna

said, "It was Jeff, Meilee. Jeff is the father."

"Why, how wonderful!" Meilee exclaimed. "Jeff is a marvelous friend and a very good man. Do you honestly believe that Dolph will be anything but pleased?"

"I'm really not sure," said Alahna, for the first time voicing her worries aloud. "Sometimes Dolph is the kindest, most understanding man I know. But he's human, which means he's not perfect, although," she smiled, "it took me many years to realize that. Having a child was his idea. When I said no, I didn't want to try anymore, I defied him and so he hurt me back. Now I'm terrified that he'll see my becoming pregnant as another show of anger and defiance. Even if the father is one of his closest friends."

"Was it defiance?" asked Meilee gently.

Alahna's eyes filled again with tears. "I don't know . . . I honestly don't know."

"Then perhaps the better question is, does it matter? Listen to me, Alahna," she said briskly, "Let's be practical. What the gods have in store for you will become clear in time. For now, you must take very good care of yourself and think happy thoughts about the safe future of your child. And," she said teasingly, "you must let me come with you for your maternity clothes. Yes?"

"Yes, yes," Alahna laughed. "Meilee, what would I do without you?"

"The very question your father often asked me. Fortunately, I've no intention of giving you the opportunity to find out."

When the changes in her body were becoming too obvious to ignore, Alahna took a deep breath, counted to ten, and knocked on the door to Dolph's study.

"Come in," Dolph called.

"Alahna . . ." he said, surprised to see her.

"I . . . I hope I'm not disturbing you. . . ."

"No, not at all," he said politely. "Please, sit down."

"Dolph," Alahna began. "Oh, Dolph, this feels so strange. I hate what's happened to us, I feel as if we've become strangers. Look," she held out her hands. "I'm shaking with nervousness. How did we ever let it get to this?"

"Stupidity and stubbornness," Dolph said, getting up to join her on the couch. "I admire your courage, Alahna, for coming in here. You're right. This has gone on for far too long."

"Yes, it has. I've missed you so much, Dolph, and," she said, her voice faltering, "now there's another reason why we have to try to mend the broken parts of our lives."

"What is it, Alahna? What's wrong? You're not ill, are you?"

"No, no, it's nothing like that." Alahna was relieved to see the concern and love in his eyes. "No, it's that . . . I'm going to have a baby, Dolph."

"A baby? How do you know? Are you sure?"

"It wasn't difficult to figure out. And I had a blood test. Dolph, I know this is a shock . . . but . . . please, be happy about it, Dolph," she pleaded. "I need you to be happy with me."

Dolph stood up and began to pace nervously. "I assume the fellow from Aspen is the father."

"No," Alahna said quietly.

Dolph stopped suddenly. "Who is then?"

"Jeff."

"Jeff Gotley?"

She nodded, not trusting herself to speak.

He turned and faced her, his face drained of color. Suddenly, he looked like an old man.

"Did you do this to get your revenge, Alahna? To repay one act of humiliation with another? Did you stop even for a moment to consider the consequences?"

"You wanted a child, Dolph. Jeff is one of our dearest friends. You've told me again and again how much you love him, what a fine human being he is."

"He's black, Alahna. This baby you're carrying will be half-black. Are you prepared to saddle your child with that burden? How could you be that selfish?"

"Selfish?" Alahna's voice rose in anger. "Selfish? Is it an act of selfishness to decide to love and nurture the child I conceived? Does it really matter so much what my motives were? What about your motives that night in Aspen? Did you stop and consider those consequences? And while we're at it, what about me? What about the fact that I'm only half-white? Did you have to force yourself to accept my Chinese blood? We've never really gotten into that, have we?"

"Alahna . . ."

"No! Let me finish! We both know why we never talked about my mother. My father warned me not to raise the subject with you. But you've always known, haven't you, Dolph? You've always known that Ohna was my mother. Ohna . . . you were her lover, weren't you?'

She stood up and crossed the room, then turned back to face him. "I know that you and Salah meant only the best for me," she said, calmer now. "But perhaps all the evasions and half-truths have finally caught up with us. Think about it, Dolph."

The door shut behind her with a dull thud that echoed in Dolph's ears. He looked around the room, staring blankly into the shadowy corners, as if searching for an answer to Alahna's angry accusations. But all he found there were memories—and more questions.

He shook his head wearily, knowing he should go after her, try to talk to her. Tell her he was sorry, that he had spoken in haste. Instead, worn out with emotion, too exhausted to move, he sat down heavily and cradled his head in his arms.

Alahna had said she wanted to try to put the pieces back together.

Never, he thought, *it was too late.*

Chapter Eight

"You know where he is, Ace, don't you?" Alahna said.

Ever since the other morning, when Dolph had phoned him at six A.M. to say he was off to Indonesia, Ace had been waiting for Alahna's question. He'd been wondering what he would tell her. Now he fidgeted with the papers on his desk, for once lacking a glib answer to smooth things over.

For the last several months, he'd felt caught in the

middle. He knew that Alahna and Dolph were having problems. He even had a pretty good idea what those problems
were about.

It was a damned shame, he'd told Jana again and again.
Two people who loved each other so much. What could
have gone wrong? But he was paid a lot of money to do his
work and not pry into their private business, so he'd kept his
mouth shut, hoping they would come to their senses.

It was nothing new or unusual for Dolph to go off by himself. But he'd made such a point this time of insisting that
nobody try to get in touch with him.

"Especially," he'd said, a little uncomfortably, Ace had
thought, "not Alahna."

"What if we need you?" Ace had asked.

"In case of emergency—and I do mean emergency,"
Dolph had said emphatically, "you can leave word with
Greg Andrews. I'll check in with him every once in a
while."

"He wrote me a letter," Alahna was saying now, holding
up a couple of sheets of paper, as if Ace needed to see the
evidence. "He must have mailed it from the airport. I'm not
to try to contact him—and he says he left you the same
instructions."

Ace shrugged his shoulders. "You know how he is," he said
unhappily. "Leave it alone, Alahna."

"But you do know where he is, don't you?" Alahna asked
sharply. Suddenly she slumped down in one of the leather
armchairs. "I'm sorry, Ace. I shouldn't give you a hard
time. You're only doing what you have to do. It's just
that—"

Her voice broke and she covered her eyes with her hand.
"Excuse me, please," she said after a moment or two and
abruptly left the room.

Back in the privacy of her office, Alahna read Dolph's
letter for the third time. She almost had it memorized.

"Beloved," Dolph had written, "you are my dearest treasure, and you have devoted your life to pleasing me. Now the
time has come for you to please yourself by moving forward
without me.

"Please believe me, Alahna, it's not that I can't accept a

child of mixed blood. I know that's how it sounded, because my anger, born out of hurt pride, erupted as prejudice.

"Of course, I've always known that Ohna was your mother. How privileged I have been to have loved you both! But I never actually faced that fact directly. When we quarreled tonight, I finally confronted the truth, and in so doing, I have had to face other, more difficult truths about our marriage.

"We have always said that age is merely a number. But I see now how wrong I've been. Age is a reality, a fact of life. Another fact of life is that your child deserves a father who is young and vital, someone you can count on, as much as anyone can be counted on, to be present while your child is growing up.

"I am also writing to Kevin Olsen, not only because I owe him the deepest of apologies, but because I want to share these thoughts with him.

"Please, don't think that I'm turning my back on you out of anger or jealousy. Know that I am doing what I feel in my heart is best for you. Dolph."

His words were only now, gradually, beginning to sink in. Alahna could imagine him after she had left the room, her angry words still hanging in the air. He must have reviewed the whole situation, adding the announcement of her pregnancy to all the other data he had been accumulating. And somehow, out of the tangled mess of their disappointments and hurt feelings, he had arrived at this conclusion: That if he were to remove himself from the picture, Kevin Olsen would move right in to take his place.

Oh, Dolph, she thought angrily, *you still haven't learned, have you, that life isn't all black and white? How typical of you to have considered all the possibilities and decided what was right for me. Dammit, Dolph! If only you had talked to me. You could have asked me what I wanted! But that's not your style.*

It never had been.

The phone rang, jolting her back to reality. Her intercom buzzed sharply.

"Meg," she said with a sigh of annoyance, "hold all my calls, please. No matter who or what."

"Alahna, this man is very insistent. His name is Kevin Olsen and—'"

Kevin! Already?

"Meg, this is very important. Make sure I'm not disturbed."

"Kevin?" her voice trembled.

"Alahna, do you have any idea how the hell nervous I am at this moment?"

"Me, too," she said. "You got the letter, didn't you?"

"Yes."

"I have a fairly good idea of its contents," she said, twisting the cord around her finger. "My husband has a rather exaggerated view of my charms. He expects that any man will simply come running into my arms—"

"Yeah," Kevin interrupted her, "I never thought I'd agree with that guy, but this time I think he's right. Hell, why are we doing this on the telephone? I'll grab the company plane and be in New York tonight."

"What?" Her head was aching so that she could hardly follow him. All she wanted to do was lie down and pull the covers over her head, just to escape from everything.

"I'll be at your place around eight. I can't wait to see you. And Alahna?"

"Yes?" she said, not sure whether she was going to laugh or cry.

"I've missed you."

Kevin had done his homework about the mysterious Robichecks. Despite their extraordinary wealth and power, they were very private people. Yet everyone seemed to know them.

"Brilliant . . . terribly attractive . . . he seems to pull the strings, but she certainly has built a brilliant career . . . very generous to all sorts of charities, though they'd be the last to tell you . . . so interesting . . . their home? magnificent, simply magnificent. . . ."

Nothing he could dig up fit his memory of the Dolph Robicheck who had appeared out of the storm that night in Aspen. The Dolph Robicheck he had encountered could have been the devil himself, urging Kevin to partake of the devil's own brew—a pleasure too sweet and tantalizing to resist.

The vivid memory of that night had remained with him, a memory too haunting to erase from his mind. A thousand times he'd asked himself why he had dumbly followed Alahna into the back seat of the limousine.

Because all that week he had dreamed of making love to Alahna. And he had been too mesmerized by Dolph Robicheck to give up the chance—even if it was an opportunity that seemed to have been created in hell.

But the devil was not supposed to have regrets. And the letter in his hand sounded genuine.

"Dear Mr. Olsen," it read, "Writing a letter of apology is not meant to be an enjoyable experience. But the burden of my abominable behavior in Aspen is so great that I welcome the relief of confessing my guilt.

"I don't know how much Alahna told you about the events leading up to her decision to go to Aspen. Assuming you are in the dark, I will tell you that we had a terrible misunderstanding—the first in our sixteen years of marriage.

"Alahna had no idea that I was keeping track of what she was doing and whom she was seeing. I convinced myself that I wasn't spying on her, merely watching out for her safety. When your name was reported to me, I had you checked out and discovered that you are a man of estimable qualities and abilities. I am not by nature a jealous husband (quite the contrary, actually). But rather than being happy for Alahna, as I have been in the past, I reacted out of jealousy, like a crazy old man who cannot bear to see his wife with a younger, perhaps more virile man.

"Since that night I have spent many hours thinking about what is best for Alahna. I am therefore releasing her from her obligations to me. By the time you receive this, I will have left New York.

"I hope that you can accept with forgiveness whatever has happened in the past.

"Again, my sincere apologies—

"Yours, Dolph Robicheck"

Riding in the elevator to Alahna's apartment, Kevin

wished he could have met Dolph Robicheck under different circumstances. By all accounts, he was an extraordinary man.

He rang the doorbell, impatient to be face-to-face again with this woman who had fascinated him from the moment he first saw her in Monte Carlo. He'd felt the attraction between them that had pulled him to her, despite her reluctance. As the door swung open, his first impulse was to hold her. But he checked himself, uncertain of what her reaction would be.

She looked different. A little more fragile. Suddenly he couldn't help himself, and he took her in his arms.

"Oh, Kevin," Alahna said.

They stared at each other, too uncomfortable to speak.

Following her through the foyer, Kevin almost whistled aloud. "And I thought I had a palace! This is some place you have here."

But once they were alone in her sitting room, he felt unsure of himself, of what he wanted to say to her.

"I think I have a lot of explaining to do," Alahna began, sounding as awkward as he felt.

"Alahna," he said, "whatever you're about to tell me, I want you to know that I had to see you again. Ever since that terrible night in Aspen, I've been fighting the impulse to call you. I'd give anything to be able to undo what happened between us in the car—"

"Kevin—" Alahna said miserably.

"No, no, let me finish. I haven't stopped thinking about you and I want you to know how important you are to me. I'm here for you, Alahna. I want to be your friend. Hell," he said, laughing weakly, "I want to be a great deal more than your friend. But for God's sake, please tell me what this is all about."

"It's a long story," Alahna said.

"Hell, that's okay." He settled himself on the couch. "I have all the time in the world, and there's nothing I'd rather do than sit here and listen to you."

She began slowly, telling him all about her childhood in Hong Kong.

"You're Salah Shawak's daughter?" Kevin exclaimed.

"Quite a man! I almost did a movie about him a few years back. Well, now the pieces begin to fall into place!"

"Wait," she continued, "there's much more."

Kevin kept quiet, only shaking his head from time to time and getting up once to pour himself a drink as Alahna talked about Dolph's insistence that she accept his idea of the shape their marriage should take. Her voice faltered when she explained Dolph's decision to have a child, and his single-minded search for the perfect sperm donor. She painfully recalled the four encounters, each more ridiculous than the last.

"That was when I said no to Dolph for the first time. The next morning I left for Aspen—and you know the rest," she said. "Except for one thing. I'm pregnant."

"But the child? Whose is it?"

Alahna stood up and began to pace the room. "I don't know what came over me, except that Dolph and I were having such a hard time. I was so lonely—he was away a lot and even when he was around, we hardly spoke. One night when Dolph was gone a close friend of ours dropped by, a wonderful man with whom we've shared a lot. It just kind of happened," she said, shrugging her shoulders.

"No, that's not true." She stared defiantly at Kevin. "I made it happen, partly because I needed to be with a loving man that night. Partly," she held her hands out, as if asking forgiveness, "to get revenge. I suppose I knew I might get pregnant. It was the right time of month. And I knew how angry Dolph would be. I had taken matters into my own hands, instead of allowing him to make all the arrangements. I think . . ." her voice faltered, "I think I was also testing him. Jeff—the father—is black. Dolph was looking for perfection. We'd never discussed the fact that I'm half-Chinese. If he couldn't accept a child who was half-black, that would mean he had never really accepted me."

"What did you find out?" Kevin asked gently.

"Oh, Kevin," Alahna said, weeping quietly, "he loves me so much. I should never have doubted that."

"Where do I fit in to all of this?" Kevin said, fearing to hear her answer.

She wiped away her tears and took the handkerchief he

offered her.

"Kevin, I can't deny that I enjoy being with you. Perhaps I love you, but I'm so mixed up that I just don't know. Nothing's clear anymore. What Dolph and I shared was wonderful and special, but the last half year we seem to have lost touch with each other. And now, with the baby coming . . . too much has happened. But I do know that seeing you again makes me feel so happy."

Before she could say another word, Kevin had his arms around her, holding her, kissing her, telling her without words how important she was to him.

Kevin's boyish enthusiasm and charm gave Alahna the emotional nourishment she needed after the loneliness of the last few months. He made her feel like a kid let out of school. Careful, she cautioned herself. You have lots to face ahead. But today, this week, she would indulge herself.

They devoured New York, as if they were discovering it for the very first time. The summer weather was glorious, and they spent hours in Central Park, walking, talking, people-watching. They visited museums and art gallerys, each delighting in the other's enjoyment. In the late evenings, they strolled hand-in-hand through Greenwich Village, stopping to buy pastries and cold drinks at the sidewalk cafes in Little Italy.

Was she falling in love with Kevin? Alahna wondered. Or was he a place to flee to, a refuge from her unhappiness?

He was so much fun. And he had an inner strength and integrity that she found very compelling.

On a sultry August evening, they rode the Staten Island ferry, holding hands as a glowing red and orange sunset enflamed the lower Manhattan skyline. Darkness began to fall like a blue velvet canopy above their heads.

Alahna could feel Kevin's pulse beating beneath her fingers.

She moved closer to him in the dark. "Kevin," she said tremulously, "I think it's time we made love."

They needed to exorcise the past, and lying naked together in bed felt strange at first. But the urgency of their desire pushed them into the present, overcoming the lingering reminders of that other time.

Kevin had business in New York, so he stayed on another week. He rented a suite at the Mayfair Regent Hotel and spent his days there, "financing my new movies, Alahna. It's not glamorous, but I need a lot of room to spread out."

Alahna went back to work, feeling more rested and energized than she had in months. At the end of the day, she found herself looking forward to coming home and spending the evening with Kevin.

Nevertheless, she missed Dolph. She tried not to think about him, but more than once found herself about to walk over to his office. She missed hearing his music fill the apartment, longed to walk into the library and find him seated at the piano.

Sixteen years together, she scolded herself. What did she expect?

Finally Kevin could no longer ignore the frantic phone calls from the studio.

"I'll be back in two weeks," he assured her. "That's a solemn oath. And if you need me sooner, don't hesitate to call. Any time of day or night. Deal?"

"Deal," Alahna said gratefully.

He called her twice during his flight, then again as soon as he landed in L.A. "I miss you already," he said. "Hey, I have a great idea. Why don't you come out here for the weekend?"

"Oh, Kevin, I can't," she groaned. "I've so much work to catch up on. I really need a nice, quiet couple of days at home."

He surprised her, appearing at her door Friday night, a huge bouquet of white roses in his right hand, a gallon of orange juice in the left.

"I know you said you need to work, but I happened to be in the neighborhood," he said. "I would have brought you champagne, but I called a friend of mine who's a gynecologist. He said alcohol for pregnant ladies is out of the question."

He was irresistible, and she told him so.

"I'm sure glad you think so," he grinned. "I knew I was

taking a chance coming by unannounced, but I figured you wouldn't turn away an out-of-town guest."

In fact, he had called Meilee to check that Alahna didn't have plans. He and Meilee had become allies, each sensing how much the other loved Alahna. They had that in common, that and their intense concern for her well-being.

"You are very good for her, Kevin," Meilee said, when they had a moment alone on Sunday afternoon. "I see how her face lights up when you walk into the room. I think she loves you."

"That's exactly what I had in mind," Kevin said. "Meilee, you take care of her this week. I'll be back on Thursday—and every Thursday after that."

Kevin kept his promise. Alahna wondered how he was able to organize his time so that he could spend every weekend with her. "Don't worry, hon," he said in his easygoing way. "So far there haven't been any complaints."

The two of them often spent their hours together working. It was reassuring for Alahna to look up from her papers and see Kevin, in his favorite chair across the room, scowling and biting the tip of his pen. Sometimes he would glance up, catch her gaze, and wink.

"Hungry?" he'd ask.

Kevin loved to cook, and he had taken it upon himself to make sure she ate properly. "I asked my friend the gynecologist, and he said . . ." became his familiar refrain.

They never talked about the future. Kevin sensed that to do so would open up a Pandora's box of questions too complex and painful to answer. Deep in her heart, Alahna still cherished the hope that Dolph would return and that . . . what? She didn't know, and therefore she couldn't fully give herself to Kevin.

"When do we begin our Lamaze classes?" Kevin asked at the beginning of her eighth month.

"You've been talking to your gynecologist friend again. And what do you mean 'we'?"

"Well, who were you planning to have with you in the delivery room? You didn't think I'd let you go through labor alone, did you?"

"Actually, I hadn't given it much thought," Alahna said.

"Don't you think it's about time you did?"

"Would you really be willing to play father to my child—my half-black child?" she asked him.

" 'Be' a father, not 'play' at it, Alahna. And yes, I would. As long as it's your child, it could be born purple and I wouldn't give a damn. By the way," he said casually, "what *about* the baby's father? You said he was a close friend of yours. Where is he in all of this?"

"He doesn't know," Alahna said, nervously clearing her throat. Seeing Kevin's look of astonishment, she explained, "He lives in Los Angeles, and he travels a great deal. He hasn't been back in New York since we . . . since the night the child was conceived. But I don't think he'd be upset," she went on, hoping she was right. "He's not the sort of man who wants to take responsibility for a child."

Kevin insisted that Alahna and Meilee join him for a day of shopping for the baby's layette. His limousine whisked them down to Saks Fifth Avenue, where he astonished the saleswoman by buying every item that took his fancy.

"Twins?" she asked, as he added yet another soft white receiving blanket to the pile that was spilling across the counter.

"I hadn't thought of that," Kevin declared, reaching for another tiny little nightgown.

"Enough, enough," Alahna groaned three hours later, as Kevin was trying to decide between the two top-of-the-line baby carriages.

"Better to be prepared," he said. "You could give birth tomorrow, and then what would you do?"

As it turned out, Alahna went into labor a week ahead of schedule, on a cold Monday in January. Kevin had left early that morning.

"I know you have things to do in L.A.," Alahna told him. "Don't worry. Nobody delivers on time, especially not the first time."

"Okay," Kevin said reluctantly. "But call me if anything happens—anything at all."

Typically, he didn't wait for her call, but telephoned from the plane.

"Oh, shit," he said, "and we haven't even reached

Chicago yet. Listen, honey, I'll take the first flight back as soon as I get to L.A. Try to hold on, okay?"

"Okay," Alahna said, gasping as another contraction began.

Kevin arrived before the baby did and coached her through her last hours of labor.

"Great, you're doing great," he cheered.

"Congratulations," said the doctor a minute later. "It's a boy."

Alahna fell instantly, madly in love with her son.

"He's beautiful," she said. "Look at him, Kevin. Isn't he beautiful? My sweet baby . . . Seth."

"Seth?" asked Kevin.

"In memory of my father . . . Seth Shawak Robicheck. His Hebrew name will be Salah. Kevin, hurry and tell Meilee. She must be so worried. Tell her I'm fine, and that I have a beautiful, healthy son and that I can't wait for her to meet him."

Kevin kissed her and whispered, "I love you, Alahna."

"I love you, Kevin. And thank you for being here."

But as she was being wheeled upstairs to her room, her last thought, just before she drifted into an exhausted sleep was, *"Dolph, where are you? Why haven't I heard from you?"*

Seth Robicheck was one day old when he met his father for the first time. Visiting hours were nearly over when a familiar face appeared at Alahna's door, smiling broadly behind an enormous teddy bear and the biggest bag of popcorn she'd ever seen.

"Congratulations," said Jeff, his large frame seeming to fill the room.

"Jeff!" said the startled Alahna. "When did you get back to town?"

"Just this morning. I called your office, hoping to find either you or Dolph. After getting a runaround from both your secretaries, I decided to drop by and get the real story from Ace. He's a great-looking kid, Alahna."

"Who?"

"Seth, who else? I stopped by the nursery down the hall.

So," he said, settling himself into the chair by her bed and stretching out his long legs, "is there anything you want to tell me?"

She'd been dreading this moment for so long that now she felt almost giddy with the relief of telling Jeff.

"You figured it out," she said quietly, never taking her eyes off him.

"I did my math on the way over here, Alahna. And then I took a long look at him, just to make sure. Why didn't you tell me?"

"I wanted to, Jeff, honestly I did."

"Alahna, every time someone uses that word, 'honestly,' I know there's nothing honest about what I'm about to hear. You really didn't want to tell me, did you? Come clean."

"You're right, Jeff. I should have told you, but Jeff," she said, tears in her eyes, "Dolph and I were in such a muddle . . . so much was happening so quickly. And besides," she said, almost defiantly, "this baby belongs to me. I was afraid, afraid that. . . ," her voice faltered.

"Afraid of what, Alahna? That I would insist on doing the honorable thing and marrying you? Or that I would demand joint custody of the kid?"

"I wasn't thinking very clearly, I suppose," Alahna said wearily.

"How did Dolph react when you gave him the news? Was he pleased? Or is that why he's not here?" Jeff asked, his eyes suddenly flashing anger. "Hey, did he cut out on you because the kid's half black?"

"No, it's much more complicated than that. I don't know what disturbed Dolph more—that I made a couple of my own decisions, without consulting him, or that he had such a hard time adjusting to my having taken matters into my own hands."

Suddenly overwhelmed by how much she needed Dolph, how much she wanted him here with her now, she began to weep uncontrollably. Jeff handed her some tissues and sat quietly, waiting out the storm of emotion. After a bit, when she had calmed down, he said, "You really miss him, don't you, babe? But Ace told me you have a nice guy."

Alahna smiled through her tears and shrugged her

shoulders. "Kevin is a very special man. But I'd give anything in the world to have Dolph here with me right now."

"Well, where the hell is he? Swallow your pride and give him a call."

"He's disappeared. I think Ace knows where he is, but he won't say. Dolph left orders that we're not to be in touch except in case of dire emergency."

"Shit, Alahna, you need him. Isn't that emergency enough?"

"Dolph thinks I'm better off without him. And you know how stubborn he can be."

A nurse poked her head in the door. "Sorry, but visiting hours are over."

Jeff stood up. "Hey, don't you worry," he said, kissing Alahna. "It'll all work out. I'm on my way to London, so I'll be gone for a while, but here's my number if you need anything."

"Thanks, Jeff," Alahna said. "I really appreciate that. I'll send you pictures of Seth as soon as we have some. I . . . I really am sorry."

"Hey, forget it. But listen, the kid needs some family. How about if I appoint myself his uncle?"

"Okay," she said, and blew him a kiss.

Halfway down the hall, Jeff stopped again at the nursery and stared through the window at little Seth, lying peacefully in his bassinet.

"Hey, little guy," he whispered. Then he turned on his heel and walked away.

The next morning, on his way to the airport, he stopped by Ace's office. Their conversation was short and to the point. When he wanted to, Jeff could be very persuasive.

"Sorry, Dolph," Ace thought afterwards, *"but there are some things in life you gotta do."*

Chapter Nine

Kevin could not have been more excited if Seth had been his own natural child. In fact, despite the baby's mocha skin coloring, the puzzled hospital staff assumed that the freckled-faced Mr. Olsen was the real father. He showered Alahna and the baby with flowers, toys, and gifts of every description. When they were released from the hospital, he worried over them all the way home as though she were an exotic princess who had just given birth to a crown prince.

He fussed over her so that she was almost relieved that he had to go back to California for several days.

"Don't worry," she said laughingly. "We'll be fine. Won't we, Meilee?"

Meilee, who could hardly tear herself away from Seth, nodded. "I'll take good care of both of them," she promised. "He's not going to do anything but sleep and eat for a while, and Alahna needs plenty of rest, too."

"But call me if he does anything exciting," Kevin said.

Alahna and Meilee exchanged amused glances.

"Just promise me one thing," Alahna said, kissing him goodbye. "Please, no more teddy bears."

Dolph had been so right. Alahna did love being a mother. She loved holding Seth, loved playing with him and feeding him, loved watching him discover his fingers and his toes and the rest of the world around him. Sometimes, when he fell back to sleep after his three A.M. feeding, she would lie awake for a few minutes, and talk to Dolph.

"If only you could see him," she'd whisper into the stillness of the apartment. "You'd fall in love with him, Dolph, I know you would."

But in the daylight, she gave little thought to her absent husband. With Seth to occupy her and Kevin's frequent phone calls and visits, she had no time for daydreaming. Ace needed her back at work, and she had decided, despite Meilee's protestations, to hire a nanny.

"Seth is already nine pounds, seven ounces," Alahna said practically. "Another month and he'll be much too heavy for you to carry. You need help with him, Meilee."

She found an Englishwoman who had twenty-five years' experience and excellent references.

"I suppose she'll do," Meilee sniffed. "At least she's not young and flighty."

When Seth was two months old, Alahna went back to working full-time at the office. The first week, she called home five or six times a day. By the second week, when even Meilee was beginning to sound exasperated, she limited her calls and dug into her work. She'd almost forgotten how satisfying it was to run her company.

She and Kevin fell into a comfortable routine. They spent much of their free time playing with Seth or taking him for walks in his carriage down Fifth Avenue and through Central Park. Kevin had endless patience with him.

It was a happy time for Alahna. Her life felt full—with Seth, with work, with Kevin and Meilee. The nights that Kevin was in Los Angeles, she often climbed into bed right after dinner to catch up with paperwork and read until she couldn't keep her eyes open.

When Meilee began to scold her for not taking good enough care of herself, Alahna took a long look in the mirror and imposed a new rule. Once a week, she banished the papers from her bedroom, soaked in a fragrant bubble bath, and was asleep by ten o'clock.

Perhaps if she got more rest, the dreams would stop.

But they kept coming back, variations on the same theme: Dolph—standing outside their house in London, in her father's study in Hong Kong, at the top of their favorite ski slope in St. Moritz. Each time, as he beckoned to her, just as she was about to throw herself into his welcoming embrace, Jeff would appear.

"No," he'd say sternly. "Not yet, Alahna."

Alahna frequently woke herself up crying, and would lie awake long afterwards, shaking with rage. Getting through the next day was always difficult, because her anger over Dolph's desertion stayed with her.

That summer Kevin rented a house on Nantucket Island

for a week and persuaded Alahna to leave Seth in the care of Meilee and the nanny, Miss Roberts.

"You and I need to be alone," he coaxed her.

Their last night on the island they took a moonlit stroll along the beach. Kevin spread his jacket out on the sand and uncorked a bottle of wine.

"I love you, Alahna," he said, "and I'm a patient man. I'm not asking for any promises you can't keep. But I need to know, do you ever think about getting a divorce?"

She loved Kevin far too much ever to tell him anything but the absolute truth. "Kevin, I never thought it was possible to love two people at the same time. I know this past year would have been infinitely more difficult without you. But I'm not ready to say goodbye to my marriage. I can't give up yet—even if that might seem the logical thing to do. I'm sorry. I wish I could give you a different answer."

"Honey, one of the things I love about you is your honesty. I tell you what," he said, refilling her glass, "when it starts to feel too difficult, I'll let you know and we'll reevaluate then. In the meantime," he clicked his glass against hers, "here's to us, and to Seth, and to all that we share."

Arriving at the offices of Shawak International on her first day back, with the temperature just hinting of autumn, Alahna looked up at her building and smiled proudly. Kevin had been smart to choose Nantucket. She had needed to be somewhere neutral, somewhere that didn't hold any memories of Dolph. Now she felt relaxed and ready to take on whatever crisis Ace had been saving for her return.

"Did you think I was keeping anything from you?" Ace asked. "You did call every day, Alahna. You look terrific, by the way."

"Thanks, Ace." Alahna laughed. "Maybe I'm looking for a problem to sink my teeth into. It's all going too smoothly here."

"Sorry, kiddo, but no emergencies," said Ace, and went off to brew his herbal tea.

No emergencies—and no messages from Dolph. Without realizing it, she'd been all the while hoping he'd been in touch. All right, Alahna, she told herself sternly. The hell with Dolph. He had made his decision. Now she had to make hers.

Exciting things were happening for the Pretty Face Division—licensing agreements, new product lines, trying to stay ahead of competitors who were watching their every innovative move. And then there was the rest of Shawak International.

Sometimes she didn't know how she managed it all, except that she was blessed with topnotch people—like Ace and the next-level of executives she and Dolph had hand-picked. People who drove themselves as hard as she did.

Seth made it all worthwhile. What had her life been like without him? she wondered occasionally. Without his sunny, dimpled smile to greet her when she walked in the door at night . . . his gurgles of delight, now sounding almost like real words when she picked him up and kissed his chubby cheeks . . . his awkward first attempts to walk . . . his excitement about showing off his latest discoveries—how the toilet paper unrolled, how cupboard doors opened, revealing hidden treasures like pots and pans to bang and put on his head.

The first time he said, "Mama," she burst into tears. No annual report had ever given her such intense pleasure.

Before she knew it, she was planning Seth's first birthday party. She scoffed at Miss Roberts' reports about the kinds of parties that were held for the other neighborhood children. Just a family party would do, something simple that would be fun for Seth.

"Happy birthday," she greeted him with a kiss that morning. "Mama's staying home so we can play today."

At noon, the doorman rang to announce a visitor. Her hands sticky with the applesauce she was feeding Seth, Alahna called to Meilee, "That must be Kevin. He must have caught the earlier flight. Will you open the door for him?"

"Forget your keys?" she asked, hearing his step behind her. "Would you look at how this boy is eating his birthday lunch?"

"He sure has grown since the last time I saw him."

"Jeff!"

Alahna whirled around and found herself, sticky hands and all, caught in one of Jeff Gotley's famous bearhugs.

"I had no idea you were coming to New York!" she said when he finally released her.

"How could I miss the kid's first birthday?" he asked. "Hey, let me take a good look at him."

He knelt in front of Seth's highchair and said, "Hello, little Seth. I brought you a present from London."

"Spoon," chirped Seth, showing off his newest word.

"He's even cuter in person than in his pictures," Jeff said. "You both look like you're thriving."

"We are," Alahna said, wiping off Seths' hands and face and lifting him out of the highchair.

"All right, Sethie, let's ask Nanny to change your diaper, so your Uncle Jeff and I can visit for a minute, and then we'll see what a nice present he brought you."

"Can you stay for lunch and Seth's party, Jeff?" Alahna said.

"Wish I could, but I have to be in L.A. tonight—or else! You know these movie people, it's all life and death and 'I need it yesterday.'"

"I know only one movie person and he seems much too reasonable to talk like that."

"Yeah, I hear good things about Mr. Olsen. How's it going between the two of you? Are you happy, baby?"

"I am, Jeff, I really am. It's been a good year—tough and exhausting, but good. I guess you could say I'm . . . content. Kevin is a wonderful man. He's given me so much."

Jeff fiddled with his gold link bracelet. "Why not marry the guy?" he asked.

Alahna looked wistful. "Aren't you forgetting something? I already have a husband."

"Yeah, baby," Jeff said quietly, "yeah, I guess you do."

Chapter Ten

Three months later Ace walked into her office and turned her world upside down. He appeared in the doorway, his mouth moving in a funny way that she had never seen before.

"Alahna," he said, and then he seemed not to be able to continue.

"Ace, what's wrong? What's happened?"

He closed the door and walked over to where she was sitting behind her desk.

"I . . . uh . . . I have bad news, Alahna."

"What? What is it?" she asked, her voice rising nervously.

"Alahna, it's Dolph. He's dead. His body was found somewhere in the middle of the jungle . . . on Sumatra."

"That's impossible," Alahna said flatly. "Ace, he's not dead. They've made a mistake."

She sounded so absolutely sure that for a moment Ace wanted to believe she was right. But there was the evidence.

"I'm sorry, Alahna. His bod . . . he's been identified."

She stared at him blankly, trying to make sense of his words. Angry that Ace, of all people, dependable Ace, should now be talking such nonsense.

Just at that moment, her office door opened and Jana walked in.

"Jana," Alahna said indignantly, "thank goodness you're here. There's been a terrible mistake. Jana? Jana, why are you crying?"

She looked at the stricken, tear-stained faces of her two dear friends.

"Oh, Dolph," she whispered, and then she knew there was no mistake.

The next few hours were a confusion of grief and horror. Someone—later she realized it was Ace—had taken charge and sent her home with Jana. Someone had gently broken the news to Meilee and helped her into bed. Someone had made sure that Seth wasn't frightened by all the comings and goings and crying and phone calls.

At some point in that long, long day, Kevin had appeared by her side.

All he said was, "I'm here for you, Alahna," and then he held her hand all through the night.

Sedated with Dalmane, Alahna slept for twelve hours straight. When she woke up, Kevin was lying next to her, fully clothed, fast asleep. She crept out of bed, went into her dressing room, and picked up her phone.

"Operator,' she said, her voice hoarse from crying, "I'd like to make an overseas call to Tel Aviv, Israel. Person-to-person, to Christopher Brooke."

Just seconds later, Chris's familiar voice answered, "Hello?"

"Oh, Chris," she said, starting to cry again, "Chris, I need you."

Kevin wanted to accompany her to London, but this was one trip she had to make alone.

"Don't worry," she said. "Chris arrives before I do. He'll meet me at the gate. Kevin, thank you, really. I promise I'll call as soon as we have some news."

Dependable as ever, Chris was waiting for her at Heathrow.

"Alahna," he said, stepping forward to hug her, and then she was sobbing against his shoulder, and it felt so good to be in his arms.

They had several hours to spare while the Shawak jet took on a fresh crew and more fuel for the leg to Indonesia. They found themselves a secluded corner where they could catch up.

"It's rather complicated," Chris explained. "They're having political troubles over there right now—lots of tribal rivalries, so nobody wants to take responsibility for any of the mayhem. Everyone I've spoken to is ready to point a finger, but that's about all, so far."

"Ace spoke to Greg Andrews, our project manager over there," Alahna said, "but Greg hadn't seen or heard from Dolph in weeks, not since the beginning of January, I think it was. We're to be met by a government representative but . . ." she shrugged helplessly. "I don't know, Chris, but I have to do *something*. You understand that, don't you?" she asked urgently.

"Of course, you must. Otherwise we'd never be able to forgive ourselves."

As if by unspoken agreement, they soon began talking about less painful topics—news of themselves and their old friends. Chris admired her latest photos of Seth and then handed her several pictures of his two-month old daughter, staring into the camera from the safety of her mother's arms. Chris' Israeli wife was blond, and almost as tall as he.

"She was an officer in the Israeli Air Force," he said proudly. "Have you heard from Jeff recently? He sent me a Christmas card, but I've not even had a postcard since."

Alahna remembered how happy and safe she'd felt the last time she'd seen Jeff on Seth's birthday. "Ace tried to find him to tell him about Dolph. His secretary in L.A. said he was in London, and his service in London thought he was en route to Japan. We left word everywhere."

"Same old Jeff," Chris said with a tired smile. "He'll be the last of us to settle down."

A second later he looked regretful and wanted to kick himself, for his "us" hung in the air. In some ways, he and Jeff and Dolph had been a team—each in his own way so debonair, so full of adventure, so ready, at a moment's notice, to help out one another.

He put his arm around Alahna and said, "Promise me not to give up hope. We'll do whatever we must to get to the bottom of this."

Alahna leaned her head against his shoulder. "Thank you, Chris. It couldn't have been easy, dropping all the pieces of your life to come with me."

"I made you a promise years ago, Alahna. Remember? That night in Paris?"

"How could I ever forget?" She smiled for the first time since she'd heard the news about Dolph. "Lucifer Lust . . . I was terribly innocent back then, wasn't I? Well," she said, blinking back tears, "I've learned a thing or two since then, and I'm a whole lot tougher than I used to be."

"Good girl! We'll make things so difficult for those chaps

in Djarkata that they couldn't possibly refuse to give us whatever help we need."

But their brave resolutions hit the stonewall of the Indonesian bureaucracy. The government officials were polite and eager to offer their heartfelt condolences. But one after another, they insisted they had not a shred more information than what she already knew.

"It's a very dangerous area," they told her gravely. "He should not have been there."

"There must be someone else we can talk to. We keep getting the same answers over and over again," Chris told the American ambassador who had offered his services.

The ambassador shook his head grimly. "If they seem reluctant, it's because they're worried about discouraging American companies with stories about disappearances and epidemics in the interior. Especially when the victim is someone as prominent as Mr. Robicheck. So they're not about to pursue a full-scale investigation. It's more prudent, they feel, to let the world hear the sanitized version."

"But this is my husband we're talking about, not some anonymous person," Alahna said bitterly. "And why was there no talk of danger when they first approached us to invest in their natural resources? We're now a major investor in this country. Certainly we can apply some sort of pressure. You are, after all, the American ambassador!"

"Our hands are tied, I'm afraid. This is not our country, and there's simply nothing more we can do," the ambassador replied.

Chris leaned forward. "You said that no one, either from the Embassy or from Shawak, identified his body before he was cremated. How did that happen? And why are you so sure that the body was Dolph Robicheck's?"

"Apparently he'd spent some months in that area. I imagine he was trying to put a stop to the troubles his company was experiencing. He'd become a familiar figure to the people in the villages along the edge of the jungle. They were the ones who found him. As for the cremation, that's standard procedure out there for people who've died of typhus."

"I want to go there," Alahna said suddenly. "I want to see where he died. I want to talk to the people who knew him."

Chris and the ambassador exchanged glances.

"Mrs. Robicheck," said the ambassador, "I'm afraid that's quite impossible. Mr. Robicheck had been living in a notoriously dangerous part of the island. Aside from the political problems they've been having, and the constant threat of attack from wild animals, you'd be exposing yourself to the possibility of coming down with the same highly contagious disease that felled your husband."

"Alahna, you simply can't risk it," Chris said. "If anything happened to you, there'd be no one to take care of Seth."

There was a long silence, and then the ambassador spoke again. "I think I mentioned to you on the phone that what we believe to be two of your husband's personal belongings were found not far from his body. Do you feel well enough to look at them and tell us?" He gazed at her questioningly.

Alahna nodded faintly and clenched her hands in her lap. "Please," she prayed silently, "please don't let them be Dolph's."

The ambassador opened his desk drawer and pulled out a manila envelope.

"Mrs. Robicheck," he said gently, "have you seen this before?"

He held up a heavy malachite ring set in white gold, one of Dolph's most cherished possessions. The ring had been a wedding gift to Dolph from her father. As far as she knew, Dolph had never removed it from his finger.

"Yes," she said, almost inaudibly. "That's Dolph's ring."

She picked up the ring and touched it lightly to her lips. Then she walked over to the window and looked down at the perfectly manicured lawn spread out below her. Her father had often talked about the grounds around his house in Shanghai. From his description, she imagined that they must have resembled the rich green carpet of grass, the well-tended gardens and paths that she now found herself staring at. Perhaps Dolph had once stood like this, gazing through one of the windows in her father's home, thinking about how much his life had changed because of his having met Salah Shawak.

Though tears were flowing down her cheeks, Alahna was

hardly aware that she was crying. A battle was raging inside her—a battle between her mind and her heart.

"He's dead," her intellect told her. "You must accept that. You're holding the evidence in your hand."

But her heart refused to believe it was so. That a man like Dolph Robicheck—so willful, so determined, so constantly ready to meet new challenges—could be gone from the world . . .

No. It wasn't possible.

She mourned him then, standing by the window, watching the gardener trim the border along the stone path. After a while, the sky clouded over and a light rain began to fall.

She turned away from the window.

It was time to go home.

Chapter Eleven

Alahna slowly began to put back the pieces of her life.

"If not for yourself," Meilee told her gently, "then you must carry on for Seth. He didn't choose to be born, just as Dolph didn't choose to die."

Meilee had aged years in the last several days. She had loved Dolph as a son. He had been her one last link to the past she had shared with Salah.

Alahna could see the lines of pain and loss that were newly etched on Meilee's wrinkled face. Yet somehow, Meilee was finding strength not to give in to her grief. The old woman was setting her a courageous example. Alahna realized that Meilee's advice was for the best. Seth was a gift to her, a gift from whatever higher powers there were. She had to be strong, to justify Seth's trust in her.

Kevin called her every morning to say, "Hello, how are you? I love you."

He had decided to take his cues from her. When she told him she needed the weekend to be alone with Seth, he said sweetly, "Of course, hon. I totally understand."

But he called twice on Saturday and twice on Sunday to make sure she was all right.

The following weekend he flew in to attend Dolph's memorial service. "I thought I'd stay at the Mayfair," he said casually when he and Alahna were discussing his plans.

"All right," Alahna replied. She wasn't yet ready to resume their old routine.

On Sunday morning the auditorium at the Shawak International building was filled with men and women who had come to show their love and respect for Dolph Robicheck. Flanked by Kevin and Meilee, Alahna came in through the side door and gasped when she saw the size of the crowd.

Jeff was waiting for them in the first row. Ace had finally caught up with him in Singapore, and Jeff had rearranged his flights to attend the service. He embraced Alahna and kissed Meilee, then shook Kevin's hand.

"Jeff Gotley," he introduced himself. "I wish we'd met under other circumstances, Kevin."

Though Alahna had thought there were no tears left in her, Jeff's eulogy had her weeping again.

"I've known Dolph Robicheck for more than thirty-five years," he said, fixing his eyes on Alahna, seated just below the podium, "and he never once disappointed me. Nor anyone else, as far as I could tell. Dolph was the stubbornest man I ever met, and he could make me mad as fast as he could make me smile. He was my best friend, my best collaborator. He had a generosity of spirit as vast as the ocean, and I'll never forgive him for dying."

After the service Kevin, Jeff, and the Taylors went back to Alahna's apartment. Seth was shy with his uncle Jeff, but he couldn't get enough of Kevin. When Jana and Meilee insisted that Alahna lie down for a while, Seth looked hopefully at Kevin.

"Park?" he asked.

"You bet, Seth," said Kevin. "We'll go to the swings. Maybe your uncle Jeff would like to join us."

"Sure thing," Jeff said.

With Seth babbling excitedly in his stroller, the two men headed across the street to the Central Park playground.

"The kid's crazy about you," Jeff said.

Kevin laughed with pleasure. "The feeling's mutual. I feel

like he's my own son. Oh, shit," he said, his face turning bright red with embarrassment.

Jeff clapped him on the back. "Forget it, Kevin. All I did was provide the inspiration, you know what I mean? But he sure is a great kid. Alahna's a special lady," he said, changing the subject. "I hope it works out for the two of you."

"You were one of Dolph's closest friends, weren't you?" Kevin asked, lifting Seth out of the stroller and buckling him into one of the toddler swings.

"He was as special as everyone says he was, if that's what you're wondering. Those eulogies weren't just a matter of not speaking ill of the dead. But one thing's for sure. Alive or dead, he wouldn't want Alahna to be without a man who loves her. I think you qualify."

"Yeah, I do," Kevin said. "She means the world to me."

"To me, too," Jeff said soberly. "Let's stay in touch, man. Here's my card. Track me down if you need to."

Kevin pocketed Jeff's card and shook his hand. "Thanks for the pep talk. I didn't want you to think I was horning in on your friend's territory."

"Go for it, baby. She needs you. Trust me, that's exactly what Dolph would have wanted."

The problem was that Alahna didn't know what she wanted. She felt unmoored and confused. Although for the past two years she'd lived without Dolph, she had never been forced to face the finality of his absence. Now, for the first time, she had to accept the reality that she would never see him again. Grieving for him, she retreated inside herself, to face her anger over the fact that he had doubly deserted her. That he had done so out of love comforted her not a bit.

The Thursday following the memorial service, Kevin arrived on his usual early evening flight, in time to play with Seth before he went to bed. Later they ate a quiet dinner in front of the fire. Kevin did most of the talking, hoping to get a smile out of Alahna, who seemed edgy and distracted.

After the third yawn she said, "I'm sorry, Kevin. It's not you. This week has been exhausting."

"I'm ready for bed myself," Kevin said. "I think I'll join you."

When they were both undressed Kevin kissed her tentatively, not wanting to press her. But making love was impossible. She was too tense, and his efforts to relax her only made her feel worse.

After Kevin fell asleep, she got out of bed and went into the living room. The view from her windows was spectacular—a jewelbox of glittering lights all the way up to the George Washington Bridge, which hung like a necklace of diamonds across the Hudson River.

"I need to give it time," she told herself. "Time to get used to the idea that he's not out there somewhere."

She tiptoed into Seth's room and kissed his baby cheek. Then she went into her study, opened up her briefcase, and sighed. She'd discovered that paperwork was the best cure for her sleepless nights. And then she laughed aloud.

Just like when I was a little girl, she thought. *When my mother died, the only thing that stopped me from crying was going to work with Papa. And eventually I stopped missing Ohna. But will I ever stop missing Dolph?*

She tried to imagine the future. Seth. Her work. Kevin? He had made it clear that he was ready for a more permanent arrangement whenever she was. But her life was in New York, and his was in California.

Once she had said that very thing to Meilee, who had looked at her sharply and said, "If you love someone enough to want to share his life, you can find the solution."

Now she realized that as long as Dolph had been alive, she hadn't ever seriously looked for any solutions. Ignoring the issue wasn't fair to Kevin, or to her, for that matter. That would change, she resolved.

It seemed to rain almost every day that April, but May was glorious, sunny and warm. Alahna, Kevin, Seth, and Meilee spent the Memorial Day weekend at the Connecticut house. Watching Seth playing in his little plastic pool next to the swimming pool, Alahna couldn't help but remember another Memorial Day. Had it only been three years ago that she and Dolph had lain here in the sun and optimistically discussed their plans about having a baby? "Take a lesson from Lot's wife," Dolph had often told her. "Don't look back. Only look forward."

Sometimes that was easier said than done.

Kevin finally convinced Alahna to come out to Los Angeles for a long weekend at the end of July. They played tennis and rode horses, and in the late afternoons they swam in the Pacific. With the sun still streaming in through the open windows and the breeze fanning them, they drank wine and made love slowly, teasing each other as they licked the salt off each other's body.

"Oh, Kevin," Alahna said afterwards, luxuriating like a well-cared for cat, "I could get used to this life."

"That's what I had in mind," Kevin grinned mischievously. "Come again, anytime."

But somehow she could never find the right weekend to get away, and it was September before she managed to squeeze in another trip to California. Landing in Los Angeles, she wondered whether she could ever live there permanently. The city didn't feel quite real to her—almost like a fantasyland with its palm trees and the ocean almost at the doorstep and its balmy desert nights. Besides, she had a company to run in New York.

Of course, people did commute between the two coasts. Kevin had been doing just that for much of the past two years. But that had always felt so . . . temporary. After the intensity of her marriage to Dolph, could she settle for what would be in effect a part-time marriage?

Just after Thanksgiving, she flew out to Aspen to join Kevin. It was their first time back there together since they had met. The previous winter, by unspoken agreement, they had avoided confronting the past and skied instead in Europe and Utah.

"Are you okay about this?" Kevin asked as they drove through the town and up the mountain to his house.

"I think so," Alahna said, swallowing hard. "It feels rather like an exorcism."

"Let's get rid of the demons, shall we?"

She brushed her cheek against his arm and nodded. "It's about time, too."

Was it the ski trip, she wondered later, that had been the turning point? Though they tried to ignore it, that first evening they had felt the strain. But the next day, the sun was shining and the slopes were gleaming with freshly fallen snow. They skied Ruthie's Run in the morning and stopped for lunch at the same mid-slope restaurant where she and Kevin had had their first real conversation.

"Should we buy you a *Wall Street Journal* for old time's sake?" he joked.

Alahna peered at him from behind her sunglasses. "That really intrigued you, didn't it?"

"I've never met another women like you, Alahna," Kevin said, suddenly turning serious. "I hope you know what you mean to me."

"I do," she said and reached for his hand. "I really do."

The rest of the trip passed quickly. Some of Kevin's friends from Los Angeles happened to be in Aspen, and the group of them spent a day skiing together. Kevin invited them for dinner afterwards at his house.

"Okay with you?" he asked Alahna when they had a private moment.

"Of course," she said, touched that he would check with her. It *was*, after all, his home.

"Lovely people," she told him later, as they were getting ready for bed.

"I'm glad you had a chance to meet them. I see them fairly often in L.A., and they've heard a lot about you."

Her first night back in New York, she tucked Seth in and kissed him goodnight, then settled into bed herself with a stack of papers Ace had sent over for her to review. At eleven o'clock, Kevin called.

"I miss you," he said. "It feels strange to be here by myself."

"I know what you mean. I miss you, too."

That was the truth—she did miss him. And yet, this evening she had also been savoring her solitude. She looked around her bedroom. She and Dolph had decorated it together—picked out the bed, chosen the color scheme, and the rug for the dark wood floors.

How peaceful it was . . . how much it spoke of her tastes

and interests. And Dolph's.

How hard it would be to move to Los Angeles and leave all this behind.

"Bring Seth to California for Christmas," Kevin urged her.

"But I've already invited Ace and Jana and their kids for Christmas Day. Besides," she said, chagrined that she'd made plans without first consulting him, "it would be too confusing for Seth. Christmas trees and Santa Claus in the midst of all that sunshine and warm weather."

The excuse sounded foolish even to her ears, and she laughed weakly.

"I'm sorry, Kevin, I should have talked to you first. But please, do join us."

"Of course I will, Alahna. But you're right, you should have talked to me first."

She hung up the phone, upset by his rebuke. He had no right . . . or did he? How would she and Kevin ever build a life together if she didn't stop to think about what he might want?

Strange, she mused. She had always, automatically deferred to Dolph's wishes and desires. What made it so different between Kevin and herself?

That spring, Alahna worked harder than she ever had in her life. Months later, she would realize that she had gone looking for a new challenge as a way to justify her almost single-minded involvement with Shawak International. But in February, when she initially considered buying the Meadowfresh Corporation, all she saw was the sales potential.

Meadowfresh was a five-year-old company struggling to establish itself in the natural face and hair care market. Their packaging was excellent, and their products were all high-quality. But the owners of the Colorado-based organization were running out of capital and lacked the marketing skills to push themselves into the black.

Scrutinizing the analysis she'd had prepared for her on Meadowfresh, Alahna experienced the same jolt of excitement she'd felt when she'd discovered Pretty Face. Here was another company begging to be acquired and integrated into the Shawak International corporate structure.

Working closely with the Meadowfresh people, three young women who'd met in business school and decided to establish their own company, Alahna would come home exhausted but elated. She had almost forgotten how it felt to start from scratch and develop marketing and ad campaigns, to map out future growth and consider new products.

What little energy she had left at the end of the day she saved for Seth.

"You're working too hard," Meilee chided her.

"I have no choice," Alahna snapped and was instantly contrite. But really, what alternative was there if she wanted to make the venture succeed?

Kevin agreed with Meilee, and pointed out to her that when he did manage to drag her to the theater on a Saturday night, she was usually asleep by the third act.

"Don't you think you're taking this too seriously?" he asked her. "You do have executive vice-presidents who could share some of the responsibility."

She was too tired to try to explain, and she was annoyed that she should have to justify herself. So all she said was, "I don't want to argue with you, Kevin, but perhaps you shouldn't come next week."

Kevin's jaw set in a way she hadn't seen before, and he took her at her word. He waited until the middle of May to come back to New York, and stayed only two nights instead of his usual four.

Kissing her goodbye early Monday morning, he said, "I'm thinking about renting that same place on Nantucket for the Fourth of July weekend. Can I count on you to be there with me? You can even bring along your briefcase if you need to work."

"Oh, darling, that's a month and a half away. I just don't know—"

"I've had it, Alahna," Kevin interrupted her. "It's time we talked this thing through. We're drifting apart, and dammit, I want to know the reason!"

Startled by his sudden outburst, Alahna took a step back and said quietly, "You seem so angry, Kevin. I don't understand."

"Alahna," he went on, trying to speak calmly, "Do you realize that in the last few months you always seem to have a reason to keep us apart?"

"That's not fair! You know how busy I've been."

"It's been three weeks since we've seen each other. Doesn't that bother you?"

"Of course it bothers me," she protested, beginning to bristle.

"Alahna, I run a pretty successful business myself—maybe not as large as Shawak, but certainly not small-time by anyone's standards. But I always find time for you. I can't even remember when you were last in L.A."

"What would you like me to do, Kevin?"

"For starters, Alahna, you don't have to go on proving yourself. You have a well-paid staff, and Ace could certainly handle most of the areas you're so intent on controlling yourself. But you consistently refuse to take advantage of that and leave yourself free."

"Free?" She looked at him blankly.

"Free to move to California with me. So that we could get married and raise children together and live like normal people. I love you so much, Alahna. This cross-country romance isn't working anymore. At least no for me."

"But I can't simply pick up and leave and let Ace take care of it all. What an absurd notion! I've spent my life working with Dolph to build Shawak International."

"Wait a minute," Kevin said, taking her hand. "We're getting carried away here. I love you, Alahna, and I would never ask you to give everything up. But don't you think there's a way we can compromise, so that we could start building a real life together?"

"Look out there," Alahna said, pointing to the cityscape beyond her window. "That's my life—here, in New York. Just as your life is in California. . . . You know, Kevin," she continued slowly, "I once gave up all that was familiar to me to start over with the man I was marrying. I'm realizing now that Dolph was—and is—the only man for whom I would ever do that."

"Alahna, you can't mean what you're saying?"

"I do, Kevin. I've never been more positive than I am at this moment."

"But don't you see where that leaves us? You're going to throw away everything there is between us, just like that?"

"It isn't 'just like that.' You said it yourself—this has been coming on for several months. Face it, Kevin," she said, facing it herself for the first time, "we live in two different worlds, and neither of us has any desire to change."

"But we love each other, Alahna. Don't we?"

She stared out the window a moment longer, then turned to face him. "There are all kinds of love, Kevin."

"Ah," he said softly. "I suppose that says it all."

After that there was nothing left to say.

She closed the door behind him and went back to her bedroom to finish dressing for work.

That had to happen, she told herself. Perhaps someday she would find a man she loved enough to take Dolph's place. But not now . . . not yet.

For now she should take comfort from the fact that she and Kevin had done the right thing by facing the inevitable. But she was too unhappy, too overwhelmed with pain and self-doubt, to find solace in that thought. And when she pricked her finger on the clasp of her jade pin and a tiny trickle of blood spurted out, staining the collar of her silk shirt, she burst into tears and began to sob as if her heart had been broken in two.

Chapter Twelve

It was the morning of Seth's fourth birthday. Alahna awoke to the sound of the intercom next to her bed buzzing insistently. She sat up and forced herself to consciousness.

"Mrs. Robicheck," said her housekeeper, "I hope I didn't disturb you, but it's Mr. Gotley on the telephone."

"Thank you, Harriet. Please put him through."

"Good morning, Alahna."

"Jeff, are you really in New York? And what are you doing up so early?"

"Don't you read the papers? I have a show opening on Broadway in a couple of weeks."

"Oh, Jeff, I'm so happy for you. That's just what you and Dolph always wanted."

"Well . . . I guess I finally did it. But the real reason I'm calling at this hour is to wish Seth happy birthday."

"Come for lunch, Jeff. We're having a birthday party this afternoon and you're welcome to stay for that, but you'd better bring a pair of earplugs and your strongest set of nerves."

"Thanks for the warning," Jeff chuckled. "Tell you what—I'd rather have you and the kid all to myself. I'll take a pass on today and drop by for lunch tomorrow."

Alahna laughed. "You're a wise man. Look, I better run if I want to kiss the birthday boy before he leaves for nursery school. But we'll see you tomorrow, around twelve."

Punctual as ever, Jeff arrived with a huge plastic automobile for Seth and a dozen red roses for Alahna.

"Seth, do you remember your Uncle Jeff?" Alahna asked.

The child peered shyly at Jeff from behind the safety of Alahna's skirt. Then he nodded and said, "Yesterday was my birthday. I'm four and I had a magician and chocolate ice cream. Did you bring me a present, too?"

"Seth," Alahna began to scold him, but Jeff interrupted her.

"I know it was your birthday, man, that's why I'm here," Jeff said. "And yes, I did bring you a present. It's in the livingroom."

"Can I see it now, Mommy?" Seth asked excitedly. "Please?"

"Did you finish your lunch? Yes? All right, but first let Meilee wash your hands and face. And later you can come give Uncle Jeff a proper thank you for whatever he's brought you."

Alahna and Jeff went into the library where the table was set for an informal lunch.

"You've done a great job with him, Alahna," Jeff said. "He's a terrific little kid."

"Thank you, Jeff. You can't imagine the joy he gives me."

There was a silence as she leaned back in her chair. After a moment she said, "I never realized it, but I did need a child to make my life complete. As usual, Dolph was right. He taught me so much, Jeff. All this time and he's still so much in my thoughts."

"I guess that's natural," Jeff said, "but Alahna, I get the impression that, except for Seth, you spend an awful lot of time living in the past."

"That's not fair," Alahna protested, stung by his criticism. "Look at Shawak International. We're doing all kinds of new and exciting things there."

"Ah, yes. Your child and your work. But what about your free time? What do you do then?"

"I'm terribly busy. I don't have much free time," she said shortly.

"No social life?" He stared into her eyes.

"I have my family, and my close friends. That's all I need."

"What about a man who can give you love and companionship? Don't you need any of that?"

"I've had love, Jeff. My memories will sustain me for the rest of my life."

"That's ridiculous!" he said impatiently. "You're much too young and sexy to live like a recluse, Alahna. I didn't believe the stories I've been hearing, but I guess they're true."

"What stories?" Alahna demanded angrily. "What are you talking about?"

"We do have friends in common," Jeff said drily. "They happen to be concerned about you. Especially when they can't get you to come to dinner or to meet an interesting single man. And speaking of interesting single men, what went wrong between you and Kevin?"

Alahna raised an eyebrow. "What makes you think that's any of your business?"

"Hey, lady, I thought we were close friends. I care about you."

"I'm sorry I snapped," Alahna said. "I guess I'm a bit sensitive about Kevin. He's a wonderful man, but he wanted more than I could give him. Besides, I told you before, I'm content. My life is very full."

"Are you happy?"

"As happy as I can be without Dolph."

Jeff shook his head stubbornly. "You should have married Kevin, Alahna."

"No, Jeff. I don't suppose you'll understand this, but I had one great love in my life. I'll never have another. Dolph was and always will be the only man for me. I can't pretend and make do with someone else. That wouldn't be fair—to either of us."

"I can't figure it," Jeff persisted. "Olsen told me he was crazy about you, and I thought you felt the same way."

Alahna stared past him and said pensively, "I loved Kevin. I still do. But being married to Dolph was so . . . exciting. He put so much effort into every area of my life— whether it was choosing my clothes, or teaching me how to be an adult, or making sure I was happy. He challenged me to grow in every possible direction. In business, in my personal life. . . .

"He encouraged me to sleep with other men, because he knew that the more experience I had, the more we would enjoy each other. It's only when you realize that you have the best, that you appreciate its value. And if he hadn't insisted that I have a child . . ." she shrugged. "I can hardly imagine my life without Seth. Dolph was quite simply the most interesting person I ever met," she went on. "We had such marvelous times when we travelled. Once, when we were on holiday in Hawaii, Dolph suggested we try an experiment. Neither of us would exchange one word with another soul for the entire week we were there. We had a beachfront suite, and we left standing orders for our food to be delivered outside the door. We spent our days sunning ourselves on the beach, swimming, and making love. At the end of the week, it was hard to get back to reality. Memories like that aren't easily forgotten."

She smiled sheepishly.

"I also took two hundred and eighty-eight dollars from him playing gin rummy. Oh, Jeff, I do miss him so."

There was a long silence. Her cheeks wet with fallen tears, Alahna played with the silken fringe of a throw pillow. "It used to be wonderful, wasn't it, Jeff?"

"What did?"

"The life we had."

"Mine's pretty good right now, actually. And what was that long song and dance you just handed me about being happy?"

"I am," she said. "I have my child who is a gift from God—and you, of course," she smiled meaningfully. "I'm happy with my work. If Dolph were alive, he would be so proud of how much the company's grown. We're now a major presence in the cosmetic and perfume industries, and our career apparel division has been a pioneer in the field. The figures are terrific, Jeff. Dolph always encouraged me to expand my horizons, and that's exactly what I've done."

Jeff stood up and stared out the window at the network of cars gridlocked on Fifth Avenue, fourteen stories below.

"Dolph used to say—"

"Hell, Alahna," he exploded, "for crying out loud, I'm sick of hearing what Dolph used to say. Oh, shit," he said, "I'm sorry. It's just that I'm under so much pressure. You know how it is . . . with the show opening up and all."

A crystal cigarette box was sitting on the coffee table. Jeff opened the box and helped himself.

"I thought you quit smoking," Alahna said.

"I did."

"Come on, Jeff. It can't be that bad."

He stood looking at her silently, his handsome dark eyes boring into hers.

"Alahna, there are times when you have to use your own judgment. You agree with that, don't you?"

"That depends, Jeff, on what you're judging."

He walked over to the cocktail bar at the far end of the walnut-paneled room and fixed two straight whiskeys.

"Here," he said, handing one to Alahna. "You'd better drink this."

"You know I don't drink whiskey, Jeff."

"Well, drink it anyway, because you're going to need it."

"Jeff," she said, fidgeting nervously with her silver bracelet, "what's going on here?"

Jeff sprawled his big frame in the chair opposite hers,

leaned forward tensely, took a long sip of whiskey, and said, "I never told you that I visited Dolph in Indonesia after Seth was born."

"What? How did you find him?"

"I wormed the information out of Ace. It wasn't easy, tracking him down, but I had to talk to him. I blamed myself for having gotten you pregnant and giving Dolph a reason to walk out on you."

"Jeff, it wasn't your fault," she said sadly.

"I had to make sure that Dolph didn't think so. Forgive me for saying so, but Dolph was really kind of nutty then. He was spending endless hours at the piano. I can't tell you how weird the whole scene was—this big, empty house in the middle of the jungle reverberating with his moody compositions. Before long, even I caught the fever and began to write. Serious stuff, I mean, not just the glitzy numbers I usually do. Shit! I went to Indonesia for a week and ended up staying five."

Jeff shook his head at the memory. "He was so wracked with guilt and shame about that night in Aspen that it bordered on insanity. 'How could I have degraded her like that?' he kept asking me. He thought it was a piece of luck that you'd met Kevin, because he was convinced that you and the baby needed a man you could count on. Someone closer to your own age. He didn't want you to wind up as a nurse in his sickroom."

He looked over at Alahna who was weeping quietly.

"Alahna, I know this is difficult to listen to, but—"

"No, no," she protested tearfully. "Go on, please. You were the last person to see him alive. It helps me, even though it hurts."

"I hope you won't hate me, Alahna, for what I'm about to tell you. You see, Dolph was intent on your putting him out of your mind and marrying Kevin, but he couldn't stop thinking about you. He made me promise to keep an eye on you, so that I could report back to him about you and Seth. All those baby pictures you sent me? Half of them ended up on Dolph's piano and desk."

"Dolph . . . he would have kept tabs on me from the grave, if he could."

Jeff stood up and began to pace. "Funny you should say that. Do you remember the conversation we had on Seth's first birthday? You reminded me that you were still married and that's why you couldn't marry Kevin. Made sense to me, and to Dolph, too, when I told him."

"You spoke to him so soon before he died?"

"I was with him the week after I saw you. By then he'd moved further into the jungle, because he'd gotten interested in some of the tribal rituals and wanted to find out more about their music. Man, talk about voodoo. I thought my granny knew it all, but Dolph immersed himself in it. One night we were sitting on his veranda. The moon was so huge you could have rolled it like a ball down the beach. It was one of those moons you only see in the tropics. And you know how obsessed Dolph was about the full moon."

Alahna closed her eyes, remembering. "We always used to make love at the full moon. We really used to do some crazy stunts in the moonglow."

"He thought of the craziest one that night on Sumatra. He decided it was time to die."

"No!" she protested, shaking her head vehemently. "Dolph would never have killed himself. You can't make me believe that!"

"He considered suicide, but he wasn't the kind of man who could kill himself, so he devised an alternate plan. He would make you—and the rest of the world—believe he was dead. That way you'd be free to marry Kevin, Alahna. But he needed help—and that, I regret to say, is where I came in."

Jeff grimaced. "I was an unwilling accomplice. I told myself, sure it was crazy and cruel. But what the hell? Your marriage was already over."

"But I don't understand," Alahna said, shaking her head in confusion. "He died of typhus."

"No, Alahna. That's the story the Indonesian government handed you. Remember, cross enough palms with silver in a place like that, and they'll agree to any kind of cockamamie tale."

He stood up and nervously flexed his fingers. "Alahna, there's no easy way to tell you this, but Dolph's not dead.

He's alive."

"Alive?" Her whisper was barely audible.

Jeff sat down next to her and put an arm around her trembling shoulders. "It's true. He's very much alive."

Alahna struggled free of Jeff's embrace. "Where is he? I have to see him! Is he all right? Dammit, Jeff, tell me where he is!"

"Please," he said, "I promise to tell you everything."

"Is he well and happy? That's the most important thing."

"Yes, he's well. I wouldn't exactly say he's happy. He was reasonably content until you and Kevin split up. But these last couple of years have been difficult for him, especially when he heard that you were alone. He was getting a little crazy, trying to figure out how to push you back into the mainstream without surfacing himself. I was worried for a while, but I finally figured out how to keep him sane."

"Go on," Alahna said urgently.

Jeff looked shamefaced. "I got him to agree to compose the music for my new show."

"Do you mean to tell me, Jeff Gotley," Alahna said, her voice rising in anger, "that you stood up at that memorial service and eulogized my husband, knowing he was alive? And that he's off somewhere, writing music for your Broadway show? You're both mad!"

"He's not off somewhere. At the last minute, I realized that the show needed additional scoring. I begged him to come out of the jungle—and he agreed. But I couldn't convince him that you'd still want to see him, even though he's here in New York."

"He's in New York?" Her face went pale. "Where?"

"At my place . . . on Central Park West."

"Let's go," Alahna said. "I want to see him, Jeff. I want to see him now."

The cab ride through Central Park seemed interminable. The five minutes felt like five hours.

Jeff paid the fare and hurriedly followed Alahna to the elevator. But he stopped suddenly.

"I'm going to let you go it alone, baby," he said. "Right now, you don't need a crowd."

He reached into his pocket and handed her his key.

"Thanks, Jeff," Alahna said, smiling faintly.

The elevator door opened directly onto the front entrance of Jeff's apartment.

Alahna took a deep, deep breath before she turned the key in the lock. From the foyer, she could hear the turbulent sounds of the piano. She followed the music, stopping at the entrance to Jeff's living room.

Then she stood perfectly still, her feet glued to the floor. Dolph was seated at the piano, his back to her. Her eyes greedily devoured every inch of his body, as if to reassure herself that he was not a mirage.

Through the windows beyond the piano, Alahna could see the towers of their Fifth Avenue apartment, just across the park. She wondered whether Dolph was staring at them, as she was, thinking about the life they had once shared.

As a young girl, she had waited for Dolph to walk through the door of her father's house in Hong Kong in answer to a summons.

That moment seemed like centuries ago, but perhaps it was only yesterday. She had dreaded, then loved, then sometimes even hated this man. Father, mother, lover, friend. No single person could fulfill all those rules, no matter how hard he tried. And certainly no one human being could measure up to all those expectations.

And yet Alahna remembered the many times when Dolph had succeeded in doing the right thing, even though it was for the wrong reasons. Little Seth was living proof of that.

She knew she had every right to be angry. To hate him for what he had done. But hadn't he given up his life for hers?

She listened a moment longer to the music, Dolph's own music, savoring the familiar sounds.

Then she took a small step forward.

"Dolph . . ."

There was an abrupt silence. Dolph turned slowly to face her.

"Dolph," she said, "you once told me that all of life was a learning experience. Well dammit! You had better come home. You haven't finished my education yet."